Praise for *Take the Lead*

"Filled with a collection of intriguing characters, this is a light, vibrantly written romance from an author who clearly adores the world she's developed—and the characters she's matched."
—Sarah MacLean, *New York Times* bestselling author, in *The Washington Post*

"Believable, emotional, and hot—everything you want from a story about dance partners!" —Jasmine Guillory, *New York Times* bestselling author, in *O, the Oprah Magazine*

"*Take the Lead* is everything I look for in a romance—lovable and layered characters, sizzling chemistry, and a charming and authentic voice." —Sonali Dev, author of *Pride, Prejudice, and Other Flavors*

"[Stone and Gina's] sexy secret romance is tested not just by the crazy world of reality TV, but also by that classic obstacle to HEA—reality." —Maya Rodale, *USA Today* bestselling author, on NPR

"A sparkling debut . . . Daria's story of this behind-the-scenes romance is a perfect ten." —*Entertainment Weekly*

ALSO BY ALEXIS DARIA

You Had Me at Hola
A Lot Like Adiós

Take the Lead
Dance with Me
Dance All Night (novella)

What the Hex (novella)

Amor Actually: A Holiday Romance Anthology

Take the Lead

A DANCE OFF NOVEL

ALEXIS DARIA

ST. MARTIN'S GRIFFIN
NEW YORK

Published in the United States by St. Martin's Griffin, an imprint of St. Martin's Publishing Group

TAKE THE LEAD. Copyright © 2017, 2023 by Alexis Daria. All rights reserved. Printed in the United States of America. For information, address St. Martin's Publishing Group, 120 Broadway, New York, NY 10271.

www.stmartins.com

Designed by Gabriel Guma

The Library of Congress Cataloging-in-Publication Data

Names: Daria, Alexis, author.
Title: Take the lead / Alexis Daria.
Description: First St. Martin's Griffin edition. | New York :
    St. Martin's Griffin, 2023. | Series: A dance off novel ; 1
Identifiers: LCCN 2022035457 | ISBN 9781250817969
    (trade paperback) | ISBN 9781250848703 (ebook)
Subjects: LCGFT: Romance fiction. | Novels.
Classification: LCC PS3604.A7433 T35 2023 | DDC 813/.6—dc23/
    eng/20220815
LC record available at https://lccn.loc.gov/2022035457

Our books may be purchased in bulk for promotional, educational, or business use. Please contact your local bookseller or the Macmillan Corporate and Premium Sales Department at 1-800-221-7945, extension 5442, or by email at MacmillanSpecialMarkets@macmillan.com.

First published in the United States in 2017 by Swerve, an imprint of Macmillan, New York

First St. Martin's Griffin Edition: 2023

10 9 8 7 6 5 4 3 2 1

To Mike.
This first one is for you.

DEAR READER,

Take the Lead was my debut novel, the one that started my journey as a published author. Originally released as an ebook in 2017, it's been given new life in paperback with a beautiful illustrated cover, updated text, and bonus material. Whether you read the original or are discovering it now for the first time, I'm so grateful this book has found its way into your hands.

At its heart, *Take the Lead* is an opposites-attract romance about living life on your own terms. The story begins when professional dancer Gina Morales teams up with Stone Nielson, a TV survivalist, for a celebrity dance competition. While I'm not a dancer myself, I admire the skill and dedication it takes, and I've always been fascinated by what goes on behind the scenes in film and television. I wanted to explore how someone ambitious might balance success and love, and how someone reserved would navigate familial expectations and the spotlight of fame. And of course, how the two of them could eventually find their happily ever after together.

Thank you for picking up this book and giving these characters a chance. My hope is that Stone and Gina will make you laugh, make you swoon, and—dare I say it—dance their way into your heart.

Wishing you all the best,

ALEXIS DARIA

The Dance Off

Season 14 Cast List

Welcome to THE DANCE OFF!

Season 14 brings together a star-studded collection of celebrities for a sizzling competition on the dance floor, featuring elite athletes, TV personalities, movie stars, and more. Meet the cast and their dance partners below, along with *The Dance Off*'s judges and hosts. Then get ready to vote for your favorite couples!

THE DANCERS

Alan & Rhianne

Alan Thomas
Claim to fame: Gold-medal-winning Paralympian
Alan is a Team USA Paralympian athlete with three gold medals in Track and Field events. When he's not training, he works with veterans.
Dance partner: Rhianne Davis

Beto & Jess

Norberto "Beto" Velasquez
Claim to fame: Reality star and athlete
Argentinian millionaire Beto Velasquez is the latest star of
the reality dating show *Your Future Fiancé*. Before that, he
had a successful soccer career, and he now owns a high-end
menswear fashion empire. .
Dance partner: Jess Davenport

Dwayne & Natasha

Dwayne Alonzo
Claim to fame: Athlete
Fresh off a Super Bowl win, NFL star Dwayne Alonzo is known for
his boldness and energy, as well as a few memorable sitcom cam-
eos. Will his end-zone victory dances translate to the ballroom?
Dance partner: Natasha Díaz

Farrah & Danny

Farrah Zane
Claim to fame: Actress and singer
The youngest of the cast at nineteen, Farrah starred in the
hit kid's TV movie *I Spy a Star,* where she played a spy going
undercover as a pop singer. Her first album will be out soon.
Dance partner: Danny Johnson

Jackson & Lori

Jackson García
Claim to fame: Actor
Jackson's a star on the rise, achieving acclaim for his role as a
vampiric werewolf on the sexy TV drama *Bite Me*. What fans
might not know is that Jackson is also an accomplished singer.
Dance partner: Lori Kim

Keiko & Joel

Keiko Sousa
Claim to fame: Swimsuit cover model
From the runways of Paris and New York to the covers of
magazines, up-and-coming model Keiko is emerging as the
new face of fashion. Her parents, tech mogul Terry Sousa and
supermodel Miaka Kano, must be very proud.
Dance partner: Joel Clarke

Lauren & Kevin

Lauren D'Angelo
Claim to fame: Olympic figure skater
A two-time Olympic figure skater for Team USA, Lauren
D'Angelo is known for her boldness on the ice and her out-
spokenness with the press. Lauren has never won an Olympic
medal, but will she win *The Dance Off*'s trophy?
Dance partner: Kevin Ray

Rick & Mila

Rick Carruthers
Claim to fame: Singer
Rick has a music career spanning decades as the lead singer
of the multiplatinum 1980s rock band Carruthers & Co. He
still tours, and runs a nonprofit organization that supports art
and music programs in public schools.
Dance partner: Mila Ivanova

Rose & Matteo

Rose Jeffers
Claim to fame: Actress
Rose starred on *The Lab*, a hit TV show about teenage scien-
tists that ran for many seasons in the 1990s. She hasn't acted

much since then, but fans still hold fond memories of the glamorous chemist she played.
Dance partner: Matteo Ricci

Stone & Gina

Stone Nielson
Claim to fame: Reality star
Stone stars on the popular reality show *Living Wild*, which follows the day-to-day life of the Nielson family as they live off the grid in the Alaskan wilderness. Among his six siblings, Stone is known as the strong and silent one.
Dance partner: Gina Morales

Twyla & Roman

Twyla Rhodes
Claim to fame: Actress and activist
Best known for her role as Queen Seraphina of the Elves in the blockbuster Elf Chronicles movies of the 1980s, Twyla has also worked as an activist for LGBTQ+ rights. Perhaps she'll confirm the rumors of an Elf Chronicles sequel . . .
Dance partner: Roman Shvernik

THE JUDGES

Chad Silver

A former club dancer, music video choreographer, and internationally known drag queen, Chad keeps busy as a host and judge on many competition shows. He currently serves as *The Dance Off*'s head judge.

Mariah Valentino

Mariah is a pop singer and classically trained dancer who now channels her musicality into choreography. The "Love You Always" songstress lends her compassionate nature to *The Dance Off*'s contestants as well as to causes benefitting the safety of animals.

Dimitri Kovalenko

Known for star turns in movies like *Aliens Don't Dance* and for choreographing various stage shows, Dimitri brings a critical eye and high standards to *The Dance Off*'s judging table.

Melissa "Meli" Mendez

The Dance Off is lucky to have international superstar and singer/actress/mogul Meli appear as a guest judge this season.

THE HOSTS

Juan Carlos Perez

Former teen heartthrob

Reggie Kong

Celebrity stylist

THE CREW

Donna Alvarez

Producer

Jordy Cohen

Field producer

Aaliyah Williams

Story assistant

One

Gina Morales clutched the edge of her seat in a white-knuckled grip and gave her field producer a side-eyed glare as he and the camera crew sorted through equipment.

A seaplane. They'd stuffed her into an honest-to-god seaplane.

The aircraft was painted bright yellow and blue with a tiny propeller stuck to the nose, cute little wings, and pontoons positioned underneath. It looked like a model toy, not something rational human beings who valued their lives should travel in.

Yet here she was, flying in a tin can over a large body of water somewhere in Southeast Alaska, while the motor droned on like a monstrous mosquito and the faint scent of fuel tinged the air.

Now she understood why her mother used the rosary in airplanes. It was to keep your hands busy so you didn't chew off all your fingernails in nervous terror. Noted. Next time Gina was on a seaplane, she'd bring a rosary.

For now, she prayed to the gods of reality TV.

Please, please, let him be a Winter Olympian.

A skier would be good, or a snowboarder, or better yet, a figure skater. Olympians were the holy grail of celebrity dance partners. If one of those awaited her when she landed, this whole harrowing journey would be worth it. After all, what other kind of celeb would be hanging out in the uncharted Alaskan wilderness?

When Gina finally dared to peek outside, she could admit the view was picturesque. A rippling ribbon of water unfurled below. Tall evergreens speared a brilliant blue sky crowded with puffy white clouds. A gust of wind teased the treetops, making the seaplane bounce in the air.

Gina clenched her jaw and looked away. Even the pretty scenery didn't distract from the bouncing. Where the hell were they going? And if they were meeting a skier or snowboarder, shouldn't there be more snow?

A tap on her arm drew her attention from the window to Jordy Cohen, her field producer. He was a slim man with olive-toned skin and a ready smile, and he covered his thinning brown hair with a worn UCLA cap. Jordy pointed at the camera, and his voice came through the headset she wore.

"All right, Gina. Ready to start?"

Taking a deep breath, she nodded and gave her shoulders a quick roll to relax them. Nerves notwithstanding, she had a job to do. When Jordy gave the go-ahead, she waved at the camera.

"I'm Gina Morales, a pro dancer. I'm on my way to meet my celebrity partner for season fourteen of *The Dance Off.*" She gave the intro in a loud, clear voice. Or so she thought.

The sound guy looked up from a device in his hand and shook his head.

After adjusting the mic on her headset, Gina repeated the lines at a volume closer to a shout. When she received a thumbs-up, she continued.

"We're in a seaplane flying over a river in Alaska, and I'm a little worried my producers are trying to kill me."

Next to her, Jordy covered his mouth to stifle a laugh. He gestured for her to keep going.

"I've been on three planes so far, each one smaller than the last." She gave an exaggerated shrug and a grimace that wasn't faked. "What's next, a hot air balloon?"

Jordy smacked his forehead like he should have thought of that. Gina resisted the urge to flip him the bird.

The pilot cut in. "We're beginning our descent."

The plane dipped. Gina spun to face the window again, her pulse racing as the water zoomed closer. Were they going to make a water landing? They had to be. Despite climbing aboard at a marina, she hadn't allowed herself to imagine the landing. With every second, the glistening surface of the inlet raced closer, but Gina kept her eyes open. She could do this. She was strong.

And if she died, at least she'd see it coming.

The pontoons hit the water, skimming along and kicking up a wave under the wings. Her stomach bounced, but she'd braced herself for a rougher landing. As the plane pulled alongside a small floating dock made of barrels, Gina pried her fingernails out of the seat cushion. She focused on getting her breathing under control while they disembarked. Once off the plane, they climbed into a waiting skiff and motored to shore. The air carried the scent of salt and wet soil, along with a crisp freshness she could taste on the back of her tongue.

Fresh air. What a novelty.

Once they were ashore, Gina and her crew gathered on a pebbly beach that led right into the water from a clearing. Ahead stood a line of trees the seaplane pilot had called Sitka spruce, the state tree of Alaska. Behind her, the water. Nothing else, aside from the seaplane, the skiff, and a second camera crew she didn't recognize. No stores. No houses. No cars. Just trees, water, and dirt. And sky. Lots and lots of sky.

Too much nature. Not enough civilization. Was it possible to feel claustrophobic in a big empty space?

Gina hunched into her coat. "Where are we?"

Jordy didn't look away from the tablet he shared with the other crew's producer. "Alaska."

"I know that, but . . ." Searching the unfamiliar crew's clothing for logos revealed nothing. Gina pulled out her phone. No service. Of course not. Why would there be service in the middle of fucking nowhere?

Better not to think about how far away they were from the rest of the world. Except now it was all she could think about. What if there was an emergency?

Eyeing the trees warily, she inched toward the boat. Growing up in New York City had given her a healthy distrust of forests. Forests had animals and serial killers hiding behind every tree. Didn't these people watch movies?

Before she could stop herself, she blurted out, "You know I'm from the Bronx, right? I don't do nature. I've never even been camping."

Damn it. Gina bit her tongue as one of the cameras swung her way. It was the perfect sound bite and would without a doubt be aired during the premiere. This was exactly what they'd hoped for—drag her out to the wilderness, film her freaking out, then toss her at her partner before she could get her bearings. The producers would do everything they could to throw her off-balance in the name of good TV.

Gina took a deep breath, then another. The air chilled her lungs. It was colder here than it had been in Juneau, but so fresh she couldn't stop swallowing it in deep, cold pulls. It helped focus her, but also made her giddy.

"You all right?" Jordy actually looked concerned.

"I'm fine." *Just having an existential crisis over the complete and utter remoteness of this location. No big deal.* She shoved her hands in her coat pockets and balled them into fists. "Let's go meet him."

The crew checked her lavalier mic and gave her a minute to touch up her hair and makeup. After she fed a few more lines to the camera about how excited she was to meet her partner, they started the trek through the trees.

"Don't break an ankle," Jordy warned.

Gina pressed her lips together and didn't reply. If she'd known where they were going, she would have worn different shoes. The soles of her shiny black boots were better suited to sidewalks than wet docks or dirt trails. They were already caked in mud and sand, which crunched under her feet with every step.

Jordy was right, though. It would be awful to get injured right before the new season started. With her eyes on the trail, curiosity about the man she was about to meet consumed her thoughts. What kind of a celebrity would he be? Would he be able to dance? And more importantly, was he popular enough to get lots of votes?

On Gina's first season, her celebrity partner was a young singer who'd started his music career on social media. While he'd been a great dancer—if a little too energetic—with a vocal fan base, he didn't have the recognition factor needed to win over *The Dance Off*'s older audience. They'd only made it halfway through the season. Nostalgia could help, too, but Gina's partnership with an aging actor from a popular action movie franchise had ended after three episodes due to his arthritis.

Despite entering her fifth season, Gina didn't have the fan following some of the other pro dancers did. Kevin Ray had been on the show since season one, and *The Dance Off* was now approaching season fourteen. Kevin had won four times. With his easy charm and incredible choreography skills, people voted for Kevin no matter who his celebrity partner was.

It made Gina want to pull her hair out. Kevin had reached the finals in season thirteen with a sixteen-year-old Internet makeup artist, while Gina and her partner—a popular football player who'd shown marked improvement—had been cut in the semifinals.

At least she wasn't the newbie anymore—that spot went to Joel Clarke, a Jamaican dancer who'd joined the cast a month ago.

Since it couldn't hurt, she sent up another prayer that her new partner would be up to the challenge. If he had even a modicum of dance skill and audience appeal, she'd do whatever it took to reach the finals and get a shot at *The Dance Off*'s gaudy golden trophy.

The trail ended in a large clearing with a two-story house made from planks of yellow lumber. A smaller house of dark, weathered wood sat to one side, and a hut made of . . . branches, maybe . . . sat on the other. A treehouse painted with a camouflage pattern perched in one of the tall trees.

Gina stared, taking it all in. *What ... the ... fu ...*

This was ... well, she didn't know *what* this was exactly, but there was no way this collection of makeshift homes was the training camp of a Winter Olympian.

As her plans for an Olympics-themed first dance turned to dust, anger kindled in the ashes.

Damn her producers. They could have warned her. When Jordy said they were going to Alaska, Gina had dressed for a meeting at a ski lodge or an ice rink, or at least somewhere *indoors.* And they'd told her to do full hair and makeup. She was going to look ridiculous wearing false eyelashes to a rough Alaskan homestead.

Bye-bye, trophy.

"Reaction, Gina," Jordy said.

There was no way she could say how disappointed she was. Instead, she took a deep breath and was assaulted by a medley of rich, earthy scents she couldn't even begin to classify. Somehow, the natural aroma soothed her, and she found her voice.

"Wow." It was the first word that popped into her mind. "This is like stepping into another time. I mean, look at these structures. And is that a treehouse?"

There. The editors could splice her words with shots of the buildings, if they chose. It was the best she could do under the circumstances.

A loud, rhythmic thudding came from behind the biggest house. Gina didn't bother to ask what it was, as the other crew's producer was now guiding her toward the noise.

Years of stage training kicked in, washing away her irritation. She grinned at the camera, infusing her voice with excitement. "I hear something over there. I think it's him."

As she turned the corner around the back porch and got her first look at her new partner, her pulse pounded in her throat and stole her breath. She blinked and spoke without thinking. "Is he ... is he mine?"

Mine. She hadn't meant to say that, didn't want to examine the mixed emotions the word sparked.

"Yes," Jordy said from behind her. "That's your partner."

Hot damn.

The bare-chested man chopping wood behind the main house was six-five if he was an inch, covered in rippling, bulging muscles and smooth, tanned skin. Obliques and delts flexed and released with each swing, highlighting his pure strength and perfect form. The rustic axe acted as an extension of his beautiful body and hit its mark every time.

He was the kind of man who'd look remarkable doing any activity, but he fit here, as if he'd sprung from the earth fully formed—and conjured by Gina's wildest fantasies—for the express purpose of chopping wood.

She wanted to lick him just to make sure he was real.

Jordy gestured her forward to confront the magnificent wood-splitting specimen. The camera crews fanned out. Gina's heart rate had yet to return to normal, and she seemed to have swallowed her own tongue, but she obligingly took a step.

A twig snapped under her boot.

The small *crack* stopped the man at the top of his swing. His head whipped around in her direction. As he straightened, the hand holding the axe fell to his side, and he scooped back his long dark blond hair with the other. Their gazes met, the bright blue of his eyes visible across the clearing.

Chest heaving, he swung the axe into the wood stump, leaving it embedded and quivering.

If Gina wasn't careful, she'd start quivering, too.

A light brown beard covered the lower half of his face, amplifying his intense masculinity to a thrilling degree and making him look wild, unpredictable, and . . . delicious. The defined muscles of his torso made her mouth water. She swallowed hard.

Work. Cameras. *Job.*

Ignoring her thudding heart and warm cheeks, Gina marched toward him. Around them, camera operators shifted to capture every nuance of their first meeting—every word, every reaction, every sign of nerves.

Despite her calm expression, Gina's mind whirled, connecting the dots as she approached her new partner.

First, her producers had made sure she was perfectly groomed and looking her best.

Following that, they'd thrown her off her game with an unsettling seaplane ride.

And now, they were surprising her with half-naked wood-chopping and so many muscles it bordered on rude.

Gina's steps faltered as the truth hit her. *Shit.* She should have seen it right away, and would have if the first sight of him hadn't short-circuited her thoughts.

This man would likely be the hottest guy in the cast, and Gina was young and single. It could only mean one thing.

They were being set up as this season's showmance.

Two

Well, Stone had expected a city girl. And he'd gotten one.

With the axe safely in the stump, Stone caught his breath, unable to take his eyes off his dance partner as she approached him. She'd appeared in the clearing like she'd taken a wrong turn in Los Angeles and ended up in Alaska. Wrapped in a pale pink wool coat and high black boots, with her long brown hair spilling out from under a matching knit hat, she looked polished, puttogether, and *small*. Next to her, he was a great hulking brute. How were they supposed to dance together? He'd crush her.

She was pretty, of course. Her eyes were dark and thickly lined, her lashes long, her golden skin reminiscent of the cones of a Sitka spruce after they had matured. Her full lips were painted the color of winterberries and caught his attention more than they should have.

Yeah, definitely pretty, but she didn't belong here. Why the hell had the production dragged this delicate Hollywood dance diva all the way out to Alaska to meet him? Stone had to fly to Los Angeles for rehearsals anyway. They could have easily filmed their first meeting there.

But if a few years on a reality show had taught him anything, it was that TV producers didn't care about convenience. Meeting in the remote wilderness, as opposed to a bright, stark rehearsal room, would make for better behind-the-scenes footage. The contrast between their appearances was purposeful, a deliberate move on the part of the producers, and Stone hated them for it.

Hated himself for taking part in this madness. A dance show, of all things.

His partner stopped a couple feet away from him. If she was nervous, she covered it well. Her grin lit her face, showing all her teeth and transforming her beauty into something more approachable and real.

"Hi there, partner." Her voice had a musical quality he hadn't expected, and a slight accent he couldn't place. "I'm Gina Morales."

"Stone Nielson." He stuck out his hand, then froze when she opened her arms. She wanted a hug? Was this for the cameras? He was three times her size, sweaty and filthy, and he didn't often hug people. But she was waiting, so he reached down and awkwardly embraced her. She gave him a peck on the cheek before pulling away, leaving behind the scent of tropical flowers and a tingling sensation where her lips had touched.

His eyebrows popped up in surprise, and she waved a hand dismissively. "I'm Puerto Rican. We kiss hello and goodbye." Her gaze flicked over to the members of his camera crew, mixed in with hers. "So, I guess you're filming a show here?"

Relief flooded through him. Good, she had no idea who he was. This whole thing was embarrassing enough without her having watched him on TV, playing out the silly storylines his father and the production team brainstormed in their weekly meetings.

Since he was shirtless and didn't have a lav mic clipped to his waistband, Stone raised his voice so the boom mic could pick up his answer. "We're filming the fourth season of *Living Wild*. My family and I live off the grid here on Nielson HQ, where we build our own homes, hunt, and live off the land."

The premise was ridiculous and hokey even to him, and he could never explain it without sounding like a robot. How much worse would it sound to her? She probably thought they were all wacky forest folk.

But Gina only nodded as she surveyed the makeshift compound. "You're like a wilderness expert or something?"

Stone shrugged. "Or something."

She sent him a teasing wink. "Well, soon you'll be a dance expert. Ready to learn a few moves?"

"I'm game," he said, because it was expected of him. The absolute last thing he wanted to do was learn to dance. "You probably haven't taught anyone to dance in the forest before."

She cast another glance around, scanning the trees. "I haven't, but there's a first time for everything."

"Nervous?"

"A little." She ducked her head like she was embarrassed. "I'm more comfortable in big cities."

"I bet." She stood out like a palm tree in the middle of the tundra.

"Is there somewhere around here with level ground?"

"We can use the porch. It's the closest thing we have to a dance floor." Stone led the way, pointing to where Gina should watch her step, while the cameras circled them like planets in orbit around twin suns.

The clearing behind the house was a veritable obstacle course of outdoorsy shit, thanks to his brothers and their multitude of half-finished projects. The producers believed it made the set "visually interesting." Stone just thought it looked like a mess.

Gina's producer cupped his hands around his mouth and called out, "Tell her why you're joining the show, Stone."

Oh, right. What the hell was he supposed to say again? They'd told him not to mention the money, but it was the only reason he'd agreed to this. If his mother hadn't owed an exorbitant amount in medical bills, he would have turned it down. His family made a good income from *Living Wild*, but his parents had already been in debt before his mother's procedure. Stone would feel better if he could help them reach financial stability, and pay off his own student loans while he was at it.

"I'm joining *The Dance Off* for my mom." Stone cleared his throat and recited the lines his producers had crafted. "She had a hip replacement last year. It was scary for all of us, and it would make her happy to see me dancing and having an experience totally different from everything we know."

He winced. The lines sounded unnatural. He just wasn't any good at these canned responses.

But Gina pressed a hand to his arm. "I'm so sorry. Is she better now?"

Her concerned expression seemed genuine, but it was impossible to know for certain in the world of reality TV. Stone nodded, not sure how else to answer.

"That was great," Gina's producer shouted. "Keep going."

God, this was weird. After four years, Stone should have been used to having normal human interactions dictated by committee, but he wasn't. And he'd been out of the game so long, hiding away in this little corner of Alaska, he barely knew how to make small talk with a woman.

On the porch, Gina unzipped her coat and shrugged it off, revealing jeans and a fluffy gray sweater that accentuated her shape. She was curvier than he expected, with a strong, solid build. Maybe he wouldn't break her after all.

The thought took his mind down another path that had nothing to do with dancing. Stone cut it off at the pass. Gina was his dance partner—nothing else. A woman from the land of smog, traffic, and fake people. They were from different worlds, and he had no business thinking about her as anything other than a means to an end. They would dance, he'd collect his paycheck, and then he'd return home to Alaska. End of story.

Gina shivered as she draped the coat over the porch railing. Stone guessed it would be easier for her to dance without it, but she didn't look like the kind of woman who liked to be uncomfortable. "Aren't you going to be cold?" he asked.

She rubbed her bare hands together to warm them. "I'll manage."

He hooked his thumbs through the loops on his jeans. If she'd put the coat back on, he could stop worrying about her. "It's a bit colder here than in Los Angeles."

"True, but I'm from New York, which has four seasons."

New York. That explained the trace of accent.

When she turned around, she gave his bare chest a once-over. "You're one to talk. Aren't *you* cold?"

He shrugged. He was, but he'd survive. Besides, he had a down jacket hidden in the house for after she left.

"So." Gina braced her hands on her hips. "Have you ever danced before?"

"Not really." His brothers Reed and Wolf were the party animals, the boisterous ones. Stone was the strong one. The quiet one. The serious one. It even said so on the *Living Wild* website, under his photo: "Stone is strong, quiet, and serious."

In a family of seven kids, birth order mattered. Stone, at thirty, was the second oldest, and he and his siblings had been locked into their roles long before the show aired on TV. Maybe if his older brother Reed were different, Stone could have loosened up a little, instead of taking on all the responsibilities of the oldest without the parental attention. But as always, he put family first. Right now, that involved embarrassing himself in front of a gorgeous woman.

"Um, but I can learn," he added. "To dance."

"Don't worry, I'm a good teacher." Gina flashed him that grin again, the wide, toothy one that almost made him forget about the cameras. *Almost.* "Besides, everyone has danced in some form or another."

"Only if you count clapping and stomping while my brother Winter plays the fiddle."

"The fiddle?" Gina snorted, covering her mouth with one hand.

At least she was laughing about the fiddle and not Winter's name, like most people did. And she hadn't batted an eyelash when he'd told her his name was Stone, so that was a point in her favor.

Gina recovered without any further comments about the fiddle. "Yes, I would say clapping and stomping *do* count, because they require a connection to the music."

"Don't we need music now?" When Stone crossed his arms over his chest, Gina's gaze followed the movement. It took everything he had not to say, *Hey, my eyes are up here.* The producers would love it, which was all the reason he needed to hold back. Besides, teasing suggested intimacy, and they were still strangers.

She moved closer, invading his personal space without a *Do you mind?* He didn't mind, though. She smelled nice. Sweet and floral.

"Not yet," she said. "I'm going to give you some pointers on frame and hold first."

This was already over his head and they'd barely begun. "What does that mean?"

"In ballroom dance, the man—or the person dancing that role—leads. He creates a frame with his body for the person in the woman's role to dance within."

Gina poked and prodded at Stone's shoulders, spine, and jaw, positioning him like a mannequin. It reminded him of the photo-shoots he'd done and when the PAs prepped him for filming. Working in TV involved being touched by strangers more often than he'd expected, but it was different with Gina. Her touch was strong and sure, and her cool fingers left a trail of fire and goosebumps in their wake.

She lifted his elbow, then pressed down on his shoulder when he raised it too high. As she circled him, the camera operators—hers and his—swarmed the corners of the porch. This footage would wind up on both TV shows.

"If you're the pro," Stone said, doing his best to hold the position she'd put him in, "how am I supposed to lead you?"

Gina ducked her head under his arm, embarrassingly close to his armpit, and peered up at him with an impish smile. "I'll teach you." Her palm rested on his lower back, his skin growing warmer where they touched. Better to focus on the potential for embarrassment, not her closeness, her scent, or the way her shiny hair slipped over her shoulder. And definitely not her hands or how much more touching they'd have to do before this was all over.

"We're expected to have our first dance ready in three weeks?" Even to his own ears, his tone was skeptical.

"We'll be ready."

"Assuming I don't break your toes first."

She suppressed a laugh. "You won't."

"And after the premiere we only have one week for each rehearsal."

"Uh-huh."

Now he didn't need to distract himself. Panic threatened, and Stone let out a slow breath. This was a fool's errand. He should stay in Alaska and call the whole thing off. But no, that wasn't an option. The contracts had been signed. Barring an injury, he was locked in.

Easing back, Gina looked him up and down, then nodded. "You'll do." Before he could prepare himself, she stepped into his arms.

She was right. Even though she was a foot shorter than he was, when she rested her left arm on his and took his other hand, she fit perfectly into the frame he created.

In hold, Gina's shoulders dropped, her neck elongated, and she tilted her head at a precise angle. For the first time since she'd entered the clearing, it was obvious she was a dancer.

Stone's heart pounded. Suddenly, he didn't feel so cold anymore. From the rise and fall of her chest, she was breathing fast, too.

"This is the hold we use for the waltz." Despite the elegance of her pose, her direct, authoritative tone didn't change. "Do you know anything about the waltz?"

What was this, a pop quiz? "Um, it's old?"

She grinned. "Well, yeah. It's the oldest of the current ballroom dances. It's a romantic dance, slower and more emotional than, say, a samba, which is a fast Latin dance."

Dread skittered along his spine at the thought. "Are we going to have to do that one, too?"

"Not for the first week."

What the hell was he getting himself into? His muscles locked, afraid to ruin the hold, afraid she would make him move in some way. His mind supplied the image of him falling, crushing her, and both of them tumbling down the steps.

He swallowed hard. Why had he agreed to this? Wasn't one reality show enough?

Oh, right. The money.

"Relax." Gina gave his shoulder a brisk pat. "You've already nailed the hold. All you have to do is step and turn." She nudged him in a way that jostled him into motion. Counting the steps, she led him in a circle, then stopped.

Stone waited for her to do something else. She didn't. "Was that it?"

"That was it." She smiled. "Good work."

He narrowed his eyes. "It can't be that easy."

"It's not. But that was the basic step. The Viennese waltz is a series of rotations, interspersed with change steps and a few others."

"If it's so simple, how do we make our waltz look different from everyone else's?"

Gina threw her head back and laughed full out. Underneath all the makeup and perfect hair, the sparkle in her eye and exuberance in her laugh struck him like a kick to the gut. Despite the cold, sweat tickled the back of his neck.

When she caught her breath, she gave his hand a squeeze. "You leave that to me, mountain man. Come on, let's do one more."

The camera operators scrambled out of the way as she led him through another turn. The boom mic bobbed over their heads.

"The waltz marked a big *turning point* in dance. Pun intended." She stopped their turn and leaned back with one leg extended, her booted toes pointed.

"How so?" Getting the hang of it, Stone led her in a rotation to the other end of the porch.

She gave him an approving nod. "In Europe, before the waltz, people at parties danced in groups and didn't touch each other a whole lot. They also faced outward during part of the dance."

"Seems strange now." They spun again, eyes locked.

"Right? People thought it was either scandalous—*bodies touching*—or boring, because they only faced their partners."

When they came to a stop, Gina stepped away. Cold air rushed in to fill the space where she'd been. Stone dropped his arms before he did something stupid, like pull her back to him.

It was his turn to say something. "Uh, you know a lot about the waltz."

"I know a lot about dance, period." She leaned against the porch railing. "This will be my fifth season on the show, and I've been dancing since I was three." She gestured out at the wilderness around them. "I'm sure you're an expert on all this."

"You learn a thing or two when your survival depends on it."

"I wouldn't know where to begin."

Miguel, the *Living Wild* producer, gave the signal. It was the perfect lead-in. Ignoring his uneasiness, Stone asked, "Hey, you want to try chopping wood?"

G ina hesitated. It would be rude to turn down the offer, but she'd been clear with her agent and *The Dance Off*'s producers about her aversion to showmances. As much as she wanted Stone to feel comfortable working with her and for them to have an easy rapport, providing fodder for the editors to cut and splice into a faux romance was *not* on her agenda. Her career was her number-one priority, and she wouldn't jeopardize it by getting a reputation for messing around with her coworkers.

Stone was still waiting. Politeness won, tempered by a determination to keep her distance.

"Um, sure." Gina followed him down the porch steps. The cameras on the ground spread out and the ones on the porch slipped quietly down the stairs behind them.

At the stump, Stone wrenched the axe free and held it flat in both hands. "You've seen an axe before?"

"Yeah, of course. On TV." Gina pointed to the blade. "This is the part you hit the wood with."

He let out a sound that was part laugh and part sigh. "Fair enough. The axe has a particular design, and the names of its parts are easy to remember because a lot of them correspond with body parts."

Body parts? Great. "Uh-huh."

His big hand skimmed the handle of the axe as he talked, drawing her attention to the scars and dirt marring his skin. His hands were those of a man who worked hard and pushed his body and strength to the limit, yet he'd held her with care and respect on the porch. In her second season, she'd been paired with a comedian who'd hit on her at their first meeting—on camera. This was an improvement over that, at least.

Even if he wasn't an Olympian.

Stone adjusted his grip on the tool and pointed to the metal part. "This part of the head is called the bit." He tapped the sharp edge. "Or as you called it, 'the part you hit the wood with.'"

"Ha!" She snapped her fingers. "I knew it. See, we city folk know something about country living."

For the first time since they'd met, he laughed. His lips stretched in a smile, showing straight white teeth, and his blue eyes crinkled at the corners.

Damn, he was handsome.

"City girl, this is way beyond country living," he drawled. "This . . . is living wild."

It was *such* a line, said to slip the name of his show into the conversation. Gina knew that. And still. The words, uttered in that deep, growly voice, reminded her that she was so far outside her comfort zone, she might as well kiss it goodbye forever. A curl of desire rippled and thrummed inside her. Breathing became difficult, the air filled with the scent of freshly cut wood and sexy man.

She cleared her throat. "You were saying?"

Stone described the different parts of the axe, and he hadn't been kidding about the correspondence to body parts. Hearing him talk about toe and heel, or cheek and face, was fine. But then he mentioned shoulder, beard, and butt, and he might as well have been talking about himself because his body was all she could concentrate on.

"Are you ready to give it a swing?"

Gina stared at the axe. She'd spaced out while he was demonstrating, distracted by his naked torso. "Oh, um . . ."

Crash.

Heart in her throat, Gina whipped her head around toward the trees. "What was that?"

Stone's broad chest swelled as he sucked in a breath. "Don't move. I think I see something."

The urgency in his voice cut through her haze of arousal. He swung the axe into the stump with a thud and put out an arm to herd her behind him.

The crashing continued. Branches snapped and cracked, and leaves swished, like something big was moving through the forest.

"What?" Alarm squeezed the word into a squeak. Her gaze skimmed the trees at the edges of the clearing, searching for the threat. Since Stone wasn't wearing a shirt, Gina grabbed the waistband of his jeans like it was a lifeline. "What do you see?"

"Stay behind me." His voice, deep and commanding, was also steady. This was his world. He knew what to do. She pressed closer to him as a growing sense of horror raised goosebumps over her back. Stone jerked his chin toward the line of trees at the opposite end of the clearing and spoke in a low voice. "Gina, I don't want to alarm you, but there's a bear in the woods over there."

Terror streaked through her. *"A bear?"*

"Yes. In this area of Alaska there are more bears than people. This is their turf."

Gina sucked in a breath. She knew it. She fucking knew it. *This* was what happened to people who went into forests. They got eaten by *bears.* "What do we do? Make a run for it? Aren't they fast?"

"I'll protect you." Stone reached around the woodpile and brought out a gun. *A fucking gun.* Gina let out a strangled squeal, then clapped her hands over her mouth.

She'd only ever seen guns in the possession of police officers,

and she didn't know a damn thing about makes and models. This
was some kind of shotgun, with a strap and a long barrel. Stone
held it comfortably, more comfortably than he'd held her during
their waltz. It fit in his big, scarred hands, fit with his long hair
and shirtless, muscled upper body. He was like an action movie
star ready to save the day against some villain.

Except they were filming a *reality TV show,* not an action movie.

"You're going to *shoot* it?" Holy *fuck.* She didn't want to get at-
tacked by a bear, but she didn't want to watch an animal get killed,
either.

If it came down to a choice, though . . .

Stone pumped the shotgun, the *ca-click* loud in the silence
around them. "No, I'm just going to scare it away. But I need you
to cover your ears."

Gina clapped her hands tight over her ears and hunched behind
Stone's broad back. As she squeezed her eyes shut, the image of
him raising the barrel of the gun toward the sky burned into her
memory. The blast of the shotgun echoed through the crisp Alaskan air, impossibly loud even through her hands. Long after the
echo of the shot died away, she stood with her chin tucked into her
chest, hands over her ears and eyes closed, until Stone's big, warm
hands curled over her shoulders.

"Gina. Gina, it's okay." His voice was close to her ear, close
enough for her to feel his breath on her cheek and catch the fresh,
piney scent that emanated from his skin. "You're safe. I scared it
away. Please, open your eyes."

"It's gone? You're sure?" She cracked open her eyelids and found
his face just a few inches from her own, his eyes as clear and blue
as the sky above.

"I'm positive."

She didn't say anything when he took her in his arms and held
her.

It was only then that she realized she was shaking.

Three

Stone wrapped one of his arms around Gina. "I'm sorry. You're okay now. It's safe."

She sagged against him, curling into his chest, her body shivering. The scent of tropical flowers invaded his senses.

"Gina? Are you all right? Talk to us." Her producer at least had the decency to appear worried, although he kept the cameras rolling. Stone wanted to punch the guy. And his own producers, who'd come up with this stupid scheme.

When Gina continued to tremble and stare at the trees with naked fear in her eyes, Stone cupped her cheeks and waited until she looked at him.

"Gina? I'm going to pick you up and bring you inside, okay?" When she gave a shaky nod, he scooped her up and carried her to the main house. If he'd thought waltzing with her was intimate, it had nothing on holding her in his arms while she pressed her face to his bare chest.

The crew leapt into action, running ahead to keep Stone's face in view. He maintained an impassive expression, just to thwart them. Inside he seethed, burning with the need to tell them all off.

In the living area, Stone settled Gina into his mother's armchair while the camera operators hovered around them. When he stood, her hands clung to his arms, and she met his gaze with a look of terror.

Guilt stabbed through him. This was his fault. When Miguel approached him with the "bear" idea, he'd shrugged and said it sounded fine, like he did with all their other idiotic plans. He'd never expected that Gina would respond this way. It made sense, though. She was an urbanite, through and through. Frightening her like this was just cruel.

"Pass me that blanket," he told one of the PAs, pointing to his grandmother's handmade quilt draped over the back of the narrow sofa. "And get her a bottle of water."

Stone sank to his knees beside Gina and tucked the quilt around her legs. He rubbed her shoulders and stroked the hair out of her face while she drank the water in halting sips. Maybe it was weird to be touching her with such familiarity, but from the way she gripped his wrist on her quilt-covered lap, she didn't seem to mind.

"Are you okay now?" he asked in a low voice, ignoring the two camera crews surrounding them. She bit her lip and nodded, but he didn't believe her. Her eyes, when they met his, were still too wide, too glassy. If he could just make her smile again, like she had on the porch, he'd know she was all right. But he didn't know how.

Her producer approached. "Ready to go, Gina?"

Wait, she was leaving? Already?

Stone wanted to ask her to stay, to do the whole thing over. He wouldn't act like such a robot this time, and they'd nix the bear interruption. They'd dance on the porch and laugh like they weren't surrounded by other people. Like they weren't being paid to talk to each other.

But what was the point? He'd be in Los Angeles soon enough. Their initial meeting was over and the crews had the footage they wanted. Better that she leave now, before the *Living Wild* crew came up with some other way to traumatize her.

Stone pulled on a quilted plaid jacket and followed *The Dance Off*'s crew through the forest to the beach. One of the *Living Wild* helicopters waited for them on the sandy spit. They loaded Gina in and took off, soaring away over the water.

After the helicopter and the seaplane were gone, Miguel kept Stone on the beach for a reaction interview.

"What did you think of Gina?" Miguel prompted.

Stone jammed his hands into his jacket pockets. Fuck. What did he think of her? In reality TV, it was hard to know what was real and what wasn't, and she'd left him with a contradictory mess of impressions.

Most of all, he felt like a dick for scaring her.

But Miguel was waiting, so Stone went with something non-committal. "Gina was cool. For a city girl."

Miguel's eyes lit up. "Explain."

Stone shrugged. "Most people aren't used to the way we live at Nielson HQ. Things are wild out here. There's no Hollywood or Disneyland. We don't have manicures or hair salons."

Stone held up his hands to show his dirty fingernails, remembering the way Gina had stared at his hands when he'd shown her the axe. What must she have thought of him?

Building steam, he kept going. "Alaskan life is difficult for folks from the lower forty-eight. They can't hack it."

"Do you think Gina will want to come back to visit?"

It took everything Stone had to keep a note of accusation out of his voice. "I can't imagine Gina will ever want to visit again, not after the bear thing."

"Are you looking forward to moving to LA for rehearsals?"

Stone suppressed a grimace. Being on *The Dance Off* required him to live in Los Angeles for however long he lasted in the competition. It could be *months*.

"I'm going to miss my family, for sure," Stone said, since he couldn't admit how much he dreaded the move. "And all of this." He spread his arms wide to encompass the beauty and nature surrounding them. "Who wouldn't? It's beautiful here."

"Are you nervous about learning to dance?"

Like he was going to answer that. With his hands on his hips,

Stone smirked a little, posturing for the camera. "I scared off a bear today. You think there's anything in Los Angeles that could scare me?"

Miguel sighed. "Is that the best you can do?"

Stone threw up his hands. "What do you want me to say? That I'm glad my partner is terrified of me? I'm sure it's going to make my experience in Los Angeles so much easier, thanks."

"Relax. It was a great scene. You played it perfectly." Miguel conferred with the rest of the team to come up with better answers for Stone.

The break gave him time to rein in his anger. It was useless, anyway. He'd signed up for this bullshit. He'd known what he was getting into.

It's not forever. That was what Stone told himself when the pressure, the cameras, and the manipulation got to him. *It's not forever.*

When Miguel came back, Stone dialed down the sarcasm, listened to their notes, and dutifully recited his lines back to the camera. After a few more questions, he got the signal that his family was returning soon.

Back at Nielson HQ, Stone dropped onto one of the benches surrounding the fire pit and scrubbed a hand over his face. This whole thing was a fucking disaster. There had to be other competition shows he could join to earn enough to pay for his mother's medical bills. What happened to the show where people ate bugs? He could do that.

Since the cameras were still rolling, he started a fire, then sat back to sharpen one of his hunting knives. It was the kind of B-roll footage they could intersperse into any episode or commercial.

Stone heard his family coming long before he saw them. Reed and Raven had loud, carrying laughs, and Wolf was prone to howling. It wasn't for show—it was just Wolf, living up to his name.

Living Wild had picked up the nine Nielsons in a package deal. Jimmy and Pepper Nielson had seven children with names inspired by the natural world. Four boys, followed by three girls: Reed, Stone, Wolf, Winter, Raven, Violet, and Lark. Their hair ranged from Pepper's pale blond to Jimmy's coppery brown, aside from Lark, the baby of the family, who was a true redhead. Most of them had Pepper's bright blue eyes, except for Reed and Raven, whose eyes were hazel. When Jimmy approached the network with his pitch, it had been too good for the producers to pass up.

Stone's shoulders tensed as his family entered the clearing. Cameras stood at the ready to catch the barrage of questions.

Wolf approached first, giving Stone a slap on the back. "Bro, who'd you get?"

Stone kept his attention on the knife. "Gina."

Whoops and hollers followed, which would have happened no matter which dancer he'd been assigned.

His mother, Pepper, sat beside him on the rough-hewn bench. "What was she like? Was she nice?"

"Yeah, she was nice." Before he'd pulled out a gun and scared the wits out of her. "She's from the big city, though. We saw a bear, and she left early."

Reed snickered. "People like her are bear bait."

They teased him a bit more, and Stone tuned most of it out, like he always did. When the cameras shifted away to follow Reed and Wolf's antics, Jimmy sat on Stone's other side and spoke into his ear, even though the lavalier microphone he wore picked up everything. The editors would cut out whatever didn't match the *Living Wild* narrative.

"Don't get too close to that dancer," Jimmy said. "And keep your mouth shut. You're a terrible liar. If you let something slip, this whole house of cards is gonna fall. I'd send Reed if I could, but they wanted you."

Stone's guts turned to ice at his father's words. Still, ice was better than red-hot fury, which had grown harder to ignore as of late. He'd done everything they'd asked of him for *Living Wild*, including leaving behind the life he'd built in Juneau. And since when was being a bad liar something to be criticized for? Sure, Reed was better at acting the role of the cool off-the-grid survivalist, but he also struggled with addiction. Sending him to Los Angeles would be a disaster.

Stone kept his tone mild. "Gina and I have nothing in common. We won't have anything to talk about, aside from our dances."

"Make sure of it. We got a good thing going here. Don't need you screwing it up." Jimmy heaved himself to his feet and ambled off to steal the spotlight.

Pepper patted Stone's knee. "Just stay quiet, honey. You're good at that."

"Yeah. Sure." He was "the quiet one," after all.

Miguel gestured for Stone to get up. "Let's get some shots of you practicing those waltz moves with the girls. And try to look excited about this, okay? We're going to do a lot of cross-promo to build ratings from the network exposure."

While the camera operators buzzed in the periphery like all-seeing, ever-present gnats, Stone summoned a smile he didn't feel and twirled his sisters around the bonfire in the gathering dusk.

In a few short days, he'd be in Los Angeles, twirling Gina. He just had to find a way to apologize for the bear without cluing her in to the truth.

G ina used the helicopter ride to pull herself together. At least it wasn't a hot air balloon, like she'd joked. By the time the crew arrived at the Glacier Valley Inn, which was advertised as being Alaska Native owned and operated, Gina was ready to film her reaction interview on the inn's wooden deck. It overlooked sparkling water and an island full of huge evergreen trees. They stood tall and straight, their pointed tops reaching toward the picturesque sky.

Behind her, the sun set over the inlet, painting the sky above the mountains in vivid streaks of orange, pink, and deep purple. It was without a doubt the most beautiful sunset she'd ever witnessed, but after her encounter with Stone, all she wanted to do was hole up inside her hotel room and decompress.

The man must think she was some kind of high-strung urbanite. *Not* the image she wanted to project anywhere, on camera or off, and especially not with her new partner. Her *hot* new partner.

Once the crew had finally set her free—and removed her mic—Gina retreated to her room. She wanted to call her family, but she'd be too tempted to tell them about her experience, and she wasn't allowed to divulge the identity of her celebrity partner until the cast reveal in a few weeks.

Still, there was one person she could tell. After washing her face and changing into sweats, Gina initiated a video call to Natasha Díaz, her roommate and fellow pro dancer on *The Dance Off*. Propping the phone on the pillows, Gina stretched out on the bed and waited for Natasha to pick up.

After a few seconds, Tash's smiling face filled the screen.

"Hey, Gina G." Natasha's long curly hair was pulled into a high bun and she wore her glasses, which meant she was in for the night. "Cuéntame. Who did you get?"

Gina rubbed her temples. "Girl, you are not going to *believe* what happened to me today."

When Gina finished recounting her first meeting with Stone, Natasha's dark eyes were wide behind her glasses and she pushed her face close to the camera. "A *bear*? You're shitting me, right?"

"A motherfucking bear."

"Where the hell are you?"

"Somewhere in Alaska. Near Juneau."

"Where's that?"

Gina shrugged. "Hell if I know."

"Okay, enough about the bear and Alaska. Get to the good stuff. Is he hot?"

With a groan, Gina flopped over onto her side. "Super hot. Like steam rising in the cold air off his ridiculously huge muscles hot. I'm not convinced he's a real person."

"Mm." Natasha licked her lips. "I can't wait to meet him. Especially since you won't make a move. Not after that whole fiasco with dumbass Ruben."

"Don't remind me. I think they're setting me up for a show-mance. And we just gave them a ton of footage."

"Shit, they should have paired him with me if that's what they want."

Gina pinched the bridge of her nose. "Part of me can't believe the producers played me like that, and the other part totally believes it. I bet you anything it was Donna's idea."

"Fucking Donna." Natasha *tsk*ed. "Still, what's the worst that could happen if you go along with it?"

"The worst?" Gina blew out a breath. "The worst would be playing into the 'sexy Latina' stereotype, setting a bad example for my nieces, and losing out on future jobs because they think I'm unprofessional."

Natasha rolled her eyes. "Gina, you *are* a sexy Latina. And everyone in this industry sleeps with each other. Hell, I do it all the time."

"It's different when it's private," Gina protested. "An onscreen showmance makes it the most interesting thing about us. Stone and I will be able to create exciting storylines without it. He's used to reality TV. He knows how this works."

Besides, a showmance had the huge potential to backfire on her. She'd seen it before when fans, pissed off by the "will they or won't they" dynamic, stopped voting for the couple in question. Every step of her career, Gina had succeeded through talent and hard-earned skill, and she would do the same with Stone.

And she would do her best to forget about how sexy he'd looked chopping wood, or how sweetly he'd cared for her after the bear incident.

Natasha raised her eyebrows. "You might change your mind when you hear who Kevin got."

Gina groaned. "Is it going to make me mad?"

"Yup."

"Tell me anyway."

"An Olympic figure skater."

Gina rubbed her temples. *Of course* Kevin got the Olympian.

"That guy has the best freaking luck. I've got a wilderness surviv-alist who's more comfortable around bears than dancing in hold."

"Don't worry about it so much. Once you're both in LA, you'll be on your own turf. And at least you've met him. I don't find out who my partner is for another couple of days. I'm itching to get started."

"Me, too."

As beautiful as the forty-ninth state was, Gina was ready to say goodbye to Alaska and get back to Los Angeles, where she'd be faced with the singular challenge of turning a mountain man into a ballroom dancer.

Piece of cake.

Four

Butterflies quickstepped in Gina's belly as she waited for Stone to arrive for their first rehearsal. Freaking out over a bear was *not* the kind of first impression she'd wanted to make, and she hoped it didn't make things weird between them. Natasha was right, though. They were on her turf now, and she was determined to come across as professional and in control.

Gina practiced a few moves in front of the mirrors in the rehearsal room they would use for the rest of the season. Some of the other pros had started to practice already. Natasha had met her partner—star football player Dwayne Alonzo, fresh off the Super Bowl—the previous morning for a short rehearsal. According to Tash, Dwayne was good-looking, but boring.

Maybe Stone would turn out to be boring. That would certainly make things easier on a personal level, although it wouldn't help their chemistry as partners. As she did a few foxtrot steps, Gina squinted at her feet, picturing Stone's much longer stride. She had her work cut out for her.

Off to the side, Aaliyah Williams, a young Black woman with long box braids and stylish glasses, sat in a folding chair. As story assistant, her job was to live log the rehearsal on her laptop and send her notes to the editors.

Jordy came in then, a camera perched on his shoulder as he faced the closed door. "Here he comes."

The door opened, revealing Stone in all his rugged Adonis-like glory. His long hair was pulled back in a man-bun—a style Gina hadn't found sexy until that very moment—and he wore navy basketball shorts and a white V-neck tee.

Gina suppressed a dreamy sigh. It was highly inconvenient to have such an attractive partner. Meeting him in the middle of a forest had made him appear almost otherworldly. A few days in LA had convinced her he couldn't really be as handsome and muscular as she remembered. Seeing him here, in the most mundane of settings and outfits, yet still larger than life and stupidly handsome, was like a slap in the face to her libido.

Haha, his body seemed to say. *I really am that sexy. Deal with it, suckah.*

Whatever. She'd danced with plenty of good-looking men. Granted, most of them had slim dancers' builds, but so what? She could be an adult about this. Even though she wanted to giggle like a thirteen-year-old meeting her favorite boy band.

Yikes. She needed to get a grip. Between Aaliyah and Jordy, everything that happened in the rehearsal room would be captured, and was fair game to end up in the show. The overhanging threat of the showmance meant Gina had to keep her reaction to Stone in check.

"Hey there." Trying for nonchalance, she strolled over and gave him a kiss on the cheek, as she did with all her friends. As if the scent of him—pine and fresh air and man—didn't make her want to close her eyes and breathe deep. She pulled back, ignoring the urge to roll around in his warmth like in a big fuzzy blanket.

Looking into eyes the same blue as clear Alaska skies, it took her a minute to find her wit. "My goodness, you're big. How tall are you exactly?"

He scratched the back of his head. "Six-seven."

"Shoot." Gina cringed. "Sorry. It's just . . . you're even taller than my initial estimate. I'm five-foot-six, and it's a challenge to choreograph a dance in hold when the partners have such a huge height difference." She grinned to put him at ease, like her nervous babbling was normal. "Don't worry. I'm an excellent choreographer, and I wouldn't have gotten this far if I were afraid of high heels."

He eyed her feet and his brow furrowed. "Are those . . . highheeled sneakers?"

She lifted a foot to show him the side view. "They're wedge high tops."

"You can dance in those things?"

"Dude, I can dance in anything."

"I'm not sure I can." He cast a skeptical glance down at his own feet, clad in shiny black dance shoes.

Gina bit her lip, searching for a reply that couldn't be misconstrued in editing. Ballroom dance required intimacy, and they didn't have long to form a bond as partners. As much as their initial meeting had unsettled her, she was the expert here. It was up to her to make him comfortable, even though just looking at him gave her butterflies.

Fucking butterflies. *Jeez.*

"How are you settling in?" she finally asked. "Did you have a good flight?"

He shrugged, the fabric of his T-shirt pulling tight over his muscles. "Uneventful flight. The hotel is nice. Different from what I'm used to."

She sent him a teasing grin. "I can't imagine a bear is going to pop out from behind the ice machine."

Instead of a laugh, he pressed his lips into a firm line and looked away. His brows knit together like he was angry.

As if sensing deep emotions, Jordy crept closer with the camera.

Gina ignored the field producer and put a hand on her partner's arm. "Stone? Everything okay?"

"Are *you* okay?" he shot back, startling her.

"Sure." The butterflies picked up the pace, dancing a salsa. "Why wouldn't I be?"

His fingers tapped a nervous rhythm against his thigh. "The last time I saw you . . ."

Gina rubbed her hands over her face. "Yeah, about that. Look, I'm sorry for the way I overreacted. First the seaplane, then the wilderness, then the bear . . . It was a shock, to say the least, and not at all what I was expecting."

Stone cocked an eyebrow. "What were you expecting? Not a bear, I'm guessing. Or me."

Should she answer? She didn't want him to think she was disappointed to have him as a partner. "I don't know, a ski lodge, or something."

The corners of his eyes crinkled like he was amused. "You think all people in Alaska do is ski?"

"How should I know? I'm not what you would call 'outdoorsy.'"

Stone's gaze darted to the camera before he leaned closer and lowered his voice to a deep rumble. "I'm sorry I scared you, Gina. I don't want you to be afraid of me."

Oh, sweet man. All this time, she'd feared she'd ruined her credibility as a teacher, while he'd been worried about what *she* thought of *him*. If he were any other partner, if it were any time other than their first rehearsal, she would have given him a hug. He seemed to need the reassurance and she believed in giving affection freely.

Except the camera was too close. Jordy's eyes held a gleam of anticipation. No matter what she did—a hug, a pat on the shoulder, a squeeze of his hand—it would be twisted to create a story where there wasn't one.

Gina nudged Stone's arm with her shoulder and whispered, "I wasn't scared of you." It would have to be enough.

"We should really get right into learning the dance, but first let's talk strategy." She turned him so his profile was reflected in the wall of mirrors. Big and strong he might be, but he went where she led him. It was a good trait, since she might have to drag him around the dance floor while making it look like he was the one leading.

She peered up, taking in his height and bulk. On second thought, there would be no dragging this man anywhere.

"You have perfect posture," she said, running a hand down his spine. The bumps of his vertebrae, embedded in thick cords of muscle, invited her fingers to linger and explore. She snatched her hand away. "This is going to come in handy. When you're dancing in hold, keep your spine straight and your shoulders back and down. Not up near your ears." She demonstrated by hunching her shoulders in an exaggerated fashion. "There's nothing graceful about this."

Stone barked out a laugh and to her surprise, he imitated her silly move. "Not exactly the epitome of grace and charm."

He flashed her a devastating smile and Gina took a deep, deliberate breath. Would it kill him to be a teensy bit uglier? She shook it off and kept going.

"Instead, we stand like this." As she had on his porch, she positioned his body into the pose he would use for the foxtrot, keeping her touch professional and impersonal. "Our first dance is the foxtrot. It's a lively, smooth-flowing ballroom dance that requires us to match our steps while in hold."

"Is this anything like the waltz you showed me?"

"I like to think of the foxtrot as the waltz con sabor. With flavor. It's a good first dance because our bodies aren't touching."

His brow creased as she stepped into the frame he created with his arms. "What do you mean? We're touching."

She grinned. "This is nothing. Dance partners are very familiar with each other's bodies. There's no getting around it. If you hold back, it ruins the dance."

Stone pressed his lips together and didn't say anything. His gaze lifted over her head to their reflection in the mirrors.

She tapped his left foot with her right. "Now, the basic steps. Always start with your left. I'll be doing the opposite of what you're doing. The foxtrot is about smooth, gliding steps and perfect frame."

After taking him through a few sequences of *slow-slow-quick-quick,* she said, "We're going to showcase your posture and form while contrasting them with your virility and humble background."

He coughed and his steps faltered. Above the beard, his cheeks reddened adorably. "With my what?"

"You're a big burly mountain man," she said.

"I don't even live on a mountain. It's an inlet. At water level."

"Doesn't matter. We'll let that side out in the Latin and jazz dances. With the more classical styles, like the foxtrot and the waltz, we're going to show a contrast—the elegant and refined side of the Viking."

"*Viking?*" He looked like he was going to choke. She broke hold to pass him a water bottle from the small cooler.

"Don't tell me you don't know what you look like," she said, pointing at his reflection. "We're going to use those muscles and that beard to our advantage."

He took a long swig of water, chugging more than half the bottle in one gulp. "I didn't realize this was so tactical."

"What, you thought you could just show up and dance?" She snorted. "Think again, buddy. This is a competition, and a lot of strategy goes into it. Come on. We have work to do."

For the next two hours, Gina dragged him around the room, correcting his steps and his stance. If he didn't learn to lead, she was going to end up doing all the work of getting him through the dances, and he was far too big for her to keep adjusting him as they moved. And while Stone followed instructions, he also sighed, eyed their reflections skeptically, and blinked for a little too long, like he wanted to roll his eyes.

Exhausted, Gina called for a hydration break. Without a word, Stone broke hold and dropped onto the edge of the small stage with an exaggerated exhale. Gina sucked on her bottom lip. If he sighed one more time . . .

The rehearsal room door opened and Donna Alvarez walked in.

Just perfect. Now Gina held back an eyeroll. She didn't have the energy to deal with Donna right now.

Donna was most likely the producer who'd chosen to pair Gina with Stone. She was manipulative, and she had an in with the higher-ups who made those decisions. A second camera crew trailed behind her, consisting of a camera operator and a mousy assistant who hugged a tablet to her chest like a shield.

"Hi, Donna," Gina said, aiming for pleasant. No need to get off on the wrong foot.

"Gina." Donna's smile was wide, but thin. Her hazel eyes were like a shark's, flat and deadly. "Good to see you."

Gina gestured Stone over. "Stone, this is Donna, my producer."

Stone held out a hand to Donna and said, "A pleasure."

"The wild man sure has some pretty manners." Donna smiled again as she shook his hand. Stone's face turned red.

"Donna oversees a few of the couples," Gina explained for Stone's benefit, and to cut through the tension. "Jordy's only assigned to us."

Jordy joined them, and they split up for individual interviews. Gina went to one corner of the room with Donna and the new crew, while Jordy and Aaliyah took Stone to the opposite end.

"How's your first rehearsal going?" Donna asked.

Gina flashed the camera a big grin. "Our first rehearsal is going great," she lied. "Even though Stone has never danced before, he's willing to learn and picking up the steps quickly." Also false. "It's really the best you can hope for in a partner with no previous dance experience."

"What do you have in mind for your first dance?"

"I've never danced with someone this big before." Gina raised a hand over her head to indicate Stone's height. Her football player the previous season had been a quarterback, and smaller. "We'll do something to show off his form, strength, and skill, with an element of fun. I want to give the viewers a side of Stone they've never seen before."

Donna's shark-eyed gaze intensified. "And what do you think about his looks?"

Gina smiled through the urge to grit her teeth. How was she supposed to answer that? *Of course he's good-looking, damn it!* "Don't worry, the viewers will definitely see Stone shirtless, although not for the first dance. It wouldn't be appropriate for the foxtrot. But keep voting for us, and we'll be sure to show you the goods." She winked at the camera.

Donna crossed her arms. "It seems like you two have a lot of chemistry."

Did it? Shit. Gina played it cool in her response. "We're still figuring out our dynamic. I'm sure our connection as dance partners will grow the longer we work together."

Donna's lips twisted like she was disappointed in the answer, but she let Gina get back to work.

Gina met Stone in the center of the room. His forehead was furrowed, and he looked as annoyed as she felt. Jordy had probably grilled him on whether he thought she was pretty or not. She'd have to warn him the questions would only get more invasive as the weeks went on.

She jerked her head to the side to indicate the crew. "You okay?" she whispered, even though the mic would catch it anyway.

Now he rolled his eyes full out. "Are those interviews really necessary?"

"Channel it into the dance. Anything that's happening, in any part of your life, channel it into the dance and let it be transformed." She shrugged. "At least, that's what I always do."

Stone held her gaze for a long moment, his expression clearing. When he nodded, she nudged his elbows. He snapped to attention, his form perfect. She gave him an approving nod. "Good. Now we focus on footwork. Ready?"

He sighed. "Ready."

She counted down and they took off across the room.

Five

G ina had claimed the foxtrot was similar to walking—one foot in front of the other. It wasn't. Hours of learning moves like the promenade, ad lib, and Park Avenue step left Stone once again rethinking his decision to join this stupid show.

Dancing was *hard*. The basic steps had been one thing, but learning choreography was a whole different beast. His muscles ached from staying in hold, his feet hurt from the shiny black shoes, and he was starving. When he complained that he was hungry, Gina tossed him a protein bar and told him to "take it from the top."

And it was all being filmed. Every stumble and misstep, Stone's curses when he slipped, Gina's innocuous touches.

How was he supposed to concentrate on learning to dance with Gina's light, capable touch a constant source of distraction? Quick touches, barely there and then gone. A fingertip on his chin to change the angle. A nudge with her wrist to raise his elbow. Even her small feet kicking his to get them to move the right way.

Were all dancers like this? Whose brilliant idea had it been to stick him with someone so touchy and talkative? *Or so pretty.* This wasn't what he'd signed up for.

And despite Gina's earlier assurances, he still felt bad about scaring her in Alaska. It hadn't been right. Pretending to see a bear in the woods was a dick move, and he shouldn't have gone along with it.

Worst of all, the producers interrupted him for interviews left and right. On *Living Wild,* his family and the crew knew he was a terrible liar, and he participated in fewer individual interviews than his siblings did. *The Dance Off* was supposed to be about dancing. Why did they want him to talk so much?

Stone stepped wrong again, nearly losing his balance. "Sorry."

The corners of Gina's mouth turned down and she threw her hands up. "Don't be sorry. Be serious."

He narrowed his eyes. "What are you talking about?"

She strode over to the cooler and grabbed a bottle of water. "You're not taking this seriously."

The accusation burned in his gut, and the words spilled out before he could think them through. "How much more seriously do you want me to take it?" He followed her and grabbed another protein bar from the box next to the cooler. "I'm here, wearing these ridiculous shoes—" He lifted one foot and gave it a disgusted sneer. "—and doing everything you've asked of me."

"Everything," she said, in a tone that sounded suspiciously agreeable, "*except* take it seriously."

Frustration made his voice come out sharper than he intended. "I come from a survival background. In the grand scheme of things, dancing has ranked low in priority. I'm doing the best I can."

Gina was unfazed. "Aren't you lucky you don't have to hunt and chop wood in LA? Now dancing can be your number-one priority. Do better."

Before Stone could come up with a reply, someone knocked on the door. Stone ripped open the protein bar and took a big bite.

A blond woman with deeply bronzed skin poked her head into the room. "Hey there," she said. "Who's first?"

"Ah, the spray tan magicians are here." Jordy turned to Stone. "Time to strip."

Stone choked. "What, here?"

The woman entered the room with a team of young, attractive assistants and began constructing something that looked like half of a black nylon tent with a large, egg-shaped opening.

No longer hungry, Stone tossed the rest of the bar in the trash. "I thought we'd do this somewhere more . . . private."

A list of instructions had awaited Stone when he moved into his hotel room the day before. Exfoliation techniques, tips on spray tan maintenance, and instructions to wear dark underwear and use the dark sheets and towels they provided. What the list had *not* mentioned was that he'd be doing this with an audience. The room was full of people. Jordy and Aaliyah conferred over a laptop, while the spray tanner and her assistants checked their equipment.

And then there was Gina. She sat on the stairs leading up to the low stage. Leaning back on one hand, she chewed on her own protein bar and eyed him thoughtfully.

"Don't be modest." She waved a hand in dismissal. "I've already seen most of what there is to see, and I'll see the rest before we're through."

Her words—and flippant attitude—didn't comfort him. Sure, she'd already seen him naked from the waist up, but that didn't mean he was ready to drop trou on their second meeting. Or in front of the others.

Stone put his hands on his hips. "Is this really necessary?"

Gina shrugged. "Fact of life around here. You'll get used to it."

She was still fully dressed and didn't seem in a hurry to be sprayed. Her skin already had a beautiful golden hue, so maybe she was exempt from this fresh form of torture. He tried another tactic.

"I'm already tanned." *Living Wild* made him use a self-tanning lotion since he was so often shirtless, but he would never admit that out loud.

The spray tan lady sputtered out a laugh. "Not tan enough. Get in here." She switched on the tanning gun with a low buzz.

Stone cursed his tendency to blush as his cheeks grew warm. Gina's accusation nagged at him. The need to prove his commitment shoved him into action. He toed off his shoes and grabbed the back of his T-shirt, yanking it over his head. From the corner of his eye, he caught the way Gina's lips parted, the slight widening of her eyes.

A hot rush of satisfaction swept through him. So, she wasn't completely immune to him. At least there was that.

No longer annoyed at having to strip, he bent at the waist to tug off his socks. When he straightened to his full height, he flexed his abs and dropped his hands to the waistband of his shorts. Gina's eyes followed his movements. Even with everyone else in the room, the moment was just for her. He kept his attention on her as he drew the shorts down his legs and stepped out of them. Standing in the middle of the rehearsal space in nothing but a pair of navy blue briefs, he met her gaze head on.

Her eyes narrowed, then she raised an eyebrow and mouthed, "touché." Then she looked away. Satisfied, Stone strode over to the egg and stepped inside.

He lost track of Gina when the spray tan lady stepped in front of him.

"I'm Martina. Have you ever been spray tanned before?"

Stone shook his head.

Martina explained the procedure as she worked, coating him in layers of tanning solution. Apparently spray tans made everyone's bodies look more idealized on stage, adding definition and shine. On *The Dance Off*, the tanner, the better.

The entire process went faster than Stone expected. Each layer took about five minutes, and he was given four layers.

"You've got some great definition in your muscles," Martina told him as she lined his pecs. "The tan will add to that and make you look even more amazing."

Stone ducked his head, muttering his thanks. He turned to face the inside of the egg-shaped tent while she outlined his back muscles. When he turned around again, the door opened and Gina walked in wearing nothing but a strapless purple bikini.

Stone nearly swallowed his tongue.

When he'd entered the rehearsal space that morning, the Gina who'd awaited him might as well have been a completely different person than the one he'd met in the woods. Teacher Gina wore her hair up in a high ponytail and her face free of makeup. Her eyes still sparkled. Her smile still drew him in. But she looked more approachable, more touchable. More real.

Dangerous thoughts for a man who'd convinced himself Hollywood girls were a bad idea.

The purple bikini was bringing up all kinds of dangerous thoughts now. Extra dangerous considering he was clad only in a pair of briefs, and the spray tan fairy had just yanked at the waistband over his hip.

To make matters worse, Gina stood nearby, hands propped on her hips, watching him with open interest.

"See?" she said. "Spray tanning isn't so bad, is it?"

Stone grunted. If he looked at her, he'd risk embarrassing them all.

"All done," Martina said. "Gina, you're up."

Stone made a beeline for his shorts.

"Wait!"

The shriek made him freeze. He turned, and Martina scowled at him. "What are you doing? You can't get dressed yet. Stand still until you're dry."

Torture. This was torture. Perhaps he'd done something in a past life to deserve the exquisite pain of watching Gina climb into the egg and turn in slow circles while being coated with tanning solution. When Gina turned to face the inside of the egg, Stone's gaze dropped to her ass, firm and round, barely covered by the purple spandex of her bikini bottoms. When she tugged the waistband down an inch so Martina could spray under the fabric, Stone ground his teeth against the fresh wave of desire that slammed into him, his blood pulsing hot through his veins. His mind supplied images of Gina's slender fingers drawing the fabric down further, inch by tantalizing inch.

No. He couldn't think that way. She was his partner, his teacher.

They had weeks of work ahead of them, work that required close contact and intimate touch. He'd never survive if he let himself entertain such thoughts.

He'd never survive if he got a hard-on in the middle of his first rehearsal—*on camera.*

Instead of Gina, he focused on how disgusting the whole reality TV circus was. He'd thought *Living Wild* was bad—hello, shirtless wood-chopping—but this was ten times worse. The manipulation, the utter lack of privacy, and the obvious efforts to throw the dancers off-balance. At least in Alaska, his producers were up front with him about their machinations.

"Stone!"

His head snapped up. Gina beckoned him from the egg. "Come on. Let's take a selfie."

Sighing, he trudged over barefoot and leaned into the egg next to her, as she directed. Gina stretched out a hand, holding her phone sideways. Their faces appeared on the screen.

"Smile!" Gina said.

Stone bared his teeth in some approximation of a smile. Gina's closeness—the sweetness of her scent, her warmth hovering next to him in the curve of the nylon egg—shot tension into his muscles. He got out of there as fast as he could, but Gina followed.

"You want to grab food?" she asked, shaking her arms while the spray tan crew packed up. "After I'm dry, of course."

All he could do was stare as her words went in one ear and out the other. Her arm movements made her breasts jiggle above the purple fabric cupping them. He wanted to replace the fabric with his hands.

Damn it. He had to stop thinking about her breasts. "No. I'm, uh . . ." He grabbed his shorts and yanked them up his legs. "I've gotta go work out." It was the first excuse he thought of, but it was a good one. He had to burn off some of this tension or he was going to explode during their next rehearsal.

"Oh, no, you're not." Martina paused on her way out the door and wagged a finger at him. "No sweating, swimming, or showering for the next six to eight hours. You'll wash off the tan before it has time to set." She gave him an appreciative glance. "I think you can skip this one workout. And don't put your T-shirt on, if you can help it." And then she was gone.

Fuuuuuck. Resigned, Stone stuffed the T-shirt into his gym bag.

"So . . . food?" Gina asked, popping up beside him in that damned purple bikini.

He shook his head. "No, thanks. I'll see you tomorrow."

Running out before she could say another word, Stone inwardly cursed *The Dance Off* and everything associated with it. He was on fire, and now he had no way to cool the flames.

After Stone left, Gina waited for her tan to dry, then put on a lightweight beach cover-up so as not to put fabric lines into her tan.

Maybe she shouldn't have accused Stone of half-assing it, at least not on the first day. But if they were going to begin as they meant to go on, she couldn't let him get away with anything less than 100 percent. He was going through the motions and doing what she said, but his lack of enthusiasm was obvious. It happened with some male celebs when they were asked to move in ways that were uncomfortable for them. If they felt silly, they didn't try. Toxic masculinity at its finest.

If she and Stone were going to win, he had to do more than try. He had to want to win, too. The trick was finding the key that would unlock his competitive spirit.

As Gina was packing her bag, Jordy flagged her down. "Donna wants to speak with you," he said. "She's in her office."

Dreading whatever Donna had to say, Gina headed downstairs and into the hall of offices. Donna ushered her inside and invited her to take a seat in the dark, cramped room, little more than a closet.

Donna was wearing her smarmy smile, which meant this conversation was going to suck.

"How are you getting along with Stone?" Donna waggled her eyebrows. "You gotta admit, he's handsome."

Ugh. Gina took a deep breath. "As you saw, we're focusing on the dance and figuring out strategy. I think—"

"Yeah, we saw that." Donna frowned. "It looks like you're holding back, though. You're usually friendlier with your celebs. And Stone seemed frustrated. Is there some tension between you two?"

Gina shook her head and smiled broadly. "Nope. No problems." Aside from Stone's gigantic, distracting muscles and reluctance to do more than the basic steps. She'd lost track of the number of times he'd asked, "Is this really necessary?" And it was only the first day.

Donna leaned in with a conspiratorial smile. "Maybe you could warm things up a bit. It would make him feel more comfortable, I'm sure."

What the hell? Lips pressed together, Gina sucked in a breath through her nose. She counted to five as she let it out, then spoke clearly and evenly. "As we've discussed in the past with my agent, I have a hard stop on the fake romance narrative."

Donna rolled her eyes. "Oh, come on, Gina. Look, we know you're attracted to men—"

"Ex*cuse* me?" Gina's eyes went wide, her lungs swelling like a balloon as disbelief surged through her.

"So I'm not sure what your problem is," Donna barreled on, ignoring the outraged objection. "Stone's hot. Just flirt a little more, give us a few soundbites to imply there's something brewing. Viewers love sexual tension. It will get you tons of votes, and possibly even the trophy."

Low blow. Donna knew how much Gina wanted to win, but she also knew Gina was adamantly opposed to pretending she was hooking up with her celebrity.

Gina got to her feet. "Don't worry. We'll get lots of votes, and we'll get them the old-fashioned way—through amazing choreography and strong technique."

"But will it be enough?" Donna pressed.

"It'll have to be. Because I'm not going to pretend I'm fucking Stone."

Donna shrugged, unoffended. "You should. I'd fuck him."

Gina opened her mouth to make some retort she'd probably regret later, but Donna's next words left her speechless.

"I'm just looking out for you, Gina. The fact of the matter is, if you don't make the finals, I'm not sure we'll have a place for you next season."

Gina's mouth snapped shut. Her skin prickled like she'd jumped into an ice bath.

"What do you mean?" The words came out raspy.

Donna lowered her voice. "I like you, Gina. You're smart and you know how to play the game, even if you refuse to do the one thing that would almost assure you the win. But you've got to make the finals if you want to stick around."

"Donna, my nieces watch this show."

With a shrug, Donna flipped open her laptop. "Figure it out, Gina. And make sure those promo shots are sexy as hell."

Gina walked out.

She seethed all the way to her car, using a pair of giant black sunglasses to shield her from the crowd of paparazzi hanging out across the street from the parking lot. Once inside, she gripped the steering wheel hard. She wanted to scream, but those assholes with the cameras would hear her.

For years, she'd worked her butt off to build a name for herself in an industry that was cutthroat and unforgiving. She'd done it through talent, skill, and determination. She continued to take dance classes, along with singing and acting lessons, to brand herself as a triple threat.

It burned to have all of that reduced to the lure of her sex appeal. As if that were her only worth, the only reason viewers might vote for her and Stone. Not because she was a qualified teacher and an accomplished choreographer with a good personality. Donna's statements implied that all the viewers cared about—all the producers cared about—was who she was screwing. This was exactly why Gina had insisted her agent tell *The Dance Off* upfront that she was not willing to be used for romantic storylines.

She pulled out her phone and called her sister. It was well after work hours in New York, so Araceli would be home, probably making dinner for the kids.

Araceli picked up on the second ring. "Hey, Gigi."

"They want me to fuck him."

"*Who?*" Celi's outrage and disbelief blasted through the speaker.

"My partner." Gina rubbed her eyes under the glasses.

There was a long pause. "You mean, they want you to *pretend* to be involved with your partner?"

"What's the difference? I'm not doing it, and I'm not going to act like I am, either."

"You got this. Don't let those Hollywood bigwigs push you into anything you don't want to do."

Gina felt her big sister's unwavering support coming through the phone, and it made her grin. If the grin wobbled a little bit, who cared? She was allowed to miss her family. "Thanks. I've worked too hard to screw it up now."

"Today was your first day?"

"Yeah."

"You'll have to call Ma. She's going to want to hear about it. How did it go?"

"Pretty well. He's not a bad dancer, just reluctant." Gina paused, then voiced the hope that had been steadily growing all day. "I think . . . I think if I can get him to take this seriously—ignite his competitive spirit, so to speak—we can go far."

Celi snickered. "Lucky for him, you have more than enough competitive spirit to spare."

"Nothing wrong with being ambitious. This is just one step of many."

"You'll get there. No rush."

But there *was* a rush. Dancers didn't have long careers. They were hard on their bodies, and injuries were an ever-present concern. In show business, age and looks mattered, too. Gina wanted to build a career that would stand the test of time, one that would allow her to continue growing her skill set and wasn't completely reliant on the smoothness of her skin or how she managed her weight.

"I don't want to be a dancer on TV forever. Even if I did, I can't. I'm already twenty-seven."

Celi scoffed. "Damn, you say that like it's old. I've got five years on you, *and* three kids." A crash in the background punctuated her words, followed by an indignant claim of "You *ruined* it!"

Gina snorted as her sister let out a long-suffering sigh. "You better go see what that is."

"Yeah, but I really don't want to." Araceli rustled around, probably on her way to check on the children. "Don't worry. You'll get through this the way you always have, by being an amazing, hardworking dancer. Keep it up."

"Thanks, Celi."

When Araceli gasped and yelled, "Look at this mess!" Gina hung up.

The call had done the trick. Her big sister believed in her. What else did she need? Gina started the car and headed home.

Six

Stone showed up to the wardrobe department the next day for his promo outfit with images of sequins and fringe flashing through his mind, so it was a relief to be handed black slacks—stretchier than they looked—and a black button-down shirt. Of course, they instructed him to leave the top buttons undone to his sternum. The costume crew hovered around him, checking fit and drape, and someone hustled him into a black vest, darker than his shirt. As he turned in the mirror, hidden sparkles flared to life all over his outfit. Tiny black rhinestones trailed down the outer seam of his trousers and tastefully lined the lapels of his vest, if such a thing could be considered tasteful.

One of the PAs led him to the photoshoot backdrop. "Gina should be out soon," they said, and Stone sat in a folding chair to wait. Even though he'd already been through hair and makeup, a woman with brushes tucked into her plastic half-apron applied another layer of powder to his face. He'd done enough promo shoots for *Living Wild* to be comfortable with this part, at least.

A few minutes later, Gina skipped over to him, wearing a spangly silver bathing suit and nothing else. Well, that wasn't entirely true. On her feet were strappy dance heels.

Stone stood, taking her in. The silver outfit covered her important bits, but her arms, legs, and back were bare, as were the sides
of her trim, deeply tanned torso, giving a good view of the indents
at her waist. The silver fabric glittered, and tiny dangling sparkles shivered and caught the light as she moved. Longer sparkles
dripped from the hem of the costume, doing a poor job of covering the tops of her thighs.

"Ready to pose?" She tugged him over to the white backdrop set
up nearby.

Ready? Boy, was he ever.

Shit, he really had to quit this line of thinking. Was he interested
in Gina? Of course he was. Was he going to act on that interest?
Nope. All of this was fake—hell, they were covered in sparkles
to present an image of beauty and excitement, while surrounded
by scaffolding, camera equipment, and people dashing around in
jeans and T-shirts. It was everything he hated about *Living Wild*,
but worse, because he was stuck in LA. Yes, Gina was sexy, sweet,
and funny, but they were from different worlds. He didn't fit in
hers, and her trip to Nielson HQ made it abundantly clear she'd
never want to fit in his. And if she knew the bear had been a PA
crashing around in the underbrush just to get a reaction out of
her, she'd never forgive him.

Oblivious to his inner turmoil, Gina discussed potential poses
with Jordy. When she turned to Stone, her tone was all business,
just as it was during rehearsal. "We're going to film our intro
first, since they have an opening at the other set." She dropped
her voice. "Sounds like one of the celebs threw a fit about her
costume."

"Do you know who?" he asked, curious in spite of himself.

She shook her head. "This footage will air during commercials
and before we dance in every episode, so it's important to film
something good."

"Like what?" He followed her as she strode down the hallway at
a fast clip.

"It has to look like you're having fun, like you want to be here."

She shot him a sidelong glance. "Voters respond to enthusiasm. If they get the impression that you think you're too good for *The Dance Off,* they'll send your ass home."

"Wait a second." Stone stopped walking and took her by the elbow. For once, they weren't mic'd, and there were no producers or cameras hovering around them.

"Look," he started, not knowing exactly what he was going to say. "Do I feel silly about all this? Yeah." He gestured at his hair—styled into smooth waves—and his sparkly vest. "But I have a good reason to be here, and I can tell this is important to you, so I won't fuck it up."

Her lips flattened and she crossed her arms. "That's the best you've got?"

He shrugged. "For now? Yeah, it is."

She sucked her teeth and started walking again. "I guess it'll have to do. Come on."

Blowing out a breath, Stone rushed after her. He could have handled that a lot better. He'd meant to convey that he was willing to try his best, but it had come out all wrong. Instead, he would just have to show her, and in doing so, reveal a little more about himself than he'd intended.

"You know, I wasn't completely honest before," he said as they approached the film set. Cameras, lights, and people surrounded a mini version of a dance floor and stage. Another costumed couple stood in the middle of it, talking.

Gina cut her eyes to him. "No?"

"I do have some dance experience."

"Oh yeah?" Interest sparked in her eyes, and she slowed down. "What kind?"

"Breakdancing."

"No!" Her mouth dropped open. "Are you kidding? Show me."

"What, here?" Stone raised a hand to run it through his hair, then dropped it before he could mess up the careful style.

"Yeah. I wanna see your moves." A playful note had returned to her voice, and he was glad for it.

He rested his hands on his hips and surveyed the space around them, assessing whether it would be enough room for him to move around. He'd feel terrible if he knocked over the cameras or took out the lights.

Gina flashed him a teasing grin. "Do you need me to beat box or something?"

He raised his eyebrows, more relaxed now that she was back to her old self. "Can you?"

Her shrug was sheepish. "No. My singing lessons don't cover that particular skill."

He wanted to ask her more about that, but she moved out of his way and said, "Come on, show me what you've got."

"It's been a while. I used to do this in high school, and I was a lot skinnier then."

Her nose scrunched in confusion. "I thought you were living in the outback or whatever."

Crap. "High school age, I mean."

"Excuses, excuses." She nodded at the open space before them and clapped out a beat. "Do it."

A fire ignited in him at her words. This wasn't the time to examine the impulse, but he wanted to impress her. Starting with some basic toprocking, Stone crossed his arms and stepped side to side before dropping down into a six-step. Whoever had made his outfit was a damn genius, because it had the perfect amount of give to account for his moves.

Others gathered to watch, so Stone stuck a handstand freeze—and didn't fall on his face, hallelujah—and followed it up with a suicide spin into a standing position.

A small crowd had formed around him. They broke into applause and cheers when he finished, but Gina drew all his attention. She bounced on her toes, clapping her hands and laughing full out. The pure joy on her face struck him like a blow. He fought to catch his breath when she rushed forward and threw her arms around his waist in a hug.

"That was *amazing*, Stone."

Damn, her sequin-clad body felt good pressed against him. Since she was close, and since he was still breathing hard, he stroked a hand down her arm in reply.

She tensed and abruptly pulled away.

Ooo-kay. Her reactions were hard to track, but it was better that they keep it professional.

Gina stepped aside, and others moved in to praise him, including—oh shit, that was *Rick Carruthers.*

Stone blinked, starstruck, as Rick Carruthers patted him on the shoulder.

"Sweet moves," the other man said. "I couldn't do that even when I was your age." Rick's full head of hair had gone gray, but he still had the same charming smile and blue eyes that graced the covers of the CDs Stone and his siblings had listened to when they were younger.

"Um, thanks," Stone managed to mutter.

"I'm Rick." The older man stuck out his hand.

"Stone Nielson." Sweat broke out on Stone's brow. He was shaking hands with *Rick Carruthers.* His brothers were going to flip. "I, uh, I'm kind of a fan."

"Oh yeah?" Rick grinned. "Glad to hear. Although I can tell you're going to be some stiff competition for me. What's your first dance?"

"Fox . . . something."

Rick chuckled. "Cool, cool. We're doing the jive. It'll be interesting to see how these old knees hold up." He clapped a hand on Stone's shoulder again. "See you on the dance floor, Stone."

As Rick moved away and the crowd dispersed, someone else approached him. Stone knew it was Gina even before he glanced down at her.

"Welcome to *The Dance Off*," she said in a low voice. "It's pretty surreal, isn't it?"

Stone shook his head in awe, watching Rick join his partner before leaving the set. Off to the side stood a short woman, her brown hair cut into a blunt bob, her lined face as familiar to him as his own mother's. "Oh my god. Is that Twyla Rhodes?"

Gina leaned against him as she checked out the middle-aged

actress, teasing his senses with her warmth and her scent. "Yes, that's her."

"My siblings and I watched the Elf Chronicles movies all the time when we were kids."

Gina pulled him down to whisper in his ear. "I heard she's the one who was a diva about her costume. Apparently, she thought it was too modest and wanted to show more skin."

His body tightened at Gina's nearness. "Do you ever get used to it?"

"To what?"

"Brushing elbows with celebrities."

A smirk played on her lips as she gazed up at him. "Need I remind you that you're a celebrity, too?"

His face heated. "I don't feel like one."

He wasn't famous for being talented, like Rick, or even Gina. Looking at Twyla, who was iconic for her portrayal of an elf queen more than thirty years ago, he couldn't help but wonder what the hell he was doing here. He was a regular guy. He hunted and built stuff with his hands, and someone had come along and wanted to film him doing those things. For that, he was here, with the opportunity to earn a ton of money and attention.

The money. He had to remember why he was mixed up in all this. Money for his mother and his family, who waited for him back in Alaska. Nothing else. Not fame, not mingling, and definitely not a fling with his partner.

"People are people." Gina shrugged, pulling him from his thoughts. "You'll see that soon enough. Behind the scenes, it's hard to keep up the celebrity facade." She touched his arm lightly. "Let's go. It's our turn to film."

As they took their places on the set, Donna entered the space and whispered something to the director.

Stone had once come face-to-face with a cougar while hiking in Canada. Its green-gold eyes had fixed on him with an intensity that sent chills down his spine and screamed *predator*. Its whiskers shivered as it assessed him, and he never forgot the slinking

feline curves of its spine and tail, and the speed at which it retreated when he shouted and fired a shot, scaring it off.

Donna reminded him of that mountain lion. Despite her wide
smile, she had a hard look in her eyes. The times she'd interviewed
him during rehearsal, the sharpness of her demeanor and questions had made him anxious to get away.

He glanced down at Gina in time to see her lips tighten at the
corners. So, Donna rubbed her the wrong way, too.

With a soft sigh, Gina gave his arm a squeeze. "Let's get this over
with and get back to dancing, okay?"

He nodded. "Okay."

For the next two hours, Stone stood in the middle of the set
with Gina while Donna, the director, and the photographer instructed him to lift her, hold her, and grab her. Finally, he understood Gina's comment about this show making them intimately
acquainted with each other's bodies. Their foxtrot was tame in
comparison.

It wasn't that he had a problem with having Gina drape herself
all over him. On the contrary, he liked it far too much. Filling his
hands with her hot, tight body while she curled her strong limbs
around him? Not the worst way to spend an afternoon. If they
hadn't been surrounded by production people, he might have enjoyed himself.

Except Donna's hungry eyes kept him on edge, and it seemed
like she had the same effect on Gina.

Gina was the consummate professional, of course, completely
unfazed by anything Donna asked her to do. Sit on Stone's shoulder? Sure. Wrap her legs around his waist? No problem. Rub
against him while whipping her hair? On it.

But there was a tension in Gina's body that hadn't been there
during their rehearsal, and a tightness to her smile. He also got
the feeling Donna was pushing Gina to do sexier moves on purpose. Still, Gina handled herself with grace.

He, on the other hand, sweated through it, and needed his
makeup touched up multiple times.

At the end of it all, Gina chugged a bottle of water and flashed him a wry smile. "You holding up okay?"

"I guess so." He could barely look her in the eye, feeling like they'd just fucked in front of an audience. How the hell was he supposed to get through a dance in a ballroom full of people, on national TV? "Is it always like that?"

Gina was quiet for a long moment. "No," she said in a low voice. "Not quite."

Before he could ask why she thought Donna had been pushing them so hard—he'd lost track of how many times the producer had shouted "More sexy!" at them—Gina said, "How much you wanna bet they're going to go with the footage of you breakdancing?"

"No way." He chomped on a protein bar. "Really? After making us do all that?"

She shrugged, like what they'd done had been no big deal. "They try to get as many options as they can. But unless Jackson García can also breakdance, my guess is that's the footage they'll use for our intro every episode."

"Who's Jackson García?"

"One of the other celebrities this season. TV actor. Also young and fit." She gave Stone a once-over. "Younger than you, but not as fit, I have to say."

His cheeks warmed. "I'm not sure if that was a compliment or not."

"Something in that realm." She grinned. "Come on, let's change and get back to working on your footwork. It's atrocious."

"That definitely wasn't a compliment."

"Nope. But it's true."

As they left the studio, Rick's words came back to him. This *was* a competition. And Gina was the only one fully invested in his success. Despite his conflicted emotions toward her, he and Gina were a unit. For at least the next month, they were partners.

He'd better get used to it.

Seven

"Hey, Gina! Hold on a sec."

Gina paused outside the door of the rehearsal room as Lori Kim, one of the other pro dancers, jogged up to her. Lori was a petite Korean American woman with a bubbly personality and an extensive collection of baseball caps. Today she wore a black one with the word HYPE spelled out in silver studs.

Gina leaned in and kissed Lori's cheek. "What's up?"

A big grin lit Lori's face. "We're going out tonight."

Gina put a hand to her forehead and exaggerated slumping against the wall. "Oh, thank god. I need a break."

After a week of rehearsals, everyone had cabin fever. The celebrities were feeling the wear and tear of full-time dance practice, and the pros were pulling their hair out trying to teach ballroom dance to a bunch of newbies with big personalities. Even the producers had all but given up on coaxing soundbites out of the cast.

Lori nodded emphatically. "We all do. That's why I got the whole season fourteen cast onto the guest list for Club Picante."

"Your ex-girlfriend's still working there?"

"Yep. We've got VIP space at the end of the bar. Say you'll come."

"Come where?"

A shiver went up Gina's spine at the rumble of Stone's voice behind her. For a big guy, he walked lightly.

"We're going to a salsa club tonight," Lori told Stone. "Want to come? You're on the list, too."

"Stone, this is Lori. She's won *twice*." Gina hip-bumped Lori, who playfully elbowed her back.

"Hey, you'll get there soon. I've just been on the show longer."

"A salsa club?" Stone repeated, skepticism heavy in his voice. He turned his sky blue gaze on Gina, and she sucked in a breath. "Have I learned how to salsa yet?"

Lori snickered and gave his arm a shove. "You're not going to be judged on it, and you'll have to learn it eventually, if you stick around. Might as well pick up the basics at a club."

"It's just for fun," Gina said. "We could all use the break, and you don't have to dance if you don't want to."

Stone narrowed his eyes, searching her face. The look was so sexy it had her heart racing.

"I don't believe that for a second," he said, voice edging toward a growl. She didn't think he realized he did, but every time it gave her a bad case of cha-cha-ing butterflies in her belly. "Going to a salsa club with a bunch of professional dancers will result in dancing, whether I want to or not."

Lori shrugged. "We can't force you. You're too big. It would take all of us to drag you onto the dance floor."

Gina imagined dancing with Stone in the close confines of Club Picante. Crowded, hot, loud, dark—

Wait a second. This was a terrible idea. "You don't have to go if you—"

"All right," he said. "I'll go."

What? No. "Really?"

"Sure." He jerked a shoulder. "It'll be a good chance to get to know the other cast members, right?"

"Cool. It's gonna be fun." Lori took off down the hallway. "See ya!"

"Ready to practice?" Stone asked when Gina just stood there, staring after Lori.

"Yeah, of course." They entered the room and set up their mics. When she stepped in close to him, he put his arm around her in perfect hold, wrapping her in his strength, his warmth, and the fresh, piney smell a week in LA hadn't diminished.

Her heart rate spiked. Sweat prickled at her hairline. Bringing Stone to the salsa club was a very bad idea, but maybe she could get through the night without dancing with him.

She signaled Jordy to move out of the way or risk being run over. "Come on, let's practice grapevines again."

At the end of the day, they parted ways at the parking lot.

"See you at the club?" Stone asked.

Still kicking herself for giving him the club address, it was on the tip of Gina's tongue to say no, to make up an excuse. As if she needed to spend more time around him. She was already on the verge of spontaneous combustion. Could people explode from lust? She was about to test the theory.

She wanted to go out, though. Part of her wanted the chance to blow off steam with her coworkers, and another part didn't want to leave Stone alone to deal with all the other dancers.

Yet another part of her really wanted to salsa with him away from the watchful eyes of Donna and Jordy. It tipped the balance.

"Yes. See you there."

She rushed home to take a shower—a cold shower—and maybe change into something sexier.

Stone maneuvered his way through the crowd at Club Picante toward the VIP section in the back. The dark club was lit red and purple, and crammed with people dancing in the space between a stage and the long, shiny bar. The blasting air conditioner did nothing to dispel the scents of sweat, liquor, and cologne. Loud music vibrated up through his feet. He received a number of appreciative stares, but the crowd parted and Gina was there, leaning against a high table. She spotted him and raised her hand in a wave.

Everyone else fell away. Stone wasn't stupid enough to convince himself that he was drawn to her because she was the only face he recognized. It was just because she was her.

It wasn't smart to be here, but after a week of dancing around each other—literally—he wanted to see Gina away from the cameras. So far, he'd only gotten contradictory glimpses—polished Gina in Alaska, teacher Gina in rehearsals, and superstar Gina at the promo shoot. Sometimes warm and flirty, sometimes cool and professional. Maybe tonight he'd finally get to know the woman behind the dancer.

When he approached her table, she scooted over to make room for him and lifted her cheek for a kiss, as she always did. Under the "nightclub smell" permeating the air, her signature scent teased his senses. He was closer to deciphering it—something flowery, with a hint of earthy spice, plus ginger from the candies she liked to eat during rehearsals. She'd put on light makeup, let her hair down, and changed into a red dress that hugged her body and drew his eye down her toned curves.

Her hand snaked into the crook of his arm and exerted slight pressure, indicating he should lean down. On her other side, a pretty woman with heavy-lidded eyes and a red-lipped smirk leaned her elbows on the table.

Gina raised her voice over the pulsing music. "Stone, this is my roommate, Natasha Díaz. She's also on *The Dance Off,* but she's been rehearsing at one of the other studio spaces."

"Nice to meet you," he said, ingrained manners feeling both out of place and necessary in this loud, obnoxious setting.

"My pleasure." Natasha sent him a slinky, feline smile. She was taller than Gina by a few inches, with a lean ballet dancer's build and tawny brown skin. Her eyes cut to Gina's. "I'm going to get a drink."

Natasha sauntered away, leaving them alone.

Alone, aside from the hundreds of other people in the club. Still, this was the first time they were together without producers or cameras.

Gina looked up at him through her eyelashes. "Don't be nervous."

His gut tightened. "I'm not."

"You are. I can tell." She rubbed his lower back, something she'd taken to doing in the last few days when she thought he needed soothing. If anything, it set him more on edge, her casual touch stoking the flames of desire.

Fuck. This had been a mistake. He should have stayed at the hotel and hit the gym, instead of coming to this club with the misguided notion that he needed to make friends, or that he could get to know Gina better without wanting her more.

It would never work. There was no point in even trying.

Her hand dropped away. "Oh, look. Natasha found room for us at the bar."

Sure enough, Natasha was waving them over with one hand, her other arm draped over the backs of a couple of seats.

Kevin Ray stood at the bar next to Natasha, easily recognizable with his light brown hair and pale skin freckled by the California sun. According to Gina, Kevin had won more times than anyone else in *The Dance Off*'s history, and his pictures were displayed all over the rehearsal studio's halls.

Stone gestured at Kevin's tumbler of amber liquid. "What're you having?"

"This?" Kevin raised his glass. "Lagavulin."

"Good enough." Stone indicated to the bartender he'd take what Kevin was having.

"Wouldn't have thought a guy from Bumfuck, Alaska, would drink scotch."

Stone tried for an easy smile. How would Reed respond? "I get into town occasionally. Not much else to do in winter but get drunk."

A petite woman slipped between them. It was Lori, the dancer who'd invited him to the club. Behind her was a guy who greeted them with a wide smile.

Gina made the introductions. "This is Lori, whom you've met, and her partner, Jackson García."

Stone ducked his head and lowered his voice so only Gina would hear. "The one who's supposedly younger than I am, but not as fit?"

She clapped a hand over her mouth to stifle a snort. Her eyes gleamed with mirth. "That's the one."

Stone sipped his drink, rolling the strong, smoky flavor over his tongue. He glanced back down at Gina's empty hands. "Are you having a drink?"

A quick, silent exchange passed between Gina and Natasha.

"Yeah," Gina said. "I'll have—"

"Let's do shots!" Lori thumped a fist on the bar to punctuate her words. "You in?"

After a short hesitation, Gina nodded.

Stone pretended to be interested in his drink while Natasha grabbed Gina's elbow.

"You never drink during the season," Natasha hissed.

Gina shrugged. "I know. It's fine."

Her roommate backed off, holding up her hands. "Mira, no soy tu mamá. Just reminding you of your own rules."

"I know."

Stone leaned down. "What did she say?"

With a huff, Gina translated Natasha's words. "She said she's not my mother. Come on." She grabbed a shot from the cluster set out by the bartender. Stone took one for himself, and when Lori counted to three, they all slammed them back.

It burned going down. Nowhere near as good as the scotch. And when was the last time he'd done shots at a bar? College? It wasn't something he and his brothers did. Reed didn't know when to quit, Wolf was a lightweight, and Winter said his body was a temple and he wouldn't poison it with alcohol.

Gina sucked in a breath as she returned her glass to the bar. Her eyes watered a little.

Stone rested a hand on the bare skin of her back and stroked gently with his thumb. "You good?"

"I'm fine."

Her skin told another story. "You have goosebumps."

She held his gaze for a long moment, her expression unreadable.

Kevin appeared at her side and grabbed her arm. "Yo, Gina, let's dance."

For a heartbeat, Stone thought she would stay. But when she nodded at Kevin, Stone let his hand drop from her back.

She wasn't his. It was stupid to feel even the slightest bit possessive over her. Still, he kept his eyes on her as she followed Kevin onto the dance floor. The music had switched from DJ-spun beats to a live salsa band, and it seemed like all the dancers knew the right steps. Since he didn't, Stone picked up his scotch and watched Kevin lead her around the floor in tight circles.

Jackson joined him at the bar, clutching a gin and tonic. "You're the breakdancing one, right? That was a hard act to follow."

"I thought I was 'the Alaskan one.'" Stone cracked a grin and made himself turn away from the dance floor. "Don't worry, there's no breakdancing in our foxtrot."

"That levels the playing field somewhat."

"You're a TV actor, right?" Since they were competitors, Stone sized him up. Jackson was a good-looking guy, objectively. Fashionably dressed, with broad shoulders, black hair buzzed on the sides, light brown skin and eyes. But could he dance?

"Yeah. My show's in its second season."

"What's the name of it?"

To Stone's surprise, Jackson ducked his head like he was embarrassed. "Bite me," he muttered into his glass before draining it.

Stone squinted at him. "Excuse me?"

With a sigh, Jackson set down his empty glass and picked up the next one the bartender had waiting for him. "It's the name of the show," he clarified. "It's called *Bite Me*. I play a vampire werewolf."

Stone couldn't help it. He burst into laughter. It was the funniest thing he'd heard since arriving in LA, and he was so fucking relieved that someone else had a more embarrassing byline than he did. He put down his drink before he dropped it, and missed seeing Gina return until she was standing right in front of him.

That damned red dress taunted him. His fingers itched to hold her as he had all week.

No, not like that. He wanted to hold her closer than the foxtrot warranted.

She cocked her head. "What's so funny?"

On Stone's other side, Jackson rolled his eyes. "He's laughing at my job. I'm a serious actor, I'll have you know."

The others returned from the dance floor and Lori called over to Mimi, her ex, for another round of tequila shots, which appeared immediately. Knowing the bartender had its advantages.

Stone accepted his second scotch, sipping and listening with one ear while Gina and Kevin talked shop, trying to gauge the nature of their relationship. There'd been nothing sexual in the way they moved together when they danced, and it wasn't like Stone had any designs on her, but still. He just wanted to know.

"How was New York?" Gina asked Kevin. "You just did a show, right?"

"Cold. And I was only in the role for a few weeks. Had to come back for *The Dance Off*."

"God, I want to be on Broadway so bad." Gina's tone was wistful. "First some hosting gigs, then Broadway. Then I want my own TV show. Oh, and movies."

Kevin grinned. "How are you going to fit movies into that schedule?"

"I'll manage." Gina blew out a breath. "Work always comes first."

Kevin gave Gina a long look, then asked Mimi to bring her a glass of water.

Stone scowled into his scotch. Gina's words confirmed what he'd already known about her—she was hell-bent on making it in this industry. But from the sound of it, she and Kevin were just friends. There was that, at least.

Mimi poured another round of shots, and everyone reached in to grab one. Lori and Jackson crowded in on either side of Stone. When Gina grabbed one, Stone sighed and took a glass.

What the hell was he even doing here? He was all for hitting a bar and having fun, but a club of this magnitude, with people plugged into the pulse of the entertainment industry ... that wasn't him. He didn't belong here.

Maybe it was time to go home. Well, back to the hotel, in any case. But then Jackson asked Gina to dance, so Stone stayed to watch them.

Natasha took the empty space next to him. "He wants to win."

"Who? Kevin?"

She shook her head and pointed to Jackson. "Look. He's asking Gina for instruction. He did the same with me earlier."

Sure enough, Gina's lips moved in a running stream of commentary as she danced with Jackson. She even kicked at his feet the way she did with Stone during rehearsal.

Natasha shrugged again. "He's a good-looking young actor at the start of his career. If he wins, it'll make him a household name and open all sorts of doors for him."

"Huh." So, even at a social outing, Jackson was playing the game. And Stone was standing off to the side watching his partner help someone else.

He didn't care. He only had to stay on for a few episodes to earn the cash for his mother's bills. But shit, if he stayed on longer, he could knock out his own student loans, too. How much did the winner stand to make?

Didn't matter. He wasn't going to win.

"What are you drinking?" he asked, since Natasha's hands were empty.

"Coke."

"Coke and ..."

She jerked her chin in Gina's direction. "Just soda. Looks like I'm the designated driver tonight."

Was Gina drunk? He couldn't tell from her dancing. She was just as graceful as ever. "You want me to keep an eye on her?"

Natasha smiled and patted his arm. "Thanks, guapo. But I got this."

Kevin scooted in on Natasha's other side. His glass was nearly empty, and his signature grin, while still in place, was starting to look a little lopsided. "What are you guys talking about? Oh look, it's my partner." Kevin lifted a hand and shouted, "Hey, Lauren, over here."

A pretty blonde in a short black dress approached them. She shot Stone a sassy grin.

"Ooh, check you out," she purred. "Are you one of the pros?"

"Nah, he's one of the celebs. A wilderness survivalist." Kevin drained his drink and called for another before finishing the introductions. "This is Lauren D'Angelo, Olympic figure skater."

Lauren slipped an arm around Stone's waist and winked up at him. "Damn, you've got even more muscles than I do."

"I . . . I guess." She was flirting, which would have been fine, in most circumstances, but she was coming on strong, and Gina was just a few yards away, spinning around the dance floor with Jackson. Even though they were just dance partners, it felt wrong to flirt with another woman.

Lauren's gaze sharpened. "Can you dance?"

Kevin cut in. "Rumor has it that Stone's got some sweet break-dancing moves."

Rolling her eyes, Lauren released Stone to take the beer Kevin handed her. "Yeah, but can you *dance*? Ballroom style."

"That's what we're here to learn, aren't we?" Stone sipped his scotch just to have a reason to break eye contact with her.

"That means you can't." Lauren shrugged. "No offense meant. Just taking stock of the competition. You know how it goes."

Stone drank again to avoid answering.

"Since I don't have to worry about you as competition . . ." Lauren's voice turned silky again, and she set the beer aside to wrap her arms around him.

She'd gone from flirty to competitive and back again in less than five minutes. Were all Olympians this intense?

Her hand slid down to his ass and Stone almost choked on his scotch. Unsure how to proceed, he sent Jackson a wide-eyed plea when he spotted the actor returning from the dance floor with Gina.

To Stone's eternal gratitude, Jackson stepped in, grinning and holding out a hand to Lauren.

"Hey, I'm Jackson. You're Lauren, right?"

She swept him with a cold, assessing gaze. "That's right."

"You want to dance? Gina and Natasha have been giving me salsa pointers. If I'm going to win, I need all the practice time I can get."

It was the perfect thing to say. Lauren's eyes flashed with challenge, and she let go of Stone. "You're on. But you're not going to win."

Gina sipped from the glass of water Mimi handed her and turned to Stone. "Getting a little close there, weren't you?"

Her tone was unreadable. Before Stone could explain, a commotion to his left drew his attention. A bearded guy wearing a scowl and a Knicks cap joined their group, greeting everyone loudly and kissing all the women on their cheeks. The guy spotted Stone and swung over, extending a hand.

"How's it going?" the guy asked in a deep, accented voice. "I'm Dimitri. You must be Stone."

Stone nodded, shaking hands, and the name clicked. Dimitri Kovalenko, one of the judges on *The Dance Off*. "How'd you know?"

Dimitri's dark eyebrows rose under the hat. "Are you kidding me? You must be the tallest celebrity we've ever had on the show, even counting football players. The wardrobe department is shitting their pants."

Mimi set out another row of shot glasses as the dancers returned from the floor. When Gina reached for one, Stone almost said something, but he caught Natasha watching.

Gina had a friend here. Lots of friends. She didn't need him looking out for her, and there was no reason why he should feel obligated to. She was just his dance partner. That was all.

"Gina, sweetheart, come dance with me." Dimitri snaked an arm around her as soon as the shot glass left her hand.

"Okay." She was giggling as he hauled her back to the dance floor.

It took every ounce of Stone's self-control to keep from charging after them to break in. But what would he do then? He had no claim on her. And he couldn't salsa.

Instead, he watched. His drink was gone before he knew it, another in his hand, thanks to Mimi's watchful eye. As he sipped, he noticed something.

Dimitri and Gina dominated the dance floor. Whereas Kevin had been equally quick and masterful, there was a difference to the way Dimitri danced with Gina. Every eye was on them as Dimitri swirled her around, his arms trailing along hers, his hand resting on her back. And touching, constantly touching her—her shoulder, her arm, her back.

He was *leading.*

So, this was what it looked like when a man led in the dance. When Gina danced with him, and with Jackson, she had to lead, because she was the teacher. Stone finally understood how hard her job was. Not only did she have to teach him the dance, she had to make it look like he was leading, when in reality, she was the one in charge. Even when she danced with Kevin, they were so evenly matched, it seemed more like an equal partnership. But with Dimitri? Dimitri was clearly in charge, every step of the way.

Maybe Stone was on his way to getting drunk, because the idea didn't sit well with him. He was supposed to lead? Then damn it, he would lead.

As if she'd heard his thoughts, Natasha snuck up beside him and nudged him toward the dance floor. "I think it's time you learned how to salsa, guapo."

Eight

The next time Dimitri spun Gina out, she came face-to-face with Natasha and Stone.

"Dimitri, I need Gina back." Natasha cut in and grabbed Gina's arm. "Go dance with Lauren."

Dimitri gave Tasha a long look, then shrugged and headed to the bar.

"Stone, are you going to dance?" Gina's thoughts were fuzzy and confused. Shit, how many shots had she sucked down? Three? Four? She couldn't remember.

"We're going to teach him to salsa," Natasha said. "Come on, you be his partner, and I'll maneuver him."

"Good luck." Gina moved closer so Natasha could put Stone's right hand on her back. "He weighs a ton."

"I can hear you," he said with that delicious growl. She shivered, then mentally slapped herself when she realized her shiver was visible.

Yup. She was drunk.

No matter. She was a professional, and she was Puerto Rican. She could teach salsa in her sleep.

Her thoughts turned to Stone in bed, and she shook her head to clear them.

"Hey, are you okay?" He leaned down so she'd hear him over the music.

Too close. He was way too close. And handsome. And delicious-smelling.

"I'm fine." She had to hold it together. She put her left hand on his shoulder and gripped his left hand with her right. "Listen to the percussion. Stone, you're going to step forward on two, the second beat of the music."

"This is closed position," Natasha said from behind Stone, kicking his feet to get him to step where she wanted him. "You do this when you're dancing close, facing each other, like in the New York style."

"New York style?" he repeated. "I didn't know there was more than one."

Natasha gripped his hips to shift his weight while Gina tugged on him with her hands. Natasha explained, "In salsa clubs, unless you're really trying to show off—like Dimitri always is—New York style is the way to go. The dancers use their momentum to create elegant movement. It's all about precision and control."

"And the man leads," Stone said, Natasha's words seeming to resonate with him. His gaze cleared, and he nodded. Gina stopped pulling on him, and he used his hands to direct her movements.

Natasha kept up a running commentary, helping Stone learn the footwork, while Gina gave herself over to the dance. Dancing in the arms of someone who could lead was thrilling and sensual. She could turn off her mind and just *move*. To be in the moment like that, fully inhabiting her body, filled her with a sense of beauty and excitement.

Stone released her back, trailing his big, hard hand down her bare arm to grip her fingers. His hands dwarfed hers, and she followed his guidance into a spin.

It was unbelievably sexy.

Gina lost herself in the music, in the movement, in the heat of Stone's body and the warming of her own muscles from physical exertion. She kept her eyes trained on his, the clear blue reflecting the purple of the club's lighting. He trapped her with his gaze, with the simmering, banked heat that made her heart thump erratically in her chest. The now-familiar scent of Stone's Alaskan freshness lulled her into forgetting everyone else around them, and it was a while before she realized Natasha had disappeared.

They danced, his hands strong but gentle. His rhythm and footwork weren't perfect, but his masculinity and dominance in the dance were really doing it for her. She edged closer as she followed the steps she knew by heart, and felt the tightening of his hold in response.

This. This was what she adored about dance. To dance like this with a man as handsome and compelling as Stone, to be this close and intimate without words, to let their bodies do the talking . . . it was the most perfect thing in the world.

Time lost its meaning. The beat changed, and she used her own body to communicate the shift to him. After a week of dancing in hold together, he figured it out without her having to say it.

God, she loved that.

With each song, they moved closer. Their bodies touched and rubbed, all hot sweat-slicked skin, her red dress vibrant in the changing lighting, his white T-shirt turning red, then purple, then blue, and back to red.

She arched and rolled, aware of every inch of her skin, and his. She wanted to climb him like a tree and wrap her legs around his waist. He'd cup her ass with those massive hands—something he was very careful to avoid doing, although tonight they wandered just a bit more than they ever had during practice.

Stone was so respectful of her. He knew he was big and burly, and since their first meeting, he'd done everything in his power not to frighten her again. Sweet, sweet man.

She just wanted his hands all over her.

The music changed again. They were barely dancing salsa now. Their bodies were too close, as if he were also reluctant to put space between them. His chest heaved, and god, she just wanted to dig her fingers into those impressive pecs, and no, she wouldn't stop there. The man had abs for days, leading down to those sexy, sharp indents at his hips . . .

Sticking around for his spray tan earlier in the week had been a terrible idea. She knew everything under his clothes—well, almost everything—and it had fueled her daydreams all week.

But they weren't at work now. There were no cameras, no nosy producers. Gina indulged herself and sank her fingertips into his shoulder, trailing them down to feel the muscles outlining his upper arm. He flexed, and she closed her eyes.

He was just holding her now, not moving. One of his arms wrapped around her waist, pressing her against him. Somewhere along the way, she'd reached up and thrown an arm around his neck, the height difference forcing her to arch her back. Her breasts pressed against his chest and her leg—what the hell?—one of her feet was on the floor where it belonged, but her other leg was bent and hitched up on his hip, held in place by his hand gripping the bare skin of her thigh.

Gina opened her eyes. Stone's face was close, his nose touching her cheek, his open mouth just to the side of hers. Her body trembled in his arms, urging her to close the remaining distance. Her chin tilted a fraction of an inch, bringing their lips that much closer. His lower lip brushed the corner of her mouth. She breathed him in deep and let out the breath on a moan.

The song ended. In the moment of silence, Stone's eyes met hers. They stared at each other, breathing hard. He was so close, close enough to kiss.

Except Gina didn't fuck around with her dance partners.

"I have to go home." The words fell out of her in a rush, her voice low and breathy.

He nodded and released her immediately. She untangled herself, her body already going into shock from the loss—cold sweat, rubbery legs, trembling nerves.

How much had she had to drink? Too much. Way too much.

She stumbled off the dance floor and found Natasha at the bar. Tash took one look at Gina's face and grabbed their purses.

Without even saying goodbye, they hustled out of the club and into the lot for Gina's car. Natasha fished the keys out of Gina's clutch and slid into the driver's seat. Gina sank into the passenger side and blinked slowly.

"You're okay with that?" Gina gestured at the wheel.

Natasha sent her a bland look. "As soon as you took that first shot, I knew our designated driver roles had switched. Kevin was drinking my shots." She gave an evil grin as she started the car. "He's going to have a wicked hangover tomorrow."

"Good." Gina shut her eyes. "He deserves it for winning the trophy so many times."

Natasha chuckled and pulled out of the spot. "You're probably going to have a wicked hangover tomorrow, too. You want to tell me what that was all about?"

Gina leaned her overheated forehead against the cool window. Her ears still pulsed from the music, despite the quiet car. Stone's scent clung to her.

"No."

She didn't have an answer anyway.

A fter Gina got home, the first thing she did was change out of the sexy red dress she'd borrowed from Natasha. She was never letting Tash dress her again. While she changed, Natasha yelled at her from the kitchen.

"By the way, I'm mad at you."

Gina's heart sank. "Uh-oh. Why?"

"Come back out and I'll tell you. I'm making guac."

Sure enough, when Gina entered the kitchen, Tash was smashing avocados in a silver mixing bowl.

"Why are you making guacamole?" Gina glanced at the clock. "At one in the morning?"

Natasha shot her a look. "Are you ready to sleep?"

"I guess not." Gina was amped from dancing and buzzed from those fucking tequila shots.

"The real question is why am I mad at you."

Gina sighed. "Fine. Why are you mad at me?"

Natasha stuck the masher in the lump of avocado and turned around with her hands on her hips. "Coño, you didn't tell me he looked like *that*."

"Oh my god." Gina pulled out a chair from the kitchen counter and perched on it. "I told you he was hot right after I met him."

"Nuh-uh, girl." Tash wagged a finger at Gina before turning back to her snack-making. "Oye, get the cilantro and stuff from the fridge."

Grumbling, Gina pulled out the necessary ingredients and started chopping.

"That man is more than hot," Natasha said, adding diced tomatoes to the bowl when Gina passed them over. "I think we can safely say he's super caliente. Like, for real."

"That's why you're mad at me? Because I didn't make a bigger deal of how hot he is?"

"No. Yes. That's part of it."

"Okay, what's the other part?" Gina dumped in a handful of cilantro and took a deep breath. The smell reminded her of her mother's kitchen.

"You said he's on a TV show?"

"Yeah. It's called *Living Wild*."

Tash let out of a frustrated sigh. "Have you even *watched* it?"

"No." Gina pursed her lips as she smashed a clove of garlic with the side of her knife. "I've been too busy teaching him to dance."

"Coño." Natasha shook her head. "I can't believe you. This has to be fixed immediately."

"It's one in the morning!"

"No me importa. We're watching that show *now*. And then I won't be mad at you anymore."

When the guac was ready, they bypassed the counter and bar stools and sat on the sofa with a bowl of tortilla chips between them. A few seasons of *Living Wild* were available, so they picked an episode from the middle of season two, settling in to watch.

There was something voyeuristic about watching Stone on TV, almost like she was spying on him, but Gina couldn't turn away. Contrived as it must be, the drama and setbacks drew her in. During that one episode, Stone hauled lumber with his brothers—to disastrous results—built a greenhouse with his sisters, and patched up his dog's injured foot. Around him, the rest of the Nielson family attended to other tasks that were deemed necessary to "living wild." Over it all hung the constant threat of oncoming winter.

It shouldn't have been a surprise that Stone was the "hot one" of the brothers—probably why he'd been picked for *The Dance Off* over Reed, Wolf, and Winter. They were all good-looking guys, tall and strapping from manual labor, but Stone stood out from the pack. He was also the quiet one, the serious one—as they called him. The look of intense concentration he wore while making the greenhouse was one she'd seen a few times when they rehearsed.

In spite of herself, Gina was impressed. Stone had skills, *real* skills that meant the difference between life and death in the Alaskan wilderness—the "bush," they called it.

She and Natasha had grown up in the same neighborhood in the Bronx, and moved to LA together as soon as they could. They giggled and goggled through the episode, amazed at what it took to live like the Nielsons.

At the end of the episode, Natasha hit "play" on the next one.

"How many are we going to watch?" Gina asked, polishing off the last of the guac.

"I want to see if they manage to build that treehouse or not."

"Spoiler alert: they do. I've seen it."

"Pendeja. I'm watching anyway. The description says they do something with a boat."

Halfway through the next episode, Tash was swooning over Stone's younger brother Wolf.

Gina glanced at Tash out of the corner of her eye. "Really? Wolf?"

Tash shrugged. "He's a weirdo. I like him."

"I didn't meet any of his family while I was there. They were filming somewhere else." What must it be like to have so many siblings? Gina missed her brother and sister, so she could only imagine how Stone must feel. At least she had Natasha with her.

At the moment, Tash was giving her a dirty look. "I can't believe you aren't going to make a move on Stone."

Gina huffed and leaned back into the sofa cushions as the man himself appeared on the TV. Shirtless, of course. "I'm not interested."

"Yes, you are."

"No." Gina crossed her arms. "I'm not getting involved with anyone in the industry. Been there, done that, got bitten on the ass. I don't care to repeat the experience, no matter how hot he is."

"Or no matter how much he wants you?"

"He hasn't made a move, either." She wasn't going to count whatever the hell had happened on the Club Picante dance floor. That was just dancing. And tequila.

"Come on." Natasha rolled her eyes. "You're not gonna try to tell me you haven't noticed his reaction to you. Dwayne barely has any interest in me as a person and he's still semi-hard every time we get too close."

"Ew, Tash."

"What? It happens. They're new to this. You're telling me Stone has never . . . you know what, the innuendo is too easy with a name like that. I can't even go there. He's never sported a stiffy while you're dancing?"

Gina sighed. "Not usually."

"But he has?"

"Well . . . he was kind of hard during our photoshoot, but I think that was because Donna was there and she told the directors to have us do extra sexy poses. We were closer there than we'd been in practice."

Tash smirked. "You were certainly close tonight."

Gina covered her face and groaned. "I hope I didn't give him the wrong idea."

"That you want his body?"

Gina whacked her with a throw pillow. "Yeah, basically. I was a little drunk. And in the moment. That's all. Anyway, our lives are too different."

"You're both on reality shows," Natasha said. "Not that different, from where I sit."

"Different enough for it to never work. Besides, he'll be gone in a few months."

Natasha held up her hands in defeat. "Whatever you say, nena."

Despite Stone's wariness of accidentally revealing something about his family, he couldn't deny he was tired of spending all his free time working out, hiking, or sitting around his room watching movies. So when Jackson García invited him out for drinks before their overnight flight for the cast reveal, Stone said yes.

Stone was worried they were going to the fancy 1920s-themed cocktail bar down the street from the hotel, and he was pleased to see they were instead meeting at a no-frills bar with an extensive beer selection, big messy pizzas, and a relaxed vibe.

Jackson was already there when Stone arrived. He waved to Stone from a square table, where he sat with Alan Thomas, one of the other celebrity contestants. Stone hadn't met Alan yet, but he knew the guy was an athlete. Stone went over to them, and Jackson made the introductions.

"Alan, this is Stone Nielson," Jackson said. "He's on a survival show called *Living Wild*. Stone, this is Alan Thomas, a gold medal–winning Paralympian in track and field."

"Impressive." Stone raised his eyebrows as he shook Alan's hand. The other man had brown hair, blue eyes, and a ruddy complexion. His features were somewhat nondescript until he grinned.

"Nice to meet you, man." Alan's grip was firm, and there was a slight twang of Texas in his voice. Something about his friendly demeanor made Stone feel at ease. "I've seen you in the hotel gym a few times."

"Are you staying there, too?" Stone asked, taking the empty seat across from Alan.

"That I am."

Stone glanced at Jackson, sitting to his right. "And you?"

Jackson shook his head. "Nah, I live nearby. You all should come over sometime. I splurged on a pool table when *Bite Me* got renewed for two more seasons."

"Glad to hear you're not getting staked yet," Stone joked. "Or taken out with a silver bullet."

Jackson made a show of huffing in indignation. "For your information, it would take a silver-tipped stake to kill my character. Needs to be both."

Stone and Alan laughed, and Stone found himself feeling more relaxed than he had since he'd left Alaska. Or maybe it had been longer than that. He didn't tease his brothers often—Reed got too mean, and Winter was sensitive to perceived criticism—and it had been a while since he'd lived close enough to his old friends to meet for drinks like this.

It was . . . nice.

Stone ordered an IPA on tap and a platter of wings to share. He had realized the best way to avoid letting something slip was to keep the others talking about themselves, so he peppered Alan with questions about his training regimen and quizzed Jackson on the number of dance classes he'd taken as an actor.

"Not as many as you'd think," Jackson admitted. "Unless there's a week where we tap or do jazz hands. Ballroom's a whole other beast."

"How about you?" Stone asked, turning to Alan. "Any dance experience?"

Alan shook his head. "Running is my life. I thought the training would've prepared me for this, but damn, dancing is *hard.*"

Stone chuckled. "I hear you. I'm exhausted every day."

"I don't know how these dancers do it," Jackson chimed in. "Moving nonstop for hours on end, and aiming for perfection every time."

"The perfection part I understand," Alan mused. "Otherwise why do it?"

"Okay, Mr. Three-Time-Gold-Medalist, we see you," Jackson said with a grin. "What's your partner like?"

"Rhianne?" Alan shrugged. "She's a drill sergeant. Aren't they all?"

Jackson nodded. "Lori kicks my ass and I love it. I haven't worked this hard since I was in drama school during the day and waiting tables at night."

"What about you?" Alan asked Stone. "How are you getting along with Gina?"

Before Stone could answer, Jackson slammed his empty glass down on the table and gaped at him. "Are you *blushing*?"

"No. Absolutely not." Stone ducked his head and drank deep from his beer, hoping it would cool his face.

It didn't.

Jackson leaned in, squinting at him. "You *are*."

Stone tried to steer them away from talking about Gina. "It's just . . . you don't find the whole dancing thing a little embarrassing?"

To his surprise, the other guys shook their heads.

"Dancing is a sport," Alan said. "Just as much as track or football."

"And this show is going to make us famous." Jackson's voice was as serious as Stone had ever heard it. "*The Dance Off* has ten times as many viewers as *Bite Me* and *Living Wild* combined."

Alan pointed at Stone with a hot wing. "But I don't think that's why you're turning red."

"I agree." Jackson flagged down the waiter. "I saw you two at the salsa club. That didn't look like practice to me."

"We're—" Stone broke off, not sure what he was about to say. Ever since that night, Gina had been all business, as if their near-kiss at Club Picante had never happened. The cameras probably wouldn't pick up on it, but he could feel the difference between them. While he missed her easy warmth and joking manner, it was for the best. He didn't need the distraction.

"She's a good teacher," he finally said.

"So are Lori and Rhianne," Jackson pointed out. "But you didn't see us blushing when their names came up."

"Let's leave him alone," Alan said. "This competition is hard enough as it is without bringing *that* into it."

"Bringing *what* into it?" Jackson asked, his tone sly.

"Whatever it is he doesn't want to say." Alan shrugged and finished his beer.

"Fine." Jackson clapped a hand on Stone's shoulder. "But if you ever want to talk, we're here."

"Thanks." But Stone knew he wouldn't take them up on it. They didn't need to know how attractive or intriguing he found Gina.

"Have either of you ever been to New York?" he asked, changing the subject.

"I lived there for a little while to try my hand at Broadway." Jackson shrugged. "Ended up bartending in the Village and singing at shitty clubs on the Lower East Side. The winters sucked, so I moved to LA and started booking TV spots right away."

Stone smirked. "I'm sure the winters aren't that bad."

The other two guys laughed. "Probably not to you," Jackson agreed.

They chatted amiably for about an hour. Stone sidestepped questions about work he'd done before *Living Wild*—engineering—and his childhood—in Seattle—but he was at least able to share anecdotes about his experience working with a reality TV crew before joining *The Dance Off*.

Overall, he had a good time, better than he'd thought he would. They kept it short—they were all leaving for New York late that night—and Jackson made him promise they'd all hang out again.

Stone and Alan walked back to the hotel, where the concierge waved Stone over.

"I have to pack," Stone told Alan. "See you in a few hours."

Alan waved and headed for the elevators.

"You're Mr. Nielson?" the man at the front desk asked, and when Stone nodded, he continued. "We have a message for you."

Stone glanced at the guy's nametag. "Thanks, Omar. My mother?"

Omar smiled. "Yes, sir."

"I'll call her."

Stone was of the opinion that he made himself available enough by being on camera most of the day, and he didn't need people bugging him during his off time, too. As a result, he often left his phone in his hotel room or let the battery die. Besides, it went with the *Living Wild* image.

His mother, however, wasn't a fan of his avoidance methods, and she'd taken to leaving messages for him at the front desk.

Upstairs, he found his phone in his gym bag—dead, of course. With a sigh, he opened his laptop and video called his mom. His mother's face popped up on the screen immediately, and she smiled when she saw him.

"Hi, son. How's everything going?"

"Ah . . . fine. Everything's good." No point in telling her about the tension underlying his rehearsals with Gina.

"I hear you're off to New York to do that morning news show?"

Stone didn't ask how Pepper knew. She could make anyone spill the beans about anything. "Yeah, I am. We're one week away from the premiere. Can't talk long—I'm leaving for the airport soon. We're taking an overnight flight on *The Dance Off*'s private jet to do the cast reveal."

"That's what I want to talk to you about."

He held back a sigh. *Here it goes.*

"Your father and I just want to remind you how important it is that you not say anything that could jeopardize our show. We're relying on this, and we've all worked hard to build this image."

"I know, Ma. I won't."

"Okay, then. Have a great time in New York City. Safe travels."

Once her image disappeared, Stone scrubbed his hands over his face. This was a nightmare. He had no idea what to expect the next day and his whole family was counting on him not to mess up.

He glanced at the clock. Shit, he still had to pack. He grabbed his suitcase and got to work.

Nine

Being packed into a private plane with more than a dozen dancers, ten other celebrities, and the show's two hosts—Juan Carlos Perez, an Afro Dominican former teen idol, and Reggie Kong, a Taiwanese American stylist to the stars—reminded Stone of crowding into small spaces with his family. Everyone joked and teased each other with an easy camaraderie, and groups split off for private conversations. Since Gina and Natasha were huddled into their seats next to each other with eye masks and ear plugs, Stone sat with Alan and Jackson.

People were filming videos on their phones and snapping selfies left and right, but no one was mic'd. A team of producers and stage managers would meet them in New York.

"It's like being on the school bus without the teacher," Jackson said, glancing around the plane.

Lauren wandered over to them. "Hey, boys."

She leaned over the back of Stone's seat and twined her fingers in his hair. Stone bit back a sigh, wishing he'd thought to tie his hair back into a bun.

"Do you two know each other already?" Jackson asked, pointing to Lauren and Alan. "You're both Olympians."

Alan shook his head. "Winter and Summer. Big difference."

"And technically they're separate events, with separate committees." Lauren sent a pointed glance at Alan's prosthetic leg, visible below his cargo shorts.

Stone's blood boiled at her insinuation, but Alan only shrugged and said, "For now."

"Well, we're all on equal ground in the ballroom," Jackson said, drawing Lauren's attention.

She scoffed. "That's what you think. Only one of us here has spent her whole life learning to dance on ice skates. This show is going to be a breeze."

Jackson flashed her a sharp grin. "It's not just about the dancing, sweetheart."

"I know, *sweetheart*," Lauren shot back. "It's a fucking popularity contest, and I'm already a household name."

"Because you're a gold medalist, right?" Jackson tapped his chin, then snapped his fingers and pointed to Alan. "No, wait. That's him."

With a snarl, Lauren stalked off to the other end of the plane.

"She's got a rep for being nasty," Alan said in a low voice once she was out of earshot. "Watch out for her."

"Bring it," Jackson said. Then he nodded at Stone. "Maybe you're the one who'd better watch out. That girl's got her eye on you."

Stone sighed. "What am I supposed to do about it?"

Jackson shrugged. "Just saying. I wouldn't touch her with a ten-foot pole. Her partner, though . . ." He twisted in his seat and waved to Kevin, who was taking pictures with Rick Carruthers. "That boy can get it."

Stone put Lauren out of his mind and slept for a few hours before they landed in New York. Everyone donned baseball caps and dark sunglasses, like it was some kind of "I'm incognito" uniform, which Stone would have found funny if he weren't so tired. A party bus waited to drive them to the *Morning Mix* studios in Midtown Manhattan. Since *Morning Mix* and *The Dance Off* were owned by the same network, the lively morning news show always got the scoop on the cast announcement.

The next two hours were a rush of activity. The drive into Manhattan offered a brief glimpse of the Empire State Building from the car windows, glinting in the dawn. From the bus, they were hustled into the studio building for a whirlwind turn through hair and makeup, before receiving barked instructions on how they should enter the set.

Stone waited backstage with Gina, who managed to look fresh as a daisy despite the early hour. His own eyes were gritty with lack of sleep, and his back hurt from being jammed into a plane seat for six hours.

Gina's hand rubbed small circles on his lower back. She hadn't done anything like that since the club. "You ready for this?"

"No. Not at all."

Her brows dipped in concern. "What do you mean?"

He struggled to put it into words. "I'm not good with interviews. Promise you'll do all the talking?"

"I—okay." She smiled and touched his arm. "I'll handle the questions. You've got the strong, silent type thing down pat."

Of course he did. It was his role, and he'd learned to play it well, even when it rankled.

The Dance Off's hosts, Juan Carlos and Reggie, went out first to chat with the *Morning Mix* hosts about the upcoming season. Juan Carlos had been on a number of soaps and sitcoms when he was a teenager, and though he was older, his brown skin was unlined and he still had the smile and dimple that had made him famous. Reggie was petite and pretty, with skin like honey and signature blue streaks in her dark hair. Finally, the couples were called one by one.

"We go in order of fame," Gina whispered. "Least to most. We're somewhere in the middle, I think, because you're on a cable show."

Keiko Sousa, a Japanese Brazilian model with famous parents, went first with her partner Joel Clarke. They were followed by Rose Jeffers, a Black actress in her forties, and her partner, Matteo Ricci. Rose's claim to fame had been as one of the main characters on *The Lab*, a hit TV show in the nineties about teenage scientists.

Stone's younger brother Winter had loved the show, but Stone couldn't tell her that.

Alan went third with his partner Rhianne Davis. Stone would have thought a gold medal–winning athlete would be considered more famous than a cable TV survivalist, but who could make sense of these things?

Next out was Farrah Zane, a short Lebanese American teen who'd starred in the popular kids' TV movie *I Spy a Star,* about a spy going undercover as a pop singer. Stone had never heard of it. Farrah's partner was a pro named Danny Johnson.

"She's supposed to be really good," Gina said in a low voice. "We'll have to watch out for her."

Stone didn't like the idea of being rivals with a nineteen-year-old girl, but he didn't reply. They were going out next.

Gina tucked her hand into his elbow and fixed a big smile on her face. The stage manager waved frantically at them, and they strode out onto the set.

The live audience packed onto a set of bleachers cheered, and Gina waved at the crowd while Stone walked them to their seats, which were positioned stadium style on three levels. Since Stone was so tall, they were given seats in the back. He helped Gina, who wore monstrously high heels, onto the platform and took his spot next to her.

They were followed by Norberto "Beto" Velasquez, an Argentinian millionaire and the most recent "star" of *Your Future Fiancé,* and his partner Jess Davenport.

The other celebs followed with their dance partners—Jackson and Lori, Dwayne and Natasha, Twyla and her pro partner Roman Shvernik, Rick and dancer Mila Ivanova, and Kevin and Lauren.

Stone would have picked Twyla Rhodes or Rick Carruthers as the most famous, but he was biased.

The rest of the morning passed in a manic blur. The hosts asked him all of two questions, and he supposed he answered them. Gina did most of the talking, smiling through the whole experience. This was her fifth time doing the media circus for a new season, and she was probably used to it. More than that, she *shined.* It hit him suddenly that she loved this stuff. Being in the spotlight, feeding off the cheers of the crowd—she'd said as much the other night while talking to Kevin. She wanted more of this. This was her life.

Meanwhile, Stone was itching to get away. The live audience, the glaring lights, and being packed onto a stage with the rest of the cast made him claustrophobic and distracted. They couldn't have been on set for more than five minutes, but it felt like hours. Finally, the hosts cut to a commercial break.

Gina let out a deep breath and grinned. "Isn't this exciting?" She must have seen the answer on his face because her smile dimmed. "Stone, are you okay?"

Aware that there were microphones everywhere, he just gave her a tight smile and nodded, patting her hand. "Tired."

He could see by the concern in her eyes that she didn't believe him, but she let it drop. The commercial break ended, the hosts asked questions of the other dancers, and at the next break they were all rushed off set.

"Is that it?" Stone asked, relieved he'd gotten through it without embarrassing himself.

Lori overheard him and chuckled. "No way. We still have to get through the interviews. Put your game face back on."

She was right. Each couple was seated in their own small room, while a parade of reporters passed through asking the same inane questions over and over. Again, Gina did most of the talking, mostly about how excited she was for the new season, and for the audience to see Stone dance. They were seated close enough that she could nudge him when he should answer, and he thought he managed not to sound like a total idiot.

Donna popped in a couple times between interviews. "Make it good, Gina," she said, her smile sharp as a blade.

"Always," Gina replied, with a tight smile of her own that made Stone want to massage the tension from her neck.

And then, miracle of miracles, they were done. A PA entered the room to unhook their mics before handing them fresh bottles of water and bidding them good day.

When they were alone in the room, Gina kicked out her legs and pressed her fingers to the bridge of her nose. "Thank god that's over," she mumbled. "I love it and wouldn't change a thing, but damn if it isn't draining."

"You handled it well." Through every insipid interview, she'd responded with resilience and enthusiasm.

She shrugged and got to her feet. "Part of the job. Come on, we have the rest of the day to ourselves. I want to show you my city."

"I hear you have to walk a lot in New York." He glanced down at the sexy sandals that made her legs look a million miles long.

She followed his gaze and laughed. "Don't worry. I'm going to change into sneakers."

"And we need our disguises, too, I guess." At her puzzled frown, he grinned. "Sunglasses and hats."

She linked her arm with his. "Look at you. You're already a pro at this 'being famous' thing."

"Heaven forbid." Stone gave a mock shudder to make her laugh, just because he liked the sound.

He was in too deep, but too tired to care. It was easier to like her, easier to enjoy her company and focus on pleasing her.

When she smiled, he forgot why he was fighting so hard.

O
utside, the weather was cool and sunny, the perfect spring day. The air was as clear as it got in Manhattan, but it had nothing on Alaska. After being there, Gina was spoiled for life.

They were still deep in Times Square territory, which meant hordes of tourists and people trying to make money off tourists— hawkers for Broadway shows, street salespeople with tables taking up sidewalk space, and creepy costume characters who'd pose for pictures at five bucks a pop. Or was it ten now?

"Where are we going?" Stone asked.

"Let's take the train to Central Park," she said. "You're too conspicuous, and the people walking around here have their eyes peeled for celebrities." They'd lost his hat somewhere in the *Morning Mix* building and had to buy a baseball hat for him in one of the many souvenir shops. Still, the sunglasses and hat did nothing to disguise him. He was massive, with a blond-streaked ponytail and full beard. It was like trying to hide a time-traveling Viking in a kindergarten class.

He shrugged. "Whatever you say."

They were close to Bryant Park, which would be populated with slightly more businesspeople than tourists, so Gina hustled them over to the subway station there and led the way underground.

In the station, Gina bought a MetroCard from one of the machines and swiped them both in. The B train waited at the platform, and she shoved Stone onto it before the doors closed.

"Hold on," she warned. He had good balance, but she didn't want him to bust his ass on the train. It was full, and at the next stop they moved farther in to make room for the people coming and going.

Stone removed his glasses and shoved them into his back pocket. "Too dark in here," he muttered. He sent a restrained glare around them and hunched his shoulders inward, as if trying to take up less space. "And crowded."

The stop at Fifty-Ninth Street–Columbus Circle arrived faster than Gina anticipated. She headed for the doors, shouldering through the people in her way until the crowd spat her onto the platform. She moved aside to get out of the flow of people.

"The park is right upstairs," she said.

No answer.

When she turned around, Stone wasn't there. She whipped off her sunglasses and stood on tiptoe, searching for him over the heads of everyone else on the platform.

Shit. He was still on the train.

She rushed back to the doors, yelling his name, and was caught between the currents of people exiting and entering the train. Inside the subway car, his head snapped up. They made eye contact, and he started to edge his way through the crowd.

It was no use. The guy was built like a fucking linebacker, but he was so worried about hurting people with his size that he wouldn't knock them aside. Before Gina could get back on, the doors slid closed right between them.

"No!" Gina pounded a fist on the glass. She raised her voice and rushed to give him instructions as the train prepared to move. "Get off at the next stop and wait for me there!"

He nodded as the train sped up and pulled out of the station.

"That sucks," the woman standing next to her said. "You should call him, just to make sure."

"Yeah, I . . . thanks." Gina stood by a steel column and tried to catch her breath.

Shit. She'd just lost her celebrity dance partner on the subway, a guy who had never been to New York City before and who *didn't carry his phone.*

She'd teased him about the way he left it places or didn't charge it, but it hadn't been a problem because he was always either at his hotel or at the rehearsal studio with her. Now, it seemed dangerous. How did you walk around without a phone? In New York City of all places?

Her own phone buzzed in her pocket with an incoming text. For a brief, elated second, she thought it might be Stone. A glance at the screen showed it was her mother, Benita, wanting to know when Gina would be coming up to the Bronx to visit and if she'd be bringing "Rock" for dinner. Of course her family had watched the *Morning Mix* reveal.

She'd answer her mom later. For now, she tried calling Stone's phone anyway, just in case.

It went straight to voicemail.

Gina's heart leaped when the telltale rush of air swept along her side of the platform, along with the rumble of an approaching train. Excellent, another B. She'd be at the next station in under two minutes. She rushed to stand by the doors when the train came to a stop. Inside, she squashed herself into a corner by the empty conductor's booth and fanned her face while a slightly garbled announcement blasted from the overhead speaker.

More people filed on. Gina tapped her foot. The train started to move. *Finally.*

Assuming Stone had followed her instructions, they'd be reunited in . . .

The train sailed past Seventy-Second Street.

"What?" She glanced around. No one else seemed surprised. "What's happening? Isn't this a local?"

A middle-aged guy in a suit gave her a disdainful look. "If you'd been paying attention, you would have heard them announce this train is going express to—"

"To 125th Street." Stomach sinking, Gina sagged against the metal door and weighed her options.

There were none, for the time being. New York City transit was notoriously unpredictable, and sometimes local trains went express for no reason, and vice versa. She was stuck watching all the local stops go by, each one reminding her how far away she was getting from Stone.

Her freak-out meter was at eleven by the time the train stopped at 125th Street. She dashed out of the train, up the stairs into the station, and down another flight of stairs to the downtown platform.

A downtown express was pulling in. She hesitated. Seventy-Second Street wasn't an express stop. But when an automated voice announced delays on the downtown local track, that decided it. She hopped on and headed back to Fifty-Ninth Street, and this time found a seat.

She spent the entire subway ride worrying that Stone wouldn't be there when she arrived. What was she going to do if he wasn't there? Did he even know what hotel they were all staying at? How would they find him?

Tears threatened, burning her eyes and forming a lump in the back of her throat. She bit her lip against them. She wouldn't cry on the train. The last time she'd done that, she'd been seventeen and stupid, crying because a boy had broken her heart.

Memories of that time reinforced all her goals and rules. Shoot for the top, and don't let any man get in the way.

Still, this was her fault. She should've told Stone where they were getting off, or held on to him to make sure he was following her off the train. She would have, if she weren't actively trying to keep distance between them.

By the time the train pulled back into the station at Fifty-Ninth Street, Gina was vibrating with anxiety. She bolted onto the platform, ran upstairs and over to the uptown platform once again, and stood wringing her hands and breathing hard while she waited for a local.

When it arrived a minute later, she paid close attention when she got on. This time, there were no announcements. The train picked up speed, heading for Seventy-Second, and Gina's heart nearly burst out of her chest.

In the seconds that passed between stations, her traitorous, anxiety-ridden brain supplied all sorts of improbable images of what she'd find. An empty platform. Stone dead on the tracks. A huge crowd she had to fight her way through, screaming his name at the top of her lungs.

When the train stopped at Seventy-Second Street, she waited at the doors, chewing her lipstick off. Every second seemed to drag, until finally the doors slid open.

Gina stumbled out, looking up and down the platform with wild movements. She couldn't see him yet. People were leaving the train, and she searched for Stone towering over them, but he wasn't there. She'd just inhaled a shaky breath to call his name when the crowd passed, and she saw him.

Stone was sitting on a bench with his ankle propped on one knee, reading one of the free newspapers distributed daily in the subway.

When she let out the breath she was holding, he looked up. His eyes lit up, and a smile curved his lips.

"There you are." He folded the newspaper, but before he could get up, she rushed him. Her knees wobbled and she dropped onto his lap, throwing her arms around his neck.

"You're here," she whispered into his hair, inhaling the scent of him that had become so familiar and comforting to her.

"Of course I am." His voice held a note of surprise. His arms encircled her, and for the first time in . . . she didn't know how long it had been . . . but for the first time since she'd lost him, she felt okay.

She refused to examine the feeling further.

"You told me to get off here and wait for you. So that's what I did." He'd listened. She didn't know what she would have done if he hadn't. "I'm so sorry, Stone."

"Gina." He eased her back and tilted his chin down so he could meet her eyes. "I'm fine. It's all right."

She let out a shuddering breath, the stress of the day taking its toll. Her words spilled out in a jumbled mess. "I lost you, and I'm supposed to be responsible for you, and you don't even have a phone, and—"

"Hey." He cupped her face and leaned in. "You didn't lose me. I should have been paying attention. And you're not responsible for me—I'm a grown man, and I've been lost in worse places than this." The corner of his mouth kicked up. "Besides, I think I was sitting here all of twenty minutes."

Gina blinked, ignoring the way her stomach fluttered at his touch. "That was it? It felt like hours."

"I'm sorry I made you worry."

"I'm sorry I made you wait."

He shook his head. "Don't be. It was an accident. I knew you'd come back for me."

"Of course. But I need you to promise to charge your phone the next time we're here."

"All right. I promise." Then he shifted and held up the newspaper. "Do you have a pen? I've been doing this crossword puzzle in my head and it's getting confusing."

She laughed full out and hugged him, relishing the way he hugged her back.

"I'm not letting go of you again," she mumbled into his shoulder.

"I think I'm okay with that." His voice was soft, and she strained to catch his words. Time to break the tension.

"My mother invited you to dinner."

He exhaled, and she felt it throughout her entire body.

"Really? Because I would do just about anything for a home-cooked steak."

She snickered. "I think bistec encebollado can be arranged. She might call you Rock, though."

"For a steak, she can call me anything she wants."

Ten

"Here we are. Central Park."

Stone blinked in the bright sunlight as he followed Gina up the stairs that led out of the subway station. April in New York was warmer than April in Alaska by far, and it was a sunny day. Over the park, the sky stretched clear and blue over the tops of the budding trees. It was a poor substitute for Alaska, but it beat out the palm trees and smog of Los Angeles.

As they crossed the street to the park entrance, Gina took his hand and gave him a playful smile from under the bill of her Yankees hat. "I'm not going to chance losing you again."

Stone was wearing a Mariners cap. When he'd selected it from the display in the souvenir shop, Gina had sent him a puzzled frown and asked, "You follow baseball?" Her question incited a panic in him, and he'd babbled out a reply. "Yeah, I mean, when I can. We're off the grid, but not, like, on another planet. Sometimes we go into town. But not . . . not often."

In truth, he rooted for the Mariners because he'd been born just outside Seattle, but that didn't fit the Alaskan persona, so he wasn't supposed to mention it. Gina was too perceptive, and he was a terrible liar. He'd have to do a better job of keeping his mouth shut.

Dirt and asphalt trails wound this way and that in the park, and holding Gina's hand as they meandered down one of the trails was nice. Really nice. He shouldn't be getting any closer to her, but more than anything right now, he wanted the distraction of human connection.

The path turned to orange bricks. Up ahead, an ornate stone railing looked out over a large round fountain with a majestic angel rising out of the center, its arms outstretched. A pigeon sat atop the angel's head.

"Bethesda Fountain. My favorite spot in the whole park." Slipping her sunglasses into her jacket pocket, Gina boosted herself up to sit on the edge of the railing.

Stone stared at the statue in the fountain. He'd seen this before. In movies, not in person. But he couldn't ask Gina about it, because she gave him a suspicious look every time he commented on pop culture. "Nice."

"My senior photo was taken here."

"Oh yeah?" He couldn't tell her where he'd gone to high school. The official *Living Wild* story was that he and his siblings had all been homeschooled by their mother, but it wasn't entirely true. He and Reed had gone to a regular public high school in Alaska.

Gina pointed to a spot to the right of the fountain. "That's where I stood with my friends. Imagine five hundred teenagers packed into the space below, and the photographer standing right here."

Stone moved in and slipped an arm around her waist. Sure, Gina had superior balance, but it was a long drop. This close, he filled his lungs with her tropical-sweet scent. When she turned back to face him, her lips parted, and her cheeks pinked.

Every so often, he caught her looking at him like this. Usually she turned away, but not this time. This time, her gaze dropped to his mouth and she licked her lips. His pulse beat heavy in his throat.

They were close, like they'd been in the train station when she'd thrown herself onto his lap. But there was no sense of danger now. Just desire.

She slipped her sunglasses back on and slid down from the rail, breaking the moment. "Let's go down and see the terrace." She took his hand again and led him down the steps.

So, hand-holding was fine, but kissing was not. It made a weird sort of sense. After days of dancing together, something as casual as linking hands was nothing. A friendly touch, that was all. But kissing? That would complicate matters, and as much as Stone wanted to taste her lush mouth, Gina's actions made it clear kissing was off the table.

When they reached the bottom, they circled the fountain while Gina regaled him with funny stories from her high school years, like the time Natasha had fallen into the water.

"I guess I pushed her," she added. "It was an accident, though. I swear."

He let out a low chuckle. "I've pushed my brothers into lots of bodies of water. Not by accident."

"My mother would have been so pissed if my siblings and I had done stuff like that. We tried not to do anything that made more work for her. She worked hard enough as it was."

He wanted to ask what that meant, but didn't. She was entitled to her secrets.

Lord knew he had plenty of his own.

She led him underneath the terrace, where it was cool and shady. A ceiling of beautifully painted tiles spread out above them, supported by ornate columns.

She started to say something, then raised a hand to smother a jaw-cracking yawn.

Stone almost laughed, but then he caught the yawn, and they both ended up covering their mouths and wearing sheepish grins.

"You were saying?" he joked.

"I guess we didn't sleep a whole lot last night."

"Hard to sleep on a plane full of celebrities."

She tucked her hand into the crook of his arm. "Come on. I know where we can go."

They climbed the stone staircase back up to the main path. Gina led the way, but she didn't talk any more. A quick glance at the sky told him they were walking south. They passed a large gray limestone bandshell. A few people on rollerblades zipped around the open space. Nannies pushed babies in carriages. Old men slouched on park benches. Overhead, the trees along each side of the walk formed a canopy of new green.

The smells of spring were everywhere, a combo of dirt and water and plants that spoke of growth and rebirth. And the park itself was an odd mix of city and nature that managed to maintain a relaxed vibe even while bikers zipped along the main roads and cars cut through to travel crosstown. It was a haven of peace in the city that never slept, a way to witness the beauty of the changing seasons without giving up the amenities of modern living.

"I always try to visit, when I can." Gina tilted her face to gaze up at the budding trees. "The park is beautiful all year long. For spring walks, outdoor summer concerts, fall foliage, and snowball fights."

He pictured her in this park, in all seasons. "You love it here."

"I do. This is my city. I didn't want to leave."

"No?"

"Don't sound so surprised. My family's here. All my memories are here. I'm sure you understand not wanting to leave your family and home."

Stone grunted in reply. That concept was growing more complicated the longer he was away from *Living Wild*. Sure, he missed Alaska, but the rest of it? Not so much.

"But the opportunities are in Los Angeles, so Natasha and I packed up and moved. My dream is to have homes—and work—in LA and New York."

She'd moved three thousand miles across the country for ambition, for career. To follow the entertainment business to its home base. He could admire how far she'd gone to follow her dreams, even if he didn't understand the impulse.

He looked up at the sky, spreading bright and endless above them, edged in on the corners by tall buildings, and sighed. "I just want to go back to Alaska and live a quiet life."

She slipped her arm around his waist and gave him a squeeze, her warm body snug against his side. "You will."

He wanted to tell her about life in Alaska, how much he loved the place but hated filming the show, but for now, it was enough to just walk with her.

Before long, they approached a giant field.

"Ta-da!" Gina raised her arm in a flourish. "I give you . . . Sheep Meadow."

"Huh." Stone made a show of looking around. "I don't see any sheep."

She shook her head at him. "They're not here anymore, silly. It's just for lounging."

The lawn was enormous—it had to be over a dozen acres—and ringed by trees, with buildings rising beyond. It was peaceful, though. People sat in the new grass, or lounged, as Gina had said. Stone followed her over to a spot in the middle, in full sunshine.

After spreading out both of their jackets, she sat on one and patted the other for him to join her.

"Gina, I don't mind sitting on grass."

"Oh, right." She giggled. "I'm delirious from lack of sleep. Cut me a break."

But when he sat beside her, she shook her head and patted her lap.

"Lean back. And take off your hat. I want to play with all this glorious hair of yours."

He'd be a fool to argue. With his head resting in her lap, his tired body relaxed amid the smell of fresh spring grass and Gina's signature sweetness. Stone closed his eyes, soaking up the warm sun and Gina's soft, sensuous touch in his hair. Her fingers sifted through the strands with gentle tugs, stimulating the nerves in his scalp and sending answering bolts of pleasure through him. Being this close to her was an exquisite torture, but he didn't want it to end.

When her strong fingers moved to massage his scalp, he groaned.

"You like it?" she asked, her voice breathy.

"Mm." He didn't trust himself to reply. He liked it *too* much.

But the week's activities took their toll, and he started to nod off.

"Stone." Gina's voice was right by his ear.

He cleared his throat and opened his eyes. "Yeah?"

"Let's take a nap."

He shifted over to make room for her on their jackets and pillowed his head on his arms. She stretched out beside him and cuddled against his side, a warm, soft presence.

"I set an alarm on my phone," she said. "When it goes off, I'll take you to get some New York City pizza, and then we'll go uptown to my mom's place."

"Sounds like the perfect day."

He closed his eyes. Drifted off. And woke when her phone beeped.

Gina sat up to fish it out of her pocket. He wanted to pull her back down beside him.

"Huh? It's a call." She pressed the phone to her ear. "Hello? Oh, sure, he's right here." She passed the phone to Stone, her expression sleepy and puzzled. "It's for you."

Stone stared at the sky while the guy on the other end rattled a name at him that sounded vaguely familiar, along with a series of instructions. He grunted a few times in response, then ended with, "Fine, I'll be there."

He hung up and gave the phone back to Gina.

"What was that all about?" she asked.

"Dinner. With some of the *Living Wild* execs. At the hotel." He blew out a breath. "Sorry. Your mother—"

"It's okay." She cut him off before he could find the words to explain how much he'd rather have a home-cooked meal with her family. "Work comes first."

He ground his teeth. Work didn't come first, not for him. Family did. He always dropped everything to come to his family's aid. It was why he was here in the first place.

Right now, the pull of *family*—real family, crammed around a dinner table to eat and fight and laugh—warred with the commitment he'd made to his own family back in Alaska, to do whatever it took to keep their secrets safe and make *Living Wild* a success. When was the last time they'd had a family dinner that hadn't been filmed?

He also just didn't want to leave Gina. He didn't want this day to end.

"I don't want to go," he finally said. "But I have to."

"I get it, Stone." Understanding was written all over her face.

She walked him to the corner of the park and out to Columbus Circle. After giving him detailed walking directions, she sent him on his way.

Probably for the best that he wasn't going to visit her family. If her mother's steak was any good, he'd likely do something stupid, like propose marriage on the spot. And if today had shown him anything, it was that Gina would never be happy with the kind of life he dreamed of having.

Eleven

The premiere snuck up on Stone. One day they were rehearsing, and the next they were hours away from the live broadcast. People kept asking if he was nervous, and then he felt weird for *not* being nervous.

He wandered around backstage while Gina was in wardrobe for a last-minute costume adjustment. That wasn't something he needed to be present for, not unless he wanted to watch Gina being sewn into the slinky purple sequined dress. The one that dipped down low between her breasts and hugged all her curves.

Nope, he didn't need to be around for that.

He found Jackson backstage in the area where the cast gathered during the show. They called it the "Sparkle Parlor." It looked like a drunk unicorn had projectile-vomited glitter all over the walls, but it was just so indicative of the show's aesthetic, he couldn't be mad at it.

Jackson paced in front of a large flatscreen TV with *The Dance Off*'s logo floating around on it like a screensaver. He worked his mouth and jaw, stretching his lips wide and uttering strange humming sounds.

Stone approached slowly. "You all right there?" After growing up with Wolf, weird behavior didn't faze him.

Jackson spun around, then hunched his shoulders when he saw Stone. "You caught me. I'm doing vocal exercises."

"Planning to sing instead of dance?"

Jackson barked out a laugh. "You wish." He rubbed his neck. "I do these before I go on stage, even if I'm not singing. They calm me down."

"Then I'll leave you to it."

Stone headed back into the hallway, passing countless crew members dashing around with walkie-talkies and other random electronics.

Smelling smoke, he followed another corridor out to a loading dock, where he found Twyla Rhodes smoking a cigarette behind a giant metal dumpster. She already wore her costume for the night, a glittery black off-the-shoulder gown.

Twyla spared him a glance. "Oh, hey there, hot stuff. You want one?" She offered him the pack.

"No, thanks."

"Good choice. It's a nasty habit." She took a long drag, let it out in a thin stream. "You're the one who lives in the forest, right?"

He bit back a sigh. "That's me."

"Don't suppose you know who I am?"

"Oh, I know. Even in the forest, we had a VCR and all the Elf Chronicles movies on VHS tape." They hadn't actually lived in Alaska then, but he left that part out.

Twyla paused with the cigarette an inch from her lips and sent him a big smile. "Always nice to meet a fan, even after all these years. That part never gets old."

"I hear they're making another sequel."

"You hear a lot in that forest."

"I hear a lot surrounded by a production crew full of nerds," he returned smoothly.

"I would imagine so." She chuckled. "And . . . maybe there will be a sequel. But you didn't hear that from me." She winked.

Another Elf Chronicles movie all but confirmed by Twyla Rhodes herself? His brothers and sisters were going to flip.

Twyla finished her cigarette and used it to light another one.

"Don't judge me," she said in a level tone. "It's the only vice I have left, and there was a time when I did everything, and I do mean *everything*."

"No judgment."

He'd heard the rumors. Years of drugs and alcohol had taken a toll on her, making her look older than her years. Hitting rock bottom and clawing her way back up had settled a brittle sharpness about her that came out in the form of dark humor and a proclivity for speaking her mind as an activist.

As a boy, Stone had thought her the most beautiful woman in the world. Her character, Queen Seraphina of the Elves, wore robes of silver and gold that left her arms bare and offered tantalizing glimpses of her legs. She must have been so young then, her alabaster skin smooth and unlined, her eyes bright and determined, her voice clear and sweet. She'd been unknown before the first movie, and then suddenly, she was a star.

"My brothers and I carved our own wooden swords," he told her. "I can't tell you how many times we reenacted the final battle from *Queen's End*. My sisters fought over who got to play your character."

Twyla giggled. "Oh, go on."

"My older brother swore he was going to marry you."

She glanced at him from the corner of her eye. "If he looks anything like you, tell him I'll take him up on the offer. He'd make a great husband number three."

"It'd be an honor to have you as a sister-in-law."

Twyla puffed on her cigarette and gave him a long look, squinting at him through the smoke. "You're a sweet kid, so I'll give you some advice: Get the hell out of this business while you can, before it chews you up and spits you out like a piece of gum that's lost its flavor."

Her words sent a chill through him. "I'll keep that in mind."

"I'm sorry, kid." She waved him away. "The prospect of dancing in front of a live audience tonight has got me in a maudlin mood. Go find your pretty little partner. That girl's got enough good cheer for all of us."

"You're going to be great," he said, sensing that she needed to hear it. "People are going to love seeing you perform again. You'll see."

Patting his arm with one hand, she lit another cigarette with the other. "Like I said, you're sweet. Now go. Leave an old lady to her thoughts."

He left her there and headed back into the main network of hallways. He passed Farrah Zane by craft services, where she filmed a video for her fans about how nervous she was and how much she needed their votes. He heard heavy kissing from a door left ajar, and spotted Beto Velasquez and one of the makeup artists out of the corner of his eye as he hurried past. By the empty judges' table, the show's hosts, Juan Carlos Perez and Reggie Kong, told dirty jokes, while football star Dwayne Alonzo stretched nearby. It seemed like everyone was looking for ways to burn off nervous energy.

Stone just wanted to get it over with. It was only dancing, after all.

He saw Gina speaking earnestly with one of the lighting guys, and had the sense to keep his thoughts to himself, lest she accuse him again of not taking this seriously.

Catching her eye, he pointed to the balcony, which would be filled with audience members soon. She nodded, and he went to find the stairs that would take him upward. He wanted a bird's eye view of the "ballroom." In reality, it was more like a theater, with a stage at one end, a circular dance floor in the center, and the judges' table positioned opposite the stage. VIP seating crowded the edges of the dance floor, resembling a dinner club with plush chairs and small round tables. Rigging and lights hid in the shadows of the high ceiling, and regular audience members were confined to overhanging balconies.

When Gina arrived, Stone was lounging in a padded folding chair, overlooking the scene below as if he were in the audience. She looked stunning in the purple dress, and he wanted to compliment her, but he just patted the seat next to him. She sat, letting out a soft sigh as her shoulders drooped. They watched Jackson and Lori work out the camera blocking down below, while the stagehands threw together a sparkly, lit-up platform in under two minutes.

"That's impressive," he said. "I wouldn't have thought it was possible to build something so quickly."

"It only has to hold up for thirty seconds," Gina pointed out. "And they do this stuff every week—build sets, design lighting routines, and sync it to live music. Not to mention the magic done by wardrobe and makeup."

"Wow." He watched Jackson backflip off the stage. "To be fair, my producers often want us to spend as long as possible building stuff so they can draw out the story. And we always have to pretend something goes wrong."

She smothered a grin. "Color me shocked."

"Heaven forbid we should build something properly the first time." He sighed and tried to put thoughts of *Living Wild* out of his head.

"We're the eighth couple to perform. Fourth from the end," she told him, turning the subject back to the premiere. "It's a pretty good spot. People usually vote toward the end of the show, so going on later is best."

"Who's after us?"

"Farrah Zane, Rick Carruthers, and Lauren D'Angelo."

Stone jerked his chin at the dance floor. "Jackson is really good."

"He's an actor. There's a high likelihood he has dance training."

Jackson had already admitted he did. "Isn't that cheating? I thought the whole point was to cast celebrities who aren't dancers."

"No, *The Dance Off* solicits celebs with all levels of experience, and there's usually a ringer. But it's not Jackson."

"Is it Farrah? That movie she did had dance numbers in it."

"Nope. Not her."

"So, if it's not Farrah or Jackson—who are great dancers, as far as I can tell—then who is it? Certainly not me."

Gina clapped her hands over her mouth, something he noticed she did to hold back a snort. He liked it. "Sorry, dude, it's definitely not you, although you're doing very well." She gave him a comforting smile and patted his knee. "In this case, it's Lauren D'Angelo."

Stone followed Gina's gaze to the loud blonde standing in one corner of the ballroom with Kevin.

Gina ticked off on her fingers. "Lauren's an Olympic athlete, which means she's in control of every inch of her body and accustomed to the grueling hours. And she's a figure skater, which means she's flexible, strong, and basically dances on ice skates."

They watched Lauren and Kevin execute a perfect spin. Gina was right. Lauren was fantastic.

"And that's not all."

"Shit, there's more?"

"Ha. You bet there is. Unlike Alan, she's never won an Olympic medal, so she's driven to prove she can win something. She's already entering this competition with the deck stacked in her favor, and to top it all off, she's got Kevin Ray. People vote for Kevin just because he's Kevin. So, yeah, Lauren is the one to beat."

Stone let out a breath, thinking of his interactions with Lauren. If the skater was taking this as seriously as she took the Olympics, he needed to step up his game. "I guess we better beat her, then."

Gina smiled at him, a small, sweet smile that set him on fire. "I guess we'd better."

"What do we have to do?"

"You listen to me and do what I say. Focus on the footwork, hold, and technique. Let the audience see your personality and vulnerability. You have a chance, Stone. If you charm the viewers, show personal growth, and turn out good dances, we can do this." She opened her mouth like she was going to say more, then shut it.

"You really want to win, don't you?" It was a stupid question. He knew she did.

"I really, really do." Gina bit her lip, and her brow creased, like she was uncertain about something. "There's another factor, too. I didn't want to tell you, though."

"Now you have to tell me."

She slouched in the chair like the air had been ripped from her lungs. "I don't want this to affect your performance or put any pressure on you. This is all on me."

"Not true. We're partners, remember?"

"Yeah, we are." She released the next words in a rush. "If I don't make it to the finals, I'm out of the job."

His jaw clenched. "Don't you mean, if *we* don't make it to the finals?"

She closed her eyes. "I guess I do. You won't be out of a job, though."

He clasped her hands in his. Somewhere along the way, this sort of casual touch had become natural for him. At least, it was natural with her. "All right, Gina. Let's win this thing."

The way her eyes lit up, and the wide, toothy smile on her face— all of this would be worth it if he could see that look on her face again at the end. She squeezed his hands and leaned in, enveloping him in her signature tropical-sweet scent.

"Team Stone Cold, for the win."

It would have been the perfect moment to kiss her. But then she stood, tugging on his hands, and the moment was gone.

"Come on, partner. Let's work on our blocking. Tonight's the big night."

He followed her downstairs. No more thinking about kissing Gina. He was here to dance, and then he was heading back to Alaska. *Focus on the money.*

The next few hours sped by. Stone waited backstage while the judges and extra dancers completed the opening number, joining Gina to mug for the camera before everyone lined up to be announced by Juan Carlos. Stone watched the other couples dance from backstage, cheering them on and joking around with Alan and Jackson, who both delivered respectable performances. As time wore on and no one fell on their faces, Stone worried he'd be the one to do so.

When it was his turn to take the stage, a stage manager appeared to usher him to his spot on the dance floor. He stood with Gina in the dark, waiting while the behind-the-scenes package played on the giant screen hanging over their heads. He closed his eyes, mortification setting in as he listened to their awkward first meeting.

"Don't listen," Gina said in a low voice.

"How can I not? It's fucking embarrassing."

She gave his hand a squeeze. "You've already lived it. Breathe now. Be present. All you have to do is dance for thirty seconds."

He took a deep breath as she instructed, and let it out slowly. "It feels like longer." On screen, Gina freaked out about the "bear."

She smiled up at him. "It's forever and an instant, all at the same time. There's nothing like it."

Stone shook his shoulders, stretching his neck muscles as the package switched to him stumbling through the steps of the foxtrot. Around them, the stagehands darted back and forth, setting up their props for the dance. "I'm . . . nervous."

"That's okay."

"I don't want to let you down."

"Oh, Stone." Gina squeezed his hand again. "You won't. Just do your best, okay? Don't worry about me."

Before he could reply—not that he knew what to say—they got the cue and took their places. Gina lounged on top of a piano and Stone sat at a small table with two other male dancers, Joel and Roman. Stone picked up a hand of playing cards and stared at them intently. The music lead-in indicated they were back from commercial.

Juan Carlos's voice rang out. "Dancing the foxtrot, Stone Nielson and Gina Morales."

The lights went up. The music started. Three weeks of intense training took over.

No time to think. No time to worry. When Gina approached, Stone exploded out of his seat, playing his role as the love—or lust—struck gangster captivated by the sexy lounge singer. Following Gina across the dance floor, he played up his character for the camera. What felt silly in rehearsal was now done without a second thought.

Stone mimed whistling, then tossed his fedora aside and took Gina in his arms to lead her around the floor.

One step after the other. Left, right, left again. Lean, step back, spin. Gina counted the moves out loud but Stone went through the dance without missing a step. The music guided their feet. The lyrics connected them, wrapping around their bodies and anchoring them in the moment.

Gina had been right, of course. There was nothing to do but dance.

It was over before he knew it. Breathing hard, Stone held Gina in his arms as the music came to an end. Adrenaline pulsed through him, his body on fire with it and the feel of Gina against him. Half a second later, the studio audience burst into applause and cheers.

"You did it." Her smile lit up her face and she broke the hold to throw her arms around his neck, surrounding him with her scent. "You did it!"

He straightened, pulling her into a hug that lifted her dance shoes clear off the floor. "*We* did it." It had been a rush, more than he'd expected, on par with hunting and cliff diving. To his surprise, he wanted to do it again.

When he set her back on the floor, Gina pressed her lips together, emotion shining in her eyes. "You're right. We did."

Juan Carlos popped up behind them out of nowhere, blurting a cheerful, "Let's get your scores!"

Twelve

The next morning, Gina sailed into the rehearsal room, buoyed by a wave of positivity. Stone had killed it in the foxtrot, earning a respectable average score for the first episode. Better yet, the fans were talking about them all over social media. He was a hit.

Jordy awaited her with Aaliyah at his side. "Nice work last night." He handed Gina a square of cardstock with *The Dance Off*'s logo. "Here's your next dance."

"Thanks." She flipped it over and groaned. "Really? So soon?"

The door opened behind her and Stone ambled through in black sweatpants and a white tank top. Gina swallowed hard. He'd looked dashing last night, decked out in dark trousers and a white button-down with a thirties-style tie and suspenders, but really, the man made anything look sexy.

"Morning." He dropped his gym bag next to hers.

She gave him a high five. "You were *awesome* last night. That was a great score."

"We only averaged seventy percent," he pointed out while Aaliyah handed them their lavalier mics. "Lauren got eighty-two."

Well, it was about time. Apparently it had taken firsthand experience of the show's scope to get Stone's competitive instincts firing. Last night, he'd seen how much work and how many people contributed to the production, and how seriously the other contestants took the competition. She'd told him Lauren was the one to beat, and now he had his eyes on the prize.

That was good, but she needed him focused on the next dance. They'd take them one at a time and do their best with each. She couldn't allow herself to get psyched out by Donna's threat. *The Dance Off* was a huge stepping stone to the growth of her career, and she didn't want to lose it.

Gina poked a finger into the unyielding muscle of his chest. "Don't think about Lauren or any of the others. It's just you and me, dancing together."

Stone nodded, then gestured to the paper she still held. "What's that?"

"Our dance for Fiesta Night." She passed the card to him, snickering when his eyebrows shot up.

"The Argentine tango?" He goggled at her, looking like his eyes were about to fall out of his head.

"You've heard of it?"

"I've seen it in movies. It looks . . . difficult." He flipped the card over a few times, as if there might be another dance hiding on it somewhere. "And close."

"It is." No point beating around the bush. "It's a sexy dance."

The big jerk rolled his eyes and groaned.

She jabbed him again. "Hey, what's that reaction about?"

His eyes cut away from hers. "This is going to be so awkward."

"It will be if you don't do it right. Come on, let's start with the basics."

As she had with the foxtrot, Gina moved around him, poking and prodding his body into position while explaining the dance.

"In the tango, our hold is the opposite of most ballroom dances. Instead of leaning our chests away, when we're in close embrace our chests and faces will be touching."

Stone sighed. "I knew it. Already awkward."

Again with the sighing? "Shush." She kicked at his heels. "You're not going to be lifting your feet a whole lot in the basic steps. Keep them close to the floor."

She moved his body, providing instruction and slight corrections as she took him through a few passes around the room.

"Tango relies on improvisation," she said. "The person in the man's role leads, directing their partner and making sure the two of them don't bump into anyone else on the dance floor. For our performance, you have to appear forceful. This is a sharper dance than the foxtrot, and you have to nail the footwork and hold."

"And we only have a week to learn this one."

"Slightly less." Gina chuckled at his muttered curse. "Argentine tango requires a connection between the partners and the music, which is almost like a third partner for us. We're communicating the emotion of the music to each other through our bodies."

Stone narrowed his eyes. "So, tango is all about sex?"

It could be argued that all dance was about sex, but Gina didn't want to go there. "Not in the way you mean—it doesn't have to be sexy. You could do a wistful tango between star-crossed lovers, a teasing tango with a jewel thief, one that evokes a sense of steady connection between a couple, or even one that's fun and upbeat. Hell, we could do a dark tango as vampires. It all depends on the music."

"We're using sexy music, I take it."

"That's the plan. We'll see if they can clear the rights for my first song choice. For us, this is a strategic move, and we're going to go as sexy as we can on network TV. People are going to want to see this side of you, and we're going to lay it all out there in week two." It was a risk, with Donna waiting in the wings to twist their behind-the-scenes clips into something romantic. But they'd fallen into a friendly, playful pattern, which would hopefully show up in their rehearsal footage.

Stone went through the steps again on his own. "You don't think it's a little early for that?"

"I'm not pulling any punches this season. I'd rather hit them hard early in the game than get eliminated and wish I hadn't saved the sexy card for later." And then lose her job. Shit. She had no choice but to make this dance sexy.

He gave a low chuckle. "I think you're mixing metaphors."

"I know I am. But you get it. Go big or go home, Stone." She pressed her hands to her mouth, eyes growing wide. "Ooh. *Ooh*. I'm getting it. An idea is taking shape."

She paced in tight circles, muttering to herself and wringing her hands as her brain kicked into high gear. In her mind, she visualized their routine, running through options for the concept, the costumes, the vibe.

She wanted this dance to be panty-meltingly sexy. Their foxtrot had revealed Stone to be a competent dancer and established them as contenders. The next dance would secure their spot in the audience's imagination. She wouldn't fake a showmance, but she'd set Stone up as a fantasy for the viewers.

Gina had seen it work in the past, before she'd joined the show. Hernando Gomez, a telenovela star, had captured the audience's hearts and lust with his masculinity and chivalry. Even though he hadn't been the best dancer that season, he had shown tremendous growth and won Lori the trophy.

"I've got it," Gina said. "We're telling a story of raw desire. Carnal magnetism."

She leaned in and pressed her palms to his chest, demonstrating the moves as she spoke. "We want each other, but it isn't good for us. I walk away from you." She spun away dramatically and froze with her head and shoulders thrown back. "You keep pulling me back in, and I want it, so I stay." She twirled into his arms again. "Finally, I run away, out into the rain." She ran across the room, leaving him gaping after her.

"Into the *rain*?"

She dropped character. "They can make it rain on the stage."

He scratched at his beard. "This is getting complicated."

"Don't worry, they can do it. And you're interrupting my flow."

"My apologies. Proceed, dance master."

She sent him a smirk, but continued. "I run across the stage, but you don't follow. You dance halfway, then stop with your arms open, waiting for me. Before I'm offstage, I turn and run back. Then we do the remainder of the dance in the rain."

His eyebrows drew together. "Won't it be dangerous to dance on a wet stage?"

"Dangerous *and* uncomfortable. But it doesn't bother us, because when you want someone like that . . ." She gave a wistful sigh. "You just want them. Nothing else matters. We're appealing to the baser instincts of the viewers. Lots of people can relate to that kind of desire."

She sure the hell could. Every time she looked at him, he tempted her to throw caution to the wind and drag him into a private corner somewhere. On second thought . . .

"And at the last moment, right before the song ends, I break hold and run off the stage."

Stone shrugged. "Whatever you say, boss."

Imagining it in her head, that ending destroyed the emotional quality of the dance, but even in character, she needed to keep her distance. Okay. Deep breaths. No more thoughts of Stone in dark corners. "Footwork and hold. Let's go."

Three hours later, Gina's frustration levels were through the roof. Stone was managing the footwork and form, but there was a hesitancy to his movements that was ruining the routine. If their chemistry was going to set the dance floor on fire, she had to demolish the boundaries between them.

Her mind issued a warning in her mother's voice. *Cuidado. Esto es peligroso.*

Yeah, it was dangerous. But it was the only way.

"Take a break," Gina said, after countless trips back and forth across the room. "This isn't working."

His brows creased, and for a second he looked hurt. "What do you mean? I haven't done a step wrong for the past half hour."

"I know. You're doing great with learning the moves. It's not that." She uncapped a bottle of water and chugged it.

"Then what is it?" He came closer and stood with his hands on his hips.

She huffed and tossed the bottle back into the cooler. Her next words were bound to end up in the behind-the-scenes footage, but they needed to be said. "You're not going to break me, Stone."

"I'm—what?" His voice rose in bewilderment. "I don't know what you're talking about."

She waved at him impatiently. "Get in hold. I'll show you what I mean, and why the tango is a hard dance for week two." She stepped into his arms, then gestured at the way he was holding her. "See? It's this. I'm not made of glass. Tango is a forceful dance. You can't be afraid to grab me."

"I'm not—"

"You are. Do you trust me?"

His eyes narrowed. "Yes . . ."

"Then give me your hands." When he held them out to her, she grabbed his wrists and yanked his arms around her. He didn't resist, but when she clapped his hands onto her butt, his whole body jerked in surprise.

"Gina, what—"

"*Squeeze.*"

He shook his head and tried to pull his hands away. "I can't. It's rude."

She tightened her grip on his wrists and barely suppressed a giggle. "Not if I tell you it's okay. Are you uncomfortable touching me?"

She knew he wasn't, not after the way he'd held her at Club Picante—something she hadn't been able to forget, no matter how hard she tried. She just needed him to bring some of that passion to this tango.

His eyes flicked to hers, then to the cameras. "It's not that . . ."

"Then what's the problem?"

The look he gave her was stern and intense. "Is this really necessary?"

"Yes."

"Why?"

Exasperation seeped into her voice. "Because I want you to know I'm fine with it. That you don't need to be so precious with me."

He spoke low, with that delicious little growl that set her pulse racing. "I don't want to hurt you."

"You won't. But Stone, if you're scared to touch me, you're going to look hesitant in the dance. If you look hesitant, it will look like I'm leading. And if I'm leading, our tango will suck." Her voice rose with each point, until she was practically yelling. "Do you want our tango to suck?"

"Of course not."

"Then grab my ass!"

She could see in his eyes the second he decided to go with it. His big hands trembled, then clenched, his long fingers clamping around her ass cheeks and palming them perfectly.

Gina sucked in a breath. Heat flooded through her, and all her attention centered on the warmth of his palms and the strength of his fingers digging lightly into her flesh.

Oh god. This was a mistake. A giant fucking mistake. What the hell had she been thinking?

"Happy?" he snapped.

"Yes." Her voice was thick, and it pissed her off. She cleared her throat. "Now that we've gotten that out of the way . . ."

She eased back, setting them up so they were in proper hold. "Let's try this again. From the top."

Two days later, they'd received their music and Stone had nailed the choreography, but they had a new problem.

He wouldn't look her in the eye.

When they danced, he grabbed her and twirled her with such delicious force that Gina was starting to dream about his touch at night. His posture was next to perfect. Their lifts were phenomenal, and he hadn't dropped her once. His footwork was coming along, aside from a slight tendency to bend his knees at an odd angle. But he was working on it, and she was confident he'd have it fixed by showtime. He'd made incredible progress in just a matter of days.

But while he did everything she told him, tightening his hold and whipping her body around in spins and lifts, he wouldn't look at her while he did any of it.

It was better to let intimacy with a dance partner build organically, but they were running out of time. Gina had to call him out.

After their lunch break—he was always a bit more amenable after he'd consumed what looked like an entire chicken—she sat next to him at the edge of the small stage stretching across one end of their practice room.

Jordy closed in on them with the camera, as if sensing she was about to give them a show. All of this would be so much easier without the crew around. Even worse, Donna was with them today.

"Stone." Gina put her hand on his knee and gave it a squeeze. "Why won't you look at me?"

He cut his eyes to her, but he didn't seem surprised by her question. "I look at you."

Goosebumps rose on her arms. Oh, that deep, grumbling voice did lovely things to her. "Do you?"

"I'm looking at you right now."

"You're glaring at me from the corner of your eye. There's a difference."

Stone let out an exasperated sigh and leaned back on his elbows. "Gina."

Just that. Just her name. She'd always thought her name was soft—the smooth "g," the dominance of the vowels—but she loved the sound of it in his gruff tone.

"Do I make you nervous?" she asked.

This time, he shot her a dark glare from under his brows, and the answer was in full view: *Yes.*

"Stone, there's no way we're going to be able to give this dance the emotion it deserves if you won't look at me."

He sighed and rolled his eyes toward the ceiling.

She tugged on his arm to make him sit up. "Face me. We're going to do something from my yoga teacher training."

"You're a yoga teacher?" He raised an eyebrow, but let her move him.

"Being a professional dancer didn't always pay the bills." She turned them so they faced each other, and took his hands in hers. "This is called eye-gazing."

"What is it?" He sounded curious. At least he was looking at her now.

"Just what it sounds like. We look into each other's eyes." She fixed her gaze on his, holding herself still.

"Like a staring contest?"

She snickered. "No. Well, kind of? You're allowed to blink."

"So, we just stare into each other's eyes . . ." Some of his own brand of quiet humor was back in his tone.

"Yes."

"And then?"

"Just do it, Stone."

As Gina stared into his eyes, she fought the urge to swallow hard. It would be all too easy to lose herself in their blue depths.

Or so she thought. Three seconds in, she felt the first twitch in her right cheek. Half a second later, the other side twitched.

"Are you supposed to be laughing?" He spoke out of the corner of his mouth, making her dissolve into giggles.

"No. Stop it."

"I'm just doing what you said." He schooled his features into solemnity, but then a grin broke across his face and he ducked his head. "This is silly."

"No, it isn't. Keep gazing."

He brought his attention back to her. This time, she made it about five seconds before her lips quirked, and she saw an answering twitch in his. She pulled herself together, then saw his jaw trembling. She bit her lip before she could smile.

The longer they gazed into each other's eyes, though, the easier it became. Her gaze wavered slightly, from his left eye to his right, to softly losing focus while staring at the bridge of his nose so she could keep both eyes in sight.

As she gazed, she noticed new things about his face—he had slight creases at the corners of his eyes, his lashes were thick and brown, and he had a good, strong nose. He had to know how handsome he was. Surely they owned a mirror in the Alaskan bush? The swirls in his eyes evoked calming mental imagery of clear water and wispy clouds scudding across a rich sky. Yet in their center, belying the tranquility, lay a barely leashed intensity like the scorching blue heart of a flame.

What was he thinking? What was he seeing in her face?

A sense of deep and utter calm descended on her. Her muscles relaxed, and her skin took on a soft, fuzzy feeling. Laughter no longer nudged her to smile or look away, and the connection between them stretched and expanded.

Gina had never felt closer to anyone else, ever. They were the same. And there was nothing to be self-conscious or nervous about.

She could trust him.

At that, she dropped her gaze. This was too intimate. Too close. The abruptness of the disconnection stole her breath, and she struggled to reclaim it while appearing at ease.

His hand entered her field of vision.

"Let's dance," he said, the deep rumble shaking her to her core.

She nodded, unable to speak, and took his hand. His warm fingers closed around hers, and he led her into the center of the room before taking her in his arms. His hold was perfect, his grip firm, just as she'd taught him. Out of habit, she looked up to meet his eyes. What she saw there scared her.

This wasn't just about attraction anymore. This was mutual respect and trust. She *liked* him. She could tell a lot about a person by the way they danced, and everything she learned about Stone, she liked. He was steady and kind, funny and patient, and committed to being here.

Not a word passed between them as he led her into the tango. His eyes never left hers, except when the choreography called for it. This time, he held her even closer than before, but there was nothing disconcerting about it.

It felt so, so right.

He still did odd things with his knees, but the force of their shared connection exploded within her, making her skin tingle and her breath quicken. When he dragged his hands up her thighs, she imagined how it would feel to be in his arms, in his bed, with nothing between her skin and his hands.

He gripped her around the waist and swung her in circles, her back arched and her hands clasping her own ankles. Then he lifted her as if it were the easiest thing in the world, spinning her like a windmill over his shoulders and bringing her back to earth with barely a bump. He made it look effortless, and she felt supported and safe throughout. People would marvel at the lift, and swoon at the passionate, watery ending.

Gina progressed through the motions of the dance, arching her body over his shoulder, curving her legs around his hip, throwing herself into his arms and letting him drag her across the floor. She pressed her cheek to his, breathing in the light scent of his sweat, and dropped to a split between his legs that ended with her clutching his hard thigh.

The dance would end on the stage with water pouring down on them, soaking them to the skin as he spun her in his arms, their hands grabbing frantically at each other's bodies until he lifted her and she locked her legs around his waist.

She'd danced the tango countless times, with countless partners. It had never, never been like this.

This was foreplay. Stone was showing her his intensity, what he was capable of, and what he'd do to her—for her, with her—if she let him.

Right then, Gina wanted it more than she wanted her next breath. And it scared the shit out of her.

Nothing was allowed to come between her and her goals. Nothing.

She would never again allow a man to compromise her career. It was why, even at the end of the dance, she had to run away.

Thirteen

The Dance Off's backstage catacombs were crowded on show night. Pro dancers, celebrities, camera operators, stage managers, PAs, makeup artists, and producers all vied for space in the Sparkle Parlor. The nervous excitement buzzed along Stone's frayed nerves. Try as he might to block everyone out, it proved impossible.

Lauren trash-talked. Twyla tried to bum a cigarette off everyone who crossed her path and Beto flirted with all the women who crossed his. Farrah and her partner Danny made silly faces for the cameras at every opportunity.

After a week of practicing the Argentine tango with Gina, Stone was so wound up he was ready to jump out of his own skin or punch a hole in a wall. Maybe both. The waiting made it worse. He and Gina weren't going on until the end of the episode, second to last. It took everything he had to force a grin onto his face when the cameras turned his way.

Gina made it better, though. When he caught glimpses of her across the Sparkle Parlor, just the sight of her soothed him.

Jackson slipped out of the makeup chair and joined Stone against the wall. To their right, Keiko—the model—and her pro partner, Joel, were practicing their dance moves. When the couple slipped into the hallway, Jackson elbowed Stone.

"I bet you twenty bucks they're sneaking off for a quickie."

"Really?" Stone raised his eyebrows and stuck his head around the corner, but they were already gone.

Jackson laughed. "You have no idea how much hanky-panky is going on behind the scenes here, do you?"

"I hadn't thought about it." How could he, when all his thoughts were consumed by Gina?

As connected as he felt to Gina, he had to remember that it wasn't real. Backstage, everyone acted like they were one big happy family, but at the end, they'd all cash their checks and go their separate ways. This wasn't his world, and Gina would never fit into his after he left. The eye-gazing? The intimacy? None of that was why he'd come here. Better to just do the dance and look forward to the day he went home.

Except Gina's job was on the line. She needed him to be in it to win it. And as much as he was doing this for his family, he was now doing it for her, too.

And maybe also a little for himself.

Since he didn't want to examine that thought too much, he turned to Jackson and said, "I'll catch you later." Then he ducked out to wander the rigging backstage. He wasn't fit company for anyone right now.

Stone spent the rest of the show avoiding Gina—and his feelings about her—until they took their marks backstage. But when she stepped closer and twined her arms around his waist, all other thoughts flew from his head.

Skinny straps snaked over her shoulders, holding up a stingy swath of glittery black lace that stretched down over half of her taut torso and one leg. It covered the important bits, but her left side and back were bare, and the "dress" was secured at her hip with only a sparkly embellishment.

Stone tried to focus on her face, since it would be rude and obvious to stare at her body, but her eyes—already so captivating—

were lined with dark makeup, making them stand out even more and leaving him spellbound. Her lips were painted red, and they sparkled, too. Her long hair had been parted on the side and pulled back into a complicated twist on the back of her head.

She was stunning, in every sense of the word, and Stone couldn't seem to catch his balance around her.

Gina spoke in a low voice. "I'm worried about you."

The scent of tropical flowers permeated his senses and made him hyperaware of their closeness. He fought his body's reaction and growled, "Don't be."

Instead of comforting her, his words seemed to make her more agitated. Her brow creased, and she leaned in even closer. "Please tell me what's going on."

"I'm fine."

Gina stared into his eyes for a long moment, then tapped a finger to his temple. "Don't get stuck in here," she said. "Stay with me. Remember what I told you? Channel whatever's happening in your head into the dance. Into me. Let me help you carry it."

Need welled up in him, and he couldn't stop himself from clutching her shoulders, shifting her an inch closer. She moved with him, her hand resting on his chest.

"Stay with me," she said again. "It's just you and me, dancing together."

He huffed out a laugh. "And millions of people watching on live TV."

She shook her head and took his face in her hands. "You're not dancing with those people. You're only dancing with me."

When he nodded, she brushed her thumbs softly over his cheekbones. "Will you eye-gaze with me, Stone?"

An unwise move, but he could refuse her nothing. He nodded.

It was easier this time. Neither of them giggled. Their behind-the-scenes footage played and Stone ignored it, keeping all his attention on Gina, as she'd directed.

Her eyes. Deep and dark enough that he could fall right into them. She'd consume him body and soul and he wouldn't even mind.

A stage manager appeared beside them. "Ready? You guys are on, in three, two . . ."

With his mind and heart full of Gina, Stone led her onto the dance floor.

That was an excellent Argentine tango last night," Donna said the next day during Stone's reaction interview.

Stone shifted in his seat. If any producer was going to pry into his innermost secrets, it was Donna. "We averaged seventy-seven percent, which feels pretty good."

Donna leaned forward, a gleam in her eye. "It was quite a sexy dance."

Stone's cheeks warmed, and he felt like an idiot. He wasn't even wearing makeup that could cover his blush, because it was a rehearsal day.

And what the hell was happening to his life that such a thought would even cross his mind?

"Um, yeah, that was kind of a strategic move. Gina's smart. She puts a lot of thought into our dances, and what stories we're telling, and what our wonderful, supportive viewers want."

Gina had drilled into him how appreciative they had to be toward their voters, instructing him to thank them at every opportunity. It reminded him a bit of being fed lines for *Living Wild,* but with less pressure, since he wasn't lying. He really did appreciate the votes.

Donna nodded. "Was it difficult to get into the role for your tango? We saw in the package how Gina encouraged you to feel more . . . comfortable."

This woman and these questions were going to be the death of him. "Well, we haven't known each other that long, and despite being on TV, I'm not a performer."

Donna jumped on that. "Does that mean you weren't acting when you and Gina were dancing last night?"

"I just mean I'm not used to this kind of stuff." Stone rubbed the back of his neck. "I want to be respectful, and I never want to make Gina feel uncomfortable. That's all."

"Let's talk about next week," Donna said, changing the subject. "The theme is Family History."

This theme was something he'd prepared for with his producers before leaving Alaska, so he knew what he could and couldn't say. He launched into the carefully crafted remarks. "My family means everything to me. Gina and I are focusing on the decision to start filming *Living Wild*. It was a big deal for us to open our lives in that way, and it brought us all closer together as a family."

He expected Donna to call him out for sounding like a robot, like Miguel did, but she kept going.

"You must miss them a lot."

Way to twist the knife, Donna. "I do." Didn't he? "Of course I miss them. I love my family, and I love Alaska."

"What's it like for you, living in LA for the time being?"

He blew out a breath and lifted his hands helplessly. "It's different? Obviously. It's weird being alone—you know, I'm used to having my family around, and being in nature. I get away to hike when I can."

"Do you think you'll ever live here?"

He started shaking his head before Donna had even finished the question. "Not a chance."

Stone left the interview with a bad taste in his mouth. If Donna was asking him such pointed questions, how much worse must it be for Gina?

When he entered the rehearsal room, Gina, Jordy, and Aaliyah were waiting for him.

"Hey, partner." Gina smiled at him from her seat on the edge of the stage. "How 'bout those scores last night?"

He gave her a high five. "And we weren't in the bottom three."

Keiko and Joel had been the first couple to be eliminated. The pretty young model had never gotten past her nerves, which tripped her up in her samba. According to Gina, Joel hadn't been on the show long enough to build up a fan following that would keep him there with low scores. It drove home how important fan engagement was. As Lauren had said on the plane, it wasn't just about the dancing.

"I have our next dance." Gina handed him a piece of cardstock before picking up the container of fruit salad beside her.

Stone flipped the card over and read it out loud. "The jive?"

"Have you heard of it?"

When he shook his head, she explained. "In ballroom, jive is considered a Latin dance. The type we'll be doing derives from swing dancing and the jitterbug, and a few other styles. It's lively, with lots of bouncing and bopping around. Very high-energy and upbeat." She did a few moves with her upper body to demonstrate.

Stone set the card on the stage and took a seat beside her. "Where did you learn all this? At school?"

She shook her head as she pulled the foil off a Greek yogurt cup. "I had to learn about it for the show. Unlike many of the other pros, I didn't start as a competitive ballroom dancer. Some of them—like Matteo, Danny, and Mila—were world champions."

"Impressive. When did you decide you wanted to be a dancer?"

She paused with the spoon in her mouth, pulling it out slowly as she thought.

Killing him. She was fucking killing him. In bike shorts and an oversized TEAM STONE COLD tank top, with a yogurt spoon, she was killing him.

"I don't remember," she finally answered.

"You don't? That seems like it would be a big decision."

She shook her head and set the yogurt aside, thank god. "No, I mean, I was so young, I can't remember that far back. I've always wanted to be a dancer. My whole life."

Her words rang with truth, and the determination in her gaze threatened to strike him down. Had he ever wanted anything that badly? Been that clear on something he desired?

Alaska. He wanted to return to the place of simpler rules, clean air, nature, and sky at every turn. His heart felt at home there. Even now, with Gina filling his senses, Alaska called to him.

When he poked at the feeling, though, it wasn't his family call-ing him back so much as the place and the way it made him feel, the peace and tranquility it evoked in him.

"Wait a second." He returned to something Gina had said, since he didn't like rummaging around in his own feelings. "If you didn't start with ballroom, what kind of dance did you start with?"

"Ballet, like a lot of other little girls." Gina leaned back on her hands. "My older sister had taken classes at our local Boys & Girls Club, and my mom was friends with the teacher. Soon, I was signed up for every kind of dance class the club offered—jazz, tap, and Latin—and I earned a spot in their kids' dance troupe, which allowed me to travel."

"How old were you?"

"When I joined that troupe? Probably eight. Eventually, we started looking for scholarships to other dance schools. I kept going with Latin and ballet, and picked up ballroom and hip-hop, too." She gestured at her curves. "I'm clearly not built to be a prima ballerina—not like Natasha—but I was good enough to audition and get into a public high school that specialized in the performing arts. That led to more opportunities, and I was part of another troupe and booking gigs by the time I was sixteen."

She opened her mouth to continue, then shut it. Her gaze dropped. Whatever she'd been about to say, it was big. He wanted to know.

"What is it?" he asked quietly.

"I'll tell you another time." She pulled up her knees and wrapped her arms around them. "Anyway, we're supposed to be talking about the most important time in *your* life."

He pulled a protein shake out of his gym bag. "As you know, I live in Alaska."

She chuckled. "I remember."

"My family didn't always live in that spot, though. We moved there around five years ago, after a fire destroyed . . . well, almost everything. Pop had a friend who hooked us up with *Living Wild*'s network, and they said they wanted to document our move and way of life."

"A fire?" Her eyebrows nearly leaped off her head. "Was it lightning?"

"Arson."

Crap. Stone faced the camera and made a slashing motion across his throat. "Sorry, you can't use that. There was a lawsuit and . . . you can't air that."

Jordy nodded. "That's fine. We'll cut it. Keep going."

Gina's eyes were bulging with curiosity, but she only said, "A fire?"

"Yeah."

Stone didn't like remembering it. That had been such a rough time. One of the neighbors had harbored a grudge toward Jimmy over a petty feud, and torched their home while they were away. They'd had a few things in lock boxes, and a small storage unit in town, and their vehicles. Nearly everything else was gone.

"After that, my father wanted to move somewhere even more remote than where we already were. It would be hard, he said, but if we all went together, we could do it."

More like if they all went together, they'd get the TV contract.

"How old were you when that happened?" All her attention was focused on him, and he didn't think it was just for the benefit of the cameras.

"Twenty-five." And living on his own, in Juneau. Working a good job for the city, putting his degree in engineering to use. But he didn't tell her about all that. He wasn't allowed. It didn't fit the survivalist image the Nielsons represented on *Living Wild.* The deal had been all Nielsons or no show, so he'd quit his job and moved with his family.

"That must have been a big change," Gina said softly, putting a hand on his shoulder and rubbing in soft circles.

"I had a girlfriend." Shit, he definitely hadn't meant to say that. Her hand paused. "Oh?"

No backing away from it now. Stone caught Jordy's eye and

shook his head. Jordy nodded. "Yeah. She didn't want to move with me. Wanted to leave Alaska completely, in fact. So, we broke up."

Stone hadn't planned on mentioning Anna, but talking to Gina was too easy. She listened, asked questions, and showed real concern for him. When was the last time he'd had a genuine one-on-one conversation? At home, there were always other people around, in addition to the cameras.

There was a camera here, too, but the difference was Gina. He already felt closer to her than he did to some of his siblings.

And that was something else to feel guilty about.

Gina was quiet for a moment, like she was digesting all he'd said. Then she got to her feet and held out a hand.

"That's her loss," she said. "Let's dance."

Fourteen

Gina packed a lot of jive content into their dance. Stone wasn't as comfortable with the movements, but he did his best, and she was glad to see he was in a much better mood during the filming of the third episode than he'd been in during the second.

Backstage in the Sparkle Parlor, everyone chatted about their stories that would be on display, reminiscing and showing off pictures on their phones.

Stone spent a lot of time talking to Twyla, who showed him a handful of inappropriate set photos from her personal collection. Dwayne—also an Elf Chronicles fan—joined them.

Gina stood to the side with Natasha. Despite living together, they barely saw each other once *The Dance Off*'s season began.

"¿Qué están haciendo?" Natasha asked, nodding her head at their partners.

"They're fans," Gina replied in English. Even though she sometimes spoke Spanish with her family, she wasn't as fluent as Natasha, and didn't always have the vocabulary for full conversations, especially when she was preoccupied. "She's showing them behind-the-scenes pictures."

"Ah." Tash gave Gina a hip bump. "How are things going with your hot Viking?"

Gina rolled her eyes. "I think the audience will like tonight's dance. It won't be his best, but it's fun."

"I didn't ask about the audience, G."

A stage manager hurried over to them. "Gina, Natasha, I need you two to grab your partners and stand over there with Reggie. I'm going to get Rose and Matteo."

They all assembled with Reggie Kong and waited patiently for the go-ahead.

Reggie turned to Gina. "Since you and Stone are dancing next after the commercial break, we're going to ask you a couple questions."

"We're just here for eye candy?" Matteo joked, his Italian accent and charm still thick after fifteen years in the States.

Reggie laughed, the blue streaks in her updo shining in the bright backstage lights. "Basically. Also, you and Rose are dancing right after them."

They got the cue from Juan Carlos, and Reggie turned to Gina with the mic.

"So, Gina, tell me about your dance tonight."

Gina launched into her speech with enthusiasm. "We're doing the jive, which is an exuberant dance, different from our tango last week. I want it to express Stone's spirit of exploration and love of nature, and show the audience the more fun side of Stone that I get to see every day in rehearsals."

"I love it," Reggie gushed. She took a step back and gestured at Gina's body. "Now tell me about this ensemble you're wearing. You look fantastic, of course, as you always do, but you also look like a wild woman who just stepped out of the forest."

"That's exactly it." Gina struck a pose in her sparkly leaf-and-vine covered bikini. Vines twined up and down her arms, even into her hair, and a green ruffled skirt covered her butt and hips. "I'm kind of like a sexy Mother Nature."

"Ha! And I bet *you're* happy with the way she looks, huh, Stone?" Reggie shoved the microphone in his face.

"Gina always looks beautiful," he mumbled, turning red.

"Right answer!" Reggie turned to the camera and read off the teleprompter. "You'll get to see them dance, along with our Super Bowl star and our former teen scientist, when we return."

Stone leaned down to whisper in Gina's ear. "Why do they always ask the most embarrassing questions?"

She huffed out a laugh as they followed the stage manager downstairs. "That's what they're paid to do."

The stage crew rushed to get their set ready. Fake trees lined the edges of the dance floor. Three other dancers—including Joel, who was now out of the competition—waited nearby, dressed in fitted overalls and white T-shirts, like Stone. They were going to play his brothers.

The commercial break ended. Since Stone had to move quickly to hit his mark, they waited on the stage while their package played on a giant screen overhead.

It started with Juan Carlos doing voiceover, and a recap of last week's dance. Then Stone's voice rang out across the ballroom.

The most significant period of my life was five years ago, when my family decided to move further into the Alaskan bush.

"Here, let's eye-gaze." Gina cupped his chin, enjoying the scratch of his beard against her palm as she directed his attention toward her. "Listening to that always makes me feel weird."

In the inky shadows of the stage, she met his gaze.

On the screen, they practiced the jive, with Gina correcting his footwork while Stone's voiceover continued.

It's weird being alone—you know, I'm used to having my family around.

We moved there around five years ago, after a fire destroyed . . . well, almost everything.

"Stone was always an active little boy," a woman's voice said.

"What the hell?" Stone jerked his head up and stared at the screen. "That's my mom. They didn't say they were getting my family to do interviews."

Gina tucked herself in against Stone's side, feeling the tension in his body. She rubbed his back in an effort to soothe him. "It's normal. They sometimes get family members to add commentary, and yours already has a camera crew around them."

His mother—PEPPER, the label on the bottom of the screen read—had soft blond hair that fell past her shoulders. Her big, blue eyes were just like Stone's. To her side sat a man with graying brown hair pulled back into a ponytail, and a full beard that was also going gray—Jimmy, Stone's dad. He spoke next.

"It was a hard decision to make, moving further into the bush. We'd talked about it for a long time, but after the fire, it seemed like the right thing to do. And of course, we did it as a family."

Stone appeared on the screen, talking to Gina in the rehearsal room. *I had a girlfriend.*

At her side, Stone's entire body clenched.

Gina grimaced. Shit. Shit, shit, shit. This was going to be so bad.

She didn't want to move. Wanted to leave Alaska, in fact. So, we broke up.

Gina would have bet anything this was Donna's doing.

"Stone," she whispered. "Stone, look at me."

He didn't. A second later, a woman with straight brown hair and a sweet face appeared on the screen. Stone jolted in surprise. Gina threw her arms around his waist, afraid he would bolt from the stage.

"Those fucking assholes." He breathed the words, and Gina knew before she looked what she would see at the bottom of the screen.

ANNA, it read. STONE'S EX-GIRLFRIEND.

"Stone loves Alaska," Anna said, her twangy voice ringing out across the room. "But I wanted to move to Seattle. It's a shame, but it just didn't work out. He's doing a great job on *The Dance Off,* though. I had no idea he could dance. He certainly never danced that way with *me.*"

The audience laughed. Stone turned to storm offstage.

"Where are you going?" Gina hissed at him, grabbing his arm and digging in her heels. "Stone, do not let them get to you!"

He stopped abruptly and she tumbled into his back, her arms wrapping around him both for balance and to keep him from leaving.

"But they have, Gina. And it's exactly what they meant to do when they dug up my past and pulled *her* out of it." He pointed at the screen. "All my staged interviews were about the fire and the move. Not about her. That wasn't supposed to be included. I even confirmed with Jordy that it wouldn't be."

One of the stage managers gestured at them frantically, and Gina's heart pounded in desperation. She had to get Stone to his mark. "What do you want me to say? They're assholes who screw with our emotions on purpose to create good TV. I'm sorry. I really am. You didn't deserve this. But please, *please,* don't leave. If you walk out now, we're done."

He leveled a steady stare on her. "And you want to win."

"I want to win with *you.*" She pleaded with her eyes, begging him to understand the difference. "Please, Stone."

For a second, she didn't know what he would do. But then he nodded, brushing past her to leap off the stage and join the other guys on his mark. Gina hurried backstage and let the wide-eyed stage manager hustle her to where she'd make her entrance from the trees. The audience quieted as the music began and the lights went up.

Showtime.

The performance started with Stone and the other three guys working together to snap a fake house into place in one corner of the floor while lively music played overhead. When they were done, they gave each other high fives, which was Gina's cue to prance out.

Hands on hips, she sashayed into the forest clearing meant to represent Nielson HQ. Stone's "brothers" melted away, and while he went through the motions, his movements weren't as sharp as they'd been during dress rehearsal. The vibe of the dance was supposed to be sassy Mother Nature meets adoring survivalist. Instead of a wide grin, his lips were set in a closed-mouth grimace, and when they got into hold, his timing was off.

"You've got this." Gina pulled him along, beaming a big smile for the audience. "You can do this."

He didn't reply. They broke hold, and he started off on the wrong foot. *The wrong fucking foot.* He'd never done that in rehearsal.

"You know the steps. Stop thinking so much." The dance brought them together, and once again, Gina fought to get them back on track.

"Smile!" She shouted at him as he swung her body between his legs and then up into the air. "Don't give up on us, Stone. Stay with me."

That seemed to snap him out of it, and he met her eyes. They completed the dance, more or less according to Gina's choreography, and finished in a dip with their faces close together.

The music ended. Stone shut his eyes and dropped his sweaty forehead to hers.

"I'm sorry."

She wanted to kiss him, to wipe away the anguish on his face and melt the tension from his muscles. But they were on live TV, with cameras pointed at them, millions of people watching at home, and hundreds more in the studio audience.

"Thank you," she said instead.

His brows creased. "For what? I screwed up."

"But you didn't quit."

"I wouldn't do that to you." He pulled her to her feet and they headed to Reggie, who waited by the judges' table. Gina kept her arm wrapped around Stone's waist. This next part wasn't going to be fun.

There were three regular judges on *The Dance Off.* The head judge was Chad Silver, a former Studio 54 dancer turned internationally recognized drag queen known for his unique fashion sense and exuberant choreography style. Then there was Mariah Valentino, a classically trained dancer and pop singer. She was gorgeous, golden, and tall, with long black hair and dark, seductive eyes. Gina often thought she wouldn't mind being Mariah when she grew up. Finally, there was Dimitri Kovalenko, an exacting choreographer known affectionately among the cast as "the cranky one."

All the judges wore grimaces of compassion. They'd seen the package, and knew what had gone wrong, but they still had to judge the dance as it had been performed.

Sure enough, the scores were brutal. Dimitri gave them a *fifty*, which brought their average score down to fifty-seven percent.

Stone was quiet through Reggie's post-dance interview questions, and Gina babbled about how they had done their best and hoped to try again next week. When the camera's recording light shut off, Gina's shoulders slumped. "Ugh, that sucked. What did I even say?"

Reggie patted her arm. "I'm rooting for you guys." And then she hurried off to have her makeup touched up.

Stone avoided the cameras for the rest of the night, and Gina didn't blame him. Finally, in the last five minutes of the show, the stage managers trotted all the couples out onto the stage for the elimination.

During dress rehearsal, Alan and Rhianne had been the ones sent home in the fake elimination. Usually, the couple whose names were called during rehearsal wasn't the couple going home that night. Thanks to last week's performance and scores, Gina had thought she and Stone would be safe tonight, but her confidence had taken a hit.

"Since we're running out of time," Juan Carlos said, "we'll cut right to the chase and reveal which of our remaining ten couples are in danger of elimination."

Everyone stood still while the cameras zoomed in on their faces. A few long, drawn-out seconds later, the lights fell, leaving the bottom three couples highlighted by red spotlights.

Including Gina and Stone.

Gina's stomach plummeted. Stone put an arm around her and crushed her to his side. She took a deep, shuddering breath and clung to him.

This couldn't be over. They had a shot at the trophy—she knew they did. Not only that, she was just getting to know Stone. They'd both shared things about themselves this week, and she wanted to continue growing their friendship. He was a great partner, a pleasure to dance with and teach now that he was taking it seriously, and he was certainly easy on the eyes. And she saw him changing from this experience, too. At the beginning, he never would have hugged her so freely, or joked with the hosts, or palled around with Twyla Rhodes. Being on the show was helping him open up and let down his guard. It would be a shame to cut off his progress now.

Gina glanced around, checking out the other red spotlights. Twyla and Roman were also in jeopardy, as were Farrah and Danny.

Crap. Farrah was young, but she was a fantastic dancer. There was no way she was going home yet. The bottom three weren't necessarily the lowest in terms of scores and votes. Sometimes, the producers put couples in the bottom to scare viewers into voting, or to zap them out of complacency.

Only one thing was for sure: one of the couples in the bottom three had the lowest combined votes and judges' scores, and was going home. It wouldn't be Farrah, which meant it was between Stone and Twyla.

Twyla, who had a fan following spanning three generations.

"I'm sorry," Stone whispered again.

"The couple leaving the competition tonight is . . ." Juan Carlos paused for dramatic effect. Gina held her breath, squeezing her eyes shut while the silence dragged on. Stone wrapped his arms around her and pulled her to his chest, his heart pounding against her ear.

"Stop."

It wasn't Juan Carlos who'd spoken. Everyone stared at Twyla, who stepped out of the spotlight with a noticeable limp.

Juan Carlos recovered quickly, as a good host should. "Is everything okay, Twyla?"

"No, everything is not okay." She stood with her head held high, leaning on Roman's arm for balance. "I screwed up my ankle in the dance tonight. I was going to try to suffer through it, but you know what? I'm too fucking old for this."

Everyone gasped and giggled, but Gina's heart swelled as she strained to hear Twyla's next words over the laughter.

"I'm going home."

Gina exhaled in a rush, sagging against Stone. He pressed his cheek to the top of her head and ran his hands up and down her arms.

"Does this mean we stay?" he asked.

"It does." She sent up another prayer that viewers would take pity and vote for them tonight.

He lowered his voice further. "What if it was supposed to be us?"

"We'll never know."

"We better kick ass next week."

She smiled and patted his back. "We will."

Backstage, they said goodbye to Twyla. The older actress kissed Stone full on the mouth, which made his whole face turn red but only slightly diminished the tension in his stance.

Jordy pulled Gina aside and handed her a piece of cardstock. "Your next dance. Figured you might want to start planning right away." He grimaced. "Sorry about the rehearsal package. You know that was all Donna's idea."

"I know."

Fucking Donna.

Gina glanced at the card and was hit with a burst of excitement. Oh, they were totally kicking ass next week. She grabbed Stone before he went off to change. "Jordy gave us our next dance style."

"Already?"

"Yeah, and it's a good one." She showed him the card. "We're doing the paso doble."

"What's that?"

Gina launched into her explanation with enthusiasm—she *loved* the paso doble. "It's a forceful Latin dance mimicking the drama of a bullfight. The leader—that'll be you—plays the role of the matador, and I'll play the cape or the bull."

Stone shrugged. "All right."

Frowning at his lackluster response, Gina tapped the card against her leg. "Next week is also Fairy Tale Night."

"Oh great, we have to tell a story again." Stone rolled his eyes, then sighed. "Sorry, I'm not mad at you. Tonight was just . . . a lot."

Her heart went out to him. She would have died if they'd gotten any of her ex-boyfriends for a surprise interview. Trying for a joke, she said, "Just wait until we have an argument. Even if it's two minutes out of the whole week, you can bet that's what'll be shown before we dance."

"Can't wait." Stone's eyes cut over to Jordy and the camera crew. Jordy shrugged, as if to say, *Hey, just doing my job.*

Okay, so maybe that hadn't been a good joke.

"Anyway," she went on, trying to lighten the mood, "I have a fun concept for this dance."

"Oh yeah?" Stone scrubbed a hand over his face, sounding not the least bit excited to hear her idea. "What's that?"

"We have Little Red Riding Hood as our fairy tale."

Stone held his index fingers up on the sides of his head like ears. "Am I the Big Bad Wolf?"

Even his attempt at humor sounded tired and quiet. Any other day, it would have held the sexy growl that drove her crazy. Gina forced a giggle, since he was making an effort. "No, I am."

"Explain."

"You'll be a combination of Red and the Woodcutter. I'm going to be the wolf."

He nodded, but his gaze was distracted. "Sounds good."

Jackson came over to say goodnight, and Gina chewed on her lower lip while the guys chatted. Stone's movements were slow and restrained, his head bowed. Shit. He was really bummed. Between their low jive score and the surprise interview with his ex, she couldn't really blame him. Still, their dance was going to be weak if he couldn't get his head back in the game. It was up to her to help him reignite his competitive spirit. The paso doble was the perfect dance for him, and she needed him in top form.

In a flash of insight, she came up with an idea to cheer him up. After Jackson walked away, she spoke in a low, rushed voice.

"We're going to break early tomorrow."

Stone raised his eyebrows. "Why? After tonight, I probably need *more* practice, not less."

"You've been working really hard. I want to do something nice for you."

The corner of his mouth quirked up. "Another salsa club?"

Her cheeks warmed at the memory. "Ha. No."

"What did you have in mind?"

"Since our last attempt to get you a home-cooked Puerto Rican meal was thwarted, you're coming over to my place for dinner." Her stomach flip-flopped at the thought of being completely alone with him, but she grinned. "I hope you like pork."

Fifteen

The door to Gina's apartment was ajar. Stone knocked anyway, even though she'd just buzzed him into the building a minute earlier.

"Come on in," she called from inside, so he pushed the door open and entered. He was greeted with the mouth-watering aroma of garlic, spices, and slow-roasting pork, and the even more appetizing image of Gina in a crop top and cutoff jean shorts chopping vegetables in the kitchen. Pop music played softly in the background.

The floor was covered in pale beige carpeting, so he removed his boots and placed them next to the neat row of women's shoes by the door.

"Good timing," Gina said as he shut the door behind him. "The meat will be ready soon."

"You did say it would take a few hours to cook."

"It does, if you do it right." She tossed cucumber slices into a large salad bowl. "Are those for me?"

He held up the plastic-and-paper-wrapped bundle of peach tulips in his hand. "Ah, yeah."

"They're so pretty. Thank you." She lifted her face so he could give her a peck on the cheek, and then nodded her head at the fridge. "Can you take down the vase from up there and put them in water?"

Once he was done with the flowers, Stone set them on the kitchen counter and looked around for something else to do. "How can I help?"

Gina jerked her chin toward the pile of dishes on the counter. "You can take those over to the coffee table. We have chairs at the kitchen bar, but Tash and I always eat in front of the TV. Bad habit, I know. If you're more comfortable at the counter, we can sit there instead."

"Coffee table is fine." He did as she asked, taking in the apartment. It was smaller than he'd expected, but cozy. The kitchen was separated from the living room by a bar, and the living room had tall windows that led onto a tiny patio and revealed a view of the building behind hers.

The furniture, like the carpet, was beige or white. Above the sofa was a large framed print of the New York City skyline at sunset. A low bookcase sported an array of framed photographs on top.

He set out the dishes on the coffee table and returned to the kitchen. "All right, give me something else to do."

She shot him a smirk over her shoulder. "Why, because you're used to me bossing you around?"

"I'm the guest. I should help out."

She handed him the salad bowl. "Stone, I'm the one who asked you over. Besides, I like cooking, and I haven't had pernil in forever."

"What was that word?" he asked, taking the salad to the coffee table.

"Pernil." She spelled it. "It's a traditional Puerto Rican dish—slow-roasted pork shoulder. Now go relax. It'll be ready soon."

He wandered over to the photos and picked them up one at a time while she bustled around the kitchen. There were photos of Gina and Natasha together at various ages, including one where they both showed off their braces in big grins. Of the rest, half showed Gina with her family. He recognized them from other pictures Gina had shown him. Her mother was beautiful, and Gina looked just like her. And there was her brother, her sister, her brother-in-law, and her nieces and nephew.

No father.

"Ready?" Gina walked over with glasses of water. "Oh, I'm sorry, I forgot to offer you a drink. Do you want wine? Beer?"

"I thought you don't drink during the show season."

"I don't, but Natasha does, and we keep stuff on hand for guests. I don't mind if you drink."

"Beer, then."

"I'll get it. Sit down, please." She gestured at the sofa and headed for the fridge.

Stone sat and glanced at the skyline on the wall. Another reminder of their differences, though lately, they seemed less extreme. Or at least, they didn't matter as much.

Gina came back and handed him a Mexican lager, then raised her glass of lemon water and clinked it against his bottle.

"Cheers," she said, meeting his eyes. "To winning."

"To winning." He took a sip, savoring the crisp taste of hops, and sat back while she filled two bowls with spinach salad.

"You have a lot of reminders of home," he said between bites.

She glanced up at the wall print. "We do. I miss New York, and my family, but having Natasha here makes it bearable."

"You've got a beautiful family."

"Thanks." She smiled into her food, her cheeks turning pink. "My brother's in the navy. And my sister works in product design for a cosmetics company. Plus my mom is an amazing singer, but . . . things happened. She never got to have the career she deserved."

The smile dropped from her face. Stone sensed there was a story there, and that it had to do with the missing father in her photos. Now that they were away from the cameras, the studio, and the other cast members, he wanted to know more about Gina, to understand her. He waited, not wanting to push.

"My dad was kind of a douchebag," she said with a sigh, setting her half-finished salad aside. "Old-school in his thinking. He wanted to settle down and start a family, so they did. Mom gave up her singing career just as it was about to take off. They had three kids—I'm the youngest—and then he split when I was little and started a new family in Orlando."

She recited the story like it was no big deal, but Stone's heart broke for her. Despite his own issues with his father, Stone couldn't imagine Jimmy ever jumping ship. "I'm sorry."

"Don't be." She gathered up the salad dishes. "It's his loss. We're an awesome family."

"Are you still in contact with him?"

She shrugged and carried the used plates to the kitchen. "Birthdays and holidays. He says he's proud of me, but . . ." She trailed off, filling new plates from a pot on the stove and a pan she pulled out of the oven. The delicious smells amplified.

"But what?"

She huffed. "He doesn't get to be proud of me, you know? He didn't do anything to contribute. He didn't scrimp and save whenever I needed new ballet shoes. He didn't volunteer to sew recital costumes so I could get mine for free. He didn't fill out applications for every kind of scholarship and grant that would help me get to where I am now. So, no, he doesn't get to be proud, because he wasn't there for any of it." She slammed the plates down on the coffee table and balled her hands into fists.

With a gentle tug, Stone pulled her onto the sofa with him. Hugging her had become as natural as breathing. Over the weeks, Gina hadn't just taught him to dance, she'd shown him the importance of human contact. A hug could convey encouragement, support, and empathy. He wanted to give her all those things now.

She gripped the back of his shirt. "I'm sorry. I don't talk about this a whole lot. It still makes me angry. Not for me, but for my mom. She loved him, gave up everything for him, and he left her."

"His loss." Stone smoothed his hand down her hair, twining his fingers in the cool strands. "For what it's worth, he should be proud of you, even if he doesn't deserve the credit."

She leaned back, laughing and dabbing at the corner of her eye. "For what? You're always grumbling about how you hate Hollywood. You don't value this stuff."

Stone shook his head. "That's not why." Releasing her, he gestured at the food before them. "When we met, I scared the shit out of you. But you've stuck by me through every step of this process, including that disastrous jive, and then cooked this meal to make me feel better. Gina, this is above and beyond your duty as my dance partner. I never would have expected something like this."

Her lips curved a little as she passed him a plate. "You didn't have to ask."

"Exactly. You did it all on your own, because you're a good, kind person. That's reason enough for any parent to take pride in their kid." He took a bite. Delicious salty goodness exploded over his tongue, and his eyes rolled back in his head. The pork was perfectly seasoned, perfectly cooked. "Oh god. This is fucking amazing."

"I know." She took a small bite. "I make it the same way my mom does, and my abuela."

Stone scooped up a forkful of rice. It was yellow, with tiny greenish beans and chopped green olives. It had a mild salty flavor, a perfect complement to the meat. "What kind of rice is this?"

"Arroz con gandules," she said. "A staple of the Puerto Rican diet."

Stone wolfed down the food on his plate, not surprised that Gina had served him three times the amount she'd given herself. Every few bites, he paused to tell her how delicious it was, both because it was true and because he liked the pleased little grin she gave in response. When he was done, he leaned back, rubbing a hand over his stomach.

"Gina, you are a goddess."

She bit her lip and tried to hide her smile.

"I mean it." Stone rested his hand at the base of her neck, kneading the muscles there. "This whole evening . . . it's exactly what I needed."

"I'm glad." When she leaned into his touch, he spread his fingers along her skin, seeking the curve of her neck and gently working out the tension. Her hair was a warm weight on the back of his hand. She let out a small sigh, her eyelids fluttering shut.

Stone made a decision and cleared his throat. "I have to tell you something."

"Hmm?" She opened her eyes. "What's that?"

"It's a confession. One I can't tell you on camera."

Her lips curved. "A secret?"

"Kind of." He stilled his mini massage, but kept his hand on her shoulder, rubbing small circles with his thumb. "There was no bear."

Her eyebrows shot up. "*What?*"

"No bear. It was all a set-up by my producers. I had to get you over to the woodpile, pretend to see a bear, and shoot a blank."

Stone's pulse pounded in his ears as he waited for her reply. Gina stared at him, mouth agape, blinking rapidly. Then she echoed his words, "There was *no bear*?" and burst into giggles.

Years of experience with his sisters had taught him that laughter wasn't necessarily a good thing. He had to tread with caution. "You're not mad?"

"Mad?" She laughed harder. "God, no. I'm relieved."

"You are?"

"Hell yeah. I can handle being set up by manipulative television producers. In fact, I should have known. But bears are a whole different ball game."

"I felt terrible for scaring you," he admitted.

She patted his knee, and said in a quiet tone, "I know you did. I don't blame you for it."

Since she wasn't mad, Stone resumed kneading the knots at the base of her neck. "You're tight," he said, changing the subject.

Her eyelids drifted shut. "Mm, that feels good."

The energy in the room changed. Stone had been aware of her all night—her outfit, which somehow managed to be cute and sexy at the same time, was hard to ignore—but now sizzling tension pressed in on him from all sides, and all he could focus on was the feel of Gina's skin under his hand. He shifted on the sofa, turning sideways so he could reach her with both hands. She tilted her head down to give him better access.

"More?" he asked, the word deep with desire.

"Yes." Her voice was high and breathy, but clear.

He pushed the dark heavy mass of her hair over her shoulder and devoted himself to the task of making her feel good.

The air thickened. His breathing became labored, catching with every soft sigh and moan she uttered. He was working his hands down her back, his fingers tangling in the fabric of her shirt, when she surprised him by—*holy shit, holy shit*—leaning forward and pulling her shirt over her head.

Stone froze. Gina's back was to him, now covered only by the thin blue band of her bra. He'd seen her back before, of course. The show's costumes didn't leave much to the imagination, and he'd had his hands all over her during practice. Still, there was a big difference between dancing with an entire camera crew and audience present, and being alone, on her sofa, when she'd just removed her shirt of her own volition.

She grabbed a hot pink throw pillow and held it to her chest, as if waiting for him to continue.

Stone stroked a finger down her spine, partly to touch her, partly to make sure this was real. "More?"

"Yes. And harder."

He pressed his palms to her back, noting how big and rough they looked next to the smooth expanse of golden skin. She wasn't complaining, though, so he continued kneading and pressing. When she sucked in a breath, he paused with his thumb on her lower back. "You okay?"

"Sorry. Old injury."

"Gotcha."

Noting the spot, he carefully worked the muscles around it, using gentler movements. Eventually, she let out a deep breath, and more tension eased from her body.

As he worked his thumbs along her spine, he skipped over the very center of her back, where the band of her bra impeded his movements.

"Stone."

"Yeah?"

"Take it off."

Again, he stilled. Had she really . . . ?

Yes, she had. So why was he questioning it? The woman had said to take it off.

Pulse pounding in his throat, he undid the clasp on her bra. But just to make sure he wasn't reading the situation wrong, he asked once again, "More?"

Her head jerked in a slight nod, and a second later he got his reply: "Yes."

Smoothing the straps over her shoulders, Stone shifted closer. As he ran his hands up and down her bare back, he curled around her and rested his cheek against her ear.

"Gina."

She shivered. "Yes?"

"More?"

"God, yes."

She turned, her lips seeking his. He claimed her mouth in a kiss even as she twisted in his arms, pink pillow and blue bra abandoned. Her tongue was warm, and she tasted like lemons. Her scent pervaded his senses, drugging him, as he lost himself in the movement of her tongue against his.

In a move made easy from weeks of dancing together, he scooped her up and settled her into his lap, then leaned over her, pressing her into the couch cushions. She tugged at his shirt, yanking it up.

"Take this off," she said, panting. "For the love of god, take this off."

He leaned back to pull off his T-shirt and in the process got his first glimpse of her naked breasts. Her nipples were pale brown and tight, and he groaned as he fell onto her, wrapping his lips around one pebbled peak.

She whimpered and clutched handfuls of his hair, left loose to dry after his post-rehearsal shower. Her sounds of pleasure urged him on. Stone cupped her breast with every ounce of gentleness he could summon. Maybe it would counteract the roughness of his hands.

But Gina didn't seem to mind. She wrapped her legs around his hips, bringing his aching cock right against the warmth between her legs.

He groaned, tonguing her other nipple as he dragged his hands up her rib cage, a move reminiscent of their tango. Her head thrashed against the arm of the sofa, and she arched against his mouth.

He had to be the luckiest fucking guy in the world right now.

When she grabbed his cheeks to pull his face to hers for a deep, searching kiss, his brain exploded. No more thoughts. Just feelings.

The heat of her skin—smooth and sleek, toned and taut—sliding against his. Her mouth—open to his tongue and so, so sweet. Her hands—exploring every inch of his exposed skin, digging into his muscles and skimming along his abs.

He was losing his mind.

"Touch me, Stone," she said, gasping. "Please."

He couldn't deny her. In the time they'd known each other, their dynamic had always been *she spoke, and he obeyed.* He ran his hand down her body, drawing it over her hip before pressing it between her legs. Her warmth emanated through the shorts, which were high enough that he could slip his fingers under the denim and her panties to touch her.

She was hot and wet, and as he plied her slick folds with the goal of bringing her to orgasm, all he could think of was sinking inside her. He touched her clit, circling it with his fingers.

"More?"

Gina flung her arm over her eyes. "Yes. Shut up and touch me."

Again, Stone obeyed. Before he knew it, she was clinging to his shoulders and crying out in his ear. His whole body clenched with need as her core contracted around his fingers. With his other hand, he lifted her head, claiming her mouth to devour her gasps and moans with a kiss.

The buzzing sound didn't register as anything he needed to pay attention to until she pulled her mouth from his.

"My phone. It's Natasha." She scrambled to snatch the device from the coffee table, and it was only then he realized the phone was also spitting out a jingle with Spanish lyrics.

"Hey, Tash." Gina held the phone to her ear and swiped her hair from her face. She was still open beneath him, still gripping his hips with her legs, still topless. "Um, watching TV."

Gina pressed a hand to her chest, perhaps to get her breathing under control, and finally made eye contact with him. Bringing a finger to her lips, she mouthed, *She can't know.*

Frowning, Stone nodded and kept quiet while Gina rattled off a grocery list. He eased away and reached for their shirts, since it was painfully obvious the moment was over. Bypassing the bra, Gina slipped on her top without removing the phone from her ear. Stone pulled on his T-shirt, and the second Gina ended the call, he stacked their dishes.

"Sorry about that." Gina ran a hand through her hair, smoothing it down. "She's on her way home from the supermarket."

"It's cool." He took the dishes into the kitchen and set them in the sink. He turned on the water but she came up behind him and turned it off.

"We have a dishwasher," she said. "I'll load it."

"Okay." Silence stretched between them. Inside, he was a riot of emotions, and he struggled to figure out what to say next. They'd been lost in their own little world one second, then abruptly cast back into the real world the next. He was still catching his bearings. Finally, he said, "I guess I should leave before Natasha gets here."

"Yeah." Gina leaned against the edge of the counter and reached for his hand. "Stone."

He drew her to him—slowly, so she had a chance to pull away if she wanted. She pressed her body to his and lifted her chin for his kiss. This one was slower, less desperate, but no less frightening in its intensity. If anything, this softer kiss tightened his body more than all the things they'd done on her sofa.

Gina broke the kiss first. With her eyes closed, she let out a little hum of pleasure and licked her lips. Then she sighed and took a step back, away from him.

"This is a bad idea, Stone."

He didn't say anything. It was, he knew it, but he was hard and aching, and having trouble remembering why he was supposed to be staying away from her.

"I don't . . . get involved . . . with dance partners. My career is too important to me."

Oh, right. That was why. He had to keep his hands off her, because at the end of all this, he was going back to Alaska, and she was staying in Los Angeles to climb the glittering ladder of fame.

It didn't stop him from wanting her, though.

"You understand, right?" She looked up at him with those big, dark eyes, worry tightening the corners and creasing her brow. "It just . . . it looks bad."

Ah. "Your reputation, you mean."

She nodded, and he brushed a lock of her hair behind one ear.

"The spotlight of fame is always harsher on women, isn't it?"

"Why, Stone, that was almost poetic."

"I have my moments."

She huffed and glanced back at the sofa, her expression turning wistful. "Don't I know it."

He headed for the door, because if he stayed, he might try to convince her—and himself—that it *was* a good idea. A great idea. The best idea, even.

It wasn't, though. He knew that. He should be glad she knew it, too, and that Natasha's call had interrupted them before things had gone further.

But he couldn't shake the feeling of her on his fingertips, and his body still cried out for her. He'd be dreaming of her tonight, that was for damn sure.

"We're okay, right?" Gina hugged herself with her arms while he put on his boots.

"Of course." He straightened and caught the sway of her body toward him before she held herself still again. "I'll see you tomorrow."

He wanted to thank her again—for her thoughtfulness, for the food, for finding him worthy enough to want to share her body with him—but if he did that, they'd start kissing again. Instead, he lifted a hand in a wave and left.

Sixteen

Had she really let him leave?

It was all Gina could think after Stone walked out of her apartment not five minutes after serving her up a bone-melting orgasm, and the thought continued to plague her as she entered the rehearsal room the next day.

It would suck if things were weird between them. They'd finally built up an easy intimacy, and their connection showed on the dance floor. Part of the reason why she'd held back—in addition to her personal rules—was because a fling had the potential to ruin their dancing. Right now, they had a shot at the trophy. A lightning-fast and supercharged orgasm on her sofa wasn't worth the risk.

Well, maybe it was. It had been a stellar climax.

Stone arrived while Gina was chatting with Aaliyah and getting her lav mic hooked up.

"Feeling better?" Gina asked him, then bit the inside of her cheek before she could say something else stupid. Undeniable evidence of his hard-on had been pressed against her less than twelve hours earlier. The man probably had blue balls all night, unless he'd taken matters into his own hands.

The thought of Stone jerking off in his hotel shower made her bite back a groan. She'd seen every inch of him naked, except for the few covered by his briefs during their weekly spray tanning sessions, and she was certain whatever he was hiding in those briefs was more than just a few inches. From what she'd been able to glean the night before, her mountain man was truly blessed in the penis department.

Stop thinking about his penis, Gina. Just stop it.

"Much better." He leaned in to give her a peck on the cheek, as he did every day, even though it wasn't natural for him. He did it because she did it.

His beard scraped her cheek lightly and she drank in the scent of pine that clung to him like a memory. It was their normal greeting. Maybe he wasn't as affected by their make-out session as she was.

But as he shifted back, their eyes met for a split second. The fiery heat in his gaze shot straight to her core, lighting a flame within her that spread through her body like wildfire. His eyes held barely banked desire and an intensity that thrilled and shocked her.

So, he'd been affected, too.

The fire was gone a second later, replaced by friendly interest. He allowed Aaliyah to mic him up while Gina was left fighting an aroused tremor.

Jordy consulted his laptop. "Before you start, we're going to record some general soundbites to introduce next week's dance."

While Jordy and Aaliyah set up, Gina stood next to Stone, every inch of her aware of him. She could feel the heat emanating from his big body, and it took all her concentration to remain still and keep her eyes on the camera. Would it be too obvious to ask Jordy to interview them separately? Then she wouldn't have to worry about the camera picking up the flush of arousal spreading over her skin.

And then Donna walked in. Just great.

"Good morning." Donna joined Jordy off-camera. "I'll take over from here."

Donna's presence had the effect of a bucket of ice water. A cold sweat broke out over Gina's body, and her muscles stiffened. Again, she wished she could complete the interview far away from Stone. Would he know that he needed to be more careful around Donna? She should have warned him. The woman could smell weakness, and she had a sixth sense for drama. If Donna sniffed out even an inkling of what had happened between them the night before, Gina was ruined.

Luckily, Donna kept most of the questions focused on their upcoming paso doble, which was easy to talk about. The paso was one of Gina's favorite dances to choreograph for *The Dance Off*, and Stone had the potential to deliver a killer performance.

So long as he stopped looking at her the way he had when he entered the room. If he kept that up, she was going to burst into flames before they even filmed episode four. And that would be really hard to hide from Donna.

"Where did you get the idea for your dance?" Donna asked.

"Honestly?" Gina grinned at Stone, recalling his confession about the bear. "The idea came to me after meeting Stone in Alaska."

"Stone, what do you think about the choreography and the concept?"

He shrugged. "I trust Gina's vision. She's the expert. I'll be the first to admit I'm not a dancer, but we've been here . . ." He cocked his head and met Gina's eyes as he counted on his fingers. "Five weeks now? And with every dance, she manages to not only teach it to me, but to get me to show emotion. Gina deserves all the credit, and the screw-up last week was totally my fault."

Donna jumped on that. "Sounds like you have something to prove next week."

Stone nodded. "Absolutely. I messed up. I have to show what I can do, show the fans we're living up to their expectations, and I have to do right by Gina."

Gina's cheeks heated at his praise. She couldn't even look at him for fear of a full-out blush. He'd been so dismissive of her work when they started. Now, it seemed like he understood and appreciated what she did.

Donna rounded on Gina. "It sounds like it's going to be a sexy dance."

Always pushing the showmance. For this dance, though, Gina could throw Donna a bone.

"It will be," she said. "A bullfight is about dominance, power, and control. In ballroom dance, if it's between a man and a woman, the male partner usually leads, but in the paso doble, the female dancer gets to have her say. It becomes a sexual dance, the back and forth between invitation and attack as both vie for control. I love this dance—the passion, the power, and the raw sexual dynamics at play. I think the viewers will be very happy with what we bring to the dance floor."

Donna seemed satisfied by their answers. She consulted with Jordy for a minute, then headed for the door. "Keep up the good work."

Once she was gone, Stone held out a hand to Gina.

"Ready to dance?" His mild smile was at odds with the fire in his gaze.

Those damn butterflies woke up and did the jitterbug in her belly.

"Sure." Her answer came out breathy, and she prayed the mic didn't catch the nuance. She took Stone's hand and let him lead her to the center of the floor.

How she'd found the strength to let this man leave her apartment last night, she'd never know. Next time, she wouldn't be so strong.

Which meant there could never be a next time.

G ina clutched Stone's hand all through the commercial break. They were still breathing hard from delivering a paso doble that felt like fire and sex. Stone had never been more forceful and aggressive in his dancing. He'd mastered the choreography—

embodying the role of the "Red-Hooded Woodsman," as Gina had named him—and conquered Gina's wolf with every ounce of passion and dominance the paso required.

In addition to the red hood, Stone wore black "leather" pants that made his ass look fantastic, and a red and white lace-up vest that left his muscular arms bare. It was her favorite of all the costumes he'd worn. He looked like an epic fantasy hero brought to life.

Gina was dressed as a sexy wolf, with feral makeup, fake fangs, claws that made it difficult to use her phone, and a furry hood with wolf ears. The rest of her costume consisted of a sparkly gray bra, and *The Dance Off*'s typical paso doble bottoms—hot pants with a long, flared skirt attached, to mimic the matador's cape. Gina had asked the wardrobe department to line her skirt with red, to represent Red Riding Hood's cloak.

Stone gave her fingers a squeeze, and sent her the same friendly smile and heated gaze he'd been giving her all week. It didn't make her uncomfortable. She liked knowing he was still interested. But he was too tempting. All their mixed-up emotions and uncon- summated attraction had been channeled into the dance. Now that it was over, she was exhausted, and unbelievably turned on.

In her free hand, she held a prop axe. It was reminiscent of their first meeting, so she'd included it in the dance at the beginning and the end. Now, she tapped it against her thigh as they waited.

Lori came over to hug her. On her other side, Jackson gave Stone an encouraging pat on the back.

"Gina. Girl. That choreography?" Lori gave a slow clap. "Brava."

Natasha appeared behind them and echoed Lori's sentiments, followed by Alan, Farrah, and Kevin.

A stage manager rushed over to shoo them all away, and Reggie appeared to speak into the camera.

"Before the break, Stone and Gina delivered a scorching hot Red Riding Hood–themed paso doble for Fairy Tale Night. The judges praised their energy and content, but said Stone needs to work on his knees. Let's see how the comments translate into scores."

Gina gripped Stone's fingers tighter under the onslaught of

nerves. It was a good dance. The judges had to see how much he'd improved. Stone slipped his hand out of hers and hugged her against him instead. After a beat, their score flashed on the screen.

"Ninety-four percent." Reggie put the mic in front of Gina. "After last week, that has to feel amazing. How proud are you of Stone right now?"

"I'm *so* proud of him," Gina said into the mic. "We've worked so hard, week after week, to turn out performances we think our fans will enjoy. Stone is doing a fantastic job, especially when you consider he's not a dancer. I couldn't be prouder."

"And how about you, Stone?" Reggie raised the mic so Stone wouldn't have to lean down. "What was it like practicing after last week's stumble and then receiving this score?"

With Gina's coaching, Stone's answers to Reggie's backstage questions had gotten smoother. "When we started, I didn't think I'd ever score that high, so it feels pretty great. And we're grateful to all our fans who keep voting for Team Stone Cold to stay on the show. We'll do our best to keep delivering great dances."

Reggie turned to the camera to recite all the voting info. Stone and Gina stepped to the side, awaiting their turn in the makeup chair.

"You were right," he said. "I apologize for doubting your storytelling concepts. What's our theme for next week?"

Gina blinked. "Oh, you don't know?"

"Know what?"

She sucked in a breath as a hollow chasm opened in her chest, leaving her feeling empty at the thought of the week to come. "It's Shake It Up Week."

His brow creased. "Is that a dance style?"

She swallowed hard and shook her head. "It means we switch partners. The audience votes to decide the new pairings. We'll find out tomorrow morning when we show up for rehearsal."

He went still, his eyes like cold shards of ice, his voice a low rumble. "What are you saying?"

"Stone, we're not dancing together next week."

Seventeen

The next morning, Stone's driver took him to a different rehearsal space. He was hooked up with a lav mic before he even went into the room, and a field producer with a camera followed him in.

Inside, he found Natasha waiting for him.

"Hey, guapo." Her eyes lit up when she saw him, and she went over to give him a hug. "This is going to be fun."

"The way you said that makes me nervous."

She laughed like a cartoon villain. "You should be. I won't go easy on you."

"What's our dance?"

"We're doing the salsa. Lucky for you, you have some experience with that one." She winked.

"Yeah, a little." Memories of dancing in the salsa club with Gina flashed through his mind. He'd almost kissed her that night. How different would things be now if he had?

It didn't matter. He'd still be here with Natasha for Shake It Up Week.

"We're going to do a very traditional, very sexy ballroom salsa," Natasha said. "And no shirt for you. I don't know why Gina's been waiting to give the viewers what they want." She snapped her fingers and pointed to the center of the room. "We're going to do a lot of lifts, too, and those require a ton of practice to make them look smooth. Let's get to work."

For the rest of the day, Natasha ran him ragged, ordering him to go over every move repeatedly until he had it right. She was a strict teacher, but he was surprised by how much fun they had together. Natasha joked and teased, keeping his spirits up even as she wore his body down.

By the end of the day, Stone was exhausted, and he missed Gina with a keenness that scared him. Not only that, he liked dancing with Gina, and had thought she was the root of his enjoyment. Natasha had showed him that dance could be fun even without Gina, which was a strange realization.

Of course, he missed Gina for reasons that had nothing to do with dancing, but it wasn't wise to think about those with her roommate present.

Donna showed up right at the end of their rehearsal, after they'd removed their mics. She dismissed the field producer and story assistant, then took a seat on a folding chair while Stone wiped his face with a towel. Donna's expression was far too calm. He didn't trust it.

Natasha gulped down a bottle of electrolyte water. "What's up, Donna?"

"How was rehearsal?" Donna directed the question at Stone.

He focused on rearranging the contents of his gym bag. "It was fine. I'm learning the steps."

Natasha laughed. "He doesn't want to say I'm a tyrant, but it's okay. I know I am."

Donna's gaze went sharp. "Any chance I can convince the two of you to act like there's something going on here for the rest of the week?"

Natasha blinked, then cast a look at Stone from the corner of her eye. She shrugged.

Stone frowned, pretending not to understand. "I don't know what you mean."

"Yes, you do." Donna gave him a patronizing pat on the arm. "It's called a showmance. You two got along great today. Just play it up a bit more, act like there's some attraction here. The viewers like sexual chemistry—they speculate all over social media—and it gives the gossip sites something to report, all of which equals an increase in ratings. This episode marks the halfway point of the season, and we could use a bump."

Stone shot a glance at Natasha, who waited with her hand on her hip. Her eyes were wide and intense, like she was trying to tell him something, but he didn't know what.

"Uh, I'd rather not," he said, trying not to look at either woman as his face heated.

Donna sighed. "I thought you'd say that. What if I offered you a bonus? You said you're here to help pay for your mom's hospital bills, right? This could get you there faster."

The outright manipulation chilled him to the bone. It was exactly the kind of shit he hated. Before he could think of a reply, Donna kept going.

"You get more money for every episode you're on, and a big bonus if you win, but let's face it." Donna tilted her head and her tone turned nasty. "You're up against an Olympic figure skater who's already gotten a perfect score. You're not going to win."

Rage burned in his gut, but Stone clenched his jaw against it. Thanks to his dad, he had lots of practice holding back his anger.

"I'll take my chances," Stone said, grinding out each word between gritted teeth. Then he grabbed his bag and got to his feet. "Gotta go. My car's waiting. See you tomorrow, Tash."

He left the room, cursing *The Dance Off,* Hollywood, and the entire entertainment industry.

Even though there was no elimination during Shake It Up Week, the showrunners made all the dancers stand in their mixed-up pairs at the end of the broadcast. Gina stood with Jackson, who kept an arm around her shoulders in a friendly gesture. She smiled for the camera while tapping her foot impatiently.

"Anxious?" he asked.

She shook her head. "Excited."

"Can't wait to get back to Stone?"

She suppressed a smile. She'd managed all of two seconds alone with Stone backstage, but during that time, he'd leaned in and whispered, "I miss you," in her ear.

Simple words, but from him, they were everything.

Jackson laughed. "Girl, I mind my own business. Besides, you got me a ninety for that salsa, and I don't think Lori could have done it. You're my favorite person right now."

A trickle of guilt diminished her mood. She and Jackson had gotten along swimmingly, and they'd received a higher score than Stone and Natasha's eighty-four.

Nothing about it had been the same, though. The easy camaraderie and good humor, Jackson's willingness to learn and grow—and drive to *win*—were all traits Gina had hoped for in a partner at the beginning of the season. She should have been happy to work with Jackson.

Instead, all she wanted was to get back to Stone. When she danced with him, she felt more alive. She had to work harder, sure, since Stone didn't have any dance training. And to say the man didn't emote naturally was an understatement.

Except the challenge made every smile she pulled from him feel like a reward in and of itself. His quiet delight when he nailed a move warmed her jaded heart.

Jackson was polished and professional. When he looked at her, it was with attentiveness, the way an eager student turns to a teacher as if to ask, "What's next?"

When Stone looked at her, it was with fire in his eyes, and barely leashed control of the conflagration. If she got too close, she'd be burned up and consumed.

After a week away from him, she was ready to be consumed. So fucking ready.

Once the cameras had clicked off and everyone filed backstage to change out of their costumes, Gina searched for Stone.

Before she could find him, Natasha caught her arm. "I'm going out with Kevin and Lori and some of the others. You want to come?"

Gina shook her head. "I'm tired. You go."

Natasha gave a nod. "Later, nena."

Stone was head and shoulders taller than most of the cast, and easily spotted. Gina's heart gave a little leap when she saw him. It was ridiculous, really. She'd known him for a couple of months, and they'd only been apart a few days. Yes, pros became attached to their partners quickly, and vice versa, but she'd never experienced this pull toward one of her partners, as if an invisible string connected them.

She let herself be drawn toward him, picking up speed until she was almost running. Around them, other couples were reuniting, and no one paid them much mind as she threw her arms around his neck.

He scooped her up, enveloping her in the scent of clean Alaskan air as he held her to his bare chest. He was sweaty, but so was she. His hair was loose, and she pressed her face into the warm mass. Inside, her heart settled, but the butterflies in her belly danced a fast cha-cha-chá.

"I missed you, too," she whispered in his ear.

When she pulled back, their cheeks slid against each other and the corners of their mouths touched. She almost turned her head to kiss him before she caught herself.

Not here. They were surrounded by cast and crew. She had to act casual.

"That was a great salsa," she said brightly.

"Natasha's a great teacher." He lowered his voice. "But she's not you."

Well, damn. The man sure knew how to get her pulse thumping.

"Come over tonight." Her words were barely a whisper.

He nodded, his lips parting to mouth, "One hour."

"Great," she said, louder. "See you tomorrow, bright and early. Next week's theme is Broadway."

They parted ways to continue saying goodbye to the rest of the cast.

Meanwhile, Gina was ready to burst with excitement. And longing.

Tonight, she would throw caution to the wind.

Eighteen

The elevator down the hall dinged. Gina sucked in a deep breath and let it out in a rush when Stone turned the corner, sexy as hell in dark jeans and a red plaid shirt with the sleeves rolled up. His hair was damp from his shower, hanging loose over his shoulders.

Shyness and nerves set in. Silly, since he'd already touched just about every inch of her there was to touch.

"Hi," she said softly.

The banked fire in his eyes flared, and he rushed to her, scooping her up in his arms and charging into the apartment. The door banged shut behind them but his mouth was already on hers and Gina didn't give a damn what her neighbors thought.

His lips were warm, his beard scratchy yet softer than it looked. He devoured her, eating at her mouth with his lips and tongue like he couldn't get enough. Gina grabbed a handful of his hair with one hand, the other petting the side of his cheek, marveling at the contrasting textures, all while she let him take the lead with the kiss.

She'd spent weeks teaching him to dance. She was tired of leading, and more than ready to relinquish control.

Or maybe not, if it meant taking things slow.

"I want you," she said against his lips, squirming in his arms. "Get naked."

They both knew why he was here. No point in playing coy.

"Hell yes." He glanced at the sofa, where they'd last gotten hot and heavy. "Bedroom?"

"Through there." She pointed, and he carried her.

It wasn't strange, being carried by him. He'd picked her up on the day they'd met, had lifted her countless times during rehearsals. In his arms, she felt safe, protected, cared for. He wouldn't drop her.

Cuidado.

Safe as she felt in his arms, there was still a thread of danger. Not for her body, but for all the reasons she hadn't taken this step with him already.

She pushed those concerns aside. She'd had enough of fighting her desire for him.

They entered her bedroom, and Stone once again kicked the door shut behind them. Laying her down on the bed, he climbed next to her and pulled her close. Her queen mattress had never felt so small.

The bedroom was lit by a lamp on the side table, casting the space in a soft yellow glow. It invited them to go slowly, to take their time.

Fuck. That.

Gina sat up. Without a word, Stone skimmed her tank top up her ribs and over her head, muttering a reverent curse when he saw the lacy black bra she wore. She smiled, then gasped when he pressed his mouth to her breast through the lace.

She grabbed the back of his shirt. "I said, get naked."

"Yes, ma'am."

Gina joined him in undoing the buttons on his shirt. "Why on earth would you wear something so difficult to take off?"

He chuckled. "I was thinking more about getting *you* undressed." With a growl, he tugged on the waistband of her yoga pants. She lifted her hips to help ease the way.

He groaned when he saw her matching lace panties. "Damn, Gina."

"I put them on just for you."

He laid a kiss on her hip. "I'm glad to hear you weren't wearing these for your dance with Jackson."

"Jealous?"

"Damn right." He moved up to kiss her lips. "All I could think of this week was our salsa, all the way back in the beginning. It drove me crazy to think of you dancing like that with Jackson."

"How do you think I felt knowing you were dancing with my best friend?"

Caging her with his arms, he gazed into her eyes. "She's not you."

Warmth spread through Gina's chest, then lower when his hand slid down to her hip.

"I missed you."

Her heart fluttered. "You already told me that."

"It's worth repeating." His fingers plucked at the elastic of her panties. "You make things . . . easier."

She frowned. "What do you mean?"

"It's easier to talk to you. Easier to think. Easier to . . . feel."

His eyes were bottomless ice blue pools, threatening to suck her in. It was more than she could take. Her own emotions were too close to the surface, and it was *not* easier for her to feel them.

Time to shift gears. "You're still dressed."

He yanked open his shirt, sending the last button flying.

"I'll find that later." Gina knelt on the bed to help him push the fabric over his shoulders. Dragging her hands down the mouthwatering expanse of his muscled torso, she grabbed his belt and undid the buckle. "No interruptions this time."

"Thank god." He groaned as she unzipped his jeans.

She reached inside his boxers and took hold of the hard, hot length of him. This was it. The moment of no return. Taking care not to hurt him, she pulled his dick out and stared.

She'd known he was packing. It was impossible to miss it in rehearsal. She'd even touched it a few times by accident during their tango practice—and not always in a good way. Seeing it up close was a whole different story. He was long and thick, hard as . . . no, she would *not* make that analogy. He was hard as *rock*, and his pubic hair had been trimmed.

She must have taken too long because he let out a groan and sank his fingers into her hair. "Babe, you're going to give me a complex."

"Sorry, I'm just . . . impressed."

He laughed, then threw his head back when she squeezed the base of his cock. "Gina. Don't tease me. Please."

"I won't." She leaned down and closed her mouth around his girth. He let out a strangled sound, his fingers flexing in her hair.

"You're . . ." He cut off and exhaled harshly when she thrust her tongue against him.

She lifted her head and grinned sweetly. "I'm what?"

Grabbing her shoulders, he hauled her up and pressed a hard, desperate kiss to her mouth. "You're amazing," he whispered. "Absolutely fucking amazing."

Her cheeks warmed at his praise, and she took one scary step forward to see how he responded. "I like you, too, Stone."

His eyes searched hers for a moment, and then he kissed her again, tangling his tongue with hers. It was her turn to groan as he dragged her against him. She pushed at his jeans, and somehow he divested himself of them without breaking their kiss. When he was naked, she pulled back to take in the full view.

"Hot damn." Her breath exploded out of her as she gazed upon his body in all its glory. "Dude, do you even lift?"

His abs—lord, was that a ten-pack?—trembled as he chuckled. "Your turn."

He unhooked her bra with one hand while the other tugged her panties down her legs. Finally, they were both naked, with nothing between them. The appreciation in his gaze set her aflame. Gina pressed the full length of her body to his and kissed him, loving the feel of his cock, hot and insistent, against her belly. Why had she fought this for so long?

His mouth left hers to rain kisses and light nibbles down her neck. She leaned into the pillows and closed her eyes, smiling.

His body stilled, and she opened her eyes. He'd paused with his face in her neck.

"What do you smell like?" he asked.

"*Smell* like?"

"I've been trying to figure it out since we met." He picked up a lock of her hair and gave it a sniff. "Like flowers, or . . ."

"Hibiscus. My shampoo is hibiscus."

"Mm." He closed his eyes and held a handful of her hair to his nose. "I like it."

She sucked in a breath when he plumped her breasts together and pressed his face into her cleavage, inhaling deeply. "That's not it, though."

"Coconut oil." She barely managed to get the words out as the rough pads of his thumbs scraped over her sensitive nipples. "Head to toe."

His lips closed around one of her nipples, and his fingers tugged at the other one. "Is that why you're so soft?"

The warm suction of his mouth, contrasted against the light scrape of his beard and the teasing tickle of his hair, made her moan and writhe on top of the blankets. "*Yes.*"

When she was arching into his mouth, he shifted to whisper in her ear. "I'm going to taste you now, Gina."

His words, and the deep, growly way he said them, gave her a shiver. She parted her thighs to make room for him to settle between them. His eyes, so blue in the warm lighting, lifted to meet hers as he lowered his head. The rest of his body, tanned and toned, stretched out to the edge of the bed.

If she weren't paranoid about having such things on her phone, she'd take a picture of him right now. As it was, she didn't think she'd ever forget the way he was looking at her. Like their roles had switched and *he* was the Big Bad Wolf.

And she was good enough to eat.

He dipped his head between her legs and gave her a light lick.

Gina dropped back onto the pillows and surrendered herself to the sensation.

As he got down to business, he pushed her legs further apart to make room for his massive shoulders.

"Damn, you're flexible," he muttered against her pussy.

She lifted the arm she'd thrown over her eyes and gazed down at him dazedly. "You already knew that."

"Just commenting." He spread her with his thumbs and returned to his task.

With every pull of his lips on her clit, waves of pleasure scattered her thoughts. Every swipe of his tongue on her entrance reformed them to a single point of focus: this man, his mouth, her pussy. From her lips fell a single word, repeated over and over like a chant: *yes, yes, yes.*

The orgasm shimmered at the edge of her consciousness. Toes curling against his sides, she bowed her body up and gripped handfuls of his hair, crying out his name. "Stone!"

His gaze flicked up to hers, wicked humor in the blue depths. He made a sound of assent in the back of his throat, his tongue busy swirling her clit, as if he knew she was close.

"Stone, I'm . . ."

"Uh-huh?"

Squeezing her eyes shut, her muscles tensed and her hands tightened on his hair. His tongue stoked her higher and higher, and finally, oh god, *finally,* she came, letting out a keening moan. Sensation poured through her body, making her tremble and shake, wringing her out and leaving nothing but tingling aftershocks that throbbed through her from end to end.

Sated and spent, she collapsed onto the pillows and fought to catch her breath.

Damn. The man had a mouth on him. But now they were 2 and 0 in the orgasm department.

Stone crawled up her body to whisper in her ear. "Condoms, Gina."

"Bedside." She flung a hand in the direction of the drawer,

which held the condoms she'd snagged from Natasha's stash. Her eyelids fluttered as Stone rummaged around. A rip of foil, and she opened her eyes in time to see him rolling the latex down his thick length.

It was a good thing he'd prepared her so thoroughly.

She flopped like a rag doll as he knelt between her legs. He took himself in hand and notched the head of his cock in her folds.

His blue gaze captured hers. "Ready, Gina?"

"I've been ready for two months. Do it."

He flashed her a grin, and in one smooth move, slid inside her.

She sucked in a breath as he filled her. Oh *god*.

He didn't give her time to adjust. Gathering her in his arms, he lifted her into an upright position.

"What are you—?"

He knelt on the bed and pressed one hand to the wall for support. His other arm held her to him, pinned on his cock.

"Ready?" he asked again.

She couldn't form words this time, and only nodded. His body tightened, the light from her bedside lamp gilding all those delicious muscles.

And then he thrust.

Tremors of glorious sensation spiraled through her body. She clung to his sweat-slickened shoulders, her legs locked around his hips. A shiver went through him.

"Damn, Gina," he ground out, thrusting again. "You're so fucking tight."

No words to be had. She moaned in reply.

"So fucking amazing." He uttered the words with reverence, his cock pumping inside her with each word, as if to punctuate.

"Faster," she whispered.

His gaze—glued to where they joined—shot up to hers. "You're sure?"

She bit her lip and nodded.

"You gotta let me know if I'm hurting you," he said, a note of warning in his voice.

"You won't. Fuck me, Stone."

Her words unleashed something in him. Curling his body around hers, his powerful hips worked like a piston, back and forth, driving his strong cock deeper with every thrust.

All she could do was hold on for the ride. In this, she let him take the lead, gave him complete control. She was coming apart at the seams and loving every minute of it.

He shifted her—still with the one arm around her waist—and held her closer. The angle rubbed his cock against her clit with each thrust. Her spine bowed. She cried out. Cried out again. And again. Her body shimmered on the edge of ultimate pleasure, the boundary between her skin and his blurring. She was boneless, weightless, utterly supported by his strength and his desire.

She surrendered completely.

The orgasm took her by surprise. Pleasure so intense could surely not be topped. And yet . . .

He slammed into her hard, locking his pelvis to hers. And in the process, she unlocked and went flying over the edge into an abyss of pure, perfect sensation, one she never wanted to leave.

He shuddered over her, holding both of them up as he let out a deep groan. His cock jerked inside her and she gasped.

It had been a given that sex with Stone would be amazing. She hadn't expected it to be a religious experience.

Breathing hard, he lowered her to the bed—still gentle, still controlled. He didn't drop her, even though his body began to tremble. When she was settled, he crashed onto the mattress beside her and buried his face in her hair. One arm snaked around her waist and pulled her to his side.

Aww. The mountain man liked to cuddle. Pleased, she scooted closer.

His lips touched her shoulder in a light kiss. Her heart melted a little.

Don't do that, she wanted to say, but it seemed ridiculous to be scared of a simple kiss after what they'd just done.

After a few minutes, Stone propped himself up on one elbow.

His hair was a mess, so she smoothed it away from his face. With a small smile, he leaned down to kiss her mouth.

The look in his eyes was so sweet, so tender, she wanted to look away. Except she couldn't. He drew her in with his patient awareness, as if he knew she needed a few minutes to collect herself and figure out a way to make things easy and light between them again.

They still had to work together. Still had to partner together until . . . however long he remained on the show. Hopefully until the finals.

And then what? He'd head back to Alaska. Gone, as if he'd never been here. And she would . . . well, it all depended on whether she still had a job at the end of this or not.

And she'd just slept with her partner.

Again.

"Stop thinking," he said in a light voice, trailing a hand down her ribs.

"Can't help it."

"Why?" He waggled his eyebrows at her. "You're going to make me think I didn't do a good enough job distracting you."

She laughed and placed a hand on his chest, tracing the defined contours of his muscles. "You're very distracting and you did a *very* good job."

"So why are you frowning?"

"Am I?" Now she was. "Huh."

"You can tell me, Gina. Whatever's on your mind. I'm a good listener."

She played with the ends of his hair. It was so pretty. Maybe he'd let her brush it.

He was waiting for a reply. She exhaled slowly. "This isn't really a great after-sex topic."

He shifted them so they lay on their backs, staring up at the ceiling. His bicep acted as her pillow. It was like they'd finally finished what they'd started in Central Park, in the sleepy meadow. He was warm, and he smelled strong and comforting.

It was false comfort, though. There was no point in getting attached to someone who was leaving.

She might as well tell him. Nothing like talking about an ex to send a guy running for the hills.

Nineteen

There's a reason why I don't date people in the industry," Gina said. "I did it once, and it went . . . badly."

Stone tensed. Maybe this wasn't a great topic to bring up. But he wanted Gina to feel like she could talk to him. She held a lot inside, masking her anxieties and hurts under a sunny exterior. He wanted to be someone she could reveal her thoughts and feelings to.

Someday, he hoped he'd be able to do the same with her.

"Once upon a time I dated a former dance partner."

His jaw clenched audibly. "Mm-hmm."

Straddling his thighs, she ran her hands up his chest and gave him a sleepy smile. "Don't worry. You are, by far, the hottest man I have ever danced with."

"Danced with or—" He waggled his eyebrows to make her laugh. "*Danced* with?"

She giggled and settled her head on his chest. "Both."

He wrapped his arms around her. They were so used to touching each other, there was none of the usual awkwardness after a first fuck. All the dancing had led them to this point. "Keep talking."

"Ruben was in the dance troupe I joined when I was a teenager. I hadn't made much of a name for myself yet when we started dating. Ruben was more well-known—or at least, that was how it seemed to me—and he talked a lot about how we were going to take the dance world by storm together. I thought he meant it."

"I sense a rude awakening coming up."

"You guessed it. We entered a competition, and I choreographed the dance for the final showcase. Ruben took full credit for it. When I pointed out to him that it was my dance, he told me, 'Jealousy isn't a good look, Gina.' Then he told everyone else in the troupe we were sleeping together, which got me pulled from the competition because they thought it would get in the way of my ability to dance, either with him or with others, and that it might be hard for me to see him dance with other women."

Stone exhaled, more of a growl than a sigh. Gina patted his shoulder.

"I learned my lesson—don't get involved with people I'm working with."

Ah. That certainly explained some things. It didn't seem kind to point out the obvious, but he did it anyway. "You broke that rule for me."

She looked away. "So I did."

He cupped her cheek and gently turned her to face him. "Why, Gina?" He needed to know.

Her eyes were dark, as if the lamplight couldn't penetrate their depths. "I wanted you too much." She swallowed. "And I don't think you'll betray me. Besides, you're, like, industry adjacent."

He raised his eyebrows. "We're dance partners."

"I know, but . . ." She gave his shoulder a flick. "Yes, I broke my rule for you, and I don't regret it. Happy? But I don't want anyone to know about us."

On some level, it made sense that Gina would want to keep this secret. On another, Stone was so over the moon, he wanted everyone to know. Except neither of them had the luxury of anonymity anymore.

That reminded him of something, although he wasn't quite sure how to bring it up.

"Speaking of . . . Donna mentioned something to me about a fake relationship thing?"

Gina rolled her eyes. "Fucking Donna. She's a meddlesome bruja."

"She made it sound like it would get us more votes. We're trying to win, right?"

Gina's mouth flattened into a thin line. "Not like that. I won't pretend to have something going on with you for votes."

"We *do* have something going on."

"My nieces watch this show, Stone. What kind of example would I be setting for them? What kind of reputation would I be building for myself in this industry if I'm pretending to sleep with my partner—or actually sleeping with him—for audience votes?"

She sat up, gesturing with her hands as her tone grew more agitated. "I'd be playing right into the stereotype I'm trying so hard to break—the promiscuous Latina who no one takes seriously. I won't do that. Yes, I'll wear sexy costumes and do sexy dances, because it's part of the job. But there's a fine line between being *sexy* and being *sexualized*. The real me comes through in the package, and balances the characters I play in the dances. I want to be known as someone who works hard and works well with others, not for crossing boundaries and compromising my integrity to win." She stared at him for a long moment, pleading with her eyes. "Do you understand the difference?"

He nodded and brushed a hand over her hair. He hated that she had to walk such a fine line, but her argument made sense. "Perfectly."

"Good." She put her head back on his pecs and wiggled around. "Now, can we snuggle a bit before I have to kick you out? Natasha won't be away all night, and I don't want her to know you were here."

He put his arms around her and held her close. It was enough that she'd broken her rule for him. He had no right to push for more.

As much as he might want it.

S tone waited for the taxi outside Gina's building. He'd rather walk, the better to burn off his restlessness, but no one walked in LA.

Besides, he had rehearsal in the morning.

Gina's words slashed at him. He was doing exactly what she'd said she wouldn't do—compromising his integrity for money.

Well, not money exactly. For family. Still, it was close enough.

He'd always done what his family had asked of him. When they'd told him to drop everything and move to a little clearing in the Alaskan bush with nothing on it but a film crew, he had quit his job, ended his relationship, and grown out his hair and beard for the role. When the producers realized early on that Stone had a hard time playing his part, they cut back on his behind-the-scenes interviews and made him take his shirt off whenever possible. And he'd gone along with it.

He'd already told Gina about the not-bear, but he burned to tell her the rest. How *Living Wild* was all a lie. He and his family were promoting a made-for-TV image of themselves that masked the dysfunction they never even talked about. Reed's drug problem. Winter's and Raven's struggles with social anxiety. Wolf . . . actually, hyperactive Wolf was the best suited to living in the wilderness, and when they weren't filming, he ran around the hotel causing chaos.

Stone just wanted his normal, quiet life back. He wanted the peace he felt when he was alone, truly alone, in Alaska. And Violet and Lark deserved a chance at a normal life, too. They were growing up in the weird, in-between world of reality TV. The fame and deception couldn't be good for them.

It was the shit that kept Stone up at night, the shit he couldn't talk to anyone about. By filming in a remote location around people who didn't give a damn what they were doing, they'd managed to fly under the radar for four seasons. But it came with a cost. No real relationships outside the family. Especially for him, since he had such a hard time hiding the truth. And now, the closer he got to Gina, the more he wanted to tell her everything.

Would she even respect him afterward? And what difference would it make? At the end of *The Dance Off*, whenever that was for him, he was going back to Alaska. He had a contract to fulfill. Did he even care what she thought?

Hell yeah, he did. He cared a lot about what she thought of him. Right now, she thought enough of him to break her own rules and let him into her bed, into her body. It was a gift he didn't take for granted.

What would she think if she knew the truth?

Didn't matter. He couldn't tell her, even if he wanted to. The best he could do was be himself—his true self—and avoid talking about the rest.

He hoped it would be enough.

The car pulled up to the curb and he climbed in.

At least next week was Broadway-themed. He didn't know shit about musicals, so that was one thing he didn't have to pretend.

How the hell was he supposed to pretend he didn't have feelings for Gina?

At their first rehearsal, Gina had told Stone to put whatever he was feeling into the dance, and for the next two weeks, that was what he did. He and Gina grabbed time together whenever they could—away from the cameras, and when Natasha was out. When they were on camera, they channeled their crackling chemistry into the dances. It was a physical thing, a third entity dancing with them in the rehearsal room—not counting the actual physical entities of Jordy, Aaliyah, and sometimes Donna.

For Broadway Night, Gina choreographed an emotional contemporary routine with lots of lifts. Stone was shirtless for the second week in a row, clad only in gray pajama bottoms while Gina wore a tan tank top and floaty skirt. It was the simplest of their costumes, yet afforded the most ease of movement. The theme of their song was forgiveness, which struck a little too close to home.

If she ever found out the truth about him and his show, Stone hoped she'd forgive him.

Maybe she was right about emotions coming through in the dance, because it was his favorite of all the ones they'd done. The judges loved it and gave him his first perfect score. They praised his intensity and strength, and said they wanted to see him try a faster, livelier dance, to show his more jovial side and make up for his abysmal jive in the third episode.

Earning a 100 percent lit a fire in Stone. He and Gina amped up their rehearsals and their off-camera time. One night, they were almost caught by Natasha, who'd come home while they were cuddling in post-coital bliss. In a whispered argument, Stone reasoned that Natasha had probably already guessed they were together, but Gina had handed him his shoes and shoved him out the door the second they heard the shower turn on.

The next week was Silver Screen Night. They danced an upbeat, lighthearted waltz to a classic movie musical, designed to showcase Stone's hold and improved footwork.

Amazing how falling for someone like Gina lightened his step.

They wore matching gray and ice blue formal wear for their traditional waltz. It satisfied the judges, who gave him ninety percent and certified him a contender for the semifinals, but they still claimed they wanted to see more.

Meanwhile, one couple was sent home every week. On Broadway Night, Beto and Jess went home. Then, on Silver Screen Night, to everyone's surprise, Dwayne and Natasha were eliminated.

And then there were six: two Olympic athletes, two hot young TV actors, the rock star, and the reality TV survivalist.

Stone still had two eliminations to survive before the finals, including the double elimination after the semifinals, and he was the least famous celebrity left on the show by far.

He wanted Gina to win. She was the best, as far as he was concerned. Not that he was biased.

Okay, he was biased, but he cared about her, and he didn't want her to lose her job because he wasn't good enough.

And it bugged him that he couldn't turn his mind off from the idea of the showmance. Not that it would be just for show, of course. There was genuine affection between them, even though neither had voiced it.

That wasn't exactly true. He thought back to their first night together.

I like you, too, Stone.

Well, the feeling was mutual. And the word "like" was woefully inadequate for all that he felt for her.

Twenty

H e's going to be so surprised." Natasha grinned and reached for the bag of plantain chips Gina held.

Gina washed her chips down with seltzer. The night before, Natasha and Dwayne had been voted off the show, so Tash was fair game to join their trio dance for next week's episode. "He said you were a good teacher, so now he gets to experience the joy of being coached by both of us at the same time."

"Double-teamed," Tash said with a laugh.

Gina shot a glance at the camera and covered her mouth to suppress a snort. "That doesn't mean what you think it means."

"Maybe it does." Tash raised her eyebrows suggestively.

At that moment, Stone walked into the rehearsal room, and Gina dissolved into giggles.

He froze. "Wait, am I dancing with both of you next week?"

"Were you asleep when Juan Carlos explained that this is Team Up Week?" Tash teased.

"I just . . ." He looked back and forth between them. "Shit, I'm in for it, aren't I?"

Tash nodded and pranced over to him. "We have a samba, too."

"What does that mean?"

"It's a fun dance," Gina explained. "Party atmosphere. It's originally an Afro-Brazilian dance, but ballroom samba is different."

"Lots of bouncing," Tash added.

Stone bounced on tiptoe, like he was about to shoot a basketball. "Like this?"

"Sort of. You're pushing forward on your toes, but it's about the rise and fall." Gina beckoned Tash over and held her hands. Gina counted and they demonstrated a few moves, bobbing up and down as they danced across the floor.

Stone raised his eyebrows. "I don't think I can do that."

"Of course you can." Tash grabbed his hips and counted out the beat.

"Nail the bounce, and you'll nail the samba," Gina said.

Tash pointed a finger at her. "Along with threesome samba rolls."

Stone groaned and Gina shook her head. "Again, that doesn't mean what you think it means."

Tash winked. "Again, maybe it does."

They ended early after spending most of the day teaching Stone the basic samba steps. On top of the trio samba, Gina and Stone were paired with Lauren and Kevin for a team dance—and they didn't have much time to choreograph or practice.

Once Tash was unmic'd, she pulled Gina out to the tiny kitchenette while Stone made a trip to the restroom.

Tash grabbed Gina's mic cord and unplugged it.

"Hey, what're you—"

Tash pressed a finger to her lips and gestured for Gina to come closer. Gina put her head next to her roommate's, sneaking a glance at the doorway.

"What is it?" she whispered.

"How long have you been fucking him?" Natasha hissed.

Gina reared back, her heart pounding. *Damn* it. "Um . . ."

Natasha wagged a finger at her. "Don't even try to deny it."

"Fine. I won't." Even though she'd just checked, Gina glanced around again. No point asking how Tash knew. They'd been friends since they were fourteen. "Don't tell anyone."

"Pssh. I can keep a secret. Can you?" With her eyebrows raised to dangerous heights, Tash sailed out of the room with a flippant "Ciao!"

Gina met up with Stone in the hallway. He was seconds away from turning his lav mic back on. She grabbed his hand to stop him.

"Natasha knows," she said in a low voice.

He just shrugged, which did nothing to ease her anxiety. "So? Isn't she your friend?"

"Of course. She won't tell anyone."

He smiled and lifted his hands to frame her face. She took a step back and he frowned. "So, what's the problem?"

"The problem is that we're somehow being indiscreet."

He shrugged again. "Maybe Natasha just knows you really well."

"Maybe." Gina wasn't convinced. "Let's go. Lauren and Kevin are waiting for us."

When they entered the other rehearsal room to meet their teammates, the first words out of Lauren's mouth were, "Ooh, I get to dance with *him*?"

Kevin let out a bark of laughter. "I guess we could choreograph a partner switch?"

Gina tensed, her skin heating. *Over my dead body.*

"We'll see how it goes," she said, proud at how friendly she managed to sound, and not at all like she wanted to claw Lauren's pretty blue eyes out.

Gina assessed their group. She was no slouch, but Lauren, with her broad shoulders and muscular ice skater's legs, looked like she could haul lumber in the wilderness right alongside Stone and his brothers. They'd make little blond babies with sky blue eyes and do outdoorsy shit like hunting and logging.

Whoa, hold up. She didn't care about shit like that—babies *or* logging. Where did this line of thinking come from?

Oh fuck. She was *jealous.*

Not cool. So not cool.

To mask her reaction, Gina turned her back on Stone and

Lauren—the pair were discussing white-water rafting—and approached Kevin.

"So, the team medley," she said. Kevin launched into an explanation of his ideas for the dance, which he'd been brainstorming for weeks. Immense gratitude filled her—for Kevin and his professionalism, his obsession with clever choreography, and his *fans*. Kevin would keep their team—Team Ice Cold, a mashup of Team Stone Cold and Team Freeze Ray—focused on the dance.

If anyone wanted to win more than Gina, it was Kevin. And Kevin always won the team dance. As long as they survived the next elimination, there was a good chance their Team Up Week scores would help her and Stone make it into the finals.

Time to pray. And then work her ass off.

Jordy came in with their music.

"Here you go," he said, handing them a piece of cardstock. "Gina, you're going to love this one."

It was said without an ounce of sarcasm. Curious, Gina took the card, read the name on top, and squealed.

Stone was by her side in a second. "What is it? What's our music?"

"Not what, but who." Gina thrust the card at him. "It's a Meli medley!"

H uh?" Stone scanned the list of songs. A couple sounded familiar, but nothing he could admit to knowing, so he just asked, "Who's Meli?"

Gina gaped at him and snatched the paper away. "You're kidding, right?"

He gave her a friendly nudge with his hip. "We don't listen to Top 40 in the bush."

"I cannot believe you don't know who Meli is."

"Melissa 'Meli' Mendez," Kevin cut in, taking the list of songs from Gina. "Singer and actress."

"She is so much more than that," Gina protested.

Lauren looked at the list over Kevin's shoulder. "Oh cool, I do warm-ups to a couple of these songs."

Gina turned to Stone, her eyes sparkling with excitement. "Meli is my *idol*. She's a Puerto Rican girl from the Bronx—from my *neighborhood*—who started as a dancer. Then she put out a few pop albums, had a few hits, and transitioned to starring in movies. From there she scored some other gigs, including a fashion line, judging, and hosting."

"Ah." It was obvious why Gina would idolize her. They had the same roots, and Meli had succeeded in the entertainment industry in all the ways Gina aspired to succeed.

Stone's mood plummeted. It was yet another stark reminder of how different their end goals were.

"Do you know how rare it is for a Puerto Rican woman to reach this level of fame and recognition?" Gina asked.

He didn't, but it was clear this was important to her. "No?"

She blinked, brows dipping like she was disappointed. "Rare. She's the *only* one who's done it at this level."

"Let's get started with this choreography," Kevin cut in. "We only have two hours."

Kevin was a hands-on choreographer. Stone sat on the stage with Lauren while Gina and Kevin worked out the dance. Their movements were sharp and fluid, like the time they'd danced together at the salsa club. Masters at work.

"How's your trio dance going?" Lauren asked, scooting closer.

"We've got Natasha."

"We're with Matteo. Hot Italian man for one dance, and you for another?" She gave him a heavy-lidded look. "I'm a lucky woman this week."

Stone's face heated, and he kept his eyes on Gina and Kevin while he tried to work out what to say.

The dance gods smiled upon him. Gina beckoned him over to try out a lift.

Gina hadn't heard, but Lauren's words still made him uncomfortable. Stone didn't want Lauren to say something within

Gina's hearing, especially since he wasn't allowed to say he was taken.

Wait, was he? He didn't know what the hell was going on with Gina. Their tryst existed in the moment, with no thought for the future, dedicated to wringing every ounce of fun and pleasure they could from this whole weird experience.

Then what? Where were they going with this? Because no matter what happened, he was going back to Alaska, and not just for *Living Wild*. Alaska was his home, the home of his soul. He felt more at peace there than any other place he'd ever been.

And Gina had made it clear her future was in two places: New York and Los Angeles. Alaska didn't figure into her dreams.

Where did he figure in?

He was afraid to ask, afraid he wouldn't like the answer.

Following Kevin's instructions, Stone lifted Gina over his head. He kept his eyes on Kevin, while his thoughts returned to the situation he was in with Gina. He whipped her around, as Kevin directed.

And then he dropped her.

Twenty-One

Instinct kicked in, and Stone caught Gina before her head hit the floor. However, he didn't count on her own reflexes. She threw her arms out to catch herself and tripped him in the process.

They went down in a tumble of limbs, crashing to the hardwood floor of the rehearsal room.

Someone screamed.

Stone twisted at the last minute to take the brunt of the fall, landing hard on his knee and forearm. Kevin and Lauren rushed in, but Stone ignored them. Gina was the only one who mattered.

He'd dropped her.

"Gina?" Wincing, he shifted into a sitting position, cradling Gina in his lap while his knee throbbed something fierce.

Breathless, she ran her hands over his body, checking him. "Are you okay?"

"Am I?" She couldn't be serious. He touched her elbows, knees, hands, checking her joints. "I heard you scream."

"That was me." Lauren knelt beside them. "That fall looked *awful*. Stone, can you move?"

"Gina, tell me you're okay." He ran his hands over her head, her neck, down her spine. Behind him, Jordy shouted for someone to call the doctor.

"I'm *fine,* Stone. I didn't even touch the floor."

Blinking, he shoved the pulsing pain aside and focused on her face. She was looking at him with concern etched on her features.

"You didn't?" But he'd dropped her. He'd *dropped* her. Fuck. As her partner, he had *one job,* and—

"I didn't. You caught me. *You're* the one who hit the floor."

"That was amazing, dude." Kevin stood to the side with his hands on his hips. "I've seen some gnarly drops—even dropped my own partners a few times. It happens. Never saw someone make a catch like that."

Lauren inched closer while Gina gingerly worked the leg of Stone's sweatpants over his knee.

Jordy crowded in with ice packs. "We have to get him checked out."

Stone leaned back and propped himself up on his arms. His left forearm complained, but since it wasn't as bad as his knee, he ignored it. He let Gina and Jordy see to his leg, closing his eyes and tipping his head back as adrenaline coursed through his body.

Lauren rubbed his back. He wished she'd stop. Gina's touch, careful yet sure on his knee, was already soothing him.

"Stone?"

Gina's voice. He opened his eyes. "Hmm?"

Her gaze was full of worry. "Does your knee hurt a lot?"

She wanted him to say no. It was on the tip of his tongue to lie. He opened his mouth, but she pressed a fingertip to his lips.

"Don't lie," she said in a low voice. "Truth. Does your knee hurt?"

He let out a slow breath. "Yeah. Kind of."

Her mouth firmed and she nodded. "We're taking you to the hospital. Can you walk?" She glanced at Kevin, who shrugged. "Stone, you're the biggest person in this building. I don't think there's anyone here who can help you walk."

Aaliyah leaped to her feet. "One of the segment producers is a big guy. I'll go get him."

Stone shook his head. "I'll walk." He got his legs under him, wincing when his knee and arm sent shooting pain from the points where they'd made direct contact with the hard floor. Once he was upright, he felt a little better. Granted, he had yet to take a step, so that might change, but at least he could stand under his own power. Gina still looked worried, so he cupped her face and leaned down to kiss her forehead. "Don't worry, babe. I'll be able to dance on Monday."

Gina gasped. Stone blinked, realizing what he'd done. He'd kissed her face, in front of Lauren, Jordy, and the *cameras*.

Lauren propped her hands on her hips. "Since when did you guys get all lovey-dovey? You screwing or something?"

Kevin's laid-back manner came to the rescue. "Hey, Lauren. Not cool. This isn't the time to joke around."

Lauren huffed. "Fine. But how are we supposed to practice our team dance if one fourth of the team is laid up?"

It was a good question. And how the hell was Stone going to samba with a busted knee?

"Kevin, you keep working on the dance," Gina said. "I'll go with Stone to the doctor."

Stone shook his head. "No. You stay here. Work your magic—choreograph the dance with Kev. Then you can teach it to me."

"I don't want to leave you—"

"Gina." He kept his voice gentle. If only he could kiss her fears away right now. The stricken expression on her face was killing him, shredding his resolve to keep his hands off her when the cameras were on. "I've been hurt way worse than this, in locations where there wasn't a doctor around for miles. I'll be okay going to a Los Angeles ER to get checked out."

She bit her lip like she was holding back an argument, but nodded. "Go home after the doctor. We'll see where we are tomorrow."

There was something in her gaze, something she was trying to communicate to him. He couldn't decipher it. Despite his calm words, his knee hurt like a motherfucker. With a nod to the rest of Team Ice Cold, Stone leaned on Jordy's shoulder and limped out of the studio.

It was nothing. Just a bad bruise. But it meant Stone was laid up in bed, icing his knee and flicking through cable channels. There was nothing on. He couldn't exercise, swim, run, or hike.

He was bored.

His laptop sat on the room's desk, but he didn't feel like moving to get it. Maybe he'd watch a movie. He'd missed all the latest super-hero flicks while filming *Living Wild*.

Someone knocked on his hotel room door.

He frowned. Had he ordered something?

No. He hadn't hit his head. He'd remember whether he ordered room service or not.

"Who is it?" he yelled from the bed.

"It's me."

Muffled, subdued, but unmistakable. Gina.

"Hold on."

Clicking off the TV, he threw the remote aside and shifted the enormous ice pack off his knee. Whereas the laptop had seemed like too much trouble, Gina's voice brought him a burst of energy. He hobbled to the door and swung it open.

Without missing a beat, Gina crossed the threshold and wrapped her arms around him in a tight hug. He returned it with one arm, since the other still held the door.

"What are you doing here?" Paparazzi swarmed around this ho-tel, which was why they always met at her apartment.

"I had to see you," she said into his shirt. Tipping her head back, she gave him a tremulous smile. "When I heard you hit the floor . . ."

He brushed loose strands of hair back from her face, relishing the freedom of such a simple move. It was so hard holding back around the cameras. "Don't worry. It would take a lot more than that to put me out of commission. I was more worried about you."

He limped backward a few steps so she could shut the door. When they were alone, finally, blessedly alone, he leaned against the wall and pulled her in for a long, searching kiss.

The now familiar scent of coconut and hibiscus enveloped him in its sweetness.

Breaking the kiss, he dipped his head and snuffled the sensitive area behind her ear. "Mm, you smell good enough to eat."

She giggled. "You're tickling me."

"I'll tickle you somewhere else, if you want."

Her laugh turned husky. She pressed closer. "God, Stone, I was so fucking scared for you. I thought you'd hit your head."

Slinging an arm around her shoulder, he shuffled back to the bed—and only leaned a little bit of his weight on her. She helped him climb onto the mattress and settled the ice over his knee again.

"I'll be fine by tomorrow." He patted the bed next to him, and she toed off her sandals and snuggled in against his side. "We'll dance next week and get great scores, and we'll make it to the finals. You'll keep your job."

A little voice in his head chimed in with a snide, *And then what?*

He pushed it away. Even if they didn't make the finals and Gina got cut from the show, she would still follow her dreams. She wouldn't let it stop her.

More importantly, she wouldn't leave the industry, no matter what setbacks she suffered. She was too talented and too hard-working to give up on herself.

It was one of the things he loved about her.

Yep. There it was. Damn it. He loved her.

He filed that away for the time being. It would only complicate things.

She hugged him and pressed her face to his chest. "It's not just about my job."

His stupid heart thumped faster. "No?"

"No." She slumped against him. "I was scared for *you*. I care about you, you know."

He swallowed. She never would have broken her rule for him if she hadn't cared. "I know."

She idly flicked her finger along the edge of his beard. "How did we get here?"

"Here?"

"Not here in the hotel room. You know what I mean."

"It feels inevitable."

"Don't give me that nonsense. You can't tell me you didn't think I was some high-maintenance LA chick when we first met."

He chewed on the corner of his mouth. "Well . . ."

She laughed. "I know how I looked. My producers hadn't given me any indication of where we were going, except that I should dress warmly."

Now he was curious. "Where did you think you were going?"

"I thought I was getting the male version of Lauren. I had dreams of a gold medal–winning figure skater, who already knew how to dance and had a built-in fan base. A sure shot at winning *The Dance Off*'s trophy."

"Instead you got a wild man with no dance training and terrible social skills."

She frowned at him. "There's nothing wrong with your social skills."

He rolled his eyes. "Gina, I barely spoke at the beginning." He was still afraid to say something that would betray his family, but he wasn't afraid to speak anymore. Gina, with her easygoing sweetness, had opened him up. He didn't have to be "the quiet one" around her. He could be himself.

It was the only thing she expected of him, and it was a gift he could never repay.

"I can't believe I dropped you," he said in a hushed voice.

She rubbed her palm in circles over his belly. "I've been dropped before. It happens."

"But *I've* never done it. I was preoccupied."

Her hand stilled. "What were you thinking about?"

Truth, she'd said in the dance studio. She'd been talking about his knee then, but didn't she deserve more truth from him than an injury report?

"I was thinking about what happens when I go back to Alaska."

Close as they were, it was impossible to miss the way her body tensed.

"Oh."

He rubbed her back. "I have to finish my contract with *Living Wild.*"

She turned her face away. "I know." Her voice sounded small.

"You work here in LA." Who the hell was he trying to convince? "I know."

He held her and she held him, touching in gestures meant to soothe rather than ignite.

"Tell me what you're thinking, Gina." She'd asked him, and he'd answered. It was only fair she return the favor.

She released a hefty sigh. "This wasn't supposed to happen."

"Your rule."

"Not just the rule." She picked at a loose thread in the hem of his T-shirt. "The rule is to protect my career. I don't need a rule to protect my . . . feelings, because I don't usually let them get involved."

His heart thumped again. If he interrupted her now, she might change tracks. But if he didn't acknowledge that he was listening, she might stop. He settled on, "Mm-hmm."

"I . . . I have some feelings, Stone. For you."

He needed to see it. Needed to know the truth. He shifted her so she was sitting across his lap and looked right into her eyes. She caught on quick, knowing what he was after.

They gazed into each other's eyes. This time, there was no giggling. Just raw, naked emotion.

A pit opened in his stomach, a great yawning chasm of longing. He saw it mirrored in her, but there was a flicker of fear, enough that he needed to do something scary himself before he could kiss her again.

"Me, too." His voice was gruff, gravelly with emotion. "For you."

She let out a shaky laugh and pressed her forehead to his. "What the fuck do we do with this, Stone? We won't work out. I can't—I won't—Stone, my mom gave up all her dreams for a man who left her with three kids to raise on her own. And the one time I let myself get involved with someone close to my job, it cost me. I can't repeat these mistakes."

It wouldn't help to point out that one of those mistakes was her mother's, not hers. Either way, he didn't have a good counterargument. Her career was important to her and they'd known each other a few months. He wouldn't ask her to change her life for him.

But he'd made mistakes, too. He'd already fallen for—and been left by—one woman who hadn't wanted the life he envisioned for himself. He was setting himself up for it to happen again.

Was he wrong? Was it worth giving up on his own image of peace and happiness to explore what he might have with Gina?

She'd never ask it of him. Perhaps because she would never do it for him.

It was too late anyway. He was already in too deep. He'd take what he could get and suffer the consequences later.

He leaned in to kiss her.

Twenty-Two

Kissing Gina was an all-encompassing experience, and Stone never wanted it to end. She wrapped herself around him like a vine, fusing her mouth to his and kissing him back with fervor. She tasted like ginger candies and a tinge of desperation. It was the last bit that made him pull back and smooth his fingertips down her cheek.

"Shh. Slow down." He brushed his thumb over her bottom lip, which quivered. "You're always going a hundred miles per hour."

She shook her head. "I can't slow down. If I do . . ."

"What will happen?"

Melting against him, she pressed her face into his neck and whispered, "My thoughts will catch up to me."

What was happening between them was terrifying, but necessary, too. They both had stuff they needed to let out. Maybe that was what mattered more than the future—creating a safe space where they could say the things they were scared to say, and feel what they were afraid to feel.

"Why is that bad?" he asked.

"Because they're conflicting messages. Stay. Leave. I don't know what to do."

He understood. The same conflict raged in him, but on a bigger scale. "What do you want, Gina?"

She lifted her head and met his gaze dead on. "I want to stay."

"All night?" They'd never done that. She wouldn't allow it at her apartment.

She nodded. His chest swelled. Finally, he'd hold her in his arms all night.

He released the clip that held her hair in a messy bun. The dark, shiny mass cascaded down her shoulders. Sifting his fingers through the hibiscus-scented strands, he cupped the back of her head and drew her in for a kiss.

He kept the pace slow, nibbling at her with light caresses and soft licks. She sighed into his mouth and followed his lead.

"What are we doing, Stone?" Her voice was breathy, the question rhetorical. He answered anyway.

"We're kissing." He dragged his tongue along her lower lip and was rewarded with a soft moan. "Isn't that enough?"

She bit her lip, then nodded. Leaning in, she pressed her lips flush against his.

In their outside lives, they were separated by a gulf of responsibilities and conflicting goals. Here, the only things between them were a few pieces of fabric, and it was time to rectify that situation. If this moment was all he had, Stone didn't want anything between them.

Most of the time they went fast. Tonight, she would stay. They had time. No one would interrupt them.

He kept the kiss light and teasing as he skimmed his thumbs under the hem of her shirt. Her skin was warm and smooth. He wanted to flip her over and trace the path his fingers took with his tongue, but the move would dislodge the ice pack draped over his knee. Instead, he lifted her until she straddled his hips.

He'd been hard since their first kiss by the door, but with her warm ass on his lap, he was a goner. He shifted his hips to thrust against her, then winced when the movement made his knee twinge.

It was her turn to shush him. "I'll do all the moving tonight." She rocked against him, her agile spine and hips undulating in a rhythm designed to drive him mad. He groaned and gripped her thighs.

"Remember when you made me grab your ass in rehearsal?" he said with a growl, nuzzling her neck.

"How could I forget? My panties were wet the rest of the day."

He lifted his head to stare at her in surprise. "Really?"

"I didn't anticipate how much it would affect me."

"It affected me, too."

"Trust me, I could tell. Your hard-on certainly didn't help my own situation."

"I wish I'd known." Groaning, he pulled her flush against his groin, but it did nothing to alleviate the heady arousal tightening his body.

"You know now. Besides, it's happening again."

"Oh, yeah? Let me check." He slipped one hand over her hip and stroked his thumb between her thighs, tracing the seam of her leggings. Gasping, she arched into his touch. The move pushed her breasts closer to his face.

Wrapping an arm around her back to support her, he bit lightly at her nipples where they pressed against the fabric of her shirt. He moved his thumb in faster circles, and she bounced on him.

"Oh my god, that feels good." A high moan built in the back of her throat, and she pulled her shirt up over her breasts. Stone grinned and tongued her left nipple through the lacy bra—hot pink this time.

"Please tell me you're wearing pink lace panties."

"Of course . . . I am." She cried out when he growled and sucked her right nipple into his mouth, increasing the speed of his thumb rubbing her clit through the pants.

"You close, babe?"

"With you? *Always.*"

The genuine feeling in her words lit a fire in him. He switched back to her left breast and dragged the lace down with his teeth, so he could taste her with nothing in the way.

Above him, her whole body tightened. He watched her face, thrilling at the pure abandon infusing her features. Her eyes squeezed shut, her mouth opened on a hoarse cry, and before his very eyes, she shattered. This—giving her pleasure, seeing her with her guards down—was worth all the bullshit it had taken to get here. Her hips bucked against his hand, her spine shivered in his hold, and her tits jiggled in his face as she rode the orgasm. Through it all, he kept his thumb on her and didn't stop until she'd collapsed against his chest, breathing hard, her heart thudding against his. He stroked her hair and waited for her to return to him.

"Mm." She tilted her head to look up at him with heavy-lidded eyes and a sleepy smile. "You're so good to me."

There was a lot more he wanted to do, but this time, they would go slow. He was tired of rushing. Every episode could be his last. For now, they had all night. He'd do everything he could to prolong their pleasure.

She stirred, then reached between them and wrapped her hand around his dick, which had created a tent out of the loose basketball shorts he wore.

"I want to suck on you," she said.

His cock surged in her hand, rock hard. He grunted in reply, unable to speak as she shifted off his lap and untangled herself from her shirt and bra. Then she shed her leggings and panties, which were indeed hot pink.

Once she was naked, she pulled his T-shirt over his head. His shorts were more of a problem. He lifted himself up with his hands, and she dragged the waistband of his shorts and boxers down, freeing his cock. She carefully pulled the shorts over his knee and the ice pack before throwing them aside.

She flashed him a sexy smile. "This is how I like it. Just you and me, totally naked and alone."

He tossed the ice pack off the bed and held out a hand for her. "Come back here."

She crawled between his legs. He shifted his good knee out of the way to make room for her. Settling in with her face in his lap, she stroked her fingertips lightly over the crown of his cock.

The last few weeks had shown him that Gina liked tonguing his dick before they fucked. At one point, he'd tried to tell her she didn't have to do it, even though his libido attempted to stop him.

"You don't like it?" she'd said, sounding incredulous. "*I* like it. It turns me on to have your cock in my mouth."

"No, I—" Her words made him tongue-tied, and he almost said he loved it. "Of course I like it. It's fucking amazing and I can't believe how lucky I am, so I'm questioning my good fortune."

"All right then. We both like it. Shut up."

And that had been the end of that.

Now, she dragged her tongue up the length of his cock, starting with his balls.

His eyes rolled back in his head. "Christ, Gina."

"I'm going to try to get you in even deeper this time," she said, before closing her mouth around the head and sucking hard.

Sensation zinged through his body, from her action and her words. His head thumped against the headboard of the bed and he closed his eyes while she worked on him.

A few days ago, she'd said she was tired of mouthing half his dick, and she wanted to practice taking him deeper. He'd almost expired on the spot.

Bless her competitive spirit.

He had to keep his eyes closed. If he looked, if he saw her methodically lubing him up with her tongue and then swallowing him into the hot, wet cavern of her mouth, he'd lose control and come right there.

Sometimes she blew him until he came. She'd done it once while he sat on the sofa in her living room, in full view of the door, even though Natasha could have come in at any moment. That time had been like fucking fireworks going off in his balls. He still dreamed about it.

But most of the time, like tonight, he was too anxious to get inside her. To feel her hugging his dick like a glove, her whole body wrapped around him while she moaned in his ear and dug her nails into his back. They were in the city of angels and she was heaven on earth and he couldn't get enough of her.

Her mouth moved up and down on him, the rhythm of her lips and tongue in perfect harmony.

Heaven.

It was too much. Too soon. He wrapped his hand in her hair and gave a gentle tug. "Gina."

She sped up her movements, squeezing him tighter with her mouth. A tremor shook his body as pleasure spiraled along his nerves.

"Gina."

"Hmm?" Her hum vibrated through his dick, sending a shiver up his spine. He gripped her shoulders and eased her off him.

"I'm too close." He dragged her up his body and pressed a kiss to her mouth. "Are you ready?"

Before he could touch her to check, she straddled his lap and rubbed her wet, open pussy on his dick, coating him with her juices.

"What do you think?" she asked, her voice husky. "Am I ready for you?"

She was driving him to distraction. His hands clenched on her hips, halting her movement. "Condoms. They're in my—"

"I want to feel you, Stone."

He stilled as her words sank in. "Are you sure?"

She took a deep breath and let it out. "Yes. I'm on the pill, and I have Plan B at home. Plus we both had physicals before we started filming."

He knew she was on the pill. Hell, he'd seen her taking it during rehearsal when the alarm on her phone went off. But he'd never had sex without a condom before. Being one of seven kids had taught him the importance of protection.

The urge to be inside her still compelled him, but her invitation humbled him. To feel her, skin to skin, would be his undoing. And he wanted it more than his next breath.

Nodding, he took her mouth in a deep, penetrating kiss. She

clutched his shoulders, shifting so he could position himself at her entrance. She was slick and ready. His knee twinged as he slid into her warmth, pushing until he was fully seated inside her core.

She sighed in his ear. Pressed chest to chest, her heart thumped against his.

Nothing between them. *Heaven.*

True to her promise, Gina did all the work. She rocked her hips, moaning each time he filled her. She undulated her spine, shimmied on his cock, and set a slow burning rhythm that stoked the fire between them.

Face-to-face, he kissed her slow and deep. With his cock surging inside her, the tangling of their tongues was another level of connection, of closeness.

Pressure built in his balls, but he wanted her to come first. He loved to watch her break apart at his touch.

Slipping a hand between them, he ran his fingertips along her folds where they parted around him. She was wet and soft, so soft. When she moaned, he rubbed her clit with the pad of his thumb, and her moan turned to a gasping sob.

"*Stone.* Yes. *Yes.*" She grabbed his shoulders and thrust her hips harder. "God. Yes. Don't stop."

He brought his mouth back to hers for a searing kiss. With his other hand, he cupped her breast, rubbing the nipple with his thumb the same way he worked her clit.

Early on, he'd worried about the roughness of his hands. She'd assured him she liked it, and he took her at her word.

The proof was in the way her pussy tightened on his dick. He thrust upward into her, meeting her every time she slammed her hips down. His knee throbbed, but the pain did nothing to detract from the feel of her silken heat.

"Come on, babe." He sucked on her lower lip. "Come all over my cock."

The dirty talk did the trick. Her knees clamped on his hips, her spine bowed, and with a sharp cry, she shuddered and shook in his arms.

With her moan echoing in his ears and her pussy clenching rhythmically around him, Stone lost hold of his control.

"Gina, can I—?"

"*Yes.*"

He slammed his hips into her, his thrusts short as the orgasm roared through him. He locked against her, holding her tight in his arms. With his face pressed into the curve of her shoulder, he emptied himself inside her.

Gina didn't want to move. The room was pitch black and she was so relaxed she could barely feel her limbs. For the first time in weeks, her thoughts didn't zip forward and backward. In this moment, lying half across Stone's naked body in a pile of pillows on his king-sized bed, she knew utter peace.

She breathed in the scent of his sweat, as familiar to her as her own, and whatever Christmas tree–smelling soap he used, and closed her eyes to go back to sleep.

A second later, his alarm blared.

She buried her face in his hard chest and grumbled. "Way to ruin a moment."

He swung out an arm and slapped the clock. It was a wonder the thing didn't crash into a million pieces under the force of his hand. Then he rolled, pulling her closer and enfolding her in his arms.

"What time is it?" she asked.

"Five. Go back to sleep."

"Why does your alarm go off so early?"

"Gym. Hike. Whatever." He kissed her forehead. "Sleep more."

Once again, the feeling of peace descended. She melted against him and slept.

A few hours later, Stone woke her by nuzzling her breasts. They shared a shower—not easy with someone as big as Stone blocking the spray. Then he lifted her and pinned her against the tiles with his pelvis.

She gasped as he slid inside her. "Your knee."

"I'm fine." He gave her a quick, hard kiss, then fucked her sense-less.

After helping her wash off again, he wrapped her in a towel and carried her back to the bed.

"Someone woke up on the right side of the bed this morning," she said grumpily as she ran his comb through her wet hair. At least the guy had hair supplies.

"You're just mad because you haven't had your coffee yet." He busied himself in the kitchenette, wearing nothing but a white ho-tel towel tied around his waist. "I'm making it for you now."

She licked her lips as she watched him. If only they could stay curled up in bed, but they were expected at the studio, and it would be suspicious if they both showed up late together.

No, they couldn't arrive together. A car came to pick him up ev-ery morning. It would look even more suspicious if he canceled it.

Hunting down her clothes, Gina made a face at the thought of putting them back on.

"What's wrong?" Stone asked.

"My gym bag—with my deodorant and a change of clothes—is in my car."

"Oh, I can get it for you." He brought her a mug. "Lots of milk and one sugar, right?"

"Yeah. How did you know?"

"I've watched you make it enough times in the studio kitchen."

She sniffed the coffee, filling her nostrils with the rich, caffein-ated aroma, then took a sip. "Good job."

He whipped off the towel, giving her an eyeful before he stepped into forest green briefs and khaki cargo shorts. "Where are your car keys?"

"My purse." She pointed to the bedside table.

After pulling on a T-shirt and the Mariners cap he'd bought in New York, he plucked the keys from her bag and gave her a wink. "Be right back."

Once he was gone, Gina flopped backward on the bed. What were they doing? When she didn't think about the future, everything with him was great. The sex was amazing, Stone was kind and conscientious, and she liked how she felt when she was around him. He *listened*. He enjoyed hearing her thoughts and feelings.

Ruben had never listened. He'd only talked—about himself, his plans, his connections. When they did talk about her, it was in relation to his plans and connections.

And the last three . . . or five . . . guys she'd dated for longer than a few weeks hadn't been the greatest listeners, either, but she'd chosen them specifically because they weren't all that interested in her life. She'd wanted to keep her romantic entanglements as far from her career as possible, which was why she ended up dating guys who she wasn't especially interested in.

She knew this about herself. Her MO was to casually date one man at a time whenever she got lonely, while still putting her career first. She gravitated toward men who were also devoted to their work. Entrepreneurs, athletes—she'd even dated a lawyer because he spent most of his time at the office or the gym. In other words, guys who made no demands on her time, and who didn't tempt her to change her goals. And when it was time for them to part ways, she hadn't cared.

Stone was the first man in a very long time who made her wonder how they could work it out.

Too bad she didn't have an answer.

Twenty-Three

I'll walk you to your car."

"You really don't have to." Gina checked herself in Stone's bathroom mirror. Her hair was still wet, but at least she didn't look like she'd spent the night in her dance partner's hotel room, fucking his brains out. Thank goodness she kept a fully stocked gym bag in her trunk. "I'll see you soon enough at the studio."

Stone leaned against the doorframe with his arms crossed over his broad chest. Even though she'd spent the whole night with him, she wanted more. More talking, more cuddling, more kissing. Stretching up on tiptoe, she lifted her face for a kiss. With her eyes closed, she got a good whiff of his forest scent. It clung to her, too.

"Why do we smell like Christmas trees?"

He jerked his chin toward the tub. "My sister makes soap with essential oils. You used it today."

"You used it on me," she corrected. "I do not recall having the energy to bathe myself this morning after someone—who is supposed to be resting his knee—did me good against the shower wall."

His grin flashed, bright against his beard. She loved when he grinned like that—sexy, playful, and a little naughty. "You liked it."

"Of course I did." She looped her purse over her shoulder. "I'd let you do it again if we weren't expected at work."

He picked up her gym bag before she could reach for it. "Let me be old fashioned and walk my lady to her car."

His lady. The phrase made her stomach flip in a pleased sort of way. "Okay, fine."

Gina had parked in a paid spot in the guest lot outside. Stone took her hand as they walked and she smiled up at him. When they turned the corner, there was a shout.

"There they are!"

Gina blinked, stomach sinking. "Oh, *no*."

The paparazzi had formed a wall on the other side of the parking lot's fence. Cameras flashed. Skeevy-looking guys with hungry eyes shouted her name, and Stone's.

Stone put an arm around her, turning her away from them. Fumbling in her purse, Gina pulled out her sunglasses and slapped them on.

"Shit, how did they know?" She yanked her car keys out of her bag. "They're usually stationed around the front entrance."

Stone shrugged. "There were a handful out here this morning. I don't know where the rest came from."

She froze. "Wait, they saw you coming down to my car and getting a bag?"

"How do they know it's your car?"

"Because the ones who camp out in the lot behind the rehearsal studio know my license plate."

"Oh." Understanding dawned on his face. "I didn't even think of that. We don't have paparazzi in Alaska."

Ignoring the shouts, Gina forced her breathing to steady, even though her pulse was pounding like a snare drum. He hadn't known. She had. This was her own fault.

She never should have stayed the night.

Raising her voice in the hopes she could spin this and keep it from being a complete disaster, she patted Stone's shoulder and gave him a bright smile. "Glad to see your knee is feeling better. I'll see you later."

Gina got in the car and peeled out of the lot, leaving him standing there. By some miracle, there was no traffic, and she got to the studio in record time. The first thing she did was track down Donna.

Donna gave her a startled look when Gina slipped into the closet-sized office and flopped into a chair, breathing hard.

"What's wrong?" Donna jumped up and closed the door, then took a seat next to Gina. For once, she seemed truly concerned. "Are you okay? What happened?"

Gina swallowed hard. The shock still hadn't worn off. "I need you to spin something."

Donna's brow creased further. "What do you mean?"

"Some paparazzi caught me coming out of Stone's hotel this morning."

Clamping her mouth shut, Donna grabbed her laptop from the tiny desk and flipped it open. "They sure did."

Gina pressed her fingers to her eyes. "Don't fight it too much, just laugh it off. Stone was injured yesterday. Say I was making sure he was okay. That's it."

Nodding, Donna typed something on her laptop. "On it." She shot Gina a look from under her lashes. "*Is* that why you were there?"

Initially? Yes, that was what had prompted her to visit him. Last night. So it wasn't a total lie. "Yes."

Donna raised her eyebrows. "Whatever you say."

"Thank you." Gina got up to leave, then paused with her hand on the doorknob. "Please don't bring any of this up with Stone."

Donna's expression was calculating. "If you spin this differently, maybe drag out the mystery, it might help your chances of getting to the finals."

"It might hurt them, too. And I'm not willing to risk it." Gina let herself out.

"How's your knee doing?" Jackson asked. He and Stone were hanging out backstage before filming started on Team Up Night.

"Fine." Stone stuck out his leg, turned it side to side. "Samba practice was difficult at first, but we got through it."

Jackson nodded. "I pulled something in my back during the third week. Nothing to do but keep going."

Juan Carlos came over, his eyes lighting up when he caught sight of Stone. "Stone! Just the man I'm looking for. Where's Gina?"

"I think she's in makeup." He hadn't seen her all day—or most of the week, aside from rehearsals—and he was starting to get the feeling she was avoiding him. "What's up?"

Juan Carlos beckoned him to follow and hurried away. The host was over a foot shorter than Stone, but the guy walked fast.

"We have some good news for her about tonight's episode," Juan Carlos said over his shoulder. "We want to film her reaction."

Stone fought the urge to roll his eyes.

They grabbed a camera crew and headed out onto the lot and into the makeup trailer. Gina looked up when they all filed in.

"What's going on?" she asked.

Juan Carlos directed Stone to sit next to Gina in an empty chair, then slipped into host mode. "Gina, tell us about your team dance tonight."

Gina smiled for the camera without even sparing Stone a glance. "We've teamed up with Lauren and Kevin to dance to a medley of songs by my absolute favorite singer, Melissa Mendez, also known as Meli."

Juan Carlos grinned. "Gina, we've got a big surprise for you tonight. And for our viewers at home."

Gina's jaw fell open. Eyes wide, she gripped the armrests of her chair. "Don't play with me, Juan Carlos. Is it what I think it is?"

"Depends. What do you think it is?"

Gina's hands flew to her face, covering her mouth. "Is she coming *here*?"

With a nod, Juan Carlos faced the camera. "That's right. Actress and international singing sensation Meli is joining us as a guest judge tonight."

Gina screamed.

Apparently, it was the exact reaction they wanted. Juan Carlos rattled off some more info, then he and the camera crew filed out.

When they were gone, Gina turned to Stone and grabbed his

hands. Her eyes were wide as saucers, and she bared her teeth in an excited grimace.

"Stone." She squeezed his fingers. "This is, like, the most nervous and excited I have ever been on this show. Meli is my idol." Her chest rose and fell sharply.

Stone frowned. "Gina, are you hyperventilating?"

She struggled to take a deep breath. Tried again. Shook her head. "I think so?"

One of the makeup artists passed her a bottle of water.

"You meet celebrities all the time," Stone pointed out. "You're a pro at this."

"She's my *idol,* Stone! My idol. I wanted to *be* her when I grew up. I still do." Gina nearly spilled the water when she opened it. "Wait, they always say never to meet your idols."

"They who?"

"I don't know. They." She waved her free hand in the air. "I have to call my mom. And my sister. And Tash."

"Natasha is backstage, walking distance from here."

"I don't care, I'm still calling her." Gina shot him a glare. "You're not comprehending the magnitude of this news."

She was acting strange, but there were too many people around for him to address it, and he didn't want to be a buzzkill. He got to his feet. "Why don't I go find Natasha and send her over?"

"Yes. Do that. I'm calling my mother." Gina held the phone to her ear. "Ma? Ay Dios mío. No vas a creer esto."

She turned her back on him, continuing to speak to her mother in Spanish. He waited a moment, then left.

Stress, that was all it was. With his injury, two dances to learn, and extra dancers involved, rehearsals had been exhausting and they'd hardly had a moment alone.

He missed her, though. And he didn't know how to tell her.

Gina never got stage fright. Tonight, knowing that she was going to dance to Meli's songs *in front of her* made Gina jittery as all hell.

She put a hand on her stomach, left bare by the lime green samba costume. "I'm going to throw up."

"No, you're not." Natasha scrolled through her phone. "Oh snap, here's another one."

Gina waved her away. Natasha was looking for tabloid stories about Gina visiting Stone at the hotel. The photos were all over the Internet, attached to stories that were rampant with speculation, including one that suggested they'd had a secret wedding. Fortunately, Donna had agreed to leave it out of the behind-the-scenes package—they had enough footage with Stone's fall and Gina freaking out over Meli—and the publicity department's spin had dispelled most of the rumors. Had Stone not been injured, the story would have been ten times worse. For now, Natasha was the only one who knew for sure that Gina and Stone were hooking up.

It felt weird to call it that, but "hooking up" had thus far been the extent of Gina's romantic relationships. She didn't *want* anything more than that, and with good reason.

Getting caught made her realize she was playing with fire, and not only with her career. As much as she'd loved being skin to skin with Stone, it had been a risky move, even with the birth control pill and Plan B.

She also couldn't deny her growing emotional attachment to him. But he'd been abundantly clear that when his time on *The Dance Off* was over, he was going back to Alaska. If she didn't want to get burned, she had to back off.

This week had been easy. Between the two dances and extra dance partners, they'd barely had a second alone. In her downtime, Gina told her agent to book her more interviews and auditions. She hadn't been alone with Stone since spending the night at his hotel.

She missed the hell out of him. The sex, but also the companionship. And it pissed her off that he made her realize how lonely she'd been before he lumbered into her life.

No, that wasn't fair. He was surprisingly graceful for such a large man, as evidenced by their progress in the show.

Natasha tapped her phone. "This one says you're running away to Alaska together."

Gina scoffed. "Like that would ever happen. Me, in Alaska? That's nonsense."

"Why, too many bears?" Stone asked, coming up behind her.

She jumped. Shit. She wouldn't have said that if she'd known he was there. He loved Alaska, and she didn't want to make him feel bad by disparaging it.

"Even one bear is too many." She kept her voice light. "Come on, let's practice that threesome samba roll one more time before we go out."

Dancing kept her mind off Stone, off the paparazzi, and most importantly, off her impending face-to-face with Meli.

When it was their turn, they went out and did the dance. The choreography was simple—lots of ballroom samba content paired with a fun song and Stone's improved footwork. Gina and Natasha had danced together for years, and Stone was comfortable with both women. He sold the hell out of the performance.

The second the dance was over, Gina patted his shoulder. "I think that was the best you've ever danced it."

"I knew it was important to you." Putting his arms around both women—something he never would have done two months ago—Stone walked them over to get their scores.

His support—and the push toward the judges' table—was necessary, as Gina was having trouble catching her breath. Meli, looking perfect and polished in a silver gown, sat right between Chad Silver and Mariah Valentino. Meli's brown hair hung in loose waves and her pleasant smile was camera-ready.

"Stay cool, G," Natasha said under her breath.

"I'm cool."

Gina wasn't cool, not at all. But she could fake it.

Meli was everything Gina had ever aspired to be. She'd done it—moved out of the Bronx, made a career for herself, and achieved fame and fortune, most of it on her own terms.

Sure, she'd been divorced four times, but that had never registered for Gina before. Why was she thinking of it now?

Juan Carlos stepped in with his microphone. He made some complimentary, family-friendly jokes about their sexy samba, but Gina couldn't take her eyes off Meli.

Until Juan Carlos stuck that damned mic in her face and said, "Gina, it's no secret you're a huge Meli fan. What's it like for you to be face-to-face with your role model?"

"Um . . ." Gina swallowed hard. "I'm speechless."

It was one of her publicist's tricks. In a difficult interview, claim to be speechless or shocked until you could collect your thoughts.

Juan Carlos laughed and addressed the judges. "Meli, since you're our special guest judge, let's hear from you."

A fine trembling took over Gina's body as Meli turned to her with a kind smile, and she was grateful for Stone's presence at her side. They were sweaty and overheated, but his strength and familiar scent calmed her. Behind Stone's back, Tash dug her nails into Gina's palm. The sharp pain snapped Gina out of her thoughts and helped her focus.

"First of all," Meli began, "as a fellow Nuyorican, I'm so proud of you both for making it this far in your careers."

Gina bit down on her bottom lip and tried not to cry.

"I loved the dance," Meli went on. "You balanced the content and the third partner masterfully. Stone, I never would have thought you'd be able to pull off a samba, but you killed it."

"I had great teachers," Stone said into Juan Carlos's mic.

Juan Carlos said something, but Gina didn't hear it.

Meli was proud of her.

In the Sparkle Parlor, Reggie pressed her to say more about meeting Meli, but Gina trotted out "I'm still in shock" and Reggie let it drop. They got their score—ninety-five percent average, including perfect scores from Meli and Dimitri—and praised Natasha for her help during the week, before running off to change for the team dance.

Gina was flying so high, she didn't even interfere when Lauren felt Stone up outside the wardrobe room. Kevin stepped in and made an easy joke, which allowed Stone the opportunity to get away.

"The woman has hands like an octopus," Stone complained once a stage manager had ferried Lauren and Kevin away. "They're everywhere."

"I met Meli." Gina couldn't shift gears enough to be jealous. "I feel like I'm dreaming."

"Gina!" Jordy came running over, baseball cap askew. He sounded frantic. "Heads up. Donna included the tabloid shots of you two at the hotel in the behind-the-scenes package."

"*What?*" Gina froze, her mouth hanging open. "She said she wouldn't."

"You know Donna."

Fucking. Donna.

Gina sucked in a breath, but couldn't seem to let it out again except in short gasps. Stone patted her back, and she coughed.

"Um, thanks for letting me know, Jordy."

"Why weren't either of us asked to comment on it?" Stone narrowed his eyes at Jordy, who shrugged.

"My guess is it was a last-minute decision to add it in, maybe once she knew Meli would be here." The field producer threw up his hands. "I don't know. It's not the kind of thing we usually include. I tried to fight her on it, but she pulled rank. I figured I should let you know so you don't blow the dance."

"Thanks, Jordy." When he ran off, Gina turned to Stone. "Fuck."

He rubbed her arms through the stretchy black fabric of her costume. "Is it that bad? All they have are some photos of us in a parking lot."

"Yes, it's bad. I don't need everyone thinking we're sleeping together."

He blinked. "We *are*."

"My family doesn't know that," she snapped, getting riled up. "My coworkers don't need to know. Neither do the millions of people who watch this show. Plenty of them don't keep up with the gossip, but plenty do, and some of them might look down on me for it and not vote."

Stone pinched the bridge of his nose. "This is so complicated."

"I *know*. It's why I don't fuck my coworkers."

He reared back like she'd slapped him. Her stomach plummeted at the look of shocked hurt on his face.

"Oh god. I'm sorry." She threw her arms around his waist and hugged him tight, not surprised that he remained stiff. "I didn't— I'm not mad at you. And you don't deserve to have me snapping at you. I'm sorry, Stone."

After what seemed like an eternity, his arms came up and he returned the hug.

"If anything, they're going to show it after the clip of us falling," Stone said in a quiet voice. "They've got lots of footage of me saying how scared I was that I had dropped you. When Reggie and Juan Carlos ask us about it later, we'll say you were checking on me."

"That's how I told Donna to spin it after it happened."

He leaned back to frown at her. "You did? When?"

"I went to see her right after I left you that morning."

His mouth flattened into a thin line. "I wish you'd involved me in this decision."

"I had to get to her quickly, before the gossip sites influenced her." She blew out a breath and crossed her arms. "Some of them are saying we're secretly married."

A PA ran over to them, out of breath. "I have a message from Jordy. He said it's taken care of, and you owe him."

Gina's pulse thudded. "What?" When the young woman began to repeat herself, Gina waved a hand to stop her. "No, I heard you. He fixed the footage?"

The PA shrugged. "Sorry, that was all he told me."

Nodding, Gina murmured her thanks. The adrenaline roller coaster and the havoc this evening had played on her emotions left her exhausted, but she still had one more dance, and it had to be perfect.

"Well, that's taken care of," Stone said in a mild voice.

"Yeah." Gina glanced around, but there were too many people here for what she had in mind. Grabbing Stone's hand, she pulled him down the hallway to the loading dock where people snuck out to smoke.

For once, it was empty. The second the door closed behind them, she grabbed his face and yanked him down for a searing kiss.

"I miss you," she whispered against his lips. "Come over tonight? Tash always goes out after the episode taping."

He pressed his forehead to hers and closed his eyes. A second later, he nodded. "Okay."

"I know we have things to talk about." She kissed him again. "Now's not the time or place. But we'll talk. I promise."

He raised an eyebrow. "Sounds ominous."

She let out a desperate laugh. "It's not. This week has fucked with my emotions. I can't sort them all out."

He kissed the top of her head and reached for the door. "We'll do it together."

Twenty-Four

The four members of Team Ice Cold stood in the dark in the middle of the ballroom, waiting for the commercial break to end. The audience was hushed, excited to see the final team dance. Just a few yards away, Meli sat at the judges' table.

As soon as the first bars of music played, Gina's mind cleared. As always, the dance took over, washing away all her hopes and fears about Meli, *The Dance Off*, and Stone.

The beat dropped. Team Ice Cold bopped around in sync, spinning and sliding. Then they launched into the lifts, leading up to the final move—the throw.

Since Stone was so strong, and Lauren was used to flying through the air on skates, Kevin and Gina had choreographed a routine that combined acrobatics, Latin dance moves, and hip-hop to go with Meli's most famous club songs.

Gina and Lauren spun out from the guys, danced a few steps together, and swapped partners. Kevin lifted Gina, Stone lifted Lauren, and right before the song ended, they tossed the women to each other.

It wasn't a difficult throw. They hadn't had time to practice anything more impressive. But in mid-air, Lauren and Gina high-fived.

Their guys caught them, spun them in a circle, and they all landed in a triumphant pose.

Gina was proud of their dance. Lauren was an asshole backstage, but a professional as soon as she hit the dance floor. And Stone had worked harder than ever this week to learn both dances and make up for losing time to his injury.

This time, Gina was prepared to hear Meli's critique.

"I loved it." Meli tossed her notes down on the table. "I could go on about the details—you guys nailed the musicality and the vibe of the music, and took it to the next level—but really, I just loved it. I thought it was perfect. And I'm so impressed. I could never do lifts like that!"

Gina almost passed out. Only Stone squeezing her shoulders reminded her to breathe.

Team Ice Cold received a perfect score.

During the elimination, Gina couldn't stop grinning.

"You're supposed to look worried," Stone whispered in her ear.

"I can't. Meli gave us two hundreds. Nothing can ruin this night."

Rick Carruthers ended up leaving at the end of the episode. Gina was sorry to see him go—not as sorry as Stone, though—and they hugged him at the end.

But then she saw Meli rounding the judges' table and heading straight for her. Her pulse pounded, and she stepped aside to greet her idol.

They were the same height, which surprised Gina. Meli had always seemed taller in the movies.

"Gina, I want to say what a pleasure it was to see you dance tonight." Meli leaned in to give Gina a kiss on the cheek. She smelled like roses. "I have to run to catch a flight, but I'll be in touch. Be well."

"Thank you." Gina returned Meli's wave, stunned.

I'll be in touch. What the hell did that mean?

Gina met Stone's eyes over the crowd of dancers surrounding Rick and his partner, Mila. The heat was back in Stone's gaze. Tonight, they would talk out whatever was between them.

The prospect terrified her. She didn't want anything serious, didn't want to talk about her feelings or relationship fears.

But he was right. He deserved to have his say, and to know why she'd pulled away.

The thought of being close to him again filled her with warm, delicious feelings. She wanted him. She missed him. And maybe having him in her bed again, being close to him, being held by him, would be worth the discomfort of baring her heart.

Y ou want to tell me why you've been avoiding me all week?" Gina sat next to Stone on the edge of her bed, facing him. She still wore her hair extensions and full-face makeup from filming. Hell, Stone was probably still wearing makeup, too. He held himself stiffly, his lips pressed into a flat line.

She fiddled with the quilting on her blanket. This was the last thing she wanted to be talking about. It would be so much easier if she could say she was over him, that it had been a fun fling, but it was time to get back to business.

It wasn't true, though. Even now, with all her doubts piling in, she still wanted him. Not just for fun, or for sex, but for more. For the way he listened to her and respected her. For the way his strong fingers found all the knots in her back muscles and brought her relief, simply because he wanted to help. For the way he made her laugh with his moments of unexpected silliness.

Deep longing churned her insides, made her want to lean toward him until she fell into his arms. Maybe then the unrelenting yearning would cease.

But then what would happen when he left?

He was waiting for an answer, his jaw set and eyes wary.

She swallowed hard and told him the truth. "You scare the shit out of me."

His lips quirked. "Ditto."

With a groan, she gave in and closed the distance between them, cuddling into his embrace. "What do we do? Where do we go from here?"

What do I do when you're gone? She didn't say it, though. It would reveal too much, and she wasn't ready to think that far ahead.

He held her against his chest and rubbed her back with his big, rough hands. Everything about him was big and rough, until you realized he was the sweetest, most caring man you could ever hope to meet.

"We keep trying to win," he said. "The rest of this . . . we'll figure it out. We have time."

They didn't, though. It was only a matter of weeks before the season ended, and then he'd be leaving. What more was there to figure out?

She lifted her head, zeroing in on his lips. "Stone?"

His hand stilled on her back. "Yeah?"

"I don't want to talk." She crushed her mouth to his, loving how his arms banded around her. She groaned as his tongue swept into her mouth.

They tipped sideways onto the bed, tugging at each other's clothing.

"Stone, I need you. *Now.*"

It was the most she was willing to admit. Need—physical need— was something she was comfortable with. The rest of it? Feelings and shit? They got in the way, made things messy.

Gina broke the kiss, panting. "Damn. We haven't showered yet."

Stone gave her an incredulous look. "Who cares?"

She blinked. "Oh. I guess you're right. Sorry, I don't usually date dancers."

"I'm not a dancer, remember? I'm *industry adjacent.*" He dragged his tongue down her neck, pressed kisses over her chest until he reached her cleavage. "Anyway, sweat doesn't bother me. I like you sweaty, clean, dressed, undressed . . ." He yanked off her shirt and bra. "I just like you."

Emotion overwhelmed her. She shoved it back as he pulled down her leggings. Of course he'd say something like that when she was trying to lock her feelings away in a box where they couldn't interfere.

"Never figured you for a romantic," she said under her breath in an attempt to break the tension.

"I'm full of surprises." He grabbed the back of his T-shirt and drew it over his head.

"Could barely get two words out of you in the beginning that weren't a sigh or a complaint."

"What I wanted to say wouldn't have been appropriate." He pressed her thighs apart and stroked her with his fingertips. "You're already wet."

"I know." She dove into his lap and tugged at his shorts. "Off."

Once they were both completely naked, he sat on the edge of the bed.

"How do you want to do it?" she asked.

"You'll see." His sexy smile made her skin tingle and her core clench with need. He patted his lap. "Have a seat."

She went to straddle him, then noticed he faced her closet. The closet, whose sliding doors were floor to ceiling mirrors. "Oh. I do see."

He nodded, and she positioned herself on his lap, facing their reflection in the mirror. He gripped her hips and guided her onto his cock. She hissed as he sank inside, stretching her in the delicious way she'd come to crave. His heat seared into her, lighting her up from within.

Their reflections watched them move. He wrapped an arm around her waist to take more of her weight and spread their legs wide. In the mirror, his thick rod could be seen disappearing inside her.

So. Fucking. Sexy.

He rocked his hips, the move sending shock waves through her body. Shivering, she bore down on him, increasing the pace. Their reflections matched their movements. His cock slid in and out of her, the image mesmerizing her. She told him with her body what she couldn't put into words.

I want you. I need you. Don't leave me.

Behind her, Stone groaned and pressed his face into the curve of her neck. Their eyes met in the mirror. Holding her gaze, his hand dipped down and pressed on her clit. She almost leaped off his lap as fire lanced through her veins.

"Yes. Touch me. Fuck me. *Yes.*"

"Gina." His voice was a growl, the syllables yanked from somewhere deep within him. "You're killing me."

"Don't stop." A note of pleading infused her tone. Tingles shot through her. "Please, Stone. Don't stop."

"More?"

"God, yes. More. *More.*"

He gave it to her. Hard. Fast. He was consuming her from the inside out. His cock drove into her, relentless and demanding, radiating pleasure through her limbs. His arms supported her, pinning her to his lap and holding her up when she lost her strength. His hips pumped, nailing her like their lives depended on it. He surrounded her, invaded her, and she only wanted *more.*

It would never be enough. She wanted *forever.*

Full, intense pressure in her pussy distracted her, and she surrendered to it. Pleasure mounted. Passion spiked. She dug her nails into his thighs, gritted her teeth, and gave him everything she had to give, calling out his name as she came.

Stone flipped her over onto the bed. She landed facedown, but didn't move. In the aftermath, her feelings were raw and bare. She wanted him so much. But she couldn't have him. Not for real, not forever. She had to be careful.

She flapped a hand at him before he could enter her again. "Condom."

He paused. "What?" His voice sounded strangled.

"Condom. We're playing with fire."

He didn't answer. Instead, there was the familiar sound of her bedside drawer being yanked open. Frantic rummaging, a muttered curse, a rip of foil, and then he was back on top of her, pushing one of her knees up and sliding into her from behind.

It was the smallest of barriers, and it broke her heart to ask for it. To need it between them, for practical reasons and emotional ones.

He started fucking her again. From this angle, he went so deep, he wrung a breathy cry from her with each thrust. Her body no longer felt like her own. It was his, and hers, just as his body was now his and hers. She was a mass of pure sensation, and she couldn't have moved if she wanted to.

His thrusts took on a shorter, harder rhythm. The fingers of one hand dug into her hip while the other roughly caressed her ass.

"God, Gina," he ground out. "I'm—fuck. You're—damn it. I'm coming."

In the back of her mind, she wanted to know what he was going to say. But her own body was lighting up, the intense drive of his cock pushing her over the edge again. Time enough for talk later.

"Me, too." The words burst out of her in a gasp. "Don't stop!"

He growled. "Never."

His hips slammed, and her orgasm ripped through her. Her limbs shook. Her inner walls spasmed. She pressed her face into the mattress and cried out as it all became too much.

So much. He was just so much. He would be the end of her.

He groaned, his body tensing. A second later, he planted a hand on the bed. The tips of his hair brushed her shoulder blades and then he crashed down beside her. When he pulled her against him, she cuddled closer.

Snuggling his face into her neck, he whispered, "Don't shut me out, Gina. We can figure it all out together."

She exhaled. As hard as she'd tried to close herself off to him, this night had wrung her out, demolished her defenses, and left her heart open. Still, she wanted to believe him, to think they could have some kind of future.

Twining her fingers with his, she nodded. "Together."

But at what cost?

Twenty-Five

When the little plane touched down in the small coastal town on Alaska's panhandle that served as home base for the *Living Wild* crew, Stone felt lighter than he had in months. Exiting right onto the tarmac, he stopped and took a big, deep breath, filling his lungs with clean, crisp Alaskan air. It was cooler than Los Angeles, but June in Alaska was gorgeous.

He turned to help Gina down the steps. The rest of the production crew filed out behind her.

"You all right there?" he asked.

"I like planes." She sent Jordy a side-eye glare. "*Not* seaplanes."

Jordy threw up his hands. "We're taking the helicopter this time. Relax."

A bunch of the *Living Wild* crew waited to escort them to the Glacier Valley Inn, and then to Nielson HQ, where Gina would finally meet Stone's family to film clips for the semifinals episode.

As much as Stone loved his family, he didn't want Gina to meet them. Not there, not on camera, not as these personas they'd crafted for television. Sometimes, he didn't even know who they really were anymore.

Miguel, the *Living Wild* producer, pulled Stone aside. "Do any of them know?"

Stone shook his head.

"Good." Miguel clapped him on the back. "Keep it that way."

A sense of unease descended like a cloud. It was a mistake to bring Gina here. It had been a mistake the first time, but he hadn't had any say in it then. This time, Stone should have insisted. Maybe a couple of his siblings could have flown to LA for the semifinals footage instead. Then *Living Wild* could have done a special episode with it, too. *Living Wild in Los Angeles,* or something.

Perhaps his own selfishness had made him think this was a good idea. He'd missed Alaska, and he wanted Gina to see it the way he saw it, without the surprises or gimmicks from her last trip. He'd wanted to show her the place he loved, like when she'd taken him for a tour of Central Park.

Now that they were here, those desires seemed naïve. Gina was gorgeous and spirited, strong and determined. But she wasn't made for Alaska. She wanted things he'd never be able to give her, and the kind of life that was impossible here. He could never ask her to move here with him, and all he wanted was to come back home.

And Gina. Yes, he wanted Gina, too. Except there was no way he could have both.

She looked up like she felt his eyes on her, and smiled. So sweet. But not for him.

What the hell was wrong with him? He should be able to give up on his stupid dream of living here on his own terms. But Alaska was in his blood, had invaded him to the point where he was hooked on it. Even now, after being back for only a matter of minutes, he soaked in the air, the scenery, the sense of calm. He'd known LA had depleted him, he just hadn't realized how much.

The Dance Off gave him his own room at the Glacier Valley Inn. It was weird, since a different room already held the rest of his belongings, but he couldn't tell the producers that. Harry, one of the inn's owners, caught Stone coming out of his new room and gave a friendly wave. Stone froze, then checked to make sure no one from *The Dance Off* was around.

"Hey, Stone," Harry said, coming over. He was a stocky man in his sixties with tan skin, an easy smile, and short-cropped gray hair. "Welcome back. Marnie and I have been voting for you. Glad to see you doing so well."

Stone shook the other man's hand. "Thanks, Harry. Means a lot."

At that moment, Gina exited her room down the hall. She stopped when she saw them.

Harry's gaze lit up. "Oh, there's Gina. I hope you two won't mind posing for a picture later. Marnie's down at the store, but I know she'll be real happy to see you both."

"It would be our pleasure." Gina gave Harry a brilliant smile, but when he wasn't looking, she raised an eyebrow at Stone.

Stone rushed to make introductions before Harry could blow his cover. "Harry and his wife Marnie own the inn. My family has known them a long time, and they're fans of *The Dance Off*."

"We vote for you two every week," Harry said again, a note of pride in his voice.

"Oh, thank you." Gina gave Harry a one-armed hug. "I'd love to meet your wife when she's back."

"We'll do that. Bye now." Harry waved and left.

Gina gave Stone a curious look. "Why do you look so tense?"

"Do I?" He stretched his shoulders. He hadn't even noticed the tension that had settled into his upper back and neck. As much as he loved Alaska, worrying about spilling the beans in front of Gina or the rest of *The Dance Off*'s crew had him on edge. "Weird to be back."

"You must be excited to see your family again."

"I am."

"Then why are you scowling?" She pressed her fingers between his eyebrows and rubbed the crease.

"It will be good to see them, of course. It was strange being away." Shit. He was back to sounding like a robot, like he did every time someone asked about his family.

"But . . . ?"

He worked his jaw back and forth. What was it? "It feels different. I don't know how to explain."

"Well, when you figure it out, I'm all ears." She tugged on her earlobes and gave him a silly, adorable grin. "You've listened to me blather on about my family often enough. The least I can do is return the favor."

Film crews be damned. The producers in the lounge could wait.

Stone pulled Gina in for a long kiss. The melding of two worlds—his life in Alaska, and his routine with Gina and their crew—was throwing him off-kilter, but when he kissed her, the ground steadied beneath his feet. His heart settled into a comfortable, familiar rhythm, like they were in sync.

She broke the kiss first, wagging her finger at him like he'd been naughty. "Nowhere we might get caught," she said, reminding him of one of her rules.

She had so many rules. He liked that about her, but he also wanted to tempt her to break them.

She swiped a thumb over his mouth, probably to wipe off her lipstick. "The crew is waiting."

They headed down the hallway, but Gina stopped before they reached the end.

"Stone?"

He paused. "Yeah?"

"Does your family know about us?"

Her eyebrows were drawn together, and she looked like she'd be pissed if the answer was yes.

"No. I haven't told any of them."

"Oh, good." The relief that infused her features made his chest hurt. The secrets were piling up. Don't tell Gina and *The Dance Off* that *Living Wild* was a fraud. Don't tell the other dancers or his family that he and Gina were an item. Don't let the media find out *anything,* even when people were constantly sticking microphones in his face and asking questions purposely designed to throw him off-guard. It was all getting mixed up in his head and being here, back in the place that could blow it all, was making him jumpy.

Then Gina smiled, and the tension eased. Sometimes he thought her smile was the only real thing in his life.

"Come on," she said. "Let's go meet them."

S tone's anxiety deepened as they approached Nielson HQ. Gina wore hiking boots this time, and they took the clearer path, but he still stayed close.

"It would suck if you busted an ankle," he pointed out.

She gave him a half-smile. "Jordy said the same thing the first time I came here."

Jordy stopped them before they entered the clearing to give them their instructions.

"Gina, we're going to introduce you to the Nielsons in groups. There are too many of them for the cameras to catch everything. Make sure the cameras can get your reactions. Stone, you'll handle introductions. Act like we aren't here, and you don't know your parents are waiting."

The cameras panned out, and Jordy gave them the go-ahead.

Stone's stomach clenched as it finally hit that he was bringing the woman he loved to meet his parents. On *camera*. God, could his life get any weirder? He forced a smile onto his face and put an arm around Gina, leading her forward.

A chill raced down his spine as he spotted Jimmy and Pepper standing in front of the big house they'd built in season two. Shit. All this time he'd only thought about hiding the truth about the Nielsons from Gina and *The Dance Off*'s producers. Keeping his relationship with Gina hidden from their castmates was hard, but hiding it from his mom? The woman read him like an open book. She'd know, and she'd have questions, and then Gina was going to kill him.

Each step amplified his terror. His parents waited, beaming big smiles. Gina returned their smiles with a wide, toothy grin of her own.

Stone's teeth were bared, but he was positive the footage would show more of a grimace than a grin. He caught Jordy's hand signal. Crap, he was supposed to say his lines. He hated this shit.

"Mom, Pop, I'd like you to meet my dance partner, Gina. Gina, my mom, Pepper, and my father, Jimmy."

His mother spoke first. "Gina, we're so happy to meet you."

"Likewise, Mrs. Nielson." Gina took Pepper's hands and leaned in to kiss her cheek. "You've raised quite the dancer."

Pepper giggled. "Please, call me Pepper. We've gone into town every Monday to watch you two dance, and it's been such a treat."

Jimmy reached out to shake Gina's hand, but she gave him a kiss on the cheek, too. "Nice to meet you, Mr. Nielson."

"Oh, Gina, I know we're just meeting for the first time, but I hope you'll call me Jimmy. As you can see, we don't stand on ceremony around here. Besides, we feel like we know you, thanks to the show and the few times Stone has called home."

Stone ducked his head. It was true. He hadn't called as much as he'd planned. With his family's filming schedule and his own rehearsal schedule, it was hard to find times to connect.

His mother squeezed his hands, and his father gave him a slap on the back.

"Real proud of you, son," Jimmy said in a gruff voice. "Never knew you had those moves in you."

"Thanks, Pop." Setting aside the fact that his father would only ever think to compliment him on camera, Stone made a show of looking around. "Where are the others?"

"Oh, they went off in the boat."

Off in the boat meant they were hiding off-camera somewhere until they could be brought in for filming.

Jimmy continued. "They should be back soon. Gina, would you like a tour of Nielson HQ? It ain't much, but it's our humble little slice of freedom."

"I'd love one."

Pepper led Gina toward the main house, which held beds for Pepper, Jimmy, and the girls. Stone followed along with his father. They stayed quiet, so as not to create crosstalk and interfere in the audio recording while Pepper took Gina through each of the rooms, telling her how they'd built it, and some of the setbacks they'd run into. Most of it had been filmed, so it would give the editors opportunities to insert past footage.

Miguel beckoned Stone and Jimmy outside. They followed him over to the little house Stone shared with Reed, waiting while Miguel organized the cameras.

Jimmy pulled out a cigarette and lit up. He took a long drag, then tipped his head back and blew a smoke ring. "How's it really going, son?"

Stone shrugged. He and his father didn't talk much. Aside from being "the quiet one," Stone just didn't see eye to eye with Jimmy on a lot of things. And being one of seven kids, they hadn't spent a ton of time together that wasn't focused on shit like hunting or building.

Jimmy put on a good show for the cameras, but he wasn't big on talking about feelings.

"I didn't think you'd last so long." Jimmy dragged on the cigarette. "Thought you'd be back here within the month."

Nice to know his father had confidence in him. "Yeah, who knew?"

"My son, a dancer." Jimmy shook his head. "Your sisters are thrilled. Your brothers are jealous. Reed and Wolf want to go on next season."

"Maybe *Living Wild* and *The Dance Off* can do a crossover. Hell, all nine of us can fill out the cast on our own." The joke was out before Stone even thought about it, and strange, because he and his father didn't have that kind of rapport.

Jimmy let out a bark of laughter. "Wouldn't that be something? We could all compete to see who's the best dancer in the family."

Stone gave a half-smile. "It's me."

"Miguel is gonna be pissed he missed this. We should say it all again on camera."

Biting back a sigh, Stone nodded. This was his life. Finally have a real moment of connection with his father, then repeat it back like a parrot for the cameras. Totally fucking normal.

Miguel came back over. "Let's get some footage of you two talking about the past couple months."

Stone shoved his hands into his jacket pockets. "Like what, specifically?"

"Talk about the challenges," Miguel suggested.

"We just made a great joke about all the Nielsons going on the dancing show," Jimmy said, dropping his cigarette and stubbing it out with his heel. "We'll tell it again."

A PA darted in to grab the cigarette butt from the ground with a tissue. Miguel rolled his eyes but gave them the go-ahead.

Jimmy turned to Stone, immediately "on." He'd taken to acting better than any of them. Better than Stone had, certainly.

"Son, I can't tell you how much you've been missed," Jimmy said, patting Stone's shoulder. "You are a sight for sore eyes."

"I've missed this place," Stone admitted. As he said the words, they rang false. He had missed being home, but it was less true now than it had been in April. The more time he spent with Gina, the more at home he felt, even though LA was still an odd fit for him. It might have been different if he hadn't had the show to occupy his time, though.

Besides, Nielson HQ wasn't technically "home."

"Can't imagine Los Angeles can hold a candle to what we've got here in Alaska." Jimmy spread his arms wide and took a deep breath. "Smell the free—"

A racking cough interrupted his catchphrase. Years of smoking had left Jimmy with a cough that often ruined takes. When it didn't appear inclined to subside, Stone thumped his father on the back. Jimmy spat on the ground, Miguel rolled his eyes again, and they continued.

Jimmy picked right back up where he left off, though he threw his arms out with less vigor than before. "Smell the freedom!"

Stone's shoulder muscles tensed in annoyance.

This. Sucked. If he could just get through the next few hours, he could get back to what now passed for normal in his life: learning to dance.

Jimmy went off to charm Gina, and Pepper came over to stand at Stone's side.

"So, Stone, what's going on with you and Gina?" his mother asked, crossing her arms.

Shit. No, his mother had not just said that on camera. Except he turned to see her smiling at him, with no fewer than three cameras surrounding them.

Gina was going to flip out.

"We're dance partners." His voice came out a low rumble, edging toward a growl.

Pepper waved a hand at him, dismissing his quick excuse. "Stone, I'm not stupid. I know there's something between you two. You can tell me."

He shrugged. "Nothing to tell."

God, he was *such* a terrible liar.

Miguel stepped in. "The girls are on their way for the next scene."

Stone took the opportunity to get away from his mother, but this exchange was going to end up in the behind-the-scenes package, he just knew it.

Maybe it wouldn't, though. Maybe there would be enough other useful footage. Maybe one of his brothers would do something so outrageous and embarrassing, that would be the focus, instead.

He could hope. And in the meantime, he wasn't going to tell Gina until he knew it was a problem.

Twenty-Six

The next morning, Stone woke to a torrential downpour. He still had a couple hours before they were supposed to leave, so he packed his suitcase and went to the inn's tiny gym for a workout.

Once he was back in his own room, he took a quick shower. As he was toweling off his hair, someone knocked on the door.

"Who is it?" If it was Jordy, he could come back later.

"It's me."

Gina.

Stone opened the door for her. Her eyes went wide at the sight of him, wearing nothing but a skimpy towel around his hips, and her gaze traveled down the length of his body. Warmth flooded through him at her perusal.

"Can I help you?" he asked in a low voice.

She snapped her mouth shut and met his eyes. "Um . . ."

He raised an eyebrow, amused at her reaction.

"I came here to tell you something."

"Okay."

"I can't remember what it was now—oh!" She snapped her fingers. "We're stuck here. Too much rain, tiny airplane can't fly in it, and even if it could, I won't chance it. So, we're stuck. Here." She swallowed audibly and glanced down at his hard-on tenting the wet towel.

"Come in before someone sees you."

She hesitated, then stepped inside.

The second the door was shut, she ripped away his towel. A chuckle rumbled through him, cut short when she dropped to her knees and took his dick into her mouth.

Ho-ly shiiiiiit.

The sight of her pursed lips swallowing his cock sent a shiver down his back. His skin erupted in goosebumps.

She slid off him with a *pop* and tilted her head. "You cold?"

"No." He sank his fingers into her hair, which was twisted up in a messy bun. "It's you. You make me shiver."

Her lips, wet and glistening, pulled to the side in a smirk. "Good. You do the same to me." Then she opened her mouth and drew him in once again.

Throwing back his head, he gave himself over to the surprise blow job. Sensation streaked through him like lightning, making his toes curl and his pulse pound in this throat. When she cupped his balls with one hand and jerked him off with the other, he locked his knees to keep from falling over.

His worries melted away, replaced by the hope that Gina's willingness to set aside her rules for him would soon extend to going public with their relationship. He was tired of hiding, tired of pretending he didn't feel the way he did. He loved her, and he didn't want to lie about it anymore.

She smiled up at him, sweet and sexy and utterly perfect. Stone gritted his teeth, and his body tightened, the orgasm coming out of nowhere. Quick as a wink, Gina clamped her mouth over the tip and swallowed.

Once she'd drained him dry, his legs finally gave out. Staggering to the bed, he fell heavily onto the edge and sat for a while, catching his breath. Gina sat beside him, brushing his hair away from his face before putting her lips next to his ear.

"Good morning, Stone."

He huffed out a laugh and swung an arm around her. "It sure is." When she curled up against his side, he kissed the top of her head. "We're stuck here, huh?"

She sighed. "Yeah, but we can't laze around in bed all day, as nice as that would be. This place has a party room. They're putting down the dance floor so we can practice, but since it's such a low-budget affair Jordy isn't even going to bother filming it. He's giving everyone else the day off."

"Practicing without cameras?" Images of dancing naked with Gina flitted through his mind. "That could be fun."

She narrowed her eyes at him. "We still need to work. We have two dances to perfect for the semifinals."

"We will." He got to his feet and snatched the discarded towel from the floor. "Don't worry, Gina. I'll get you into the finals."

She smiled but didn't answer.

Stone entered the Glacier Valley Inn's small event room to find Gina staring out the big windows, which offered a view of the rain pelting the inlet. Tall trees swayed in the strong wind and clouds crowded the sky.

"I do see why you love it here," Gina said, glancing over her shoulder at him. "It's beautiful, even like this."

"More so when you're here." He came up behind her and nuzzled his face in her hair.

"You're going to give me a toothache being that sweet." Smiling, she took his hand and led him to the twenty-by-twenty dance floor laid out over the carpet.

"What did you think of my family?" he asked before she could launch into an explanation of their jazz routine.

"I liked them," she said. "I also have a big family. Even though I only have two siblings, I grew up with lots of cousins. Holidays and birthdays were always a mess of relatives piled into a house too small to fit us all."

"Yeah, I know a bit about what that's like."

She squinted at him. "Did all nine of you really live in that one little hut during season one?"

Shit. A direct question. He was supposed to lie. He was supposed to say, *Yes, we did, but the Nielsons stick together,* or some nonsense like that.

Except he was so tired of lying to Gina.

"Ah, no. Not really."

Her eyes widened. "No?"

He shook his head.

"Where did you stay?"

In for a penny, in for a pound. The urge to come clean welled up inside him like a tidal wave. He glanced at the door to make sure they were truly alone.

"Right here in town," he said.

Gina's hand flew to her mouth. She stared at him.

This was it. His fears come to pass. She wouldn't understand, and she'd judge him for it. Gina, who was so aligned with integrity that she wouldn't fake a relationship with him—despite really having one—even though she wanted, *needed,* to win.

"I'm sorry. I've wanted to tell you since the beginning." He was tripping over his words but couldn't stop them from tumbling out. "I couldn't, though. There are contracts, and NDAs. My family—they're counting on me. I've gotta keep this a—"

She shook her head and he shut up. Her hand dropped from her mouth, and he saw the beginnings of a smile.

"I'm just shocked because . . . this makes so much sense. All the questions I asked my TV—or Natasha—while watching episodes of *Living Wild* make sense now." Excitement shone in her gaze. "Where did you live, if not in that hut?"

He spread his arms wide. "Right here in the Glacier Valley Inn."

"Shut the front door." She let out a delighted laugh and clapped her hands. "For real?"

"Yep. It's the worst-kept secret in town."

"I love hearing behind-the-scenes gossip like this. So, wait, none of that stuff is true?"

"I mean, we stay out there sometimes, if we're filming at night. We still build and haul stuff around."

It was a relief to finally have someone know the truth, and even better that it was Gina. Stone had been so worried about her reaction, and she was handling this better than he could have expected.

She sent him a contemplative look. "I feel like I'm meeting you for the first time."

He swallowed. "I wanted to tell you. I hate lying. It's why I'm terrible at interviews. I'm scared I'm going to slip up. My family . . . the show offered a package deal. All nine Nielsons, or no show. I had to join."

"I understand." She laced her fingers behind his neck. "So, who are you, Stone Nielson? If that's even your real name."

He chuckled and rested his hands on her hips. "It is. My parents really are nature lovers, and Nielson is Swedish."

She smiled up at him. "I want to know all about you. I was watching your show to try to understand you better, but now, I can just ask."

"I feel like myself for the first time in . . . years," he admitted. "I had to cut ties with all my friends when we started the show."

Her eyebrows dipped in compassion. "That must have been hard."

"It was." He tugged on his beard. "I didn't even have this before the show started. Or the long hair."

Her eyes sparkled. "I want to see pictures."

"I have a few. Not a ton, since the fire that destroyed my family's home is a true story. I just wasn't living there at the time. I was in Juneau."

"Doing what?"

"I was an engineer for the city. I quit to join the show."

Her eyebrows rose. "Why does that sound so hot? Maybe because I'm picturing you in a toolbelt and nothing else."

He touched his forehead to hers. "That can be arranged. I do own a few toolbelts."

When her eyes went dark and dreamy, he gave in to the urge to kiss her. Telling her the truth eased the weight he'd been carrying since *Living Wild* hit TV. He and Gina were still from different worlds, and they still had a dance competition to win, but maybe, just maybe, they could figure out the mess reality television had made of their lives and find some kind of happy ending.

And maybe his mother's nosy question wouldn't end up in the behind-the-scenes package.

The truth seemed to have unlocked something in Gina, too. She kissed him hungrily and gripped handfuls of his hair. Her mouth was warm and tasted of ginger. She was desperate for him and he couldn't deny her anything. He grabbed her ass, molding her tight against him, and she moaned.

A soft noise had his eyes flicking open just in time to see the lens of a video camera disappearing before the door to the ballroom shut without a sound.

His body tensed, but Gina was still kissing him. She hadn't noticed.

In the split second that followed, Stone decided not to tell her.

Twenty-Seven

Donna's office was tiny. Stone sat on a folding chair and hunched his shoulders, trying to take up less space.

Tapping a pen on the edge of her desk, Donna raised her dark eyebrows in invitation.

Stone fought the urge to fidget. Donna's direct gaze and her silence unnerved him. But he was here for a reason. He had to find out if she knew about the kiss.

"Have you gone over the footage from Alaska yet?" he asked.

Without taking her eyes off him, she nodded. "Most of it."

Stone scratched the back of his head. A nervous tell, but he couldn't help it. "I guess you saw our rehearsal at the inn."

Again, Donna nodded. Her expression didn't change.

"Are you planning to air it?"

Now, a cold, calculating smile spread across Donna's face. "Of course I am. Jordy interfered the last time you two gave me something good."

Fuck. "Is there anything I could say to persuade you not to air it?"

"No."

"It will really upset Gina. And we were told we weren't being filmed."

"Gina knows this business. Nothing stays secret here." Donna tilted her head. "Are you going to tell her?"

That was the big question, wasn't it? The one he'd been grappling with since they'd left Alaska. There had been plenty of opportunities to come clean, but he'd convinced himself that he was wrong about what he'd seen. No point in upsetting Gina over something unconfirmed.

Now he knew the truth. Donna was going to air the footage.

If he told Gina, she'd be hurt. Sad. She'd pull away from him again, and it might affect their dancing. They were so close to the end and he wanted them to win.

"You told Gina you'll fire her if she doesn't make it to the finals."

Donna nodded. "I like Gina. She's been assigned to me since she joined the show. I want her to win. But even if she makes the finals, nothing is guaranteed."

Stone narrowed his eyes. "What would guarantee her spot next season?"

"I think you know."

"First place." He asked the question he didn't want to know the answer to. "Do you really think this footage, this storyline, will help Gina win?"

"I've thought that since the beginning. It's why we paired her with you." Donna dropped the pen onto her desk and folded her hands. "Look. I'm not the enemy here. You, Dwayne, and Twyla were my charges. I'd hoped Natasha and Dwayne would be the showmance backup if Gina refused, but Natasha's messing around with someone else on the cast, and Dwayne was never a good enough dancer to take the trophy. You're the only one left. I want you to win, to beat Lauren and Kevin. I'll never hear the end of it from Kevin's producer if he wins again."

Stone didn't care what Donna wanted. He only cared about what would help Gina. "And you think showing a clip of me kissing Gina will make us win?"

"I know it will. The viewers love a story with a happy ending. You have four dances left in the entire show. The data proves you could screw up at least one and still win, provided you have the viewer votes."

It wasn't how Gina wanted to win. But at this point, wasn't it more important to make sure she did? Her career was on the line, and that meant more to her than anything else.

Stone had started this journey for the money, and while he stood to take home a good chunk of change for winning, the money meant less to him now than Gina getting what she wanted. What she deserved.

Gina deserved to win.

Besides, Donna had the footage, and she'd already been thwarted once. She wasn't the kind of person to let it happen again.

His options were to either tell Gina about it, or not.

They still had a week left to perfect two high-intensity dances. There was nothing they could do to stop Donna, and Gina didn't need the extra pressure. She was already stressed. If a few minor paparazzi photos had thrown her into a frenzy, he couldn't imagine how actual kiss footage would affect her.

That settled it. He wouldn't tell her. Besides, she'd gone to Donna about the parking lot photos on her own, without involving him. This was the same thing.

The clock was winding down. Their time as partners would soon come to an end. Maybe having their relationship out in the open would help them be honest about it themselves, and they could figure out where they were going.

Gina would get it. She'd understand he was sparing her the stress, and trying to help them win.

Still, he left Donna's office with a sick feeling in his gut.

Stone paced while the behind-the-scenes package played before their dancer's-choice contemporary dance. After two weeks of practicing for the semifinals, he wanted them over with.

"We've never danced first before," he said in a low voice.

Gina grinned. "Sometimes it's nice to get it out of the way and enjoy watching everyone else. But we still have another dance to-night, if you want to obsess over that."

He groaned and pinched the bridge of his nose. "The stripper dance."

They'd been given a song from the movie *Boylesque*, a romantic comedy/dance musical about a group of teachers who start an all-male burlesque troupe to raise funds for their school. Stone had watched it that week and he could secretly admit it was a pretty fun movie. But he still wasn't psyched about their dance.

Gina covered her mouth to suppress a giggle. "I told you, it's *boylesque.*"

"I just never thought I'd be taking my clothes off for the delight of a room full of people."

"It's a job, just like any other."

"I know. But I'm having second thoughts about that costume."

"Don't. It looks great on you. And anyway, it's too late to change it."

On the large screen above them, they relived Gina meeting the Nielsons. Then his mother's voice echoed through the ballroom.

"What's going on with you and Gina?"

Next to him, Gina froze.

His answer came next, spoken by his image on the giant screen. "We're dance partners."

Stone's heart pounded. Maybe they'd leave it at that. Please, god, let it be left at that.

In his arms, Gina began to tremble.

The image changed: his mother, indoors at the Glacier Valley Inn, in the room where *Living Wild* filmed their interviews.

"I think there's something going on there." Pepper touched the side of her nose and gave the camera a knowing nod. "I'm his mother. I can always tell."

Gina gasped. "What—?"

"Shh. Don't watch."

Her eyes flickered in the reflected light from the screen as she stared at him. "Don't *watch*?"

On the screen, Stone's worst nightmare unfolded, the one he'd been expecting for the last two weeks. He and Gina, in the makeshift rehearsal room in the Glacier Valley Inn. Kissing.

Now, she shook in his arms, her eyes glued to the screen. When she turned to him, devastation was written all over her face.

"Stone?" Her voice was a hoarse rasp. "Did you know?"

A chill settled into his bones, and a cold sweat broke out over his skin.

He'd made the wrong choice.

If he told her the truth now, it would very likely crush whatever was budding between them. But if he lied, it would be crushed anyway.

Truth, then.

"When I spotted the camera, it was already too late. I didn't want to upset you."

She didn't reply. Just covered her eyes with her hands and took a step away from him.

"Gina—"

"Don't." She held up a hand to stop him. The other remained over her eyes, shielding her from him. "Don't say anything. I need a second."

His heart twisted, calling out for hers even as he held himself back, giving her the space she requested.

One of the stage managers approached tentatively. "Um . . . it's time."

Gina dropped her hands. Her eyes were clear, her face wiped clean of expression. She took Stone's hand and met his eyes briefly. "Let's kick this dance's ass."

They took their marks.

The music started, melancholy and dark. A man's voice, haunting and compelling, rose over it. Gina danced in the spotlight until Stone strode toward her and hauled her against him. She struggled in his arms. It was part of the choreography, but with every move they made, his heart sank further.

Gina slipped a piece of rope over his arm and threw herself out of his grasp. When they came together again, it was the same. Throughout the dance, they came together and fell apart, and each time Gina added another piece of the harness that would lift him into the air. Each rope felt like the weight of familial expectations.

Each time she ran away from him, it felt like the end.

More dancers appeared from the shadows, throwing more loops of rope around his arms and legs. They pulled, tugging him backward as he strained toward Gina, who danced in the light.

The music began its crescendo. Stone took a step with his right leg. The ropes fell away. Another step. His legs were free. When the music reached its peak, he flexed his arms and all the ropes not attached to his harness snapped.

Running across the dance floor, he leaped, and the harness lifted him. He hit his moves in midair, spinning and swinging. When his feet touched the floor, he pulled Gina to him. The ropes lifted them, and they performed the midair routine they hadn't gotten to practice as much as he would have liked.

During camera blocking, when he'd voiced his concerns—namely that Gina wouldn't be wearing a harness, and he was the only thing keeping her suspended—she had smiled warmly at him and told him three words that struck him to the core.

"I trust you."

He held her now, as they struggle-danced in the air. As close as they were physically, there was a new distance between them that hadn't been there before.

He wanted to speak, to say, "Gina, I'm sorry," but he was worried about dropping her. She was a professional and she hadn't done a step wrong through the whole dance. If he spoke, it might break the spell. It might break the brittle concentration evident in the strain around her eyes.

After all this time, and as close as they'd become, he'd gotten to know her well. She was holding it together because it was her job, because she took dance more seriously than anything else, and because this was the semifinals.

Inside, she was breaking.

I trust you, she'd said.

Not anymore.

He didn't drop her. They performed the sequence perfectly. When the ropes lowered them, the music slowed. Crouching together on the floor, Gina turned to him and undid the harness. The ropes rose into the air and disappeared.

The dance told a story of breaking free of the bonds that tied you to the person you used to be. For Stone, during rehearsal, it symbolized his feelings about his family. After visiting them with Gina, he could no longer ignore the dissatisfaction and suffocation of being part of *Living Wild*. Of being stuck as one of nine. Of being labeled the quiet one.

He'd found his voice with Gina. He'd remembered who he was.

When the ropes were gone, Gina scurried out of the spotlight. Stone got to his feet, head tucked and arms pulled in tight. As the last bars played, he threw out his arms in triumph. The spotlight winked out, leaving the entire ballroom in darkness.

He held the pose for a second, breathing hard. The dance was over. They'd sold it. But after the footage earlier, there'd be consequences.

The lights came back on and Gina joined him to walk to the judges' table. She said, "Good job," but wouldn't meet his eyes.

A sick feeling spread through his belly and compressed his chest. When they finished a dance, it usually left him energized and elated, and they couldn't keep their hands off each other.

Tonight, nerves conquered every other feeling. He'd fucked up. Royally.

Juan Carlos was waiting for them. He was smiling, but there was a flicker of apprehension in his eyes.

"That was intense," Juan Carlos said once they'd joined him. "Stone, I'm surprised you're not suffering from rope burn."

Stone swiped a hand over his bare chest. "A little."

"All right, let's hear from the judges." Juan Carlos turned to them without any more jokes. "Mariah, we'll start with you."

The judges' comments washed over Stone. Next to him, Gina

nodded and smiled, so the critique must have been positive. It was all he could do not to interrupt the entire broadcast by dropping to his knees and begging her forgiveness.

Backstage, Reggie waited for them in the Sparkle Parlor. Natasha was there, having been one of the dancers to assist during their number. She grabbed Gina and gave her a big hug. A few of the other pros gathered around to compliment them on the dance. It was customary to congratulate and hug each couple right after they came off the dance floor. Still, it was hard to miss the way Gina's smile turned brittle at the attention. Stone made eye contact with Jackson, who raised an eyebrow. Kevin sent Stone a hard look before turning away.

"Gina, Stone, over here," Reggie called, gesturing for them to join her in front of the camera. Screens behind her replayed their dance without sound.

They moved to their places by Reggie. When Stone put his arm around Gina, she let him. That was something, at least.

Reggie leaned in with her microphone and a big smile. The blue streaks in her hair glimmered in the too-bright backstage lighting. "That was some interesting footage, huh? Anything you two want to tell us?"

Gina tensed, but retained her easy smile. "Nothing to tell. It was part of the choreography we decided to scrap."

"Stone, how about you? Any juicy gossip you want to share?"

He shrugged. "When in Alaska, do as the Alaskans do."

Reggie blinked. "I don't know what that means, but I believe you. Let's get your scores."

A giant ninety-four percent flashed on the screen. Backstage, everyone clapped. Reggie turned back to the camera. "Gina and Stone received a ninety-four. They have another chance tonight to earn more points with their combo dance, but they still need your votes. Don't forget to visit our website." She gave the rest of the info, and a few seconds later, the stage manager indicated they were done.

Tucking the microphone under her arm, Reggie took Gina's hands in hers. "I'm so sorry. They told me I had to ask that."

"I know." Gina squeezed Reggie's hands. "It's okay."

Natasha appeared behind them. "I'm stealing her for a minute."
She put her arm around Gina and hustled her out of the Sparkle
Parlor.

Kevin sidled up to Stone once the women were gone. "You've got
Donna, right?"

"Yeah, and Jordy."

"Jordy's good, but he doesn't have as much power. Donna,
though?" Kevin shook his head. "Fucking Donna. I used to have
her. After I won the second time, I requested a switch. They let me
have it, since I threatened to quit otherwise."

Stone didn't say anything. Someone called Kevin's name. He
slapped Stone on the back in a good-natured way. "Just get through
the next dance, man. Only one more episode left."

Kevin seemed to take it for granted that Stone would end up in the
finals. Maybe he'd been around long enough to guess these things.
But finals weren't enough. They had to win. And Stone had to prove
to Gina she could trust him.

One of the stage managers popped up at his elbow. "We have to
get you to wardrobe to change for your next dance."

His next dance. The *Boylesque*-inspired striptease. Gina had
choreographed it to be sexy-funny, to showcase not just his body,
but his breakdancing moves and his ability to laugh at himself.

Tonight, in front of millions of viewers, he was going to use it
to seduce her.

Twenty-Eight

How dare they.

*H*A fine trembling took over Gina's body, a combination of fear and adrenaline and pure, white-hot anger.

How dare they fuck with her career this way? With her reputation, with her wishes, with her fucking *life*. Could she sue? Probably not, but her agent was getting a call as soon as this whole mess was over with.

Natasha sat with her, making sure she sipped from a bottle of water. They were sequestered away in one of the empty offices.

"You're a good friend, Tash."

"Keep drinking."

"Fine." Gina took a small sip. "I still have another dance to get through."

"Not until the second hour. And I'm not needed until then, either. For now, we sit."

Natasha didn't ask any questions, which was part of what made her a great friend. She didn't push or pester, didn't ask, "Are you okay?" Any one of those things would have probably made Gina cry, but Natasha's quiet support was exactly what she needed to stay strong.

When the shaking subsided from earthquake to rumbling sub-way levels, Gina set down the water bottle. "He knew."

"Knew what?"

"He knew they had the footage. And he didn't tell me."

Natasha sucked her teeth. "Qué jodienda, coño."

Gina massaged her temples. A headache flirted at the edges. "He's probably looking for me."

"So what?" Natasha crossed her arms. "And why? To explain why he acted like a bonehead? Too bad."

"He might have had a good reason."

"Don't defend him. What they did was fucked up. It's okay to be mad."

Natasha's words rattled around Gina's head. Yes, she was angry. And it was justified. She had every right to be angry at having a private moment recorded. Without mics, on a day when filming was supposedly canceled and she'd been unaware there was a camera present. The producers were no better than the paparazzi, sneaking around to get the dirt and then airing it without her knowledge or consent.

And Stone had known they had the footage, and he hadn't told her. When the paparazzi had confronted them outside his hotel room, he'd been present for it. She hadn't hidden that from him. Sure, she'd gone to Donna on her own, but after he'd gotten pissed off about that, they'd agreed to handle things together.

"I bet this is Donna's goddamn fault. Fucking Donna." Gina got up to pace in the small office. "How many times did I fucking tell her I didn't want the producers crafting that kind of storyline for me?"

"Our agent even told them that."

"Yeah! My fucking agent!" Gina blew out an angry breath, clench-ing her hands into tight fists. "And who cares if I am having . . . relations . . . with Stone. It's my business. We're both consenting adults. And we weren't supposed to be filmed during that rehearsal."

Natasha snapped her fingers in agreement. "Amen. Fuck who you want to fuck. Ain't nobody else's business."

Gina narrowed her eyes. "You had sex with Jackson, didn't you?"

"Sure did. And it was *uh-mazing*. But you don't see them trying to make up a story about me."

"They tried with Dwayne. And with Stone."

Tash waved a hand dismissively. "I had no chemistry with Dwayne. It wasn't going to happen. You and Stone, on the other hand . . . I saw that coming from a mile away."

Gina dropped back into the desk chair and covered her face with her hands. "Really?"

"Yeah, girl. You're obvious as fuck."

"I tried really hard to hide it."

"I'm your roommate. And that man has a lot going for him."

"How could he hide this from me, though?"

Natasha chewed the inside of her cheek. "Did you ask him?"

"No. I didn't want to talk right before we did our contemporary. I needed to have my head in the game so I didn't fall during the aerial routine."

"Which looked fucking awesome, by the way."

"Didn't it?" Gina leaned back, stretching her feet out in front of her. "We worked so hard on it."

"And you got a great score. I'll eat my toe shoes if you don't get a perfect score for your next one."

Gina grabbed Natasha's hand and squeezed tight. "I'm glad you'll be there with me."

"To watch Stone strip? I'd do it for free. Hell, I might even bring some singles with me to tuck in his little shorts." She wiggled her eyebrows. "Or some twenties. Think we could get him to do a repeat performance backstage?"

"Not a chance. I had to fight with him to get him to agree to the number in the first place." She grinned. "We might have practiced some stripping moves in his hotel room."

"You are a lucky, lucky girl."

Gina fell quiet. Sitting and chatting with Natasha made her feel normal, like the events of the night—like that goddamned footage—hadn't happened. But it had. Everyone had seen it. It was a good thing her phone was still in the Sparkle Parlor, because her mother and sister had likely sent a bajillion texts.

"I thought I was."

"You still are." Natasha got to her feet and pulled Gina out of the chair. "Stop moping. The show must go on. After the second dance, you chew him out. Let him grovel. Then you have excellent make-up sex and get ready for the finals. I'm going out with Jackson again, so I'll be home late." She winked.

Gina smiled, but betrayal weighed her down, made her limbs feel like cement.

Donna had known how she felt, and the bitch had gone and put the footage in anyway.

But Stone had known, too. And he hadn't told her.

A ngry as she was, Gina was still excited for their combo dance, which combined Latin, jazz, and breakdancing moves. It was the most fun Gina had ever had choreographing something for *The Dance Off,* and with Stone's breakdancing skills, she was pleased with the results.

He'd fought her on it, of course. The guy looked like he'd been sculpted by Michelangelo—better, actually—but he was modest as a schoolmarm. Even if the judges didn't love it, Gina was betting the fans would.

It was the last chance for America to vote. Next week, a winner would be crowned. Everything they did tonight would determine how many votes they got, so they were pulling out all the stops.

The finals were in reach. It was killing her to know their fate was already sealed, and they just didn't know it yet. Tonight, two couples would be sent home, but they wouldn't know who until the elimination at the end of the episode. In the finals, three couples would compete for the trophy.

And everyone who was left in the competition—Alan Thomas, Farrah Zane, Jackson García, and Lauren D'Angelo—could be a contender for the top spot.

Not worth thinking about. If ever there were a time to stay present, to live for the moment, it was now. Gina had no idea what repercussions the night would have on her career. She was angry, but she was also so close to the end of this ride.

Finally, it was time for her and Stone to take the floor. The behind-the-scenes package showed them arguing about Stone stripping during the dance.

His incredulous tone rang out through the ballroom. "You want me to *strip*?"

"It's called boylesque. Like burlesque, but with dudes."

"I don't care what it's called. I'll look ridiculous."

"Oh, come on. Please?" Her entreaties were interspersed by fits of uncontrollable giggling. "Do it for the fans!"

It hurt to watch it now, to hear herself so happy and carefree. The whole time, he'd known what was coming, and he'd kept it from her.

The lights came down. They took their places.

A stage had been set up in the middle of the ballroom, a long, rectangular platform that looked like a catwalk. Gina stood at the end, with other dancers lining the sides. When the music started, she did her moves, mugging for the camera. Then it panned away, and Stone hit the runway.

He came out with the swagger of a champion, like he knew every eye was on him and he loved it. Gone was the man who wouldn't look her in the face during tango practice, and the man who had barely said a word during their trip to New York. This Stone was strong and confident, and he owned that fucking stage.

Gina and the other dancers swooned at the edges, reaching for him as he hit his moves. Stone pulled Gina up, lifting her from the floor with one arm. As many times as they'd practiced, it felt easier now than it ever had. There was a glint in his eye that made her feel warm all over, aware of every inch of her skin. She couldn't take her eyes off him.

Stone spun and posed, executing perfect body rolls that would make a real stripper cry tears of pride. He ran his hands over her, executing their moves in hold with a level of force and mastery that was rare for a male celeb on this show.

He was truly leading, in complete control of this dance, and of her. Even though Gina had orchestrated the whole thing, she could only go along for the ride. When the time came, he pulled off his shirt. She took it and pretended to swoon, falling off the stage into the arms of Matteo and Joel.

When Stone reached the end of the stage, the music picked up. He pulled out the breakdancing moves they'd been saving and the audience went wild.

And then Stone ripped his undershirt down the middle.

If the audience had been screaming before, now they lost their fucking minds. Their cries reached deafening status. Stone seemed to drink it in, embodying the character like never before.

Through it all, his eyes kept finding Gina's.

The fire in his gaze, the naked desire—it went with the dance. It went with the character. But it was all for her. Gina knew that look, had seen it every time he thrust his hips and filled her.

She'd never been so turned on during a performance with literally *millions* of people watching.

For the rest of the dance, Stone showed off what his mama gave him. He leaped off the makeshift stage to dance with Gina, seducing her with his body, his hands, his eyes, and most powerfully, his ability to lead. He pulled her against him, rubbed his body on hers, spun them around, all while undulating his hips in a way that had her mouth going dry.

Natasha joined in for a few moves, she and Gina providing accompaniment to Stone, who was the real star of the show.

When they pulled off his tear-away pants, the audience lost their minds again.

He completed the dance in gold lamé hot pants and matching gold-and-white high-top sneakers. The dancers playing crowd members fawned over him, and when the song ended, Stone stuck his final pose and shot the camera a fuck-me grin.

He'd done it perfectly. Better, in fact, than in any of their rehearsals. When he hugged Gina against him, she let him, and handed him the gold basketball shorts that had been their deal, so he didn't have to receive their scores while mostly naked.

He looked damn good in that gold banana hammock, though. They'd joked about him keeping it and wearing it in the bedroom for her.

She couldn't think about that now. Well, she could, actually. She could picture it all too well. But it wasn't enough.

Already, her brain pushed away the discomfort of what had happened earlier. Already, she tried to convince herself this was normal.

It wasn't. For once, she wanted more from a man than just a casual physical relationship. She'd put her heart on the line, knowing he was leaving, knowing men ruined careers—like her father had done to her mother. As soon as the cameras stopped rolling tonight, she'd have to face the consequences.

Backstage with Reggie, their scores appeared on screen. Ninety-seven. Dimitri was the only one who hadn't given them a hundred.

"We'll take it," Gina said into the microphone. "We've worked hard on these dances, and we just hope we can show everyone what we have planned for next week."

While Reggie fed the camera the voting info, Gina and Stone moved off to the side.

The others fell on them with congratulations, but Gina wasn't in the mood for it. They'd all seen the footage. They all knew she and Stone were hooking up. It was her worst nightmare come true.

She could handle the good-natured teasing from her coworkers, but would anyone else in the industry take her seriously after this? The producers, the execs, future casting directors . . . It was the kind of thing that caused drama on set. Would they respect her now that they knew she'd gotten involved with her partner?

And the timing sucked. Even if they didn't make it to the finals, they'd still have to do the *Morning Mix* interview together the next day, and Stone would have to return to Los Angeles for the last episode. After that, he'd be gone. She'd always known this thing between them had an end date, and now they'd been exposed just in time for them to break up.

Lauren D'Angelo sidled up to her. "I knew you were fucking him," she whispered in Gina's ear. With a wink and a sly smirk, Lauren slipped away. Gina's blood boiled in response.

"Don't listen to her." Natasha stood at Gina's side, ready to do battle. "That comemierda is jealous and you know it."

Even though she didn't want to, Gina sought Stone out in the crowd and found him chatting with Jackson and Alan. Lauren's comment had pissed her off, but it also left a strange, sour residue. "I feel awful," she confessed to Natasha.

"It's stress." Natasha rubbed her back. "Only one more week, then this is all done."

"I kinda want to hide until the show is over."

"I'll go with you. Well, until Alan's second dance. I'm in the opening bit."

Gina hid in the green room, but before long, it was time to return to the stage for the elimination.

Stone gave Gina a look that managed to be both wary and full of heat. Her twisted-up emotions couldn't take it. She swallowed hard and looked away.

They took their places on the stage with the four other remaining couples—Jackson and Lori, Lauren and Kevin, Alan and Rhianne, and Farrah and Danny.

Juan Carlos talked. Gina tuned most of it out.

Lauren and Kevin were safe. Ugh.

Jackson and Lori were safe. Good for them. Jackson was a great dancer, and Lori's choreography pushed the boundaries of ballroom into performance art.

It was down to the last three celebrities: Stone, Farrah, and Alan.

Gina held her breath. From his spot behind her, Stone wrapped his arms around her and rested his chin on her head.

How could his touch make her feel so secure when he'd betrayed her like this? And why did her stupid heart yearn to wiggle even closer into his embrace? If anything, she should pull away. There was only one week left. Better to start the separation process now.

"The last couple who *will* be going to the finals is . . ."

Juan Carlos paused. Drew it out. The tension built while the low, percussive music played.

"Stone and Gina!"

Stone whooped and spun her around, lifting her into his arms. Gina clung to his neck and burst into tears.

Everything was fucked up and confusing and she shouldn't be hugging him but *damn it* she was going to the finals! For the first time ever! And her job was safe!

That thought pulled her back a step. Her job, here at *The Dance Off*, with a producer who went behind her back to dig up dirt and air it on TV. Hell, they'd done it to Stone, too, airing an interview with his ex in the third episode.

Gina slapped a lid on her compassion. The interview with his ex-girlfriend was all the more reason for him to have told Gina what he'd known. He'd experienced the betrayal and humiliation firsthand, and he still let it be done to her.

All night, she'd kept it in. And now, with the knowledge that they were safe, that they would dance another day, she lost it. Tears leaked from the corners of her eyes, and her chest heaved.

Stone put her down but didn't let go.

"God, Gina, I'm sorry. I'm so sorry I didn't tell you. Donna said—"

"Shut up," she whispered. "Don't do this here."

Hiding in his embrace, she wiped the tears from her face before turning around. She headed straight backstage, skipping the portion of the night where she took selfies with the fans. She wanted to get out of this costume, wash her face, get the fake hair off her head, and sink into a deep, dreamless sleep.

Except Donna was waiting for her backstage, wearing a self-satisfied smirk.

Gina wanted to strangle her, but there were cameras everywhere.

"Gina, I have someone who wants to meet you." Donna gestured to the man next to her. He had medium brown skin, a slight build, and short salt-and-pepper hair. "This is Hector Oquendo."

Hector gave Gina a big smile and shook her hand. "Very nice to meet you, Gina."

With a nod, Donna backed away and disappeared. Coward. Stone stayed by Gina's side.

"Thank you," Gina said. She'd never heard of a Hector Oquendo. Should she know him? "Were you in the audience tonight?"

"I was. You two were fantastic." He extended his grin to Stone. "I was waiting to see if you were going on to the finals before I gave you the invitation."

Gina frowned. "For?"

"Oh, sorry. I'm so amped up after the show—and a bit jetlagged, I'll admit—I forgot to tell you who I am." He pulled out his wallet and handed her his card. "I'm the producer for *Bronx Girl,* the autobiographical Broadway musical by Meli Mendez. We want you to come to New York and audition for the lead role. After the finals, of course."

Hold up. Had he really just said what she thought he said?

Gina stared at the card in her hand, the printed letters blurring as she replayed his words in her mind, trying to make sense of them. Meanwhile, Hector kept going.

"Meli had wonderful things to say about you after she was a guest judge here, and your producer said you'll be in Manhattan the day after the finals. You're from New York originally?"

It took Gina a second to find her voice. "The Bronx," she said. "Same neighborhood as Meli."

Hector's face lit up. "That's even better. It will be great for promo. I have to tell you, we were worried about finding someone to play Meli, and when she saw you, she came back and said, 'that's her.' We haven't even opened auditions to anyone else yet."

Gina blinked as his words sank in. A smile spread over her face and she pressed her hands to her cheeks, which flooded with warmth. "This is . . . this is more than I could have dreamed. Thank you."

"So, you'll come to audition?"

"Yes, of course."

"Excellent. Oh, can you sing?" He waved the question away before she could answer. "Not that it's a dealbreaker if you can't. That can be taught."

"I work with a vocal coach."

Hector grinned again. "Perfect. All right, well, I've got a flight to catch. I look forward to seeing you next week." He nodded at Stone. "I hope you win. Goodnight."

As he hurried off, Stone rubbed Gina's shoulder gently. As amazing and wonderful as the conversation with Hector had been, she'd never lost track of Stone's presence, solid and strong at her side.

It would have been easier to hate him, to wish him gone, or banished. The fact that she wanted him here, and was glad that he'd been present to share her wondrous moment with Hector, was only going to make the coming conversation that much harder.

She swallowed hard. "We have to talk."

Twenty-Nine

After a tense and silent drive home with Stone's big body crammed into the passenger seat of her car, Gina was vibrating with stress and ready to snap at any moment. When they reached her apartment, she headed straight for her bedroom out of habit. Stupid mistake. Stone followed her in and shut the door behind them.

"So, that was good news, right?" He crossed his arms over his chest and hunched his shoulders, something he did when he was trying to appear smaller and less intimidating. She wanted to tell him not to bother.

"It was." Shit, it *really* was. It was more than she'd ever dreamed possible, and when she did dare to dream that big, it was much further down the road. "But that's not what I brought you here to talk about."

Stone came toward her and took hold of her shoulders. "Gina."

Just that. Just her name. As always, the way he said it made her knees weak, and loosened her resolve to steel herself against him. In the past few months, he'd figured out how to bypass all her defenses and access her heart.

Tonight, she wished she'd left a few walls in place.

He rubbed her arms, warming her, relaxing her. "You deserve to celebrate a little," he said. "This is a big deal."

"It's just an audition." Inside, under the hurt, she was leaping for joy. "Stop trying to distract me from being angry at you."

"Can't." Slowly, he bent his head and brushed his lips over hers. "I'm too happy for you."

She trembled. She fucking trembled. All the reasons for staying mad tumbled aside, and she plastered herself to him, kissing him back with a vengeance.

Things moved quickly after that, which suited her fine. If they slowed, she'd think about what she was doing. If she thought about it, she'd pull away.

She should pull away. She was mad at him. And sad. And mad. Or more sad?

God. She was *both*. And not even about his mistake. He was *leaving* her, and the thought of him boarding a plane back to Alaska devastated her heart. She should never have gotten so wrapped up in him that it would hurt this much when he left.

She needed to stop thinking about it. Just feel. Let him wash it all away with his touch.

Their clothing was barely a barrier. She was wearing a skirt, which made it easy for him to yank off her panties. She unzipped his cargo shorts and pulled out his cock while he unwrapped a condom. In seconds, he'd seated himself on the edge of her bed and she'd climbed onto his lap. With her knees on either side of his hips, she sank onto him, hissing as he stretched her.

No foreplay. No dirty talk. No sighs or moans. Just growls and grunts and the slap of flesh on flesh. She dug her nails into his shoulders, balling up the fabric of his T-shirt in her fists. He skimmed his hands under her skirt and gripped her hips to bounce her up and down on him. Without their usual level of preparation, the feeling of being stuffed was more powerful than ever. He filled her, his cock burrowing into her much as he had insinuated himself into her life and made a space for himself.

Except it was like he had always been there.

It was hard to remember a time before him.

This was the way of it with partners on *The Dance Off*. The intensive nature of the training and filming schedule forced an intimacy that was unlike anything in the real world. As special as this felt now, he was returning to Alaska in a week. And now it looked like she'd be going back to New York.

This was it, then. The last time.

Pressing her face into his neck, breathing in his pine-and-fresh-air scent, rubbing her cheek against his beard—all of it would be the last time.

Gina wrapped her arms around his neck and clung tight, not wanting to let go. But she was fooling herself. She'd always known he was going to leave.

Stone shifted them onto the bed without pulling out. Holding himself over her, he pinned her to the mattress with the force of his hips. Over and over, until waves of pleasure stole her reason and her voice. Hoarse cries fell from her throat, and still, she clung to him with everything she had.

When his thumb touched her clit, she exploded. As she shuddered and quaked beneath him, he pulled her close. His big body tensed, his muscles locked, and he came with a gasp. Her own orgasm rumbled on and swept her away, leaving an overwhelming emptiness in its place.

Panting hard, she didn't move until he slipped out of her and shifted to the side. Then she rolled off the bed and grabbed the box of tissues from the bedside table for them to clean up.

If it got any more awkward, she was going to run out of the room screaming.

After pulling her panties back on and righting her clothing, she sat on the edge of the bed, looking anywhere but at him. Stone disposed of the condom and tucked himself back into his shorts. Once he was zipped up, he stretched out on the mattress and pillowed his head on his arms, staring at the ceiling.

"Now what?" he asked.

Better to cut right to the chase, to cling to the reason she'd been given. "I can't put it aside and pretend everything is normal. I'm pissed off that they got that footage of us in the first place, because I knew better. But for Donna to air it on the show, without even warning me? And then to find out you knew about it and didn't tell me? I can't get past this."

"Donna said that even if you made it to the finals, there were still no guarantees you'd have a spot next season, and this would increase your chances of winning and keeping your job. Besides, you went to Donna on your own after the paparazzi incident."

"But you knew about that. I didn't know Donna had that footage. I didn't know you had a conversation with her. And at this point, maybe I don't want to work for a show that has so little respect for me. The fact that they've been pushing the romance angle for months, when they know I don't want to do it, shows they don't care about me. I'm not okay with them making it look like I have no self-respect."

His eyebrows shot up. "Wow. Really?" He sounded offended.

She hated hurting him this way, hated dismissing what had come to mean so much to her. But she needed to end it. "Don't take it personally. I don't want anyone thinking I'm hooking up with my partner. Not you, specifically. Any guy."

His eyes narrowed. "Now I'm just any guy."

"Damn it, Stone. Stop making this about you."

"How can I not?" He threw up his hands and got up to pace in front of the mirrors. It looked like he had an angry twin, like her room was doubly full of him. She hugged herself with her arms, holding onto her anger and giving it voice. It was the only way she'd get through this.

"Fine. It is about you. You went along with it because you thought this would help you win."

He froze and gave her an incredulous stare. "I thought it would help *you* win."

"I don't want to win like this. Besides, you stand to take home three hundred and fifty thousand dollars if you win. You really expect me to believe that had nothing to do with your decision to withhold this from me? You made it clear from the beginning you were here for the money."

Chest heaving, his mouth fell open in indignation. "I can't believe you're throwing that in my face. My mother had a *hip replacement.* Do you know what kind of bills that procedure incurs? How much physical therapy she needed? I'm not ashamed of my reasons for joining the show initially, but once you told me your job was on the line, all I've focused on is helping *you* win."

His argument was too logical. He'd chip away at her resolve if she wasn't careful, so she sidestepped and delivered a direct hit. "Just because you don't care about lying on TV doesn't mean I'm cool with it, too."

"Jesus Christ, Gina. You and I are *not* lying. We have something." He scrubbed a hand over his face and resumed pacing. "Fuck. I'm falling for you and I want to shout it from the fucking rooftops, and all you want to do is pretend I don't exist unless I'm in bed with you. You want the truth? It hurts. You know how many people have propositioned me since I've been in LA?"

Her jaw dropped and a spark of jealous anger flared in her gut. It was easier to deal with than his admission, to focus on her own hurt rather than accept the responsibility of hurting him. "What the fuck is *that* supposed to mean?"

"It means that I hoped you were actually someone who was able to look past all this—" He made a vague gesture at himself. "And get to know me for who I am. Not for what I look like or the character I play on TV."

The urge to reassure him pounded through her, but she bit the inside of her cheek to hold back. She had to stay on topic and see this through to the end. "Regardless of whatever we've been doing, you knew I wanted to keep my private life private. Forgive me for not wanting millions of people to know about my sex life. I can't even look at my phone right now because it's full of questions from my family. The cast and crew know. It's going to be all over the internet and tabloids, along with those photos from outside your hotel. I'm going to be bombarded on social media and in interviews. There's no way potential gigs won't know about it, and it will color people's impressions of me."

Again, his face pinched with hurt. "I don't understand why it's so bad if people know we're together."

"It's bad because reputation counts for so much in this business, and mine has just been destroyed. It'll change the kind of jobs I'm offered, and what people will think they can ask me to do." She clenched her hands in the coverlet and played her final card, the argument he couldn't talk her out of because it had been the guiding force behind her "rule" all along. "Do you have any idea how much my agent fought them on the showmance angle when I was hired? A lot. And because I'm Puerto Rican, I've already been fighting against the 'sexy and promiscuous' Latina stereotype for my entire career, something that's hard enough when you're a dancer. You knew this when we started, and it's exactly why I don't get involved with partners. So, no, you don't get to make this about you, and you don't get to tell me that you did this for me. We're done, Stone."

Panic crossed his features. "Gina, wait."

She turned her back on him so he couldn't see the tears. "I'll see you in practice tomorrow. You know the way out."

Unable to sleep, Gina tossed and turned most of the night. The next day, she was up at dawn, staring bleary-eyed at the espresso maker on the kitchen counter, when Natasha dragged herself through the apartment door. Her long curly hair was a mass of frizz, and her eye makeup had smudged, giving her the appearance of a bedraggled raccoon.

They blinked at each other. Gina spoke first.

"Fun night with Jackson?"

Natasha toed off her silver flats and shook her head. "I went home with Dimitri."

Gina leaned against the counter. "What happened to quitting him like a bad habit?"

"I relapsed." Tash flopped onto the sofa and threw an arm over her eyes. "Can you make me one, too?"

Gina got down a second cup. When the espresso shots were ready, she carried them over to the sofa. Natasha shifted her feet out of the way so Gina could sit.

"Which one of us is going to go first?" Tash asked in a hoarse voice.

"I guess I can." Gina frowned into her cup as she stirred. "I broke up with Stone last night."

That made Natasha sit up. She held her espresso to her nose and breathed deep, eyes rolling back into her head. She took a sip, and nodded. "Now that I'm human again, I have to point out, breaking up means you were together."

"Yes, damn it. We were together. And I'm an idiot for letting it get that far when it was never going to go anywhere."

"You like him."

"Of course I like him." Gina sipped and burned her mouth. She blew on it and sipped again, the rich, dark flavor exploding over her tongue. "What's not to like? The man is nearly perfect."

"Nearly. Except for little things like not telling you Donna had video of you two kissing."

"And that he talked to her about it behind my back." It seemed petty to hold a grudge about that, since she'd done the same after the paparazzi had caught them in the parking lot, but it was easier than admitting she was using it as an excuse to break up before their careers forced them to say goodbye.

"Did he explain why?"

"He claims he did it so I would win and keep my job."

"The nerve of him!"

Gina ignored the sarcasm. "But now I'm not even sure I want it, you know? Oh!" She grabbed Natasha's arm. "I didn't tell you what else happened last night."

"Oh shit, there's more?"

"Meli wants me to come audition for her Broadway musical!"

Natasha screamed so loud, Gina fumbled her cup. They set their espressos aside quickly so Tash could give her a big hug.

"That is the best news," Natasha shouted in her ear. "I'm so happy for you! Girl, you better hook me up if you need an understudy."

"You don't sing."

"Ensemble, then. I sing well enough for ensemble." Natasha leaned back against the arm of the sofa. "You'll nail the audition and then tell *The Dance Off* to fuck off."

Gina pushed her hair out of her face. "I can't really think that far ahead, not until after we get through the finals."

"One more week."

"Yeah. One more week." One more week, and then Stone would be out of her life forever.

Even without this whole kissing footage fiasco, it would have happened anyway. He had to go back to Alaska to resume filming. She had to continue building her career. It was all she'd ever wanted.

Career came first. Always.

Gina collected their cups and brought them to the sink. "You want to tell me what's going on with you and Dimitri? Again?"

Natasha groaned and covered her face with one of the colorful throw pillows brightening up the beige sofa. "Not really."

"Should I guess?"

"Probably." The word came out muffled.

"You guys had too much to drink at the club, he turned those sexy chocolate brown eyes on you and said in that deep Brooklyn accent"—she dropped her voice to imitate Dimitri's baritone—"'Yo, Tasha, you wanna go home with me?' And you tripped and fell on his dick."

Tash threw the pillow aside and scowled. "That's exactly what happened."

"Was it good, at least?"

"It's always good. That's the problem." Tash got up to rummage in the fridge. "Did you get in one last round with Stone?"

Gina sighed. "Yeah."

"Was it good?"

"Of course. Just made the rest of it worse, though."

"One more week."

"I know."

Thirty

After an especially punishing session at the hotel gym that did nothing to keep his mind off Gina, Stone returned to his room just in time to pick up a call from downstairs.

"Yeah?" He held the phone away from him, since he was dripping with sweat.

"Hello, Mr. Nielson. This is Omar at the front desk. We have a message for you. Your mother called and asked you to connect with her on video chat."

Stone's cell phone had been off since the semifinals for this very reason. He suppressed a groan and thanked Omar.

Hanging up, Stone plucked at the wet tank top clinging to his chest. He was drenched. His family would have to wait until he'd taken a shower.

He wished he could put it off longer. Ever since he'd visited Alaska with Gina, resentment toward his family popped up at odd moments. He'd recall someone from college, and then remember he wasn't allowed to reach out to anyone from his former life. Or someone at *The Dance Off* would ask him *anything,* and he'd have to lie or clam up.

And after everything that had happened with Gina . . . shit, he just didn't want to talk to anyone.

He was hurt, he could admit that much. And angry. And he still had to fucking dance with her and pretend like everything was fine. It was fucked up.

He glanced at his laptop. As much as he wanted to ignore them, the pull of family was too strong. After a quick shower, he sat at his laptop and called his mother.

Pepper's face popped up on the screen, crinkling into a smile when she saw him. He could see her room at the Glacier Valley Inn in the background. "Hi, honey."

Stone couldn't help it. He smiled back. Yes, he was mad at her for asking about Gina on camera, and for adding to it in the interview, but she was his mom. He loved her and always would.

"Hi, Mom."

"You've made it to the finals. We're so proud of you."

"Thanks. Where's everyone else?"

"Your father's meeting with Miguel, and the others are having breakfast. I've been sitting here waiting for you to call."

The guilt trip worked. "Sorry, I was in the gym."

"Don't you think you have enough muscles?"

"Gotta keep up my appearance as the strong, silent one, right?" The words tasted bitter as he said them. It no longer felt like a joke, but an insult, a stifling of his true self.

"We all have our roles to play," Pepper answered in a mild tone. "Speaking of, I saw the footage last night."

Of course she had. Why else would she be calling? "Uh-huh."

"I thought you told me there wasn't anything going on between you and Gina?"

"There isn't." *No thanks to you.* He couldn't say that, though. Not to his mom. "It's just the producers trying to make a story out of nothing. You know how it works."

"Oh." The corners of Pepper's mouth turned down. She looked . . . disappointed. "That's a shame. You seemed so happy around her, I was hoping . . . well, never mind. You're a grown man and that's your business."

It was on the tip of his tongue to blurt out everything, to explain what he'd done and how Gina had reacted, to spill how fucking torn up he was about it. But what would be the point? None of it mattered. In a week, he'd be home, and Gina would likely be moving to New York. She'd never give up her life to go with him, and the distance between Manhattan and Alaska made for a hell of a long-distance relationship—not that Gina would even want that now.

His mother changed the subject, catching him up on what was happening with his siblings, and what the producers had planned for them when Stone returned.

"We're all real anxious to have you back," she said. "What do I say about next week? Break a leg? I can't tell that to my own son."

He chuckled. "I love you, Mom."

Her cheeks turned pink and she smiled. "Well, I love you, too, Stone. See you soon."

He disconnected the call and dropped his head into his hands. If he could, he'd leave right now. Head to LAX and hop a plane to Juneau, maybe even stay there and pick up his old life. Leave everything behind, unfinished, to avoid the pain and discomfort. If he never saw Nielson HQ again, it would be too soon.

Everyone wanted him to be silent—his family about their pasts, and Gina about their relationship. The silent protector, keeping secrets and putting his own needs aside. Well, he was sick of being the quiet and reserved one. Through dance, he had found his voice.

The gym bag he carried to practice every day sat in its spot next to the dresser, taunting him. *Are you really going to let the figure skater win without a fight?* Snatching it up, Stone headed out of the room.

Maybe his personal life was falling apart, but damn it, he had an ugly-ass dance trophy to win.

Stone entered the rehearsal room with his stomach tied in knots and his footsteps powered by determination. Okay, so Gina was angry with him and he didn't know how to fix it, but he'd made a commitment. The finish line was in sight and he was going to see it through to the end.

No matter what, he still wanted her to win.

"Morning." Gina didn't greet him with her usual peck on the cheek. Her eyes were shadowed, dragged down by dark circles.

"Hi." As much as Stone wanted to hold her close until they'd talked out all the bullshit between them and come up with a solution, he was also angry. She'd thought he was in it for the money—and yes, he had been at the beginning—but ever since she'd told him her need to make it to the finals, and her desire to win, those had been his driving goals as well. He'd wanted to do this for her, like he'd wanted to join the competition to make money for his mother, and like he'd joined *Living Wild* to help his family.

He'd spent so much of the last few years doing things for other people, he had no idea what he wanted for himself. And to have Gina throw it back in his face had been a shock.

By tacit agreement, they didn't mention anything about what had happened between them—not the kiss footage, not their relationship, nothing. More than ever, he was resentful of the cameras, but on another level, he was grateful for them. He didn't know how to address Gina after their argument, and dance rehearsal gave them a script for how to manage the day.

Gina waved the piece of cardstock that told them their new dance.

"We have two dances for the final," she said. "The redemption dance, which is chosen by the judges, and one more dance style we haven't done yet." She tapped the card stock against her thigh, her fingers clenching like she was resisting the urge to crumple it and throw it at him. "Our final dance is a rumba, a . . . romantic dance."

Her voice broke, and she turned away.

God, he was such an asshole. She was hurting, and all he had done was focus on his own bruised feelings. How could he not, though? He'd fallen in love with her, and she didn't want him. Rational thought was beyond him for the time being.

Still, he would have tried to comfort her if he thought there was even the slightest chance she'd allow it.

Instead, Gina turned back, utterly composed, and continued as if she'd never stopped. "We're doing American-style rumba, which is taught in a box step. The footwork is slow-quick-quick, on the one, three, and four. Ready?"

Her voice sounded hollow as she explained the moves, and her demonstration looked stiff as she took him through what she explained was a smooth, fluid dance.

"Hey, Gina, are you okay?" Jordy called, his face creased in concern.

She sent him a tight smile. "I'm fine."

But Stone knew she wasn't. If he were a different person, it might have made him feel better to know she was as heartbroken as he was, but it just made him feel worse.

Halfway through the day, Chad Silver entered the rehearsal room. The head judge always wore perfectly tailored suits in bright colors and patterns. Today's jacket was electric blue, over an orange-and-white-striped button-down. Stone couldn't imagine wearing such a getup, but Chad, with his russet skin, bald head, and abundance of confidence, made it shine.

"Hello, my lovelies!" the judge called in his rich, exuberant voice. He walked right over to Gina and enfolded her in a tight hug. "How are you feeling, my dear?"

She clung to him for a moment, and Stone's heart contracted. But when she stepped back, her eyes were clear.

"Fine," she said. "I'm fine. What's our redemption dance?"

Her smile was a shadow of its usual brilliance. Guilt churned Stone's stomach.

Chad waved Stone over. "How's it going, big guy?"

Stone shrugged and gave the expected answer. "Looking forward to the finals."

"So am I." Chad clapped his hands together. "Let's talk about your redemption dance. Last week you showed us sexy and cool with your jazz combo, and intensity and strength with the contemporary. In the rumba, you're going to give us suave and romantic, but we still want more of your lighthearted side. We know you can dance fast, especially after the breakdancing you did last week. That's why, for your redemption dance, we want to see you take another shot at your jive from week three."

Chad made a sympathetic grimace. "We know the package influenced your jive, and we see how far you've come from there, since last night's footage would have thrown anyone off, and you both turned out great performances. We'd like to give you another chance to show the viewers what you can do."

Stone nodded. "Jive. Okay. Which one was that again?"

Chad chuckled. "The one where you built a house in the woods."

"Oh. That one." The one where the producers had tracked down his ex-girlfriend, surprised him with her interview, then tossed him onto the dance floor.

Shit. They were in the same situation here. Gina had been blindsided by the footage last week, partly because Stone hadn't said anything. He thought he'd been sparing her the stress, but now he could see it looked like he was siding with the producers. No wonder Gina was pissed.

Chad helped Stone with the jive steps he'd struggled with the first time around. It helped to have a man demonstrating how the moves should look, and this time, they were easier. Not only that, Chad made their rehearsal easier all around, with his lively energy and positive demeanor. He seemed extra attentive to Gina's needs and complimented her choreography skills and work ethic.

When Chad left, Gina shuffled over to the cooler and pulled out a sports drink. Stone grabbed a towel and wiped his face with it.

"I'm going to take off," she said without looking at him. "I have a headache. We'll work on the rumba tomorrow."

She was avoiding him. He supposed he couldn't blame her. "I think I'll stay here to keep practicing the jive."

Her eyebrows arched in surprise. "That's . . . that's good. Do you want me to see if Natasha's around to practice with you?"

Wow, Gina *really* didn't want to be around him. "Whatever. Sure."

"I'll text her. See you tomorrow."

Ten minutes later, Natasha came in wearing a guarded look.

"You're working on the jive?"

"Yeah. Gina left with a headache."

"I know. She told me." Natasha leaned over Aaliyah's open laptop. "Can you show me the dance they're doing?"

After replaying Stone's dress rehearsal footage from week three a few times, Natasha nodded. "Got it. Let's go, guapo."

In the center of the room, Stone assumed the proper hold and took Natasha in his arms. Before she counted down, she narrowed her eyes at him.

"You fucked up. Don't think I'm going easy on you."

Shit. Natasha knew what he'd done.

This rehearsal was going to be *brutal*.

G ina arrived at rehearsal the next day determined to throw herself into the choreography and develop the greatest rumba she could. If this was going to be her last season on the show, she wanted to go out with a bang. Fans would remember this dance and put it on their "top ten" lists for years to come.

More than that, she wanted to rub it in Donna's face. And Lauren's. And hell, even Kevin's. And Stone's. She'd show them all what she was made of, that she was worth so much more than cheap gimmicks.

Gina stopped short in the doorway, a wave of anxiety sapping her strength.

Donna was waiting for her, perched on a folding chair with her laptop on her knees. She sent Gina a self-satisfied smile.

"Good morning, Gina."

Gina's hand itched to slap Donna's smug face. Fuck. *Hold it together, girl.* She straightened and entered the room with a bright smile. "Hi, Donna."

"We've been tracking social media across multiple platforms for the past few days."

Gina still hadn't checked her accounts for fear of all the fan comments. "Oh?"

"There was a spike for you and Stone the night of the episode, although Lauren and Kevin are still leading in interest overall."

Thanks, pendeja. "Oh."

"The response has mainly been positive. People want to know if you two are dating."

Gina held herself still. If she moved, she'd do something she'd regret.

Maybe Jordy sensed it, because he interrupted by showing Donna something on his own laptop.

When Donna looked away, Gina left the room. She ran into Stone in the hallway.

"Your best friend's in there." She stormed past him, heading for the tiny kitchen at the end of the hall.

"What?" Stone paused with his hand on the door. "Who?"

"Fucking Donna." Gina spat the words, the anger she'd held back in the rehearsal room spewing out at him. "Maybe you two can strategize some more about how to ruin my life."

Stone dropped his gym bag and caught up to her in the kitchen, where she rummaged in the cabinets, slamming doors. She wasn't even looking for anything, she just needed to get away from Donna and make some noise.

"Gina, come on. You know that wasn't what I was trying to do."

She did, but . . . "Your intention doesn't matter. For someone who claims to hate lying, you sure do it a lot. Look at your family's show."

"I was trying to *help*." His tone darkened. "And don't bring my family into this. You know how I feel about *Living Wild*."

Gina stopped messing with the cabinets and braced herself on the edge of the sink, breathing hard. "You know what? I hope we don't win. If we win, we'll have to do the media circuit, and we'll always be remembered. If we come in second or third? No one will give a fuck about us."

"You don't mean that."

She covered her face as all the emotions from the past few days threatened to overwhelm her. "I do. I just want to forget all of this, and I want everyone else to forget, too. I'm done here. I can't work for a show that does this kind of shit to me."

"We work in reality TV. We've chosen to put ourselves out there for the public. This goes with the territory."

She dropped her hands and glared at him, hurt anger powering her words. "One of us chose to show their life on TV and lie about it. I don't flaunt my private life, and I don't work on a show that focuses on it. I'm a dancer. That's what I let people see. You knew they had footage of us, and you chose not to tell me."

"And what would have happened if I had told you?" Stone folded his arms across his chest and leaned a hip against the counter. "Huh? Would you have stormed into Donna's office and demanded she cut the footage?"

Gina sucked her teeth. "Yes."

"And then what? Do you think she would have said, 'Yes, Gina, you're absolutely right, I won't air it'?"

"Gotta say, this sarcastic side of you is not very attractive."

Stone ignored her nasty comment and kept going. "Let me tell you what would have happened. Donna would have steamrolled you, because she's the producer and you're just a dancer. She would have flat-out refused to pull the footage, and Jordy wouldn't have been able to help you this time. You would have spent the entire week stressed out about it, and it would have affected our rehearsal, your peace of mind, and our dances."

It sounded reasonable. But Gina didn't want to be reasonable right now. She wanted to be mad and she wanted to argue, because everything felt out of control and there was nothing she could do about it. "You still should have told me."

Even to her ears, it sounded stubborn and childish. But it was the only defense she had against throwing the whole disagreement aside and begging him not to go back to Alaska.

She'd never do it. Just as she wouldn't let anyone get in the way of her dreams, she also wouldn't interfere with his. And he'd been perfectly clear from the beginning that when this was all over, he was going home.

She should have listened.

Stone threw up his hands. "You're right. I should have. I'm sorry I didn't. Next time I'll tell you so you can feel anxious and powerless all week."

She glared daggers at him. "I would have gotten my agent involved."

"And Donna would have pointed out that real footage of us kissing doesn't count as a fake showmance. You're not going to win against her."

"You didn't even give me the opportunity to try!" she shot back. "And the fact that you don't understand why I'm upset makes it even worse."

"I do understand. And I'm sorry. Maybe you should try to understand why *I'm* upset."

"You don't have anything to be upset about."

"That's it, then." His lips flattened into a line. "Your feelings are the only ones that matter here." He took a step back and held up his hands. "I get it. It's not about me, and never was. Come back to the room when you're done throwing a fit."

She sucked in a breath, but Stone was already walking away. Swallowing hard, Gina turned back to the sink. She would *not* cry, she would *not* cry, she would—

Lauren appeared in the doorway, making Gina jump.

"God, Lauren, you scared me." She put a hand to her chest to calm her racing heart.

"Trouble in paradise?" Lauren asked with a nasty smirk.

Gina huffed out a breath and went to move past her. "I'm not talking about this with you."

Lauren grabbed her arm, and Gina whirled on her with fire in her eyes. "Lauren, get your hands—"

"I know your boyfriend's dirty little secret."

The singsong whisper set Gina's teeth on edge. "Let. Me. Go."

"Oh, do you already know?" Lauren cocked her head and widened her eyes, blinking like a demented owl. "Don't worry. I won't tell . . . unless I think you're going to win. Lucky for you, I think your little 'true love' gamble is going to backfire. You better hope I don't change my mind."

Gina clenched her jaw to cover the spark of fear. "I don't have time for shit-talking. I have a rumba to choreograph."

Lauren released her and Gina hurried out of the kitchen.

"See you at the finals, Gina," Lauren called after her, followed by a cackling laugh.

Gina's first thought was to tell Stone that Lauren knew the truth about *Living Wild,* but she slowed as she reached the door.

Should she tell him? He'd kept something big from her, claiming it would stress her out. This news was almost certain to wreck his week, and maybe then he'd know how she felt.

Her mother's voice flashed through her mind. *Don't be petty.* She'd said it every time Gina or her siblings had complained about something the others had or hadn't done.

No. Her first impulse was the right one. He needed to know.

Opening the rehearsal room door, Gina stuck her head in. "Stone, can you step outside for a second?"

He gave her a dark look, but handed his lav mic back to Jordy. Good, he hadn't put it on yet.

Gina glanced over her shoulder to make sure Lauren was gone, then pulled Stone out when he joined her at the door. She shut it and spoke quickly and softly.

"I think Lauren knows about your family. The truth about them."

"Christ." Stone shut his eyes, scrunching up his face in annoyance. "What am I supposed to do about it?"

"I don't know. But I wanted to tell you, so you weren't blindsided by it." She gave him a pointed look.

He rubbed his eyes. "Okay. You're right. I should call my producers, just in case. Can I borrow your phone? I left mine at the hotel."

Gina handed her phone to him. "I'll work on the choreography. Take your time."

As she slipped back into the rehearsal room, her heart rate returned to normal and her nerves settled. The anger was still there, but it was tempered by . . .

Determination. No matter what happened in her life, focusing on her work got her through. For the next week, she would throw herself into the choreography and the training. She and Stone would go back to their teacher and student partnership. She would show Donna and everybody what she could do, based on her own merit. And then her life would return to normal.

They were done, and that was the end of it.

Thirty-One

Stone paused in the act of toweling off when someone knocked on his door. It was too much to hope it would be Gina. He stuck his head out of the hotel bathroom and called, "Who is it?"

"Room service."

Huh. He hadn't ordered anything yet. Jackson and Alan had invited him out, but since the finals were filming live the next day, he figured he'd be better off going home to his lonely hotel room.

Wrapping a towel around his waist, Stone stood to the side and opened the door a crack to peer out.

"Surprise!"

Instead of a bored bellhop, his family stood in the hallway. Half of them, anyway.

Stone's stomach jumped, and his hand clenched on the door. It would be rude to slam it in their faces, but their unexpected arrival was the absolute last thing he needed right now.

"Wow. Um, hi." He cleared his throat. "What are you all doing here?"

"Aren't you going to let us in?" his mother asked.

Stone took a quick head count. Pepper, Reed, Violet, Lark, and Wolf, plus a small camera crew.

"I'm not dressed," he said. "And you have cameras."

Pepper gestured for the cameras to wait. "Stone, let me in."

Since she was his mother, he did.

Once they were alone, Pepper took a seat in the armchair on the other side of the bed. "This is a nice room," she said, taking it all in. "Bigger than the ones at the inn back home."

The inn *was* home, since they didn't actually live at Nielson HQ, but Stone didn't correct her.

"I'll be right back." He went into the bathroom and rushed to get dressed, in case his mother started snooping. Not that he had anything to hide, except—shit, there was a giant box of condoms in the top drawer of the dresser, the first place she'd look.

He almost fell in his hurry to pull his jeans on, but when he came out, his mother didn't appear to have moved.

"Where's Gina?" she asked.

Or maybe she had snooped. He picked up a comb and ran it through his wet hair. "At her apartment, I guess. Big day tomorrow."

"I'm looking forward to watching you from the audience. Lark was like to burst when she found out we were coming. Stage-side VIP seating, too."

"I bet." He'd been like to burst when he'd seen them in the hallway.

"We were hoping you . . . and Gina . . . could join us for dinner."

Of course they were. "With cameras?"

His mother flushed. "It's the price we pay. They sent us down here so they could film us acting like country bumpkins in the big city."

It was ridiculous. Pepper had lived in St. Louis when she was younger, and the family had lived in Seattle before moving to Alaska after Winter was born. Stone scratched his beard. "And they were hoping to get more footage of me with Gina."

"You know the game."

He did. And he hated it. But compromises had to be made. *Living Wild* had lent him to *The Dance Off* for the time being, but they still owned him.

"No Gina. But I'll go to dinner with you."

"Great." Pepper stood. "We already have a reservation. Now that you're decent, come out and greet the others. We'll have to reshoot you opening the door. Try to look surprised and happy, okay?"

He grunted. "I'll do my best."

After dinner, when the cameras shut down, Stone pulled his mother aside before she could climb into the waiting SUV with his siblings.

"Did Miguel tell you I called? One of the other contestants made a threat to expose us."

She nodded, her expression turning serious. "I heard."

"What's going to happen if she tells?"

Pepper sighed and tucked her hair behind her ear. "It's always been a possibility. A few smaller blogs have already run the story, which is probably how your nemesis found out, although it hasn't affected the ratings. Your father doesn't like to think about it, but we're on borrowed time. This show won't last forever. They never do."

As much as Stone hated being part of it, *Living Wild* had been a good source of income for all the Nielsons. "That *Swamp Hunters* show is on its tenth season."

Pepper patted his arm. "I only ever wanted enough to live comfortably, on our own terms, and to help send the girls and Winter to college."

Stone was the only one with a four-year degree. Reed had gotten an associate's degree from a community college, and Wolf had said college wasn't for him. Then they'd gotten the show, so Winter and Raven had put off going to school. Everyone had made sacrifices for *Living Wild,* but the money had been too good to pass up.

Gina would have said the cost outweighed the benefits. She wouldn't sell her integrity for money or fame, even though she wanted both.

It was hard to fault her for it, especially when he was so damn proud of her. She was going to get the show in New York, he just knew it.

And then she'd be even farther away from him.

"We've got your medical bills, too," Stone reminded his mother. And himself. It was the reason he'd come to LA in the first place. For the money.

And then he'd met Gina. He couldn't bring himself to regret it.

"We'll get to those. You kids are more important. And you have your own student loans to pay off. I do wish you'd do those first."

Stone gave her what he hoped was a reassuring smile. "If I win, I'll be able to do both, with some left over. How's your hip?"

Pepper patted the hip that had been replaced. "Better than the old one."

He leaned down to give her a hug. "I love you, Mom."

"Oh, where's this coming from?" she sputtered, but she hugged him back.

"Just missed you is all."

"We all miss you, too. Now, you've got a big day tomorrow. You'd better go up and get some sleep." She climbed into the car. "We'll be in the audience cheering you on."

It should have comforted him, but it didn't. His worlds were merging. His family—and *Living Wild*—were sucking him back in. The person he'd become on *The Dance Off* didn't fit into the Nielson dynamic, which had been set decades before, changing slightly with the addition of each new child, or the show's script.

He didn't want to go back to being the person he'd been. It was already happening, though. He'd been quiet through dinner, while Reed and Violet dominated the conversation. He was quieter in rehearsals, since he wasn't joking around with Gina anymore.

His old life was calling. What would it cost him to stuff himself back into the *Living Wild* role? And was it worth it?

One more day. And then he'd find out.

G ina gave Stone a high five after they finished their redemption jive. "That was great," she said evenly. "Good job."

They'd reached a tentative peace, where they could at least work together. Despite their distance, Stone's dancing was better than ever. He'd thrown himself into rehearsals with a gusto that made his previous efforts look like those of a slacker.

She, on the other hand, felt as brittle as blown glass. Through sheer willpower, she'd managed to smile and play the role of the excited finalist, but her control hung by a thread.

Stone nodded, a glint of determination still in his eye. "One more dance," he said.

"One more." Was this night ever going to end?

They joined Reggie to receive their scores. Stone chatted with the host, which was great because Gina was barely following what they said. Before last week, she would have been proud of how he handled the questions. He'd come a long way since their first meeting, more at ease on camera and in his own skin. The *Boylesque* dance seemed to have marked a turning point for him, and while she was glad he was opening up and having fun in front of the cameras, it hurt at the same time. The impending separation would be easier if he were still the same closed-off, recalcitrant giant she'd first met.

Their score flashed on screen. One hundred percent.

Holy shit. Their first dance of the finals, and they had a perfect score.

With a cheer, Stone picked her up and spun her in a circle.

Even as Gina held on to him, her chest ached. While her anger had diminished over the week, it left in its place despair and guilt at the things she'd accused him of. After blowing up at him in the kitchen, her warning about Lauren had struck some kind of truce between them. But being this close to Stone every day, missing him and wanting him, and pretending that things were fine, was utter torture.

The show must go on.

The rest of the night was a haze. Every minute that passed brought them closer to their rumba, and she dreaded it. The dance contained everything she felt for him but didn't dare say.

All the longing, the passion, and the incredible gratitude. Stone had opened her heart and made her *feel*. He'd *seen* her, and helped her be comfortable with being seen. With him, she didn't have to hide, to guard herself. She'd felt safe with him.

And despite his boneheaded mistake, she still did.

More fool she. He was leaving soon, just as she'd always known he would.

After changing into her rumba costume—a bedazzled beige leotard with a sheer white skirt draped loosely over her hips—Gina hung around backstage in the Sparkle Parlor. She cheered for the other dancers, did funny dances for the cameras before commercial breaks, and made small talk with the celebrities who'd returned for the finale.

No matter how many times she repeated the words *one more dance* to herself, it didn't sink in that this was the end. She'd never made it to the finals before. She'd wanted to win for so long. Now, she was closer than ever, but . . . she didn't care.

Maybe some things were more important than winning.

Gina turned and caught Stone staring at her from across the room. His troubled gaze churned up her longing for him. They were both suffering. She shook her head and shrugged. What did he want her to say?

There was something in the set of his jaw that made her think he was going to come over and comfort her. But she couldn't take his sweetness right now. Not with the end so imminent. Instead, she slipped through the crowd and found Kevin. Kevin would talk, and she'd pretend to listen. It was what she needed.

Finally, it was time to take the floor one last time.

Gina took her place with Stone, listening to the behind-the-scenes package with half her attention. The narrative played up Gina's preoccupation with the choreography, her commitment to perfection, Stone's determination to win, and their journey from the beginning. It made no mention of the kiss revealed in last week's footage, or their argument in the kitchen.

Small mercies.

The music swelled, and their last dance began.

Gina folded into the first move, curling in and hugging herself with her arms. Stone tugged her back to him and led her through the steps of the rumba.

She couldn't have kept her eyes off his if she'd wanted to. He wore an intense, stricken expression, something akin to grief flashing in his blue eyes. Every time he pulled her close, her heart broke anew. When she danced away from him, it was like swimming through molasses. All she wanted to do was let him hold her. She'd taught him too well—he knew how to lead now, and whatever drew her to him was too strong to be denied.

"What do you have to lose?" the live singer crooned.

Everything.

They flowed with the music, breaking apart and coming together, pleading with their hands and bodies. For what?

See me. Understand me. Love me.

Her body rejoiced when he held her against him. Her heart hurt when she pulled away.

This was the last time she'd feel his hands on her. She cherished every moment.

Their bodies stilled as the last line of the song rang out. "What'll you do when you have nothing left to lose?"

Gina burst into tears.

She'd already lost the things she'd tried so hard to protect. Her private life, her relationships, her reputation.

Her heart.

What was left?

She'd done everything she could to win the trophy. It was up to the judges now.

Thirty-Two

The dance ended with Stone holding Gina against his chest. His heart pounded so hard he couldn't catch his breath.

He didn't want to let her go. Not now, not ever.

Gina covered her face. Her shoulders hunched and her body shook.

"Gina?" Stone turned her, cupping the back of her head.

"I'm fine." She pulled away from him and wiped her eyes carefully. "Come on."

They moved toward the judges' table to receive personal comments. The judges looked concerned. It was like a flashback to last week, after the damning footage from Alaska.

Juan Carlos stepped in and urged Gina closer. "How are you doing, Gina? You all right there?"

She nodded. "It was a very emotional dance, and an emotional journey. I just can't believe it's over."

"That was your last dance with Stone."

She bit her lip and nodded. "I know."

Helplessness washed over Stone, along with the need to comfort Gina. She was hurting, and he wanted to soothe her, even though he was hurting, too.

Instead, he had to stand there, watching as she struggled to control her reaction. It fucking sucked.

All of it sucked. He was tired of holding back from her. But a gap had opened between them and there was no easy way to cross it.

Dimitri Kovalenko went first.

"I don't really know what to say." He flipped his pen in the air. It landed on the desk and rolled off. "That was perfect."

Juan Carlos grinned. "High praise, from that guy. Mariah, tell us your thoughts."

Mariah Valentino dabbed at the corner of her eye, then leaned in, giving the camera a look down the front of her skintight dress.

"You two have danced well together all season, but this was the most connected I've ever seen you. It was like you were one being in two parts, bound by an invisible cord and a telepathic bond. Truly a stunning, emotional dance. And Gina, I think this is the best rumba choreography I've ever seen on this show."

Blinking hard, Gina pressed her hands to her chest and mouthed, "Thank you."

Juan Carlos extended a hand toward Chad Silver, all the way to the left. "Chad?"

Chad turned a kind smile on Gina. "I know the past few months have been an emotional roller coaster, but you've both handled every challenge with grace and determination." He turned to Stone, his dark eyes intense. "Stone, you're the underdog, but you've approached each dance with trust in your partner and a commitment to getting it right. Maybe you never danced before coming here, but I hope you'll continue after you leave. You're a force to be reckoned with, and we're so very glad to have had you here."

Chad's words hit hard. Stone swallowed, and nodded. "Thank you."

As if sensing vulnerability, Juan Carlos leaped in with his microphone. "Stone, do you have anything to say about that?"

Aside from the fact that it was the kind of thing Stone wished his father might someday say? "Ah, well, it means a lot to me to hear that. I respect the judges for their experience, so it . . . it means a lot. Thank you."

"All right, you two. Go meet Reggie to get your score one last time."

Stone didn't try to hold Gina's hand or put an arm around her as they ran back to the Sparkle Parlor. She looked as fragile as he felt. Nothing had prepared him for the overwhelming emotion of this night.

Backstage, they joined Reggie in front of her camera.

"That was such a romantic dance," the host gushed. "I was back here in tears. Thank goodness for the makeup department, am I right? Stone, what was it like for you to hear comments like those from the judges, after months of critique?"

This was easy to answer. "It's all thanks to Gina," he said. "She's been the most amazing teacher and partner, patient and giving. If not for her, I never would have made it this far, and I'd still just be an emotionally stunted wilderness nut." Everyone around them laughed, but Gina looked over her shoulder at him with tears shimmering in her eyes. He said the next words directly to her. "I'm very . . . very grateful, for all she's done for me."

Now, he did put his arm around her, and she gave him a squeeze in return.

"Thank you." Her voice was soft, as was her expression.

"So sweet." Reggie grinned and turned back to the camera. "Let's get your scores."

Colors swirled on the screen. Stone's heart pounded. At his side, Gina tensed.

A giant, sparkly one hundred appeared.

Reggie cheered. "Another perfect score!"

Stone hugged Gina fiercely. When the cameras cut away, he let her go. He wanted to kiss her, but didn't dare. Her eyes still looked watery.

She took a step back, averting her gaze. "Come on. Let's watch Lauren and Kevin's rumba."

"It won't hold a candle to ours."

Pride—for her, for their dance—made Stone feel ten feet tall. Kevin and Lauren wouldn't be able to match them. The rumba was a dance of love, and Stone was totally fucking in love with Gina. He'd been falling for her since the moment she'd walked into the Nielson HQ clearing and taught him to waltz on the back porch. He'd fought it for a while, but he couldn't lie to himself any longer.

Damn, and his mom and four of his siblings were in the audience. They would say something, for sure. He was in for a lot of shit-talking when he got back to Alaska.

The thought of returning home should have cheered him up. It didn't. Going back to Alaska meant leaving Gina, which had somehow become the last thing he wanted to do.

They watched Lauren and Kevin's dance on the Sparkle Parlor's screens. Technically, their rumba was perfect. Kevin was a great choreographer, and Lauren executed every move with precision. But Stone had been dancing—and watching the others—long enough that he could see how their rumba differed from his and Gina's.

There was something forced about the way Lauren conveyed feeling. As someone who'd been faking emotion on camera for four years, it was glaringly obvious to him. She made the faces, smiling when she should smile and scowling when the dance style called for it, but she was acting, not feeling.

Then there was the fact that she and Kevin had absolutely no sexual chemistry.

Dance was about intimacy and vulnerability, connection and communication. Stone's training with Gina had shown him that, and not just because of their physical relationship. Gina had insisted he get in touch with his emotions, which had been hard at the beginning, but he had to admit it made a difference. A good dance told a story of two people who connected on a level deeper than words.

Kevin and Lauren didn't have that. At all. So while Lauren didn't miss a step, Stone was sure that if he didn't feel any sort of emotional reaction while watching her, it was likely the judges wouldn't either.

The dance ended. Stone clapped, then listened closely while Lauren and Kevin received their comments from the judges. He bit back a smug grin as Mariah pointed out that their dance didn't make her feel anything.

The scoreboard flashed, showing the combined scores for the night for all three couples. Stone's heart leaped. He was on the top, with a perfect score. Jackson was three points below, and Lauren was in third place, with ninety-four percent average.

Holy shit. Maybe he could win this.

Gina appeared at his side and spoke in a low voice. "Viewer votes from last week. That's what will make or break us."

"I believe in us."

She didn't reply, but her lips pursed. The unspoken *I don't* cut deep.

It all came down to Donna's gamble. Had airing the kiss turned the viewers against them, as Gina feared it would, or had it drawn the audience into their love story?

When Stone had arrived in Los Angeles, he'd sworn to avoid the drama and the media circus at all costs. Now he was neck deep and playing to win.

Was it worth it, though? Even if they won the trophy, he'd lost Gina. At one point he'd hoped they could try some sort of long-distance relationship, but after his misstep with the kiss footage, she'd made it clear they were done.

One of the ubiquitous stage managers appeared to usher them out. They'd gone through it in dress rehearsal. The third-place winner would be chosen first, then they'd break for commercial, then the first-place winner would be named, and the hideous glittery trophy would be bestowed on the season fourteen champion.

If Stone won, someday he'd have his own house and place the gaudy thing on his mantle, front and center.

On second thought, it would only remind him of Gina. His mother could have it.

They took their place on the stage under the spotlights. Stone put an arm around Gina's shoulders from behind, holding her against him. Was she as nervous as he was? While Juan Carlos talked, Stone closed his eyes and pressed his forehead to Gina's hair. He filled his nose and lungs with her tropical scent.

"Gina?"

"Not now."

"When?"

She didn't answer. Did that mean never?

Juan Carlos threw out an arm toward the stage. "And that makes our third-place winner . . ." He drew it out. The music turned low and menacing. "Jackson and Lori!" The music lifted and soared, the crowd cheered, and Gina and Stone shifted to give Jackson and Lori hugs before they ran off the stage.

"I told you," Gina muttered when they took their places again. "It was always Lauren and Kevin."

Stone pressed a kiss to the top of her head. "Don't give up on me now."

Her shoulders tensed, and her voice came out breathy and raw. "Please don't make this harder than it has to be."

When the show cut to a commercial, Gina broke away from him to hug Lori again.

This time, when the spotlights came back up, Stone rested his hands on Gina's shoulders, needing to anchor himself. "I'm not trying to make this harder for you. I just—I'm nervous, okay?"

She put her hand over one of his and squeezed. "Don't be. No matter what, you're going to walk away from this a star."

"Not if Lauren destroys my show."

"You'll recover. Men always do."

She was talking about them, and the impact their relationship might have on her career. Regret weighed heavy on his soul.

The music lowered once again. Juan Carlos called out, "And the first-place winners and season fourteen champions of *The Dance Off* are . . ."

The cameras were right on them. Stone closed his eyes and gripped Gina's shoulders tight.

". . . Stone and Gina!"

Stone's eyes flew open.

Under his hands, Gina jerked. "What?"

The word was echoed from their left, where Lauren stared at them with wide, disbelieving eyes.

"You won!" Kevin yelled.

Gina appeared to be in shock. Everyone rushed them while Juan Carlos shouted for Lauren and Kevin to join him for an interview. Stone lifted Gina in his arms. She clung to him, gasping for air.

Her voice shook. "Did I hear that right? Did we win?"

"We won." He kissed her temple.

When she pulled back, her smile was sad. "You were right. Congratulations."

Shit. Stone didn't want to be right. He wanted *her*.

The others reached them, showering them in hugs, kisses, and congratulations. It was overwhelming. Everywhere he looked, another smiling face. He lost Gina in the crowd. After a minute, he heard Juan Carlos yelling for him.

"Gina?" Stone searched for her amid the sparkling, glittering mob. Wading in, he grabbed her hand and tugged her off the stage. As they passed Kevin and Lauren, they paused to wish them well. Lauren grabbed Stone's ass and he reared back, startled.

"Cut it out, Lauren," he growled, but the figure skater just gave him a saucy wink.

"Congrats," she said, pouting her painted lips. "Enjoy the spotlight while it lasts." Then she was swept off in the crowd and Stone and Gina were at Juan Carlos's side. In the host's hands was *The Dance Off*'s trophy.

"You two have earned this," Juan Carlos said. "Congratulations!"

Stone took the gold trophy, which was encrusted with mirrored rhinestones forming the silhouette of a dancing couple. It was disgusting. He'd treasure it forever.

"Here," he said, turning to Gina. "Hold this."

Her face lit up when she took it, but the light was still tempered by sadness. Once she had the trophy, Stone gripped her by the waist and lifted her up to sit on one of his shoulders. She let out a startled giggle, then, smiling wide, she raised the trophy over her head and gave a loud cheer.

It should have been beautiful. It should have been the most wonderful moment in his life, to have delivered this win to the woman he loved, and to have helped her achieve her dream.

Instead, this was the end.

Thirty-Three

The next twelve hours were a whirlwind. From greeting fans, posing for photos, and rushing through interviews, to boarding *The Dance Off*'s private jet for an overnight flight to New York City, Gina didn't have a second to breathe. Being packed into the little plane with the other finalists and four of the other pro dancers—including Natasha, thank goodness—didn't leave a lot of room for self-reflection or dwelling on her problems.

Delirium set in halfway through the flight. Gina didn't remember landing or the party bus ride from the airport to the *Morning Mix* studio—but there were lots of selfies and videos posted on social media, so she'd piece it together later.

After arriving in the jeans she'd worn on the plane, she signed autographs for the fans gathered outside the studio building, then hurried inside to change into a dance costume. After a quick group routine, she was dressed in her TV outfit—tight black pants, a sequined silver tank, and heels.

Exhaustion tugged at her limbs, but euphoria and adrenaline kept her focused. She laughed when she was supposed to laugh, answered questions with charm and humor, and showed off the trophy.

The last time she'd been here, she'd been so excited. Now, she couldn't wait for it to be over.

Then, of course, the conversation took a turn.

"Gina," said one of the hosts. "You and Stone had an interesting moment before the semifinals. We have a clip."

On the big screen behind them, they replayed the kiss footage. Gina's stomach knotted, but she kept her smile in place.

The host grinned. "Want to tell us what that was all about?"

Gina fed them the story she'd come up with. "We were practicing a bit for a dance. Obviously, we decided not to use it."

The hosts murmured, and one of the others leaned in with a glint in her eye. "Come on, Gina. You can tell us. Is Stone a good kisser or what?"

The arm Stone had thrown around her shoulders stiffened. Through sheer force of will, Gina continued to smile.

"Yes, absolutely." She held up her hands when everyone burst into laughter. "What? Should I have lied?"

Stone covered his face with his hands.

Satisfied, the hosts transitioned to the next segment.

Gina turned to Stone, who was staring at her. He shook his head, giving her a half-smirk.

Her heart thumped. She wanted to poke him and joke around. She wanted to know they could hang out afterward and rehash this whole absurd experience, like they had every week after each episode.

But she couldn't. Whatever TV magic had captivated them was over. The spell was broken, and now they were just two very different people with very different lives. It was time to return to the hopes and dreams that had propelled them toward *The Dance Off* in the first place.

A few more interviews, and then it would all be over.

After they'd fulfilled their *Morning Mix* commitments, Gina stood on the sidewalk with Stone and the other cast members.

He was getting on the party bus to the airport, to catch a ride back to LA on the private jet, and from there a flight to Alaska. His luggage had already been sent to Juneau.

It was hard to embrace the truth, that this was really it. It was always a shock to end a season, but not like this. She'd never made it this far—to the finals, to winning—and she'd never gotten so close to one of her partners.

Never fallen in love with one.

She hated the word, had avoided it the whole of her adult life. And here she was, twenty-seven years old and unable to think of anything else that encompassed the depth of her feelings for Stone.

Putting off their goodbye, she focused on everyone else first. Finally, Natasha stepped forward and gave her a big hug.

"I wish you were coming with me," Gina said.

Natasha let out an exasperated huff. "If my mother wanted to see me, she'd return my messages. I'm not going to show up at her apartment without notice. And for what? So we can fight? No gracias."

"My mom and sister would love to see you."

Tash cracked a smile. "Give them my love."

"I will."

They hugged again, then Natasha got on the bus.

Gina turned around to find Stone standing behind her. He held his arms out. Before she could question the wisdom of her actions, she stepped into his embrace and hugged him hard.

One more couldn't hurt.

It did, though. Oh, it did hurt. Her chest tightened, and her eyes got hot, like they wanted to spill tears. She breathed deep, filling her nose and lungs and memory with the fresh, wild scent of him, which he'd somehow never lost after three months in Los Angeles. He was so warm, his chest hard beneath her cheek. His arms, big and strong around her body, squeezed her close. Ready and willing to protect her from everything.

Except for the distance he was about to put between them. She'd always known it was inevitable, and it was stupid of her to have let herself fall so deep and so hard.

Gina eased back. With great effort, she met his eyes. "Have a good trip back to Alaska."

Stone gave her a long, steady look. His mouth opened, then he shook his head, like he was going to say something, then changed his mind. "Break a leg. In the audition, I mean."

"I know what you meant." She fought back the nervous smile that tugged at her lips. Tried to think of something else to say. Found nothing. "I guess . . . this is it."

Again, Stone opened his mouth, paused, and closed it. The awkward silence stretched between them, pulling taut, trying to drag them together. Her stomach muscles tensed against the need to close the distance. To hug him one more time. To kiss him even though they were surrounded by people.

Why the fuck was she resisting so hard?

Stone exhaled, his massive shoulders rising and falling. "Bye, Gina." His voice was low, almost sad.

"Bye, Stone." She held back everything else she wanted to say to him and collected the pieces of her broken heart as he boarded the bus.

Well, the show must go on.

After making sure her sunglasses and Yankees cap were in place, Gina gathered her emotional shields, grabbed the handle of her suitcase, and headed for the casting studio.

O ver the course of her career, Gina had been to plenty of auditions. Hell, she'd even attended auditions at the exact rehearsal space in the Garment District where she was meeting Hector Oquendo and the *Bronx Girl* team. So it was silly to be nervous. All the same, her skin hummed with anticipation as she rode the elevator up, her fingers clenching on the handle of her rolling suitcase like it was a lifeline.

When the elevator let her out, she checked the map in the reception area for the room number her agent had emailed her. Heart pounding, she made her way through a maze of hallways that smelled of floor cleaner and dodged people in dance and workout gear who were reading lines and trying to act like they weren't all nervous and intimidated, too. For once, Gina didn't have to worry about any of them. She was the only one auditioning for this role. It was hers to lose.

No pressure.

When she found the correct room, she closed her eyes for a moment and took a deep breath. All the stress of the past week—dealing with Donna, breaking up with Stone, winning *The Dance Off*, and jumping through verbal hoops on *Morning Mix*—had left her utterly worn out. Really, she wanted to sleep for a week. Or six. But this was the chance of a lifetime. It was exactly what she'd wanted ever since she was a kid. If she got this role, and if *Bronx Girl* did well, she was set. She couldn't let her mind be consumed by . . . everything else.

Stone.

It tore her up inside to think about him. He wouldn't be on the plane yet. In a movie, this would be the moment where she dropped everything and raced to the airport to stop him from leaving.

But this was New York City. One did not *race* to the airports. One sat in traffic, or squashed onto the train or bus, hugging one's suitcase between one's knees and praying the security line wasn't bonkers.

Anyway, he had his life to get back to. Just like she had hers. As always, her career came first. And she was about to take the next big step.

Gina pushed the door open.

Holy mother of . . .

Meli!

Gina's jaw dropped. Meli stood with a group of people at the far end of the rehearsal room, gathered around a rectangular folding table. Meli's brown hair was swept into a high ponytail, and she wore a white blouse, glittery jeans, and wedge sandals.

Not even in Gina's wildest dreams could she have imagined playing Meli on Broadway, and now she was about to audition in front of the woman herself. For some reason, it had never crossed her mind that Meli might be present. The nerves that had buzzed innocuously before now threatened to overwhelm.

Since no one had noticed her yet, Gina took a moment to get herself under control, sucking in a deep breath and letting it out slowly. It wasn't like she hadn't met Meli before. They'd spoken briefly just a few weeks earlier. The whole reason she was here now was because Meli believed in her.

And she had to stop thinking, or she was going to psych herself out. Better to get this over with before anxiety could overtake her.

Striding forward, Gina fixed a big smile on her face.

Hector the producer spotted her first. "Ah, Gina's here."

The others looked up, and as Hector made introductions, Gina filed away everyone's names. The director, writer, music director, choreographer, casting director—shit, *everyone* was here. The whole production team. Even more amazing, everyone was Latine. Plus the writer, director, and casting director were women, and the choreographer was nonbinary.

But then Meli came around the table and enfolded Gina in a rose-scented hug, and Gina forgot about everyone else.

"Gina, I'm so glad you could make it."

"Of course." Gina's thoughts were a litany of *omigod omigod omigod*, but she tried to play it cool. "Thank you for thinking of me for this part."

Meli waved that away. "As soon as I saw you, I knew. I wanted to ask you then and there, but I had to run to the airport. That's why I sent Hector."

Gina grinned so hard her face hurt. This whole thing was like a dream.

After the team took their seats around the table, Gina was surprised when Meli indicated she should sit and join them.

"You're the first actor we're auditioning," Meli told her. "Since you're playing me, you're the most important person in the show. Obviously." She gave her ponytail a flip, and everyone laughed.

Gina just nodded and bit her tongue before she blurted out that she hadn't gotten the part yet. This was the strangest audition she'd ever been to, but if they wanted to act like she was already part of the team, that was fine with her.

The writer explained the basic premise of the story, which would follow Meli's rise to stardom, starting in the Bronx and ending with her Vegas residency. The music director handed Gina a list of songs. About half were Meli's greatest hits, and the others were new, written to advance the narrative.

"The theme of the story is finding yourself," Meli added. "And the cost of fame. It's . . . not exactly a traditional happy ending." She wiggled the bare ring finger on her left hand. "But it's a universal story. And I'm happy with my life, so I guess it is a happy ending, after all."

After discussing a few more details with the director about staging and production, the music director finally asked Gina to sing.

"If you have prepared songs, those are fine, but we'd also like to see how you do with some of Meli's songs."

He passed her a sheet of paper, and Gina gave a strangled laugh. "Oh, I don't need the lyrics. I've sung this into my hairbrush more times than I can count."

When Meli beamed, Gina thought she would pass out. Instead, she took her spot, breathed like her vocal coach had taught her, and began to sing. And because it was a Meli song, and Meli was *right there,* she did a few dance moves, too.

When she was done, Meli clapped and yelled, "*Wepa!*"

They had Gina sing some more, and at one point, Meli got up to sing and dance along with her. Gina nearly died.

The choreographer got involved then, and when they asked for Gina's opinion on the moves, Gina almost wept with excitement. The team was really serious about letting her put her mark on this show.

Dream. Come. True.

After the casting director had Gina do a cold reading from the script, Meli called for a break. One of the assistants brought in water, coffee, and a fruit platter.

Gina sat on the floor to stretch, and Meli came over and dropped down beside her.

"You're great," Meli said. "We're offering you the part. Hector will come over at some point and make it official, but I wanted you to know."

Excited tremors rumbled beneath Gina's skin. "*Thank you,*" she said, giving the words emphasis in a vain effort to express the depth of her feeling. "I mean it. Really. Thank you."

Meli grinned at her. "This show is going to be a hit. I hope you're ready."

"Oh, I'm ready."

It was finally happening. Everything Gina had worked toward, for so many years. Her career was leveling up, faster and higher than even she, with all her big dreams, had imagined.

And yet, something weighed her down.

Probably exhaustion. She'd hadn't slept on the overnight flight from Los Angeles, and she'd been going nonstop for days. The excitement would hit her later, after it all sank in.

"How's your partner?" Meli asked. "From *The Dance Off.* You guys filmed a live show this morning, right? I thought you might bring him with you."

Just like that, the excitement bubble popped.

There it was. Not exhaustion or stress, but Stone. Missing him was like a lead weight in Gina's gut.

She fought to keep her tone light when she answered. "He's heading back to Alaska. His show is still filming."

Meli nodded like she understood more than Gina was saying, and she leaned in, lowering her voice. "I get it. It's hard to nurture a relationship in this industry."

With a rueful smile, Meli gestured toward the team, who spoke animatedly over the script. "They're debating whether or not to cast four different men as my husbands. Although for your sake, I suggested they cast one guy, and put him in different costumes and wigs. Then you only have to develop chemistry with one person, and the audience can bond with him, too."

"I think that's a good idea." Gina hesitated, then asked, "Is it difficult to put all that out there on the stage? To be open about your love life?"

Meli leaned back on her hands and pursed her lips as she thought. Finally, she said, "Not as much as you would think. Is it embarrassing? A bit. But it's my life. I'm not going to stay with someone just because of what the tabloids might say, and I'm also not going to hold back because of that same fear. You get me?"

Gina nodded slowly. "I think so."

Meli had a point, but it was easy for her to say that now—she was an international superstar. Had she had the same philosophy when she was just making a name for herself?

Gathering her courage, Gina asked, "Do you wish it had turned out differently?"

Meli looked her dead in the eye. "No. I followed what was important to me. Would it be nice to have a partner to share all this with? A family? Sure. And maybe it will happen, someday. I'm an optimist. But I went after what I wanted, and I got it."

The fame. Yes, Meli had the fame. She'd made it big, and lived life on her own terms. *Bronx Girl* was Meli's creative vision, and although she was letting the professionals do their jobs, it was clear who was in charge here. Everything about it was inspiring.

But there was a sadness in her eyes when she talked about her failed marriages. And when Gina later read the script in the taxi on her way to the Bronx, her heart broke each time one of Meli's relationships combusted. Four times she'd tried, and four times her marriages had exploded spectacularly. The men left, and Meli was alone. But she still had her career—the fame, the fortune, and the fans.

Maybe Gina shouldn't have asked Meli if she wished it had turned out differently. Maybe a better question would have been, was it enough?

Every time Gina walked in the door of her mother's apartment, she was welcomed by the smell of home, a mix of the lemon-scented cleaning polish used on the old wooden furniture, the homemade rose potpourri in decorative bowls on the windowsill, and the sazón used so often in Puerto Rican cuisine.

Gina still had keys, so she let herself in and dragged her suitcase through the living room and down the hall to the second bedroom, the one she used to share with her brother and sister. After storing her luggage by the wall, she flopped onto the twin bed, covered with a quilt made by her great-grandmother.

The toll of being awake for a day and a half pulled her under. Before Gina passed out, her phone buzzed with a text from her agent, Penelope.

How many press stops should I book for you?

Ugh. This was about *The Dance Off*. Gina had won, and everyone was going to want to interview her. She typed her response before she could talk herself out of it.

None. I need a break. Gonna stay with my family for a couple days.

Are you serious? You need to maximize the publicity to stay in the viewers' hearts and minds—and those of casting directors.

Gina didn't bother to reply that she'd already lined up her next gig. Tossing the phone aside, she settled her head onto the pillow. Yeah, she knew all about the planning, the timing, the exposure. She just didn't care. What did it matter? They'd only want to ask her about Stone. And if that was the most interesting thing about her . . . what was the point?

For three years, her goal had been to win *The Dance Off*. Now she'd done it. It was the ideal time to turn that win into opportunities. And while she was thrilled with the *Bronx Girl* job, she couldn't drum up the enthusiasm to run around to more meetings. It was hustle. It was work. Gina was *tired*.

And okay, she was lonely, too. She missed Stone. She missed strategizing with him and explaining her thought processes. He always wanted to know the *why* behind her decisions. Not to question her, but to better understand so he could help.

She'd lost her why. Whatever had driven her all this time was gone. She'd wanted to win *The Dance Off*, thinking it would fulfill some need. But now she'd won, and she still didn't feel fulfilled.

What was missing?

Stone.

No, it couldn't be that simple.

G ina woke with a start when her mother entered the room. "Oh, I didn't know you were sleeping." Benita backed out of the door. "I'll let you rest."

"No, Mami, está bien." Gina rubbed her eyes. "What time is it?"

"Five. I left work early, because I knew you'd be here. Sleep if you need to sleep."

"No, I'll get up. That was a good nap."

"I bet you needed it." Her mother sat on the edge of the bed and pulled her into a hug. "I missed you, mija."

"I missed you, too." And because it was her mom, and mom hugs beat out all other hugs, Gina let the tears come.

Benita gasped, then hugged her tighter. "¿Qué pasó, Gigi?" she asked, resorting to Gina's childhood nickname.

Gina sniffled and wiped her face. "You know."

"I don't, because you haven't returned my calls all week. You only texted, and ignored my questions about that boy."

"'That boy' is what this is about."

"Stone? The one you kissed?"

Gina let out a weepy laugh. "I'm so freaking embarrassed about that."

"Pero why?"

Gina was saved from answering by the sound of keys in the

front door. A second later, her sister Araceli's voice floated down the hall.

"Knock knock! Anyone home?"

"Aquí," Benita called.

Araceli appeared in the bedroom doorway. "Gina, are you crying?"

Benita answered for her. "Sí. We're talking about that man she kissed on TV."

Groaning, Gina covered her face with a pillow.

"Yeah, I was curious about that." Celi joined them on the bed and snatched the pillow away. "Spill it."

Gina huffed out a breath and pulled her knees up to her chest, explaining in a few brief sentences what had occurred with Donna and the kiss footage.

Araceli and Benita exchanged glances.

"Where is Stone now?" Celi asked.

"At this point? Probably on a plane back to Alaska."

Another shared glance.

Gina huffed. "I'm *right here,* you two. Stop talking about me with your eyes."

"I have a few more questions before I judge you." Celi held up a finger. "First of all, what's the real deal with you and Stone?"

"We . . ." Normally, Gina didn't mind talking about men with her sister. Granted, their mother was there, too, but still, Gina was at a loss for words. "We were kind of seeing each other?"

"You were sleeping together."

"Oh my god." Gina flopped back onto the bed and covered her face. "Yes. We were."

"Gina, I know you're a grown-up," her mother said.

"Mami, could you please just not?"

Araceli scoffed. "Get up and stop acting like a child. If I wanted to deal with kids right now, I'd go find my own."

Gina sat up. "Where are they, anyway?"

"At Abuela's house. Don't change the subject. How do you feel about Stone?"

Fuuuuuck. "Um . . ."

"For real, Gina. No bullshit."

Gina rubbed her eyes again. "I think I was falling in love with him."

Silence.

When she looked, her mother and sister were staring at each other with wide eyes, raised eyebrows, and pursed lips.

"Hey, what did I say about silent eye conversations?"

Araceli shook her head. "Sorry, but this is a first. I don't think I've ever heard you use the word 'love' about a guy before."

"That's because I *haven't.*" Gina's gut twisted at the thought of what she was losing, and her lip wobbled in response. "This thing with Stone isn't like anything I've ever felt before."

"And he doesn't feel the same way?" Celi asked, her tone gentling.

"I don't know. He said something about falling for me."

Celi slapped her forehead. "Are you kidding? Men don't say stuff like that unless they mean it."

"He knew how I felt about having our . . . relationship or what-ever it was . . . be public. He should have told me what he knew."

"Why, so you could obsess about it like a lunatic?"

Gina glared at her sister. "No, so I could have convinced Donna not to air it."

"How?" Araceli's gaze took on a challenging light. "You've told me all about that woman. What if she had completely disregarded your wishes?"

"I'd have gotten my agent involved." The argument was remark-ably similar to the one she'd had with Stone in the kitchen. The opposing viewpoint sounded increasingly rational the more times she heard it.

"And then what? If Donna didn't back down, would you have quit when you were so close to winning?"

"I didn't know I was going to win," Gina shot back. "I don't want my personal life being put on display. Who knows what it will make people think of me?"

"Why do you care?"

"Remember that thing with Ruben?"

"Fuck Ruben." Celi dismissed him with a wave of her hand. "You're in the big leagues now. Ruben was small time. Besides, you were—what? Eighteen?"

"Seventeen."

"Mistakes made as a teenager count as life experience. Learn the lesson and move on."

"I *did* learn the lesson. Never get involved with someone I'm working with." *And never get involved with someone who won't stick around.*

Celi wagged her finger. "Nope, that's not the lesson. The lesson is don't date selfish assholes."

Benita nodded wisely. "That is a good lesson."

"Besides," Celi went on. "It wasn't even that big of a deal. The kiss was shown, and what happened? Nothing. You still won."

"But I didn't want that to be the thing that made me win. I wanted it to be my talent and skill as a choreographer, and—"

"Bullshit." Celi jabbed a finger in Gina's face. "You know that's not how *The Dance Off* works. Fame and personality play a huge part. The bottom line is that it was helping you before the kiss was even aired. You and Stone have what Kevin and Lauren didn't. Real chemistry, real personality. I know everyone and their mother loves Kevin, but he's a fake-ass plastic doll. Sure, he's funny and nice and all that, but he's fake. There's something going on there behind that good ol' boy surface that I don't trust."

Gina sighed. "It doesn't matter anyway because I didn't want all this. I didn't want to fall in love with someone—anyone—right now. Or ever. Especially not someone who lives in the middle of nowhere on the other side of the country. I have too much work to do to build my career, and a man will only get in the way of that."

"Esperate." Their mother held up a hand to interrupt. "Is this because of me and your father?"

Gina pressed her lips together, but she was helpless to remain silent under the pointed stares of both her mother and sister. When she answered, her voice came out quiet and ashamed. "Yes, it's because of Papi."

"Ay, mija." Benita pressed a hand to Gina's cheek. "All this time, you've been carrying this around? The idea that a man will get in the way of your career?"

"It's what happened. You would have had a great singing career if not for Papi. And then he left."

"You can't know that. Success is a fickle thing, and the entertainment industry isn't all it's cracked up to be. Don't forget, I agreed to give it up. He didn't force me."

"Have you ever regretted it?" Even asking, Gina felt small and young. It was something she'd wondered forever, and part of her had always wanted to build her career higher and stronger so her mother's sacrifice wasn't in vain.

Benita shook her head. "Not at all. My family is the greatest gift I've ever been given. Success isn't everything, mija."

Gina chewed that over. "I still want it, though. Is that bad?"

"Not at all. You're allowed to want what you want. And you're allowed to want *all* of it, even the stuff you think you shouldn't want, or can't have."

Her mother pulled her into a hug and whispered in her ear, "He's not your father, Gina. Not all men leave. And even if he does, you'll survive." She got to her feet and tapped Araceli on the shoulder. "Come help me with dinner."

Before Araceli left the room, she stopped in the doorway. "How did the audition go?"

"Hmm?" Lost in her musings, Gina had forgotten all about it. "Oh, it went well. They offered me the lead role."

Celi gave her a thumbs-up. "Rock on."

Thirty-Four

On his first day back filming *Living Wild*, Stone managed to smash his thumb in the door of his room at the Glacier Valley Inn. After his fingernail started turning black, they had to stage a similar event at Nielson HQ to explain it. That same day, he fell over the side of the boat—*not* staged—and was knocked out with a nasty sinus infection for a week.

Sliding out of bed, Stone stumbled into the bathroom. His fever had finally abated, but he still felt like hell. He took a piss and splashed cold water on his face, which wasn't the best idea. Shivering from the chill, he tottered back to bed and rolled up in the blankets like a burrito.

Horrible as he felt, he was glad he'd gotten sick, because he had no fucking desire to return to *Living Wild*. He'd never wanted to do this stupid show in the first place. But, like always, his family had needed him and he'd set aside his own desires to help them.

At the time, Stone hadn't expected it to last. It was a dumb idea. Who'd want to watch a bunch of yahoos with silly names living in the woods? He figured he'd be back to his old life in Juneau within a year.

Inexplicably, the show had been an instant hit, and their contracts were extended.

After the fifth season, though, his current contract would be up. He just had to finish filming this one, and then get through one more . . .

No. He couldn't do it.

Stone's stomach twisted in knots, shying away from the idea of even one more episode, let alone a whole other season. Rolling onto his back, he stared at the inn's white popcorn ceiling, lit only by the thin sunlight seeping around the corners of the shades. The bed was nowhere near as comfortable as the one he'd slept on in LA, and nothing compared to Gina's mattress—with her cuddled against him, her cold toes pressed to his calf.

Missing her left a physical ache in his chest. He loved her. He could freely admit that here, far from the moments they'd shared in Los Angeles and even farther from her home in New York City. She was probably still there, making enormous strides in her career.

Stone dragged his laptop onto the bed with him and flipped it open. In his fever-induced delirium, he'd taken to watching Gina's interviews on YouTube. It made his heart hurt to see her, but he needed his fix.

After finding a new talk show clip, he started the video. Gina's smiling face appeared on the screen. Longing bloomed in his chest, leaving a bittersweet ache.

"Gina, tell us about your choreography style," the host in the video asked.

Stone listened with half an ear while Gina replied, her voice washing over him in a soothing wave.

Gina was incredibly talented, and a hard worker. She was going places. There was no room in her life for a guy with an engineering degree and a shitty reality show on his resume who wanted to live in Alaska, of all places. His ex-girlfriend, who'd been born and raised in Juneau, hadn't even wanted to stick around. Why would Gina? There was nothing for her here.

Except him. And he wasn't enough. The whole time, she'd wanted their relationship kept secret. Maybe it was because she knew he would never fit into the life she wanted.

"And how did you get started?" the host continued. "Tell us about your journey as a dancer."

When they'd first met, Stone had thought the same of her, that she would never fit in here, in his life. But it turned out the opposite was true. He could never reach the heights she aspired to attain. She had values that ruled her decisions, and as she'd pointed out, he'd sold his integrity to reduce his family's debt and fulfill his duty as the silent protector. Here he was, back in the fold, yet he'd never felt more alone. A Gina-shaped space had been carved into his life, and it was empty.

Stone had hoped the hole would be filled by all the things he'd missed about Alaska—the quiet, the fresh air, the peace and simplicity. Except it was all a lie. There was nothing simple about his life here. Everything his family did on camera was scripted. The whole time he was in LA, he'd longed to return to something that was a fantasy all along, the idea of a quiet, peaceful existence in the wilderness. He didn't even truly live in the bush, and there was nothing quiet or peaceful about being on a TV show and living in a hotel.

"And what about Stone?" the interviewer asked Gina. "You two seemed to be very . . . close, during his time on *The Dance Off.*"

Stone grabbed the laptop and stared at it through bleary eyes, all his attention hanging on Gina's next words.

On the screen, Gina hesitated. Her eyes flicked toward the camera, then down to her lap. She bit her lip.

"Yes," she finally answered. "We were. Dance partners always get close but this . . . this was different."

"What happened?"

Gina straightened her shoulders and shook back her hair. Her lips curved in a tight, closed-mouth smile, and Stone knew whatever she was about to say would be holding back a wealth of feeling.

"Let's just say letting him go back to Alaska was one of the hardest things I've ever done." Gina's hands twisted in her lap. "I feel like . . ."

"What do you feel like?" the host prompted, when Gina trailed off.

Stone's spirits fell. There was no way she was going to answer. She was too good at playing the publicity game.

But she continued.

"I feel like . . . something's missing." Gina's hands broke apart and she tapped her chest, quickly, an involuntary gesture. Then she shook her head and waved it off. "Never mind. I think it's just a lot of changes all at once and—"

Stone slammed his laptop shut.

He'd seen it. The naked vulnerability had been there for a second before she remembered where she was and shut it down, but he'd spent every day with her for three months, and he knew her tells. He knew how she looked when she was feeling more than she could put into words, more than she wanted to reveal. The lip-biting, the tapping, the compressing of her lips as if to hide what she really felt.

Letting him go back to Alaska was one of the hardest things I've ever done.

He had to get out of his contract.

As soon as Stone had the thought, something closer to real peace descended on him. Yes. That was the answer. Winning *The Dance Off* had solved the financial issues keeping him on *Living Wild*. If he could work with the show's lawyers, maybe hire a good one of his own . . .

Someone knocked on his door.

He cleared his throat. "Who is it?" It came out as a croak.

"It's Mom."

Instead of looking for underwear, Stone dragged the blankets with him as he shuffled to the door. When he opened it, Pepper's face became a mask of concern.

"Oh, honey. You're still sick?"

"Mm-hmm."

He fell back into the bed while she filled a mug of water for him from the bathroom sink.

"Reed said you were, but you know how he is. He likes to joke."

"Fever's gone, at least. I think."

Pepper brought him the water and pulled a chair closer to the bed. After he took the mug, she pressed the back of her hand to his forehead. "You still feel a little clammy, but not warm."

"I should be okay tomorrow," he rasped. "Maybe."

She dropped her hand. "Stone . . . I came to tell you something."

"What?"

"Apparently, that figure skater poked around too much." Her shoulders slumped. "Your father and I just had a meeting. They're canceling the next season."

"Wait, really?" He struggled to sit up. "This is the last one?"

"I'm afraid so." Giving his leg a pat, Pepper got to her feet. "We always knew this might happen. Surprised we made it this long, if you want to know the truth. And don't worry, your father is already pitching a few ideas for a new show."

Stone blinked.

"Feel better, son." The door whispered shut behind her.

Stone sat on the bed in a tangle of blankets, staring at the hotel room door.

He was free.

I can sublet my room," Gina said while Natasha poured two glasses of wine.

"We'll figure it out. Did you decide whether or not you're going to do *The Dance Off* again?"

"Not yet." Gina took the wineglass Tash handed her. "I know this is show business, and there will always be someone trying to manipulate me, but if I return, I don't want anything to do with Donna."

"I wouldn't blame you for telling them all to go fuck themselves, but I'll miss having you there."

"It's going to be weird being alone in New York while I'm doing the musical. I've gotten used to LA."

"And you have a kickass roommate here." Tash clinked her glass to Gina's. "Are you going to live with your mom?"

"No, I'm hoping to find a place in Hell's Kitchen, or somewhere else in Manhattan where I can get to and from the theater easily. What are you going to do in the off-season?"

"While you were gone, I booked a gig on a cable show filming this summer. Nothing big—I'm playing a teenager, if you can imagine."

Gina laughed. "A mean girl?"

Tash pursed her lips and shrugged. "I play the sassy bitch so well."

"If only people knew what a softie you are."

"Don't tell anybody, or I'll cut you."

Gina snorted and drank more wine. It was a nice, sweet Pinot Noir, something she'd missed while filming. "We live in a world of seasons, don't we? We could be living different lives every few months."

Natasha flashed her knowing grin. "You mean you could fit in a season in Alaska?"

"Maybe." Gina tried to squash a smile. "Summer, of course."

"Does that mean you forgive him?"

Gina swirled her wine, watching it splash up the sides of the glass. The dark, fruity scent filled her nostrils. She missed the scent of pine.

"My sister pointed out that it was probably for the best that Stone didn't tell me, considering how I might have reacted."

"You mean how it would have made you an anxious mess?"

Gina glared at Tash out of the corner of her eye. "Yes."

Tash grinned. "Keep going."

"And my mother . . ." Gina stopped. Absentee fathers were a sore subject in this apartment. "Mami thinks I didn't want to get close to Stone because . . ."

"Because your father left?"

"Yeah. And I knew Stone would be leaving."

Tash shrugged. "I know I have daddy issues. I was wondering when you were going to cop to yours."

"I started thinking, what if I just don't want to be alone? A few months ago, that didn't seem like a good enough life goal. But now . . ."

"Now you've met someone you wouldn't mind being not-alone with."

"Exactly." Gina sipped again, then set her glass on the coffee table next to her trophy—slightly smaller than the one *The Dance Off* gave to the celebrity winners, but no less tacky. "I think I'd like to be not-alone with Stone. I don't know how we'd make it work, but I'm willing to try."

"Aww, look at you, sounding like a rational adult." Tash smirked and raised her glass.

"Oh, I also found this on my phone." Gina pulled up a video and pressed play. Natasha leaned over to watch.

Stone's face appeared on the screen, too close, and shooting nervous looks over his shoulder. He was in the hallway of *The Dance Off*'s rehearsal studio.

"Gina, I'm . . . fuck, I don't even know why I'm doing this. I hope you never find it. Or at least, I hope you don't find it until I'm back in Alaska."

He let out a sigh and scrubbed a hand over his face.

"I just want to say, I think the world of you. You're smart and funny, beautiful and determined. For months, you've pushed me to do better, be better. You've helped me learn a lot about myself along the way. I have you to thank for that."

He shook his head and muttered something like "that sounds cheesy" under his breath. His face was bright red. When he looked back at the camera, though, his eyes were dark and filled with pain.

"I'm hurt, Gina. Really hurt. I was hoping we could . . . well, it doesn't matter anymore. I understand why you're angry, and I'm sorry. If I could go back and do it differently, I would, but . . . I don't want to hide. I want to love you in the open." He swallowed visibly. "If you ever . . . well, you know where to find me. Glacier Valley Inn, room one oh seven."

The video ended.

Natasha screeched. "When did you find this?"

"This morning. While waiting for my flight back." It still gave Gina a warm, tingling rush every time she watched it, even though she'd played it over and over on the flight to LA, grinning like a fool the whole time.

"This is some romantic comedy shit right here." Natasha flipped open her laptop on the coffee table and sat on the floor in front of it. "You know what, I think it's summer in Alaska right now. What if I just happened to look up flights?"

Gina grinned. "I have over a week before rehearsals start . . ."

"Nearest airport?"

"Check Juneau."

A heavy knock sounded from the apartment door.

Tash got up, giving Gina a quizzical look. Gina shrugged. She wasn't expecting anyone.

After looking through the peephole, Tash spun around with a huge grin on her face. "It's him," she mouthed, then grabbed her wineglass and tiptoed into her bedroom.

Him? Did she mean *Stone*?

Hands trembling, Gina set her glass on the coffee table and went to the door. After taking a deep breath, she pulled it open.

Stone stood on the other side, wearing dark jeans and a navy button-down that made his eyes look like they glowed. His hair was pulled up into a messy bun, and he carried a duffel bag slung over one shoulder.

Gina's heart gave a hopeful thump in her chest. Before she could greet him or ask what he was doing there, he spoke.

"I've been watching your interviews."

"Oh." Despite what she'd told her agent, her sense of obligation was too strong, and she'd made the circuit through all the daytime talk shows. But if he was here, that meant he must have seen the most recent one, where she slipped up and admitted she wanted him to stay. "I saw your video on my phone."

He blushed. "When?"

"This morning."

"Did you mean it?" they both asked at the same time.

Stone's brows creased. "Of course I did. Every word. I wouldn't have said it if I didn't."

And that was the truth of him. Yes, he'd lied for his family, but she'd never doubted his feelings for her were genuine.

How had she repaid him? With unfair accusations. She'd said hurtful things to push him away, all because she'd been too scared of what she saw when he looked at her, and what she felt when she looked at him.

All because she'd been too scared of what would happen when he left her.

She was about to apologize when he launched into a speech.

"Gina, please try to understand. My family has had a hold on me my entire life. I've always been the responsible one who drops everything to rush to their aid, and I'm tired of it. I hate being on *Living Wild*. I thought I would hate *The Dance Off*, too, except it was the most fun I've ever had."

She couldn't hold back a dopey grin. "Really?"

Some of the tension in him eased. "You light me up. You helped me remember who I was before, and see clearly who I am now and who I want to be."

"I like who you are," she cut in. She wished she'd reassured him the first time he'd brought this up, but she'd been too busy breaking up with him at the time. "Since the beginning. In every dance, the goal was to show who you really are—even if you didn't know who that was yet."

His eyes were earnest and clear. "You saw me. You're the first person who has in a long time. I wanted to help you win because you deserved it, but I was also trying to shoulder your burdens for you. I should have told you what Donna was doing and included you in deciding what to do about it. Maybe part of me wanted everyone to know about us, but that was the wrong way to do it. I should have respected your boundaries."

When he paused, Gina jumped in with the apology he was owed. "I'm sorry for that."

He looked confused. "For what?"

"I'm sorry I was so adamant about hiding our relationship. I'm not ashamed of you, Stone, and never was. I was scared. It was easier to focus on our differences and tell myself it would never work, rather than figuring out how it could."

His lips quirked. "Meanwhile, I kept telling myself we weren't right for each other, because our lives and goals are too different. Then I realized I'm the one who wasn't right for you. I get why you want to be in show business. You're good at it, and you didn't need that kiss footage to get votes. You deserve to be a star, and you deserve a man who will help you make your dreams come true, wherever those dreams take you."

Everything he said was magical and lovely, but Gina had made mistakes, too, and she had to own up to them. "And you deserve someone who won't try to keep you hidden behind the scenes. I was scared of what people would think of me. But it's my life, and I can't live it according to what other people might say. Not only that, I made this season all about me. I should have been more focused on your growth than on winning. My fears and ambitions got the better of me, but success is meaningless if it requires me to be alone."

"Gina." Stone's blue eyes held everything she'd come to miss in the days they'd been apart. "You don't have to be alone. I won't make you choose. I love you, and I'll follow you wherever you want to go, to the ends of the earth, if need be. Let's chase your success."

From the bedroom, Natasha let out a whoop.

Stone's cheeks flushed red—more visible than they'd been at the end of the season. "I didn't realize Natasha was home."

"Don't mind her." Gina pulled him into the apartment. Shoving the door shut with her foot, she yanked him down for a scorching kiss. He still smelled like pine and clean, crisp air, and his arms still felt strong and protective around her. How had she ever let him go? That was a mistake she wouldn't be making again.

"Did you trim your beard?" she asked, petting his cheeks.

"I shaved it off the day I quit *Living Wild*."

She squinted at him, trying to imagine him without the facial hair.

He scrunched up his face. "It looked weird. I'm not used to seeing myself without it, so I'm letting it grow back."

She scratched at his chin with her nails. "I've always liked it."

"Does this mean you forgive me?"

In answer, she led him to the coffee table and spun the laptop around, showing him the airline tickets Natasha had researched. "I can learn to compromise."

"So can I." They laughed together, and it was the most beautiful sound.

Gina closed the laptop. "How do we start?"

"However we want. My next season of *Living Wild* has been canceled, thanks to Lauren D'Angelo. Did you hear she was kicked out of her latest skating competition for using performance-enhancing drugs?"

"Kevin told me. Can't say I'm surprised."

"Anyway, I managed to get out of the rest of this season, too, since I already missed most of it. I'm *free*, Gina."

His eyes were alight, devoid of tension. But one thing worried her. "You love Alaska. I can't ask you to leave it behind."

"I love you more. I'll make do with visits. I was hoping you'd want to go with me someday, so I can show you what I love about it. Without a camera crew this time. I bought a plot of land there, to build a house of my own—or *our* own, if you want it to be. Not right away, but—"

"I'll help you." She threw her arms around him. This was a big deal for him. He'd gotten his life back and come to her door with his heart in his hands, and he was willing to travel with her wherever her career took them. The least she could do was embrace the place where he felt most at home. "I'll help you build the house. I don't know how, but I'll learn. It's a bit far for weekend getaways, but we'll figure it out."

His shoulders relaxed, and he smiled. "Thank you."

"By the way, I think I love you," she whispered in his ear.

He stilled. "Do you mean that?"

"I said, 'I think.'"

With a growl, Stone scooped her up and carried her into her bedroom. "I'll have to convince you, then, until there isn't even a shadow of a doubt."

Gina laced her fingers behind his neck. "I look forward to it." She pulled back as something new occurred to her. "But what are you going to do while I'm working?"

He set her on the edge of the bed and sat beside her. "It turns out winning a show with millions of viewers generates all sorts of interesting job offers."

"Oh yeah? Like what?"

His cheeks turned red again. "Everything from posing naked with a Sockeye salmon over my crotch for a national billboard campaign to being a 'beard ambassador' for men's hair products."

She gave him a speculative look. "I think you should do the salmon one."

"Honestly, I'm tempted. It's a *lot* of money."

"Well, if you're not going to be making sustainable salmon sexy, what *are* you going to do?"

His expression softened, and it struck her that he looked more at ease than she'd ever seen him. "An Alaskan conservation group has asked me to come on board. I'll be able to combine my degree with whatever small amount of fame I currently have in order to give back to the place that's given me so much."

"Your engineering degree?"

He nodded. "My focus was on civil and environmental engineering. I'll mostly be doing consulting, which I can do remotely, along with advocacy and outreach regarding green energy and preservation initiatives."

Gina stroked his cheek. "That sounds like the perfect fit for you."

"I love Alaska, and I want to do my part to preserve its beauty and culture. Between climate change and people trying to exploit its resources, there's a lot to protect."

And he'd always put himself in the protector role. Her heart swelled with pride for him.

"But that's not all," he said, and her eyebrows shot up.

"There's more?"

"A few designers loved the *Boylesque* routine so much, they're begging me to do Fashion Week. Your agent said there's some sort of bidding war going on." He looked mildly embarrassed, but also flattered.

"My agent? Penelope?"

"She reached out after the show ended and I signed with her. Thank god, because I don't think I could manage all this on my own. And she said if I ever want extra cash, she'll book me more gigs in New York or LA, wherever you're stationed."

"But Stone, you hated being on camera. Are you going to be happy with modeling?"

"I think so. Being on *The Dance Off* showed me I don't mind the cameras as much if I don't have to lie. And the publicity I get from staying visible will help boost the preservation work."

It was incredible how all the pieces of their lives were falling into place, but Gina needed to be sure. "You were so set on going back to Alaska."

His expression turned pensive. "You know, when I went back, I realized that while I love the place, my image of my life in Alaska wasn't real. *Living Wild* was a lie, and the life I had in Juneau doesn't exist anymore. I was fooling myself."

Knowing the truth about his family, Gina understood what he meant. "But are you going to be happy in New York? In Los Angeles? You're turning your entire life upside down just to be with me."

He cupped her face and looked deep into her eyes. "You're worth it, Gina."

The words, and the little growl in his voice, made her heart do a backflip. "You think so?"

He gave her a light kiss. "It doesn't matter where we are—New York City, Alaska, or Los Angeles. I'll be happy anywhere as long as I'm with you."

She hugged him tight. "I'm so excited to be not-alone with you, Stone."

"Huh?"

"Never mind. Kiss me."

He did.

Epilogue

Gina took a whiff of the pasteles boiling in the pot on the stove. "It finally smells like home in here, instead of paint and new wood."

Stone, as it turned out, had a taste for Puerto Rican cooking, and Gina had asked her mother and sister to help her make pasteles to store in the house she and Stone had built—with the aid of the Nielsons—in Southeast Alaska. The extra freezer was fully stocked with piles of the platano leaf–wrapped bundles of mashed malanga, calabaza, and green bananas.

"Watched pasteles don't cook." Stone took Gina by the hand and led her into their living room. He sat on the sofa and pulled her into his lap, tucking his face into her neck for a long sniff. "Besides, home to me smells like coconut and flowers."

She snuggled against him. "I wasn't going to leave my shampoo behind."

He rubbed his nose in her hair. "I like it. You're the only tropical flower in Alaska, and you're all mine." Lifting his head, he sniffed the air. "It's a good thing you didn't pop those in the pot while my family was here. They never would have left."

"They had to. They're filming tomorrow."

Stone's family had gotten a new show where they taught survival techniques to regular people. Stone wasn't on it, and neither were Raven and Winter. They'd gone off to college in Seattle.

"Trust me, they would have stuck around for food."

Gina rested her head on Stone's chest and closed her eyes, listening to his heartbeat. "Today was fun."

"I'm a little worried by how good you are at shooting a gun."

She snorted. "Don't worry. Hunting isn't for me."

"Thank goodness." He was quiet for a moment. "Is it terrible that I'm glad you're skipping the next season of *The Dance Off*?"

"No, it's not terrible. But why are you glad?"

"Because I know how much time goes into it, and I'm selfish." He squeezed her. "I want to spend more time with you."

"A Broadway show takes up tons of time, too."

"I know, but I've met your costars, and they're all afraid of me. How do I know *The Dance Off* won't give you some strapping young man—"

"You mean how they gave me *you*?"

"Exactly."

"They did that because I was single. They know I'm not single now. The whole world knows I'm not single now."

"Pop tried to pitch me the idea of us doing a reality show about living together." Stone rolled his eyes upward. "I told him I'd think about it, but if he ever brings it up to you, the answer is no. I'm sick of cameras watching our every move."

"At least there are no paparazzi in Alaska."

"Why do you think I like it here so much?"

"Ha." Gina hugged him and stayed quiet, listening to the sounds of the wind outside the house, the water bubbling on the stove, and the fire crackling in the hearth facing the sofa. The aroma of peppers and onions mixed with the smoky, earthy scent of the burning firewood—Stone would know what type of wood it was, and maybe one day, she would, too—but underlying it all was the scent of pine and fresh air.

The new scent of home.

The warmth of Stone's body enveloped her, and the fabric of his gray Henley was soft under her cheek. *Bronx Girl* was a success, and Gina's contract had been extended. Her understudy was handling the role now, so Gina could spend time in Alaska organizing the house before winter set in. Stone warned her it arrived early. They'd head back to New York in a few days, so Gina could go back to playing Meli on stage—still a dream come true, and she loved every minute of it—and so Stone could walk the runways for Fall Fashion Week. As it turned out, all the dancing had made him a stunner on the catwalk, and the attention amplified the reach of his preservation work.

"I love you," Gina murmured into his chest.

"I'm sorry, could you say that again?" Stone shifted her so he could look her in the eye. "I don't think I heard you correctly."

She scowled at him. "Stop making such a big deal about it."

"No, I'm going to make a very big deal about this. My girlfriend has finally stopped qualifying the L word with 'I think.' I'm going to take out an ad in the goddamn *New York Times*."

She flicked a finger against his rock-hard pecs. "Oh, stop it."

"Nope." Stone cupped her face in one hand and kissed her slowly, until her body heated from more than the crackling fire. "You love me. I'm going to remember this day for the rest of my life."

"Just remember who we have to thank." Gina cut her eyes to the pair of gaudy glitter-and-rhinestone-encrusted trophies resting on the center of the mantel, glowing golden in the light of the fire and the rays of the setting sun streaming through the big windows behind them.

Stone raised an imaginary glass in a toast. "Fucking Donna."

Gina laughed and lifted her hand to toast as well. "Indeed. Cheers to you, Fucking Donna."

They clinked their imaginary glasses, pretended to sip, and then proceeded to break in the new sofa.

They almost forgot about the pasteles.

Acknowledgments

Thank you for spending time with Stone and Gina and the cast of *The Dance Off.* I'm unbelievably lucky to have been able to produce the updated version of *Take the Lead* you now hold, and I hope it brightened your day. And to everyone who read the original back when it first came out, thank you for taking a chance on a debut author. You were my first readers, and it means more to me than you will ever know.

It takes a village to create a book, and mine starts with my stellar agent, Sarah E. Younger, who ticks all the boxes on my agent wish list and then some. I'm so glad I tracked you down at that bookstore event. Thank you for being such an amazing champion for this book and for me as an author.

I also owe huge thanks to my original team at St. Martin's—Jennie Conway, Holly Ingraham, Titi Oluwo, Lizzie Poteet, Kerri Resnick, and Marissa Sangiacomo—and my new team—starting with the incredible Tiffany Shelton, without whom this new version wouldn't have happened, along with Kejana Ayala, Gail Friedman, Gabriel Guma, Hannah Jones, Erica Martirano, Melanie Sanders, and Ervin Serrano. Thank you all for believing in these characters and their love, and for helping me shepherd this book into the world not just once, but twice! And the beautiful cover illustration is thanks to Chloe Friedlein, who perfectly captured Stone and Gina and their chemistry. I couldn't be happier with the update!

Much appreciation goes to Sarah Daniels, Fallon DeMornay, Elizabeth Mahon, and David Nierenberg for supplying their expertise on various topics like auditions, spray tans, ballroom dance, and seaplanes. Any mistakes are my own. Special thanks go to Ana Coquí and Keara Rodriguez for being early readers of the updated manuscript; to Lindsey Faber, who worked on both versions; to my amazing publicist, Kristin Dwyer; and to all the writing communities I have ever or will ever be part of. Art doesn't happen in a vacuum, and the support and encouragement of these groups has been vital to my journey as an author.

In that vein, I give thanks for Robin Lovett, C. L. Polk, and Kimberly Bell, who appeared in my life at the perfect moment, and without whom this book would've never been written.

And finally, I'm eternally grateful for my boyfriend, who has supported me through the ups and downs of being a writer and artist; his parents, who have nurtured my creative endeavors; and my own parents, who instilled in me an early love of stories.

Thank you all. ♥

Turn the Page for Exclusive Extras

for

Take the Lead

The DANCE OFF
Season 14 Episode Guide

Episode 1: Premiere

Meet the new cast of eleven celebrities and their pro dance partners as they compete to win *The Dance Off*'s trophy!
No Elimination

Episode 2: Fiesta Night

All eleven pairs face off for the second time, performing a variety of Latin dance styles, including tango, samba, salsa, and more.
Eliminated Couple: Keiko & Joel

Episode 3: Time of Your Life

Grab your tissues as the couples perform emotional dances inspired by the most significant times of their lives.
Eliminated Couple: Twyla & Roman (due to injury)

Episode 4: Fairy Tale Night

Hear ye, hear ye! Tonight, all nine couples will tackle dances with themes from classic fairy tales.
Eliminated Couple: Rose & Matteo

Episode 5: Shake It Up

In a twist that's sure to have them shaking in their dancing shoes, the remaining celebrities switch their pro dancers for a week.
No Elimination

Episode 6: Broadway Night

The show must go on as the couples gear up for a night of performances set to popular showtunes from Broadway musicals.
Eliminated Couple: Beto & Jess

Episode 7: Silver Screen Night

Grab your popcorn and get ready for a series of dances reminiscent of classic Hollywood movies.
Eliminated Couple: Dwayne & Natasha

Episode 8: Team Up

Guest judge Meli joins the show as the remaining six couples perform trio dances and team dances in what's sure to be an action-packed night.
Eliminated Couple: Rick & Mila

Episode 9: Semifinals

The remaining five celebrities perform a dance chosen by
their pro partners, along with a combo dance mixing up
two or more dance styles, all before the dreaded double
elimination!
Eliminated Couples: Alan & Rhianne, Farrah & Danny

Episode 10: Finals

The eliminated celebrities return for fun and games while
the top three couples perform a redemption dance chosen by
one of the judges and a second dance in a style they haven't
yet performed. After the combination of judges' scores and
viewer votes, the Season 14 winners will be crowned!
First Place: Stone & Gina
Second Place: Lauren & Kevin
Third Place: Jackson & Lori

Discussion Guide

1) *Take the Lead* provides a glimpse behind the scenes of reality television. What surprised you most about this world?
2) If you could perform a routine on *The Dance Off,* who would you choose for your celebrity partner? What dance style and song would you pick?
3) One of the themes in *Take the Lead* is the cost of success and fame. If you could be famous for anything, what would it be, and how do you think you'd handle being in the public eye?
4) Gina aims to bust stereotypes of Latinas in media and pop culture. Why is it important to do the work of dismantling harmful and offensive stereotypes?
5) Gina prompts Stone to channel his emotions into their dancing. In what ways can creative and performing arts provide emotional benefits?
6) Stone's journey takes him to Alaska, Los Angeles, and New York. Which of these locations would you most want to visit on vacation, and why?
7) If you were part of the Nielson family, what would your nature-based name be?
8) Gina and Stone are surrounded by a large and diverse cast of secondary characters. Who stood out to you the most, and why? Are there any other characters whose story you would like to see told?

9) Natasha is Gina's best friend and roommate. In what ways do they support each other, and why is it important to depict positive female friendships in media?

10) At its heart, *Take the Lead* is a workplace romance about complicated family dynamics and living life on your own terms. How would you have managed the conflicts these characters faced?

Bonus Scene

This scene takes place three years before the events in Take the Lead *and reveals the incendiary first meeting between pro dancer Natasha Díaz and judge Dimitri Kovalenko.*

Damn it. I'm all turned around, and I forgot where my producer—Donna, her name is—told me to go.

Good going, Tash—it's the first day and you're already lost!

The Dance Off's rehearsal studio doesn't look much different from the other ones I've been to in Los Angeles, but it's slightly bigger, more labyrinthine. Lots of long hallways, all decorated with framed, poster-sized photos of couples from previous seasons.

Someday, my picture will hang on these walls. I haven't met my celebrity partner yet, and I'm savoring the days until I do. Once we start training, it'll be a whirlwind of work and stress. But I'm more excited than anything else. Since I was already on *Everybody Dance Now, The Dance Off* has bumped me up to a pro, even though this is my first season. Usually I'd have to do time as a backup dancer and gain some audience recognition, but being on another TV show already accomplished that for me. Gina was tagged to choreograph some episodes of *Everybody*, so she's going to join *The*

Dance Off next season. I can't lie, it's weird being here without her. For one thing, I wouldn't be lost if she were with me.

Room B is just up ahead. Is that where Donna said I should go? I'll just pop my head in and see. If it's the wrong room, I'll apologize and duck back out.

I grasp the knob and ease the door open. Stepping inside, I spot a lone figure off to my right. Dark fabric stretches across broad shoulders that stand out against the stark white walls of the rehearsal room. It's like the shape of him is burned into my retinas. If I closed my eyes, I'd see the afterimage of him behind my lids.

He turns when he hears me, and my heart leaps into my throat. Oh, shit. I know exactly who he is.

Dimitri Kovalenko, one of *The Dance Off*'s judges. A dancer and choreographer who catapulted to stardom over a decade ago thanks to a silly dance movie I've seen approximately one million times.

He's so fucking hot I can't stand it.

Before I can open my mouth to apologize or babble or even breathe, he advances in long, quick strides. Without a word, he takes my hand, and I let him pull me toward him. I've had a crush on this man since I was a teenager, and every dancer trying to make it in Hollywood has followed his career.

And now I'm alone in a rehearsal room with him.

His hand grips mine firmly as he pulls me against his chest. His eyes are dark, lost in thought. His forbidding brow draws down, making him look severe. I can smell his cologne, something sharp and tangy-sweet, but not overpowering. It wraps around me, luring me in. It reminds me of the expensive scents advertised in the thick fashion magazines my mother sometimes brought home from the hair salon once the stack in the waiting area got too tall.

I don't question what he's doing with me. It's all too clear.

We're dancing.

He guides me with commanding touches. Not just his hands, but everywhere our bodies connect. Fingers, feet, hip, shoulder—I move with him, surrendering completely to his lead. He spins me out, tugs me back, and catches me on his hip. My hair, still loose, flips over my head and covers his shoulder and neck.

There's no music, only the sounds of our breathing, of our sneakers on the shiny floor, of fabric shifting over our skin.

My heart pounds but my breathing stays even. My body knows what to do.

I let him lead.

Still, every time he pulls me close, fire races along my nerves. My chest feels tight, my skin sensitive. It hungers for his touch, perfectly attuned to him, waiting for the next hint of direction. We sway together, leading into a low lift, then we salsa across the floor. We're moving so fast, in such unison, I feel like I'm flying. My feet barely touch the ground.

But I won't fall. He won't let me. He's in complete control.

Seconds tick past, but I have no idea how long we've been dancing. The dark intensity in his eyes fills my vision, and I lose track of all else.

I almost forget this was the wrong room.

Finally, he flings me into an ending pose. My hands brace against his chest. Our eyes are locked. He has hold of my hip and my shoulder.

We're both breathing hard. It wasn't a particularly long or taxing dance, but the heat between us . . . I know he feels it, too.

His gaze drops to my lips, parted to catch my breath. They're dry. I lick them.

His eyes snap back up to mine.

"What's your name?" His voice is deep, like a growl, or a grumble. He has a reputation for being the cranky judge.

"Natasha." Points for not stuttering.

His grin is quick, his teeth flashing against his trim, dark beard. He repeats it, giving the syllables a roll, an accent. "Natasha."

The back of my neck prickles. I wish he'd say it again. It's delicious in his mouth.

"You know who I am?" he asks, still grinning.

Oh, of all the obnoxious . . . "Yes."

"Good." He leans in close, presses his hot forehead to mine. We've both broken a sweat. Our lips are just a whisper apart when he says, "Come over tonight."

His voice is low. Even though we're alone, the words are just for me and have nothing to do with this rehearsal room or *The Dance Off*. My mouth longs for him to close the gap.

I swallow, and say again, "Yes."

He nods, releasing me and taking a step back. "Go. You're probably expected somewhere."

I am. I take a few steps toward the door and grab my bag. I don't even remember dropping it. Once Dimitri took my hand, I was his.

"Wait." He strides forward and takes the bag from me. Digging his hand inside, he pulls out my phone and holds it up for me to unlock it. Once I do, he adds his number and address to my contacts.

"Nine," he says when he drops it back into the bag.

Nine is late. I'm expected at the studio early the next morning. But I don't care. This will be worth any price.

He catches my chin in his hand and brushes his thumb over my lips. "See you."

My skin is hot, and my breath trembles out. "Later."

I dash from the room.

The second I'm in the hall, I remember where I'm supposed to be. Not Room B. Room *E*. And now I'm late.

Natasha and Dimitri's story continues in
Dance with Me

Turn the Page for an Excerpt from

A Lot Like Adiós

Now Available from Avon Books

The international bestselling author of You Had Me
at Hola *returns with a seductive second-chance romance
about a commitment-phobic Latina and her childhood
best friend who has finally returned home.*

Hi Mich. It's Gabe.

After burning out in her corporate marketing career, Michelle
Amato has built a thriving freelance business as a graphic designer.
So what if her love life is nonexistent? She's perfectly fine being the
black sheep of her marriage-obsessed Puerto Rican–Italian family.
Besides, the only guy who ever made her want happily-ever-after
disappeared thirteen years ago.

It's been a long time.

Gabriel Aguilar left the Bronx at eighteen to escape his parents' demanding expectations, but it also meant saying goodbye to Michelle, his best friend and longtime crush. Now, he's the successful co-owner of LA's hottest celebrity gym, with an investor who insists on opening a New York City location. It's the last place Gabe wants to go, but when Michelle is unexpectedly brought on board to spearhead the new marketing campaign, everything Gabe's been running from catches up with him.

I've missed you.

Michelle is torn between holding Gabe at arm's length or picking up right where they left off—in her bed. As they work on the campaign, old feelings resurface, and their reunion takes a sexy turn. Facing mounting pressure from their families—who think they're dating—and growing uncertainty about their futures, can they resolve their past mistakes, or is it only a matter of time before Gabe says adiós again?

Chapter 1

CALENDAR
One year until NYC
Today at 9:00 AM

"Fuck." Gabriel Aguilar scowled at the reminder on his phone screen before swiping it off with this thumb. He hated calendar alerts—the damned things ruled his life these days—but he especially despised this one. New York was the last thing he wanted to think about, today or ever.

Shoving the phone into his sweatpants pocket, Gabe pulled open the glass double doors leading into Agility Gym and strode inside like he owned the place.

Which, technically, he did.

Cool air and the faint scent of lavender greeted him, a welcome change from the blistering Los Angeles heat. The gym felt like home, more so than Gabe's minimalist apartment in Venice did. Located near Bergamot Station in Santa Monica, Agility Gym was well ventilated and spacious, with clean lines, high ceilings, and large front windows that let in lots of sunlight. All around, trainers and physical therapists worked one-on-one with clients on everything from stunt work to knee rehab.

There were ups and downs to being a business owner, but Gabe wouldn't trade it for anything. He'd built this. It was *his*.

The lavender scent grew stronger as Gabe neared the front desk where Trung, a former acrobat of Vietnamese descent who managed client scheduling, chatted with Charisse, one of Agility's best PTs. Trung swore by the soothing effects of the essential oil diffuser, and while Gabe didn't have strong opinions about aromatherapy, he could appreciate that lavender was an improvement over typical gym smells.

Despite the calendar alert urging him on, Gabe went over to greet them.

Charisse, a tall woman with a small fro and dark umber skin, returned Gabe's fist bump with a wide smile. She and Gabe were gearing up to co-teach a class on hand therapy for the many clients who complained of repetitive strain injury from overusing their phones and computers.

"Lots of new sign-ups," Charisse said, before turning to Trung. "Can you pull up the list?"

"Sure thing." Trung's purple-tipped nails clattered on the keyboard before they spun the screen around, revealing a color-coded spreadsheet. "Here you go."

"Almost at the stretch goal," Gabe said with a grin. "We might have to open more spots."

Scanning the long list of names gave Gabe a rush. It was the kind of thing he missed doing, since most of his time now went toward the administrative and managerial tasks of running the gym. Speaking of, he had a shit-ton of such tasks waiting for him.

"I'll see you two later," he said, and headed for his office in the back of the building.

As Gabe approached, his business partner, Fabian Charles, stuck his head out of his own office.

"That you, Gabe?"

Gabe started most of his mornings at a gym closer to his apartment, where he could be just another person sweating it out with the weights, and not the face of the business. They'd worked out a schedule where Fabian came in earlier, but Gabe stayed later.

"Yeah, it's me." Gabe had met Fabian while playing baseball for UCLA, and all these years later, the guy was still his best friend.

Fabian was Haitian by way of Boston, with coppery skin and dark locs pulled back with a rubber band. He was first-generation like Gabe, whose parents had been born in Mexico and Puerto Rico.

Fabian waved him into the office. "Did you see the calendar alert?"

Gabe bit back a frustrated growl. Thinking about New York made him think about his family, a topic that always tanked his mood. "How could I miss it?"

"I figured you'd say that. Come on, I've got some updates."

Gabe followed Fabian into the office, trying to ignore the piles of paper on Fabian's desk. And floor. And chair.

Fabian claimed having everything out where he could see it counted as an organizational system, and while it made Gabe twitchy, he couldn't deny that the guy was a genius at what he did.

They'd started Agility together when they were twenty-six and filled with the fire to build something of their own, a gym focused on physical therapy and rehab. Gabe had gotten interested in sports medicine after blowing out his knee and working on his recovery with the UCLA team doctor. After graduation, Gabe worked as a personal trainer and went back to school for physical therapy. Fabian had followed up undergrad with an MBA. The gym itself was Gabe's vision, but Fabian had the skills to make it happen. And so, Agility Gym had been born. Five years later, it was now a hot spot for Hollywood stars.

And at thirty-one years old, Gabe was tired as fuck.

But there was no rest for the wicked, and there was still work to be done. He waited for Fabian to move a pile of papers from the guest chair before he sat down. Fabian took his place behind his desk and pulled a few brightly colored sticky notes off his computer monitor. Gabe, who'd gone paperless three years ago, withheld a comment.

"Ah, here we go." Fabian held up a blue sticky note. "Today marks one year until we have to open an Agility Gym branch in New York City, as per the terms of our investment agreement with Powell."

Gabe crossed his arms and waited for Fabian to get to the point. Richard Powell, their first investor, had insisted they open a location in New York City within six years, mainly so Powell could use it while he was on the East Coast for work. They'd met Powell through an investment competition for recent grads, and he'd been the first one to give them a chance. At the time, they'd been thrilled that Powell had taken such an interest in the gym. But lately, his involvement left Gabe wondering who was actually in charge here.

"I know you don't want to, but you've gotta get started on this, dude," Fabian said, a note of apology in his voice. "I can hold down the fort here, but I can't travel back and forth like we'd planned."

Resentment simmered in Gabe's gut. When they'd made the agreement, Fabian had assured Gabe he'd handle it when the time came. He was the one with the vision for the New York location, and the drive to get it done. But Fabian's life had expanded in ways they never could have foreseen. Since then, Fabian had gotten married and bought a house. His wife, Iris, an entertainment lawyer, was pregnant with twins, and their home renovation project had turned into a beast. On top of all that, Fabian's parents had moved in with him in advance of his father's open-heart surgery, which was scheduled to take place in a few weeks.

Gabe was happy for him. He really was. Fabian had always wanted to be a dad, and even though Gabe didn't feel the same impulse, he could still be happy for his friend.

But Gabe *wasn't* happy about what it meant for him.

For all his messiness, Fabian was a great business partner, and an even better friend. He knew about Gabe's issues with his family, and he'd never have stuck Gabe with this task if there'd been another choice. Gabe hadn't been back to New York since his sister's wedding nine years ago, where he and his parents had made a scene and his father had yelled "Don't come back!" at his retreating form.

"I know I have to do it," Gabe said, shaking off the memory. Managing the New York launch was something he'd resigned himself to once he'd realized the one-year mark was coming up and Fabian was in no position to go anywhere.

"I'll help how I can from afar," Fabian offered. He held up his other hand, which had three pink sticky notes stuck to his fingers. "That's what I wanted to update you on. I've made some inquiries."

Gabe shifted in the chair, getting comfortable. "Let's hear it."

Fabian peeled a note off his finger and squinted at whatever he'd written there. His notes looked like they were written by a two-year-old who'd decided to try writing upside down.

"I've reached out to a real estate agent to help us find a space, a contractor to give us a renovation quote, and . . ." Fabian wiggled his middle finger, which held the final pink sticky note. "I found the mastermind behind the Victory Fitness rebrand."

At that last bit, Gabe leaned forward. "Really? You found them?"

Victory Fitness was a bicoastal gym chain whose clout had sky-rocketed three years earlier thanks to an ad campaign that went viral. At the time, Fabian had tacked up the magazine ads on his office corkboard, and they'd kicked around the idea of hiring whoever had come up with the concept. There were already a lot of gyms in New York, but if they could bring that person on board, it could be exactly what they needed to make the expansion a success.

As much as Gabe didn't want to return to New York, if he had to do it, he wanted to blow it out of the water, to have the name of his gym—a take on his own last name, Aguilar—splashed every-where.

Especially where his father could see it.

"It took a little work to track her down, because she's freelance now. But I got someone at her old firm to give me her contact info. Her name's . . ." Fabian peered at the sticky note. "Michelle . . . Amato."

Gabe's heart leaped into his throat and his skin prickled like someone had dumped a bucket of ice water over his head. "What did you say?"

"Michelle Amato. She used to work for a marketing and adver-tising firm—"

"Oh shit." Gabe put a hand on his forehead and fell back into the chair, the strength draining out of him. Even though they'd been out of touch all these years, the last thing Gabe had heard about Michelle was that she'd gotten a job in marketing. "It's Michelle. It has to be. Goddamn."

It was a small fucking world after all.

"What is it, dude?" Fabian tossed the sticky notes onto the desk and got up. "You look pale."

"Michelle's my . . ." What were they? "We used to be friends. Best friends. She—"

"Wait, this is *that* girl? *The* girl? The one who you—oh damn." Fabian pulled out his phone while Gabe stared into space, swamped by memories.

Of playing in their adjoining backyards. Of dinner with her family. Of her keeping him company during his shifts at his father's stationery store.

Of her taste on his lips the last time he'd seen her.

"This is the one you wrote that sci-fi fanfiction for?"

Gabe narrowed his eyes at Fabian's question. "I wrote it *with* her, not *for* her. We were fifteen. And I told you never to bring that up again, pendejo."

"Not my fault you spill your deepest, darkest secrets when you're drunk." Fabian's eyebrows rose. "Daaaamn. She's smoking hot, dude."

"What?" That snapped Gabe out of his reverie. "How do you know?"

Fabian turned the phone to face him. "Her Instagram."

Gabe grabbed the phone, suddenly ravenous for a glimpse of Michelle after all these years.

Fabian stuck his hands on his hips, mouth agape. "You mean you haven't Internet-stalked her?"

"Not . . . not in a long time." He had in the past. But it had been too painful, and scrolling through her photos without comment-ing made Gabe feel like a creep. It had been more than five years since he'd last looked her up. And shit, Fabian was right. Mich was gorgeous.

She was pale, but there was a warmth to her skin, offset by her long dark hair. Her light brown eyes held that glint he remembered, like she knew a secret and didn't you wish she'd tell you.

The photos in her feed were a collection of selfies, family pictures, a black cat, and Manhattan street photography. Gabe zeroed in on the selfies, which showed her giving the camera a range of looks that went from sultry to silly.

It was, in essence, Michelle. Just as he remembered her.

He'd always thought she was the most beautiful girl in the world, and age had only made her hotter.

"Stop it." Fabian snatched the phone back. "You're torturing yourself."

"No, wait—" Gabe reached for the phone, but Fabian held it over his head.

"I'll email her to apologize and say we found someone else," Fabian went on. "No harm, no foul."

Gabe was already pulling out his own phone to look her up through the gym's Instagram account, taking care not to accidentally like one of her photos with an errant thumb tap. "Did you mention my name in the email?"

Fabian hesitated before answering. "I might have."

Gabe sent him an exasperated look. "Is that yes or no?"

Fabian sighed. "It's a yes, but let me handle this. For your own good."

Gabe shook his head, suddenly filled with certainty, and . . . some light feeling he couldn't name. "Nah, I gotta email her."

"Son, listen to me. This is the one who got away. You're not thinking clearly."

Fabian was right, but it didn't matter. "I have to," Gabe said, getting to his feet. "The way I left things, and now this . . . I'll be a total dick if I don't even email her to explain."

He'd already ghosted her as a friend. He wouldn't add professional ghosting to the list of his sins where Michelle was concerned.

Had he really thought he could keep his old life separate from this expansion? He should have known better. It was only day one and a gigantic piece of his old baggage had already been dredged up. Now he had to address it.

Gabe grabbed the duffel bag he'd set beside the chair. "I'm gonna email her."

"Let the record state that I think this is a terrible idea," Fabian told him. "This is my fault. You should let me fix it."

"You have enough work to do trying to manage everything from here so I spend as little time in New York as possible." Gabe's phone dinged with another fucking calendar alert.

"Conference call with the managers in ten minutes," Fabian said, glancing at his computer screen.

"Yeah, yeah." That meant Gabe had ten minutes to reply to Michelle. "Forward me the email you sent her."

Fabian let out a soul-weary sigh and dropped into his desk chair. "Fine."

Gabe left his partner's office and headed to his own.

He dreaded returning to New York, dreaded facing Michelle. But somewhere deep inside, he also felt . . . glad. All the times she'd reached out to him over the years, he hadn't known what to say . . . so he hadn't said anything. Now he had a real reason to reply.

He was nervous as all hell, but also . . . he still missed her. After all this time, an ache still formed in his chest at the thought of her.

Mouth set in a grim line, Gabe sat at his own desk, which contained not a single piece of paper or sticky note, and pulled the ergonomic keyboard closer. Then he began to type.

About the Author

Alexis Daria is an award-winning and bestselling romance author. Her debut novel, *Take the Lead,* was a RITA Award winner for Best First Book, and *You Had Me at Hola,* the first book in her Primas of Power series, was an international bestseller. A former visual artist, Daria is a lifelong New Yorker who loves Broadway musicals and pizza.

For updates and exclusive content, follow Alexis's newsletter: alexisdaria.com/newsletter/.

Look out for the next book in the
Primas of Power Series

Along Came Amor

Copyright © 2023 by Alexis Daria

Available Summer 2023 from
Avon Books

*From international bestselling author Alexis Daria comes the
final installment in the critically acclaimed Primas of Power
series, where a divorced middle school teacher discovers
that her perfect no-strings fling is anything but.*

No strings

After Ava Rodriguez's now-ex-husband declares he wants to
"follow his dreams"—which no longer include her—she's left questioning everything she thought she wanted. So when a handsome
hotelier flirts with her soon after her divorce is finalized, Ava vows
to stop overthinking and embrace the opportunity for an epic one-
night-stand.

Roman Vasquez's sole focus is the empire he built from the ground up. He lives and dies by his schedule, but the gorgeous stranger grimacing into her cocktail glass inspires him to change his plans for the evening. At first, it's easy for Roman to agree to Ava's rules. But one night isn't enough, and the more they meet, the more he wants.

No falling in love

Roman is the perfect fling, until Ava sees him at her cousin's engagement party—as the groom's best man, no less! Suddenly, maintaining her boundaries becomes a lot more complicated as she tries to hide the truth of their relationship from her family. However, Roman isn't content being her dirty little secret, and he doesn't just want more, he wants everything. With her future uncertain and her family pressuring her from all sides, Ava will have to decide if love is worth the risk—again.